G000256640

The Man on a Donkey, Part 2

Books in the Loyola Classics Series

The Man on a Donkey, Part 2
A Chronicle

H. F. M. PRESCOTT

Introduction by Jim Campbell

LOYOLA & CLASSICS

CHICAGO

LOYOLA PRESS.
A JESUIT MINISTRY

3441 N. Ashland Avenue
Chicago, Illinois 60657
(800) 621-1008
www.loyolapress.com

© Copyright by J. W. Prescott and Mrs. S. C. Thedinga. All rights reserved.
Introduction and study questions © 2008 Loyola Press. All rights reserved.
Originally published in 1952 by Eyre & Spottiswoode, London. The first U.S.
edition was published in 1952 by the Macmillan Company, New York.

Picture credit:
Series art direction: Adam Moroschan
Series design: Adam Moroschan and Erin VanWerden
Cover design: Maggie Hong
Interior design: Erin VanWerden

Library of Congress Cataloging-in-Publication Data
Prescott, H. F. M. (Hilda Frances Margaret), 1896–1972.
The man on a donkey : a chronicle / H. F. M. Prescott.
     p. cm. — (Loyola classics)
   Originally published: New York : Macmillan, 1952. With new introd. and study
questions.
   ISBN-13: 978-0-8294-2639-7
   ISBN-10: 0-8294-2639-6
   ISBN-13: 978-0-8294-2731-8
   ISBN-10: 0-8294-2731-7
   1. Aske, Robert, d. 1537—Fiction. 2. Great Britain—History—Henry VIII,
1509-1547—Fiction. 3. Yorkshire (England)—Fiction. 4. Catholics—Fiction.
5. Christian fiction. I. Title.
   PR6031.R38M36 2008
   823'.912—dc22

                                                          2008006548

Printed in the United States of America
08 09 10 11 12 13 Bang 10 9 8 7 6 5 4 3 2 1

Contents

Introduction

Jim Campbell

Henry VII of England (1485–1509) was an economical and prudent man. He was frugal in his expenses and when he died had amassed a personal fortune of 1.5 million pounds. Today the amount left to Henry VIII in 1509 would amount to the equivalent of about 1.5 billion dollars. Henry VIII quickly found many ways to spend the money that his father so carefully saved. He embarked on war with France. Between 1509 and 1515 Henry spent some 1,344,030 pounds on his European wars. His Lord Chancellor, Cardinal Wolsey, spent another 400,000 pounds from 1522 to 1523. Soon Henry's personal fortune was drained away.

For the rest of his reign, Henry VIII had money problems. The sources of his income were fairly static, so he needed another source of ready cash. He found it in the eight hundred monasteries and priories of England.

The precedent of closing monasteries to cash in on them was begun by Cardinal Wolsey. Wolsey closed twenty-eight smaller monasteries and used the funds to build colleges. Over the centuries, these religious establishments had also gathered a great deal of wealth in the form of religious artifacts. Wolsey confiscated these artifacts for his personal use. After his fall from grace in 1529, all of Wolsey's possessions became the property of the King. In *The Man on the Donkey*, H. F. M. Prescott shows us Henry VIII and Anne Boleyn as they search Wolsey's palace to examine the inventory of his wealth.

1529

October 24

But the King grew impatient and let the pages go with a run.

"Where is the plate of gold and silver?"

He found the page.

A gold cup of assay . . . a crystal glass garnished with gold . . . a gold salt garnished with pearls and stones and a white daisy on the knop.

He shut the book, and, turning, shouted for one of the royal officers who had charge of the stuff. The man's voice answered him hollowly in the great empty house.

"The keys! The keys!" the King cried, and when the keys were brought they went away with them to the chamber where all this most precious stuff had been stored.

There it was, set upon benches and cupboards, and overflowing to the floor, the dim light gleaming on the bellies of gold cups, gold salts, silver cups, silver salts, and catching the facets of jewels.

"Jesu!" cried Mrs. Anne, and the King said, "Passion of Christ!" at the sight of that sumptuous spectacle. Then they moved about, touching and lifting, here a gilt charger, there a gold cup with a cover and the top-castle of a ship on the knop.

"Ah! the pretty thing," cried Mrs. Anne, and pointed her finger at a bowl of gold with a cover, garnished with rubies, diamonds, pearls, and a sapphire set in a collet upon it.

The King stooped to look at it. Just near, upon the bench end, stood a tall gold salt with twined green branches enameled upon the gold, and scrolled letters enlaced together; the letters were K. and H. He gave the salt a shove with the back of his hand and it fell from the bench and clattered to the ground.

Mrs. Anne tittered, because she knew that K. stood for Katherine, but the King's face had reddened with anger. He caught her by the wrist and kissed her roughly and went on kissing. As his mouth lifted from her throat or from her lips he was muttering—

"Laugh? You may laugh. And she. And the pope. But none will laugh when it is seen what I shall do."

As we have seen in Part 1, King Henry VIII took control of the English Church in 1534. He saw that the riches tied up in the lands of the monasteries and their centuries-old collections of artifacts were the answer to his financial difficulties.

The Religious Establishment

In 1530 there were over eight hundred religious monasteries and priories in England, housing a population of over eight thousand religious men and women. They were the inheritors of a tradition of religious practice going back to 940, when the first Benedictine monasteries were established in England, the earlier monasteries in the Celtic tradition having been destroyed by Viking invaders. Over the centuries, the religious establishment of nuns, monks, friars, and order priests received donations of land, artifacts, and money to such an extent that by 1530 they controlled from one-fifth to one-third of the land in England. These religious communities had flourished and suffered along with the general population of England during this time. Many religious establishments were underpopulated, having not recovered from the devastation of the Black Plague in the middle of the fourteenth century. This underpopulation was the reason Cardinal Wolsey gave in petitioning to close the twenty-eight monasteries that he did.

In 1535, Thomas Cromwell, Cardinal Wolsey's former secretary who had helped Wolsey dissolve the monasteries in the late 1520s, was appointed by Henry as vicar-general with authority to investigate the monasteries. After a year of investigation, Henry appeared before parliament and demanded the closure of the monasteries and priories which had income of less than two hundred pounds a year. Parliament agreed, and the King's representatives began the closures. There were 291 houses eligible for closure and dissolution involving some 1500 religious men and women. Of these, 244 were actually suppressed. Collectively the lands of these monasteries and priories produced a yearly revenue of 32,000 pounds and yielded 100,000 pounds in religious artifacts

Eastern and Northern England were hit very hard by the closures. Two-thirds of the existing monastic institutions disappeared, 87 out of 130 houses. Lands were confiscated, communities were broken up, buildings were torn down, and anything that could be moved was sold off. The people living in these areas of the country saw permanent elements of their social life disappear.

Pilgrimage of Grace

Northern England was primarily rural. The main population was farmers and sheepherders who were conservative and not open to revolutionary ideas. They had a deep devotion for Katherine of Aragon and were upset with the new policies being introduced by the King. When Henry began to execute monks and bishops for failing to take the oath declaring Henry head of the Church in England they were appalled. They blamed Thomas Cromwell for influencing the King.

The changing economic climate also upset the people. Prices were rising and new taxes were being introduced across the board.

1536

September 17

"For now there be things devised against the commons too grievous to be borne, as that every man shall be sworn what goods he hath, and if he have more than so much all his goods shall be taken away. Likewise there is a statute made that none shall eat white bread, goose, nor capon, but if he pay pennies to the King. Likewise another that none shall be christened, wedded, nor buried but at the price of a noble. For these days there is a sort of Lollards and traitors that rule about the King, and have brought him to such a covetous mind that if the Thames flowed with gold and silver it would not quench his thirst."

The county of Lincolnshire was hardest hit in Northern England. Thirty-four religious houses were suppressed, decreasing the Church's revenue by 31 percent. In October 1536, the common people (commons) of Lincolnshire began an uprising. Thousands of people gathered and threatened the King's commissioners. While there was much excitement, the people had no leader and the revolt was swiftly put down. It was during this rising that Robert Aske of Yorkshire emerged as a potential leader.

Later in October 1536, Robert Aske led a new rebellion. The commons accepted his leadership, and thousands gathered to follow him, first to York, then to capture Lord Darcy's castle at Pontefract. Lord Darcy had no arms with which to defend the castle and while loyal to the King, he detested Cromwell and his ilk. Darcy surrendered the castle to Robert Aske and later cooperated with him in the rebellion. Robert Aske then issued an Oath of Honorable Men to state the principles of the rebellion.

1536
October 16
The Oath of Honorable Men
Ye shall not enter into this our Pilgrimage of Grace for the Commonwealth, but only for the love that ye do bear unto Almighty God, his faith, and to holy church militant and the

maintenance thereof, to the preservation of the King's person and issue, to the purifying of the nobility, and to expulse all villain blood and evil councilors against the Commonwealth from His Grace and his Privy Council of the same. And that ye shall not enter into our said Pilgrimage for no particular profit to yourself, nor to do displeasure to any private person, but by counsel of the Commonwealth, nor slay nor murder for no envy, but in your hearts put away all fear and dread, and take afore you the cross of Christ, and in your hearts his faith.

By the end of October, Aske commanded 35,000 men. Henry had no standing army, and his forces were in disarray. Aske hesitated. His aim was not to overthrow the king but to rid him of Cromwell and the other ministers whom Aske saw as responsible for the new religious policies.

Henry was naturally infuriated with the rebellion, but he played for time. He offered a free pardon, which Robert Aske accepted. On December 8, 1536, Aske laid down his pilgrim badge. With the loss of his leadership, the Pilgrimage of Grace was over.

Henry's Revenge

Henry brought Aske to London to keep an eye on him and to wait for an excuse to execute him. This came in January 1537. A general rebellion broke out in Yorkshire. Henry used this as an excuse to send forces in to carry out a terror campaign against the people.

1537

February 16

They said then, Sir Rafe leading, that they were glad.

"And that you shall surely know you have done what shall please His Grace," Norfolk said, "I shall read you a letter." He took it out from his pouch, and spread it out upon the coping of the wall, and ran his finger along the lines to find his place.

"'Our pleasure,'" he read, "'is that before ye shall close up our Banner again, you shall in any wise cause such dreadful execution to be done upon a good number of the inhabitants of every town, village, and hamlet, that have offended in this rebellion, as well by hanging of them up in trees, as by quartering of them, and setting up their heads and quarters in every town great and small, and in all such other places as they may be a perfect spectacle.'"

He folded up the paper again, and then looked into their faces.

"So," said he, "you see that both you and I have well served the King. Lawyers may say, '*Fiat Justitia, ruat coelum.*' But it is better that these, whom blind Justice might have spared, should suffer, when by the example of such a dreadful severity, many more may be prevented from light doings."

They said, the two Yorkshire gentlemen, that it was better, and that the King was a most gracious, godly, and wise Prince.

In July 1537, Robert Aske was executed for committing high treason.

It is at this point the events described in *The Man on a Donkey, Part 2*, end.

Aftermath

The Pilgrimage of Grace was intended to preserve the monastic institutions of England. There is no doubt that Henry used the rebellion as an excuse to dissolve the remaining religious institutions. By 1540, all the monasteries and priories were dissolved. Six hundred years of religious life in England disappeared.

Henry received some 171,312 pounds, a gross income more than three times that of all crown estates on the eve of the Dissolution. The value of the melting down of religious artifacts added another 100,000 pounds. All of this Henry frittered away. By the end of his monarchy, two-thirds of the monastic lands that Henry confiscated had been sold outright at bargain prices to cover his debts.

The Man on a Donkey

In *The Man on a Donkey, Part 2*, we see the events of the Dissolution and its effect on the people whose lives we are following.

Christabel Cowper as prioress of Marrick Priory does everything she can think of to stave off the closure. No matter how she works the numbers, Marrick Priory cannot produce the 200 pounds necessary to forestall closure. She does her best to pay off Cromwell and anyone else who might keep the priory open. She achieves a temporary reprieve, but the threat of closure remains strong. As a last resort, she goes to London to meet with Cromwell personally and to bribe him with her most precious possession, a golden pyx used to bring Holy Communion to the sick. With her mind only on the survival of the priory by any means, Christabel ignores all who would see the closing of the monasteries as God's will so the monks and nuns would cleave to God alone.

1537

March 29

The prioress of Marrick let her lip curl. She had Moses and the Prophets; half an hour ago she had had mad Malle babbling of the insatiable tender love of God. Now she had the old prioress of St. Helen's. She had not listened to any of these, nor would she have listened though one rose from the dead.

Thomas, Lord Darcy, is caught up in the rebellion. He works with Robert Aske and refuses to betray him. After the Pilgrimage of Grace, he is brought to London and to the tender mercies of Cromwell. Darcy cannot countenance Henry as head of the Church of England, and he accepts the consequences of his decisions.

Julian Savage is not permitted to become a professed nun at Marrick. Her sister marries her off to Laurence Machyn, a London merchant. Laurence proves to be a gentle man and loving husband. Julian becomes reacquainted with Robert Aske when he comes to London, however, and her love for him leads her to help while she can. Her love also leads her to deep sorrow and despair at his death. She cannot help but continue to believe that God made pain and chose it for himself.

Gilbert Dawe continues the downward spiral of self-loathing and rejection of the faith. He runs and runs from God, thinking in his final spiral that while God could save every other man, God could not save Gilbert. Gilbert sees himself as a leaky bucket from which God's grace has drained away.

1537
November 4

[Gilbert] did not know that though the bucket be leaky it matters not at all when it is deep in the deep sea, and the water both without it and within. He did not know, because he was too proud to know, that a man must endure to sink, and sink again, but always crying upon God, never for shame ceasing to cry, until the day when he shall find himself lifted by the bland swell of that power, inward, secret, as little to be known as to be doubted, the power of omnipotent grace in tranquil, irresistible operation.

Robert Aske, as we have seen, is forced by his conscience and his desire to be faithful to become the leader of the Pilgrimage of Grace. He finally places his trust in a duplicitous King, and suffers the consequences of that trust. Even before he makes the decision to lead the rebellion, he has an intuitive insight into the suffering to come.

1536

September 30

"If I move," he said in his mind, "I do wrong. If I move not, wrong is done."

The other, which was a dumb thing, was fear—the fear lest he should stand alone, a man disowned by kin and friends; there in the dark he knew in a foretaste the weight and desolation of that loneliness.

In the midst of all these events Malle, the visionary scullery maid, and Wat, Gilbert Dawe's mute son, have a vision of the Man riding through the fields surrounding Marrick Priory.

1536

March 28

[Malle] plumped down on the ground, and caught Wat by his knees so that he tumbled against her. Then they sat together, rocking to and fro, and Malle kept on babbling, "We shall brast, Wat, we shall brast," while Wat made shocking faces and groaned in his throat; it hurt them so, the joy that was far too big for them, and the dread. For God, that was too great to be holden even of everywhere and forever, had bound himself into the narrow room of here and now. He that was in all things had, for pity, prisoned himself in flesh and in simple bread. He that thought winds, waters, and stars, had made of himself a dying man. . . .

They crouched on the hillside, looking toward God, feeling God under their spread palms on the grass, and through the soles of their feet. Beyond, beyond, beyond, and beyond again, yet always that which went still beyond—God. And here, with only a low wooden gate between, that thing which man could never of himself have thought, and would never come to the depth of for all his thinking, here that thing impossible was true as daylight, here was God in man, here All in a point.

Jim Campbell is a veteran religious educator and author. He is the coauthor of the Finding God *religious education program, published by Loyola Press, and the general editor of the Harper's New American Bible Study Program. He has three postgraduate degrees, including master's degrees in theology and history, and a doctorate in Ministry in Christian Education from the Aquinas Institute of Theology, St. Louis. He is the staff theologian at Loyola Press.*

The Man on a Donkey, Part 2

A Chronicle

To Dorothy Mack
because it is her book

Author's Note

The book is cast in the form of a chronicle. This form, which requires space to develop itself, has been used in an attempt to introduce the reader into a world, rather than at first to present him with a narrative. In that world he must for a while move like a stranger, as in real life picking up, from seemingly trifling episodes, understanding of those about him, and learning to know them without knowing that he learns. Only later, when the characters should by this means have become familiar, does the theme of the whole book emerge, as the different stories which it contains run together and are swallowed up in the tragic history of the Pilgrimage of Grace. And throughout, over against the world of sixteenth-century England, is set that other world, whose light is focused, as through a burning glass, in the half crazy mind of Malle, the serving woman, and in the three cycles of her visions is brought to bear successively upon the stories of the chief characters of the chronicle.

Gilbert Dawe, Priest

1536

January 7

At Kimbolton Castle the groom of the chamber and the candle maker heard the clock strike eleven as they finished the worst part of their work, and washed their hands, letting the water run over their forearms, till the basin looked as if it was full of raspberry juice. Then, having tidied up the mess, and set aside the earthen jar in which were enclosed the heart and entrails, they kicked the bloody cloths out of the way of their feet, and set to work to cere the body, wrapping it in fold after fold of waxed linen cloth, with handfuls of spices laid on, till the sickly smell of blood was overlaid by the sharp scents of cinnamon and myrrh. By the time they were done it was close on midnight, and all at Kimbolton asleep except those who waited to watch beside the bier till day. The groom of the chamber unlocked the door, and he and the other went out, leaving alone the body of Katherine who had been Queen. It lay now stiff as wood, and bulked out to unnatural rotundity by the folds of the cerecloth; only the face showed, wax white and sharp in the light of the candle flames which shivered when the wind whined through the shutters.

Outside on the dark stair the groom of the chamber let out a great sigh, and said that "By Cock! he had a sore thirst." As the chandler had the same they went off together to shake up one of the buttery lads. When he had found ale and bread for them, they blew up the cinders of the fire in the almoner's room, and sat down to warm their feet and drink their ale. A big tabby cat, dislodged from the cushion of the settle, stretched and yawned, showing teeth curved and sharp as thorns, but milk white; then it leapt, light as a leaf, on the lap of the chandler and at once fell asleep again.

Not till their cans were half empty did either of the two men speak, and even then the groom of the chamber was sparing of words. But the chandler became garrulous. He said it was a pity to see the good Queen lie dead, and no harm now to call her Queen for that Queen she had been and now was no more, nor was anything anymore, God have mercy on her soul. "And," said he, "all her ladies saying that since the Emperor's ambassador came to see her on New Year's Day, that she fared the better for it, and would recover. Aye and surely it must have given the poor soul comfort to speak to one of the Emperor's people once more."

The groom of the chamber grunted. He was a lean, sharp, worried man, never talkative, and now he would not raise his eyes from the fire. The chandler went on:

"That fat man of the imperial ambassador, the one that spoke English, told me the poor lady took heart so from his master coming, that he heard her, when they were talking, laugh, and more than once."

"Did she laugh?" the groom muttered, but it was less a question than a sort of sour comment.

"Aye—that she did. And asked for the fat man—you know what a merry talker he was—to make her sport that evening."

After a silence the chandler shifted a little on the seat to look at the groom of the chamber.

"Even last night the women were saying that she was so much better that she called for a comb and dressed and tied her hair for herself."

The groom of the chamber twitched his thin nose, frowned, squinted into the can that he held on his knee, and said nothing.

"And tonight," said the chandler, fondling the cat with one hand, but keeping his eyes on the groom, "tonight—there she lies, dead." As he lifted his chin toward the painted beams of the ceiling they both thought of the little close room above, of the reek of the blood, and of the dismal work they had accomplished on the shrunken body of the gray-haired woman that had come to England nearly thirty years before, a young girl, plump and merry, afraid a little, yet hoping more than fearing, because of the ignorance and potency of youth.

"Why," the chandler leaned along the settle and spoke softly, "why did you cut through the heart when it was forth of the body?"

The groom's eyes came quickly to his in a sharp look. But all he said was, "Because so it should be done."

"Perdy, I never saw it so done before."

The groom of the chamber got up. He said he was for bed, and went away. But before he went to bed he found the dead woman's chaplain, the bishop of Llandaff, who, with others, was watching about the body, and told him, very secretly, a dreadful thing—how that the heart of Dame Katherine, Princess Dowager, was black and hideous all through, and to the surface of it clung a small black globule. The groom of the chamber knew just so much of surgery as to be very positive. He told the bishop, who was a Spaniard, that from the state of the heart he knew that the Princess Dowager had been poisoned. The bishop wrote a letter that night to Master Chapuys, telling him what the groom had said. "And if it is poison," he wrote, "surely none other but the Concubine hath devised it."

January 8

Not only the Queen Anne but the King himself joined in the dancing this night, and both showed very good cheer. Many remarked it, and thought, if they did not whisper, of the messenger who had come that morning from Kimbolton, announcing the Princess Dowager's death. At last, quite late, the King clapped his hands to quiet the musicians and bring the galliard to an end. Then he called for wine and candles, and for his gentlemen to put him to bed. The Queen and her ladies, having curtseyed to the King, withdrew to her apartments.

In the King's bedchamber the gentlemen on duty took off the King's rings, and chain, the dagger in a crimson velvet sheath the hilt of which was frosty with small diamonds. One of them laid by his yellow satin cap with a white feather, and a sapphire brooch to hold the feather. Two others helped him to take off the yellow satin doublet. The King whistled softly a tune that they had danced to just now; he yawned, whistled again, and smiled privately to himself.

They had put on him by now his nightshirt, and the gold embroidered nightcap; when he had slipped his arms into a green and white velvet nightgown he spread them out in a great luxurious stretch, yawning again, wide as a cat, so that all his fine teeth showed, and his pink tongue.

He kept Norris behind when the others had gone, talking with him of the buck hounds, and of a new goldsmith out of Germany, a very skillful craftsman; but at last he got into bed and lay there with his eyes shut, and his face, with the fine sharp beaked nose, turned up to the celure of the bed, while Norris drew the curtains softly, and thought, with a sort of start in his mind, how the King would one day—one day—lie just so, with face composed and eyes shut; but on that day the eyes would not open again.

They opened now and met Norris's, and Norris felt his heart quicken, as though the King could read his thought.

"How," the King asked, "goes this business of your marriage?"

"But lamely," said Norris, and asked himself, "Can one have told him that I wait to stand in his shoes?"

"You should make haste," said the King, closing his eyes again, yet smiling with his mouth. "And how think you," he asked, "should a man choose a wife? For wit, or for beauty, or for what other quality in her?"

Norris, because he had been for a moment afraid, now became pert. He said that himself he favored a plump dower.

But the King, frowning a little, went on, as if he had not spoken. "Of all things," said he, "let her be meek," adding hastily, "given virtue, of course, given virtue."

Norris agreed, "Of course." And then, since Katherine, Queen or Princess Dowager, was tonight, though unnamed, in the minds of all, he began to say that though Her Highness had been virtuous, meek she had not been. But he stopped short, having remembered the awkward fact that it was not for him to consider her as the King's wife at all.

Yet the King only smiled at Norris's stumbling. "No matter—no matter. She is dead." He crossed his breast under the sheet and murmured, "*Deus misereatur . . .*"

"God be praised," he said aloud. "Now am I free from any threat of war with the Emperor. Now I shall have peace."

After Norris had left him the King humped himself more comfortably into the warmth of the bed, drowsily watching where a dimly luminous glow in the curtains showed that the great candle burned outside. "Peace with the Emperor," he thought, "peace at home."

"My little fair sweetheart," he murmured, and thought—"Meek as a dove, and as a lamb innocent."

January 18

It was Dame Margery Conyers who was the first to see the King's visitors. She was up in the Vine Chamber in the dorter which she shared with Dame Joan Barningham and Dame Eleanor

Maxwell; it was called the Vine Chamber because a long time ago the beams of the ceiling had been painted with a pattern of vine leaves and grape bunches; the paint was faded now and dark, but on a sunshiny morning you could now and then catch a gleam of gold among the leaves.

The gleam was there today, because of the brightness outside, where a white frost lay on the ground and on the roofs, and the sun shone over all, yellow and clear. The servants had lit the fire and redded up the room while the ladies had been in church, and now the flames were climbing merrily up the chimney; beside the hearth, between the settle and a stool, a table was laid for mixtum with a white fresh cloth.

The day was so fair that for mere pleasure of the sunlight Dame Margery went over to the window, which fronted the sun across the dale. The little panes were all patterned by the frost with pictures of marvelous things. Crusted upon the glass there were woods, sharp hills, lakes still and frozen, fountaining shapes of unknown leaves, all frost-white, yet lit through by the yellow sun with a warm glow of rose.

Dame Margery opened the window, and met the sunshine that came swimming into the room on a faint lit mist and with the clean smell of rime. Across the frozen grass the trees laid lavender blue shadows. Just as she drew a deep breath of the sparkling morning she caught sight of the dozen or so riders who were crossing the ford; they were almost in the sun's eye for her, but she could see one, tall and thin, who wore a big red felt riding hat; another bulky man rode a little askew in his saddle, and as she looked he raised a hand and pointed as if he had seen her at the window.

And as if he had seen her she slammed the casement to. She knew who these were. The nuns' miller had heard from one of the Stainton hinds, who had it from a lead miner, who was told by the Leyburn shepherd, that the King's visitors were come to Coverham Abbey; the shepherd had heard the monks' carter say so at the ale house in Leyburn.

Dame Margery made haste to go down, but it was as if the stone stairs had turned soft as feather pillows under her feet, and the flags of the cloister like quaking marsh land. These visitors, sent about to every monastery in the country, were here to pry, to pick on faults, to question. And at the end of it their meaning was to turn out the ladies from Marrick. She was sure of it. Houses in the South Country had been served so; now it would be their turn.

The prioress was busy counting tallies in the little office halfway along the passage between the cloister and the great court when Dame Margery found her. "Well?" she asked, without looking round, and the light slivers of wood clicked as she counted, "Four boon days; five; six," and then again, "Well?"

"Madame," cried Dame Margery, and tears of excitement rushed to her eyes. "They are coming—from Coverham. They are at the ford." She listened, for by now they must be past the ford. Her right hand, clenched among the folds of her gown, was lacking, though she herself did not know it, the hilt of the sword that her father, and his fathers before him, had carried. "Can we bar the gate and keep them out?" she asked breathlessly.

"By the rood! that we cannot," the prioress said. She laid down the tallies on the convent chest. For a moment she considered; then she told the chambress what to do, precisely and in detail; cut her short with, "Silence! On your obedience!" and turned again to her counting.

Dame Margery, crimson and smudging tears hastily from her face, went back into the cloister, and found that the news had come there already. All the ladies stood close, gabbling together like so many ducks, but much shriller. They cried out to her, and she to them, and the noise grew; most of them were sure as she was of the worst; a few were doubtful; only old Dame Joan Barningham was confident that our Blessed Lady would protect her daughters.

Dame Margery pushed through them, answering questions as she went. "Have you seen them?" "Yea." "Where are you going?" "To the kitchen." "What for? Does the Lady know? What does she say?" There was a silence when that was asked.

Dame Margery had her hand on the door of the buttery passage. She gave them the answer loudly.

"She says, 'Make ready a breakfast for them.' She says, 'Have herbs strewn in the guesthouse. Have the maids light a fire, and see they well blow it up before they leave it. Get out the silver spoons.' She says, 'Set before them the wild boar pasty.'"

She had opened the kitchen door, and now slammed it behind her. The ladies were left to make what they could of the prioress's orders. They found many interpretations of them; Dame Bess Dalton even suggested tentatively that the prioress intended to put poison in the pasty. Dame Anne Ladyman came nearest to the truth when she said, rolling her great black eyes, that, Mother of God! all men were alike. Feed them well and they'd be kind.

That would not have ended the debate, but the sound of voices, and of knocking at the gate, cut it short. The ladies, hushing each other loudly and urgently, made with one accord for the buttery which had a window on the great court.

July and Dame Eleanor Maxwell were left alone in the cloister. Dame Eleanor sat still on her bench; she had at first hoped to learn what it was that had so excited the other ladies. She had plucked at a sleeve here, a gown there, but if any had tried by shouting in her ear to make her understand, the hubbub had been too great for their words to penetrate her deafness.

So the old woman had given up her attempts, slipping back into the prison of her body, which had windows, but in which no sound, except the most muffled and indistinct, was ever heard. She sighed and trembled a little, frightened by a turmoil which had for her no meaning except that it must mean ill. Uncomprehending almost as a baby, but far more patient, she sat very still, her hands crossed upon her big belly, her lips moving in prayers that were just audible.

Behind her, and keeping out of her sight, July stood stiff as a clothes peg, looking down at the grass in the cloister garth, where frost had laid such jewelry upon every blade, dead leaf, and common stone, as none of the King's goldsmiths could by any means have equaled. Her eyes saw, but her mind did not perceive, that exquisite transient craftsmanship, being filled with a dismay too deep yet for any feeling. They would all be put forth from Marrick; she was far more sure of that than the most despairing of the ladies, because she had known always that disaster was the order of the world.

As the ladies sat down to their mixtum, very late, and most of them with the doors set a little ajar, they could hear now and then men's voices, and footsteps heavy and strange. Listening, they knew by the sounds just how the King's visitors were going about their business; the door that clapped to so noisily was the door of the frater; a board in the floor of the warming house creaked; the loose handle on the parlor door rattled, and they thought of their embroidery turned over, perhaps trampled upon by these terrible persons. When the chapter bell rang they came down circumspectly, as if wolves waited below, and sure enough in the chapter house there were two men, one standing by the lectern, the other sitting in the prioress's chair. This one was heavy and bulky, with a broad face that had purple veins like tiny worms upon his cheeks. The other, who flipped over the pages of the Rule as if he disdained it, was much longer and thinner; he was younger too, and dressed in fine red cloth and crimson velvet; he had a haughty look, and his jaw thrust out dangerously like the jaw of a pike.

When the bulky man, who was Dr. Layton, had read the Commission of the Visitation, the prioress knelt and kissed the seal that dangled from it. It was only a little seal, being Master Cromwell's and not the Great Seal of England; for it was not the King but the chief secretary who had sent out these men. Then Dr. Layton told them that the King had heard of the corruptions and wickednesses which had defiled the small houses of religion. They looked at each other and were silent; last year the bishop had visited them, but, though severe, he had not seemed to think their faults very black, so perhaps all might yet be well.

"Therefore," Dr. Layton concluded, "we shall speak with each of you severally, to learn in what state this house stands. We shall begin, as is the custom, with the youngest of you."

That was July, because the youngest novice had gone home for a christening. So they left her, standing in her place looking down at her clenched hands. She did not see Dr. Layton crook his finger to her, but when he ordered her to "Come—come near," she gave a start, and went and stood before him, but would look no higher than his boots, which were of light brown leather, rubbed dark and shiny where the stirrup irons had worn them.

The other man, who was Dr. Legh, came near, and the two of them spoke together, but not to her. "Too young to know much . . ."

"But *ex ore parvulorum* . . ." "Well, well, ask her. Little pitchers have long ears."

In the end it was Dr. Legh who began by asking her whether the divine service was fully and meetly kept.

"Oh yes," said July, and they both laughed, Dr. Legh with a thin high whinnying laugh that she much disliked.

"Too fully and meetly," he tittered. "You're not very devout, mistress. And now as to fasting . . . ?"

Dr. Layton interrupted after a little. He said it was no use "putting such questions as you put to this child. She cannot know how the officers of the house lay out the revenues."

Dr. Legh asked, "Why not? Put them all through it. Truth comes out by little and little, like whey from the press."

But Dr. Layton overrode him, and July thought for a moment that he was the more bearable of the two, while he asked her how old she was, and when she was to be professed.

She told him fifteen first, then sixteen. Then she said "Yea, sixteen, and I shall take the vows at Easter."

"God's Blood! sixteen!" cried Dr. Layton. "That's how scandals grow. My young gentlewoman, in another ten years we'll have you kicking against the vows, and maybe committing fornication with some pretty wanton priest."

He laughed, low and richly, and July thought him worse than Dr. Legh.

"Or if not with Master Priest," he ran on, "then with some fine gentleman who comes and goes, in and out of the house. For I hear from certain of the servants—" he spoke over his shoulder to Legh—"you heard it too—that your prioress will let men speak with the nuns in the cloister and the parlor. Now can you say who entertained these men, and whether any sent or received love letters or tokens, pretty trifles such as ribbon knots, or rings with posies? Or did any man haunt the church alone after dusk? Jesu! things can be done in the church after dusk that you wouldn't think for." He laughed again, and asked Dr. Legh didn't they know it by now, both of monks and nuns? Legh smiled, but sourly and as it were with disdain.

"Now," Layton said, and laid his warm fingers on July's hands, clasped in front of her. "Now can you remember of any gentlemen who came into the cloister—yea, even though you saw nothing amiss done?"

July unclasped her hands and put them behind her back.

"No," she said, "None."

"None? You're sure?"

"None," she told him again, and he caught her look and in it read hate. He could not know what she hated him for, nor that when he spoke of men it meant for her nothing but one man, and when he spoke of wantonness it was as if his soft pawing hands were feeling toward the name of Master Aske, to soil it with their touch.

They asked her more questions after that, but she shut her lips and only shook her head or nodded for answer, so they rated her for an obstinate forward stubborn wench, and after a little, since they got no more out of her, sent her away to bring to them the eldest of the novices.

January 19

Next morning, early, because they would leave Marrick at once after breakfast, the two visitors sat in the guesthouse chamber, drawing up their report on the priory. There was a fire, but, in spite of much work with the bellows, a gusty wind was puffing smoke and more smoke down the chimney and into the room. Dr. Legh flapped it from his face with a long, impatient hand. "The devil's in the fire," he said and coughed, and bade the clerk open the window, "for it's better to freeze than stifle."

The clerk, who sat much nearer the window than he, thought otherwise, but did what he was bid in silence.

"Are you ready?" Layton asked. He sat the other side of the hearth from Legh; the prioress's red buckram bag lay on his knee, and from it he was pulling out bundles of old charters with cracked or crumbling seals dangling—seals of red wax, or heather-honey brown, or oily green.

The clerk, having sat down again and tucked his left hand under his thigh to warm it, said that yea, he was ready. Layton began to dictate; this was all of the revenues of the priory from meadows and closes, sheep walks and messuages that had been given in old time to the house—at Marske, and Downholm, Richmond and Newton-le-Willows. He stopped once to flourish a small, very old charter.

"Here's a pretty thing! 'Henry le Scrope 14th year of King Edward son of King Edward'—that'll be Edward II—'holds ten acres of Margaret, Prioress of Marrick, at a rent of a red rose in the time of roses for all services.' Was she then his minion? Were nuns, think you, as loose then as now?"

Legh said scornfully that such a rent was nothing uncommon, but Layton would not be deprived of his ancient scandal. "For look you," said he, "that same payment was after commuted to sixpence."

When all the spiritual ties and temporalities of the house were written down, they came to the nuns themselves, beginning with Christabel Cowper, prioress and treasurer.

Dr. Legh said at once that there was little against her, except that it was said of her—that fat Nun Elizabeth Dalton said it—that she wore petticoats of brocade and gilt pins on her veil. "But I make little of that," said he, waving his hand against the smoke, and then holding it before him to look at a gold ring on his finger with one sapphire stone in it.

He thought that Dr. Layton did not know that the prioress had given him the ring.

"What," asked Layton, "of those mistakes in the account roll?"

Legh chuckled. "Jesus!" said he, "No mistakes. They're all on her side, and I think I know where the money went that was so subtly hidden in them. You've seen the prioress's chamber? Yea. Very fair. Very neat. Good wainscot work and made to last many a year. Indeed," he looked very superciliously at the clerk, and a little less so at Layton, "indeed, for my part, I think it a pity that this house should not continue, so I gave the Lady the best counsel that I might." He half closed his eyes to look again at the sapphire on his finger, and added, "Of course, she said the house was too poor to offer so great sum to the chief secretary for its continuance." He smiled to himself, making the same mistake with regard to Dr. Layton that the prioress had made. But he had far less excuse than she, for by this time he should have known that Layton, for all that he was a man of one idea, was no fool.

For a moment Layton said nothing, but scratched his thigh and savored his keen dislike of his fellow visitor. Then—

"What of that that was said of her as to being found with a boy in her bed one night?"

"Tcha! And how many years ago? Even that black-eyed scandal monger that told it could not say but that it was a matter of two children. And such as she—" he looked at Layton with a look that said, "and such as you,"—"would find matter to traduce a saint."

"Well, well," Layton let it go.

"Who next?"

"Dame Margery Conyers."

"That bag of bones!"

"Confederate with the prioress, I think," Layton put in, but Legh disregarded this, which might have been a warning to him. So they went on through the nuns. Nothing much could be objected against the house except that the nuns were accustomed to go out from the cloister to funerals and christenings, staying away an unconscionable time, and that it had been known for gentlemen to be entertained in the cloister and the parlor. One nun, professed two years ago, at the age of twenty-three, must go forth; they both agreed to that, though their commission only gave them power to send away any under twenty-two years of age who had taken the vows.

"As for that novice," said Legh, meaning July, "she shall not take the vows this Easter."

"And it would be well," Layton added sourly, "if she took them not at all."

At last Legh stood up and stretched himself till his joints cracked. He said, well, that was an end, and now for the mulled ale the prioress had ordered for them, and to saddle.

The clerk began to shuffle his papers together, and then Layton spoke.

"Have you forgot," said he, "this matter of the wench who sees visions?"

"Visions?" Legh was taken between wind and water.

"Or have you not heard?" Layton purred, knowing well Legh had heard. "I thought it," he said, "a grave matter."

Legh sat down again. In his mind he abandoned the cause of the prioress, and with less compunction because the ring, though pretty, was of no great value, and he suspected that it was not her best. "Tell me," he said, as if this talk of visions was news to him.

So Layton told him of the serving woman, Malle, who, certain of the servants averred, saw visions of our Savior, of our Lady, of saints and angels and devils too.

"And doth she prophecy treasonably?" Legh inquired with the due amount of apprehension that a loyal subject should show.

But Layton was satisfied; he had given the young man a lesson. He said that there were no prophecies that he could hear of, nor naught treasonable in the visions, but that it seemed the wench was but a poor, crazed, harmless creature. "Nevertheless," he concluded, "it were well that I should admonish the prioress that such things are dangerous. Write it down so," he bade the clerk.

Legh understood precisely why he said that "*I*" and not "*we* should admonish the prioress." Nor when they rode from Marrick, warmed by the mulled ale, did he need to inquire how Dr. Layton had come by a handsome brooch that he wore; it was a thing of a good deal more value than the sapphire ring on his own finger.

January 29

Sunshine was blown across the empty countryside like straw before the wind; in the great church of the Abbey of Peterborough the colored windows glowed and gloomed as the light filled them and was wiped away. As well as the changeable brightness of the day the strong tide of air found its way into the church in little trickles and eddies and swayed the flames of many torches and tapers lit for the burial of Katherine, once Queen of England. Sometimes a stronger breath moved the drooping banners, upon which candlelight and sunlight chased each other, showing the arms of England, of the Emperor, of Spain, Aragon, and Sicily; there were also little pennons bearing devices such as the bundle of arrows, the pomegranate, the lion and the greyhound, which commemorated old alliances as far back as John of Gaunt, who had married a Spanish Princess. Besides all these banners there were four great golden standards on which were painted the Trinity, Our Lady, St. Katherine, and St. George, while round about the walls hung cloths painted with the dead woman's chosen motto, "Humble et loyale," in tall gold letters. All that was left in England of Katherine, Queen or Princess Dowager, lay in the midst of the lights and the banners in its leaden coffin, under a cloth of gold frieze with a great cross of crimson velvet.

The mourners, of whom the King had chosen for chief his niece, Eleanor, daughter of the Dowager French Queen and the Duke of Suffolk, sat in black rows upon the benches, while Bishop Hilsey of Rochester preached to them against the power of the pope, and against the incestuous marriage of Katherine, widow of Prince Arthur, to Henry, then Prince of Wales. Lady Eleanor sat, hearing, yet not hearing, with every appearance of decorous attention; her mind was running upon the delinquencies and impertinences of one of her waiting women, and on the piercing phrases of her next rebuke. But the ladies and gentlemen who had been of the dead woman's household heard and attended well enough to what he was saying. Many of the gentlemen scowled; those of the ladies who were not crying shuffled their feet upon the hassocks of rushes. The imperial ambassador, M. Eustace Chapuys, who was placed among the great mourners, neither scowled nor shuffled, but sat very stiff with a face empty of expression. Only when the bishop, warming to his work, declared that the Princess in the hour of death had confessed that she had never rightly and lawfully been Queen of England, the ambassador's sanguine complexion deepened to crimson; he lifted his head and stared at the bishop, in a look giving him the lie. But the bishop would not catch his glance, keeping his eyes all the time on the words of his dissertation.

When the solemn Mass was over they buried her before the lowest step of the high altar, laying over the stone a simple black cloth.

That same day at Westminster, as rain began to slash at the palace windows in an early twilight, a man in a sober black gown came to a door in the palace, knocked, and with a backward glance to see that none watched him, slipped in.

A young man, with a long, pale, disdainful face, was writing at a table. He let his eyebrows run up toward his fair hair at the intrusion. But the other said, "My master is one of the doctors to the Queen's Grace."

"Ah." Sir Edward Seymour stood up. Under his dignity he was eager. "Well?" he asked.

"She hath miscarried."

"Of a boy or girl?"

"Of a male child."

"Not that that matters," Sir Edward corrected himself coldly, and the doctor's servant let the corners of his lips drop in a sour smile. It mattered much for the Queen's Grace.

"Tell me—" Seymour was easing a pearl ring from his fore-finger, and the other, keeping his eyes away from it, began to talk, doctor's stuff at first, which was mere words to the unin-structed, but afterward things more understandable.

"As soon as she could speak," said he, "she asked her woman, 'Knave or girl?' and when they said, 'Knave,' she let out a cry, and on that same moment swore that the fault was her uncle's the Duke of Norfolk, because he had told her that the King had fallen in the tilt-yard. 'And he looked so white and wizen,' says she, 'I thought His Grace was dead, the which pierced my heart like a dagger, and I shrieked, and the pains came.'"

"His Grace hath been told?"

The doctor's servant nodded as he took the ring from Seymour's fingers, and now he let his eyes take a look at it, before he put it by in his pouch, and tightened and knotted the strings. It was a ring of price, and according to his lights he was a man who liked to be honest, and give value for money. He came close and whispered.

"I spoke with him who brought the news to His Grace. He heard the King say that now he was sure that black sorcery had been the means by which he was brought to this present unhappy marriage."

Sir Edward put by the fellow's hand from his arm, and said stiffly that news, so it were true, should always find its reward. When the doctor's servant had gone off, circumspectly, he also came out from the room, and went up through the palace toward the chambers of the Queen's maids, to find his sister, Mistress Jane Seymour. He thought it well she should be told all that he had just heard.

February 4

Dinner at Marrick Manor began with veal chawetts, and for a while the prioress and Dame Nan talked of how these should be cooked. The priory made its chawetts with wine, a little verjuice, and dates, raisins, currants, and mace. These chawetts of the Bulmers had green cheese in them, and no wine nor dried fruits. The prioress professed herself eager for the receipt, and Dame Nan said over her shoulder, "See to it, John," and one of the men waiting answered her, "Aye, mistress."

But after that more and more the prioress directed her conversation toward Sir Rafe, so that by the time the cloths were drawn, the servants gone away, and the three of them private (which was what the prioress had asked for) Dame Nan's face was set hard as a stone, and she sat beside the prioress on the settle, remote and pale, looking down at her hands idle in her lap, while the prioress leaned toward Sir Rafe in his chair, and told him of all that the visitors had done and said, of Dr. Layton's warnings, and Dr. Legh's counsel, and thus came to the point of her errand, and the dire need of the house.

"Well," said Sir Rafe at the end of it all, "if you will sell me those closes up at Owlands—"

"No. But I will lease you the west side of Owlands Bargh."

"Sell it, and you shall have that which will content Cromwell."

They haggled about that for some time, while Dame Nan sat mute, only her chin lifted a little higher.

When they had agreed at last, the prioress got up to go, so they all stood, but Dame Nan moved a pace aside to separate herself from them, and looked out of the window at the garden deep in snow and shining in the sun. The prioress was telling Sir Rafe how his brother Sir John would not pay the dower of Julian Savage this Easter, seeing that the visitors had forbidden that she should be professed. "So how," the prioress asked, throwing her hands wide, "how can I keep a growing young wench without dower till she be twenty-four, and the house squeezing out money to buy our continuance, if it may be? Nay, marry, I cannot do it. I cannot. She must away again to Sir John."

Sir Rafe began to hum! and ha! He made it clear without exactly saying so, that he thought his brother in the right, since to pay a dower when the priory might not stand, was only to put money out of his own into the King's pocket. If the money were July's own, left by her uncle, that made no difference.

It was then that Dame Nan spoke, surprising both of the others.

"I will have the young gentlewoman here at Marrick, if Sir John and—" she paused, "and his lady allow."

"Why Nan—" Sir Rafe cried.

"I need another gentlewoman," she said, never turning her face from the window.

"Well, well," the prioress murmured. She was indifferent what became of Julian Savage, so long as she did not eat up so much as a groat of the priory revenue. She asked Sir Rafe when she might have the money in her hand for the leasehold, and they went out together, leaving Dame Nan just rising from a needlessly deep and stately curtsey.

After a few minutes Sir Rafe came in again, and sat down. He looked at his wife's back, regretted, as he often did, that things were come to be so often at cross-purposes between them, and, not being wise enough to let ill alone, said, "I cannot see for why you should need another gentlewoman, nor, if you do, why you should take that young wench who's a bastard."

"And sister to your brother's wife," Nan caught him up. "At last his wife," she added smoothly, and saw him scowl. He was not glad to be reminded that since Dame Anne Bulmer had died last autumn Meg Cheyne had become Meg Bulmer. And when Dame Nan added that she thought it not well that a young wench, who was to have been a nun, should go to such a sister as Meg, he was too much in agreement with her to find any retort.

"And I hope," Nan concluded, with jagged ice in her tone, "I hope I may at least choose my own gentlewomen."

He cried then, "Death of God! It's that, is it, that you grudge at? That I deal for you in a matter of land and leases, though before your face, mark you? Shall not a husband do so?"

"You have tried to buy that which my ancestors gave to the nuns."

Sir Rafe threw his hands wide, caught his knuckle smartly on the settle, and swore again.

"There was a time you wanted the closes at Owlands," he told her, and she, remembering that time, and all those times when they had been one in mind and in heart, was pierced by the pain of remembering.

"My ancestor, Roger Aske," she began stubbornly, but Sir Rafe cried a murrain on all Askes, and inquired whether she would not have the priory to continue.

"I would," she said in the voice which she kept for their worst quarrels.

"But you would not have me help the prioress to one hundred marks?"

"One hundred marks to bribe Cromwell with."

"Well—would you that, or that the house were suppressed?"

"I would not the King left his business in the hands of a rogue."

"Fie on such words!"

"Fie on him for a rogue! Yea, fie on the King too! My fathers gave lands that God should be served down at Marrick. Will the King do well if he take those lands that were never his?"

Sir Rafe rebuked her. Then, because in this also they did not really differ, only that he thought it unseemly for a woman to speak so bluntly against the King, he said, to turn the subject, that it was well the priory had that manner woman for its prioress these days.

"Is it?"

"God's Bread!" he cried, "is it not? You know how well she has cherished the house."

"I know how she cherishes that which is her own. I know what manner woman she is, and what it is she loves. Not God, nor poverty, nor charity. No. But her will, and her way, and her goods."

"Tcha!" was all he could say to that.

"And she says that if that poor soul Malle speak more of heavenly things she's to have a sore whipping. You heard her say it. That is how Christ is served at Marrick."

"Mercy of God!" he asked her, did she think that the woman Malle was anything other than a poor crazed fool?

"Fool or saint," she said, "it would be all one to my lady prioress."

"Oh!" he cried, and got up. "Here is but spite and ill-will and a woman's shrewishness," and he left her there. She stood for a long time by the window looking out. The sun had gone down now, and the snow was bright no longer, but only a shroud over the frozen earth. She laid her face against the bubbled quarrels of the casement, and kept it so till it ached with the cold, smelling the thin, chill smell of the glass, and feeling her heart like the flesh of her cheek, both aching and cold.

February 16

A servant had been sent down from Marrick Manor with a mule, and a priory servant was to go up with Mistress Julian Savage to fetch back the baggage pony that carried her little trussing coffer and bed, which was all she had brought to Marrick. Two of the ladies, Dame Margaret Lovechild and Dame Bet Singleton, came to the gatehouse with her, and saw her lifted up on the mule, and cried to her to come and see them often, and that she was not far away, and must not forget them. They waved their hands to her, and then turned back into the great court, because they ought not to have been there at all, but in the cloister, and the bell in the tower was ringing for None. As they picked their way through the trampled snow, which the great frost kept crisp yet, Dame Margaret was wiping her eyes.

"Poor child," said she, "poor little wench."

"But when I asked her yesterday was she sad to be gone from us, she said, 'It matters not. It is all one.' And today she did not shed a tear."

"Ah! But she was sad for all that. And perhaps she meant that it was all one, if the house did not continue."

Dame Bet cried out, "Fie! we shall continue," for the ladies were getting their courage again, and could not conceive that Marrick should be suppressed, and the priory void, and they all sent away to those homes that they had seen only now and again for many years.

Meanwhile July and the two servants went up by the longer way to Marrick Manor through the bright day, July riding a little in front of the men. She did not once look back, but neither did she look forward, only down at the mule's shoulders where the muscles slid under the mouse-gray hide.

Just about the time that July sat down to her dinner at Marrick Manor the nuns' bailiff came back to the priory; he had been on the road from London for the last three days, but he was brought at once to the prioress, delivered his message and handed her a letter.

She looked down at it in her hand, and asked again, though she had heard him well enough, "You say the chief secretary promised to be good lord to us, and bade us not to fear?"

"He said to me those very words."

She broke the seal then, and opened the letter. The same was written by one of Master Secretary's clerks, and signed with Thomas Cromwell's own hand; the ladies of Marrick should not fear if in their house God's service was well kept, "for it is not the King's intent to suppress any but abbeys in which manifest sin, vicious, carnal, and abominable living is daily used." So Master Cromwell accepted the gelding, and promised to accept one hundred marks next year.

Within the hour the news became known in the parlor where the ladies sat, and then all pretense of silence and meditation ceased.

Never, they told each other, had they believed that Marrick should fall, and that was true, but for the last few weeks they had not been easy, so that now, as their confidence returned, they grew very cheerful. Yet it did not take them long to grow accustomed to this security which was so natural to their thoughts. Before suppertime Dame Anne Ladyman was heard to lament that, it being a Friday, they would have to eat "those everlasting beans once more." And Dame Bess Dalton, who was darning a tenterhook rent in the skirt of her habit, remarked that she supposed there'd be no new gowns for them now for many a year, aye, and long after the Lady had redeemed Owlands

Bargh. "Surely," said Dame Bess, "this same pretext will serve her bravely whenever she will stint us of this or that."

March 6

The prioress looking from her window saw the bailiff talking to one of the hinds who was plowing. So she put on her pattens, and a big cloak, for the evening was setting in fine and frosty, under a clear sky, and hurried out to catch Master Bailiff before he went off to the ale house at Grinton.

She caught him, and kept him standing first on one leg, then on the other, at the edge of the field, while the hind trudged up and down the furrows. There was much to be spoken of, for barley sowing was on hand, and harrowing would follow. Then grafting must be finished in the orchard before the moon began to wane. And this year white peason should be sown in more plenty, for the prioress thought she should have enough for the pot, and to sell also.

At last she let him go, and herself came back toward the priory. Along the hedge the blackthorn blossom tufted on the dark boughs was like pearls, like stars; away on the edges of the wood it was like spilt foam. She turned into the orchard gate, and for a while walked among the trees, pausing specially long to look at the new graftings; on the big old Bittersweet apple tree she had had the bailiff set three grafts, of Pomewater, Ricardon, and Blandrelle. So in five years' time, or seven, that tree would bear his four manner apples; a great subtlety it would be and much admired.

Before she left the orchard she took a look also at the three young walnut trees, clean, slim, and silver gray. They would be slower; perhaps in twenty years the nuns would have of them plenty of nuts. She looked at them kindly; she did not wish to hustle them. She doubted if even in twenty years' time their neighbors, the ladies of St. Bernard, would have thought of planting walnut trees—that is if, in twenty years' time there were any ladies in the little house a mile down the river. And then she reflected with some satisfaction on the elimination of the ladies of St. Bernard, who had not Thomas Cromwell to their friend.

So, as she latched the orchard gate carefully behind her, her mood was contented, and in tune with the quiet evening. And she smiled to see that big lad, Piers Conyers, bumping along from Grinton on a chestnut cob. He smiled too, and pulled up to walk the pony alongside her, his blue cap in his hand.

"Well," said she, "and what mischief have you had in hand?"

He grinned, then laughed. There was down on his chin, but his cheeks were yet soft and round as a child's cheeks; and so was the nape of his neck, where the brown hair fell in a soft curve. He said, demurely, "Madame, no mischief, but an errand for my lady."

"Faith!" she told him, "I thought you had helped yourself to Mistress Doll's little cob."

"And so I did."

They both laughed, and she said, "I'll not tell. Get on. Get on with you. But rub him down well and water him, for I can see you've been riding races."

So he went, shouting, and beating the little beast to a canter with his heels, and she came on slowly, smiling at him, and smiling in her mind at another boy, younger than he, and a

long time ago. John was in her thoughts as he had not been for
many a day, he and Piers together. She felt their kindness for
her, and it was as if John and she were still as young and silly as
they had been. Then she laughed outright, as she remembered
Dame Anne coming in with the candle in her hand, and all
her solemn horror, so palpably enjoyed. She had never laughed
at that before, only, if she thought of it, had been able to smile
bitterly. But now she thought, "Mother of God! How silly we all
were!" and she laughed comfortably in her mind at all of them.
Then she thought, "It is because I grow old that I can laugh." It
did not grieve her to think of growing old, but gave her a feeling
of greater security and quietness.

As she turned under the gatehouse she heard Jankin's fire
crackling merrily, and saw the light of the flames sliding and
shaking upon the opposite wall. It was a pleasant sound, and
when she came into the great court it was pleasant and a great
surprise to see the Lent Peddler and his tall white donkey. Jankin
was unloading the donkey, but the Peddler stood near, and
Dame Margery Conyers and Dame Anne Ladyman were with
him. They saw her and they all stood stiff, as if they had been
caught at some shocking deed. Jankin stood with one of the
packs held against his stomach, Dame Margery's hand went up
to her mouth, Dame Anne and the Peddler stood still staring.

Then the two ladies cried, as if with one voice—"Madame!
Madame! Have you heard?"

They told her, the Peddler, Jankin, and the two ladies chiming together like dogs, that Parliament had given into the King's
hands all the abbeys. "No," said the Peddler louder than all,

"only the little abbeys, such as this one," to be suppressed and altogether brought to an end.

When they had finished telling her there was a silence so complete that she could hear again the crackle of the sticks in Jankin's fire in the gatehouse. She said at last, to Jankin, and pointing to the Peddler, "Give him to eat, and his beast," and then went up into her chamber. She had not told the ladies to follow her, but she was not surprised to find them in the room with her.

She sat down in her chair, and they side by side upon the bench. Dame Anne twiddled her fingers together, Dame Margery had her hands tight locked; the prioress saw them sit like that and then turned her eyes to the window; Calva lay there sharp edged and dark against the last of the dying light.

Margery Conyers suddenly wrenched one hand from the other and beat it on the bench beside her.

"Shall they do it? Will not men rise to forbid them? Oh! Shame! Then let's bar the gate. Let them take us like a besieged city if they dare."

She burst into tears then, and the prioress told her that such a thing could not be, to hold the house against the King's will. But she did not speak sharply, and patted Dame Margery on the shoulder, bidding her take heart. Margery was a fool, but she loved the priory, and Dame Christabel felt kindly toward her.

"Jesu!" Dame Anne said, "if there are to be any of such doings let me forth first," and she laughed. She had given up twisting her fingers together, and now she pinched her veil on this side and on that, and drew a little farther from under it a curl of dark hair which showed upon her forehead, where it should not, by the Rule, have showed at all.

"Well!" said she, giving herself a little shake like a bird that has just preened its feathers, "if they choose to put us forth what can we do but seek husbands. Fie on such a need! God's Mother! I shall die of shame to feel a man's hand on me."

The prioress turned and looked at her, and under the look Dame Anne grew red and giggled. Then the prioress turned her eyes away. It seemed to her now that there had never been a time when she had not detested Dame Anne. "At her age!" she thought. "Her head's like a brothel!" And she was filled with a fury of scorn and disgust.

But when the two had left her, and the warming fury had died, then the prioress knew the blank of final defeat. All the abbeys must go—all the little abbeys that is—and she had got out of Jake the Peddler that proof which should try and depart great from little. She bit at her knuckles, and at her nails. It was useless to unlock the chest and to go through the priory accounts. Never, she knew, could she make Marrick even appear to possess revenue of £200 a year. Yet she could not but try. Soon she sat at her desk with rolls and books spread out, reckoning up, and reckoning up again. It was as hopeless as she had known it would be. At last she allowed the rolls to slip away and rattle to the floor at her feet. She set her elbows on the desk, and her forehead fell into her hands.

March 28

They were winnowing in the big garner—the last of the wheat, which the prioress looked to sell at a good price at Grinton. Because of the dust it was very thirsty work, and long before noon the bailiff winked his eye to one of the men, and walked away toward the kitchen. The rest of them followed soon, keeping close to the wall and out of sight of the windows, in case the prioress was looking out. Malle trailed after them, last of all.

Cook already had his face behind a can of ale, and a man they did not know sat with him, black, shaggy haired, in patched leather hosen; a man of not much more than thirty by his look, but with lines bitten into his face by hunger, or sorrow, or by some stress beyond the common lot. Yet when those who came in from the winnowing grew merry over their ale, he was laughing with them, and more than once it was a shrewd saying of his, or a homely salty story that had set them laughing. Certainly, for all the raggedness and wretchedness of his look, he was one of those that have a way with them; even the bailiff listened when he spoke, and cook, a man of uneasy temper, treated him with unusual sweetness, so that the drinking time in the kitchen lasted longer than anyone had thought for. But at last they must go back to their work, so by ones and twos they drifted away.

Malle had not come into the kitchen. She had stood all the time at the door, gaping in. Now they had to shoulder past her, so stupid she was, and so taken up with staring goggle-eyed at the stranger. Only when all had gone except cook and him, and he got up, and came toward the door, she skipped back out of the way, standing aside in the shadowed passage till he had bidden "God be with you!" to the cook, and gone out. Then she followed him.

There was no one in the great court to bid mad Malle back to work, but the prioress herself saw her, for she stood at her window with Dame Anne Ladyman. First they saw the stranger come out. "There goes an ugly vagabond knave!" said the prioress. "Whence is he?" Dame Anne agreed that surely he was a rough one to look at. She supposed he might be Sir Rafe's new shepherd's man from over toward Lunesdale, where folk are very poor and wild.

When Malle went by following after him it was Dame Anne who said with a titter, "See the fool running after him!" The prioress "Tushed," impatient of Dame Anne's meaning, and for that reason would not open the window to send the woman back to the winnowing. Also her thought was more taken up by the man.

"Fie!" said she. "If Sir Rafe hath brought that one into the dale he hath brought a very stout rogue. See how he goes." He passed just then under the lintel of the gatehouse, and something in the way he carried himself made it seem, though it was amply high, too low and mean for him to pass beneath.

"Fie!" she said again, feeling herself strangely and strongly moved against the fellow. "I warrant this is one of those whose humor it is to grudge at rich men, and would pull down all to be as wretched as they."

When the man came out from the priory gate there was Wat, Gib Dawe's brat, sitting by the nuns' duck pond, hugging his knees. He got up at once, and came slinking down to the laneway, as the man went past the churchyard toward the nuns' steps;

he came alongside Malle, and gave her a quick glinting look, a strange look, but neither frightened, nor wary, nor wicked; his face was slobbered with tears, but that did not matter, for she was crying too. They smiled at each other, and when she held out her hand he took it. So they went both together after the man.

By now he had come nearly to the gate in the wall that divided the priory land just here from the Bulmers's. He went slowly, with his head bent, as though he marked the young grass growing, for it was a very fair bright day, and for the first time the grass smelt of spring. After him, but some way behind, came Malle and Wat. The brown ducks that had been preening and scratching and shaking themselves with much fuss and flutter on the edge of the pond went now in line, following him toward the gate, and a few of the priory sheep, which the shepherd had brought down from Owlands, moved that way too, slowly, with little pauses and starts.

When the man had gone through the gate, letting the weight swing it to after him, he turned for a moment and looked at them all. They stood still, nor did any of those creatures move again until he went on, more quickly now, up the nuns' steps and into the wood.

Only then they came to the gate, and Malle and Wat stood looking over it and watching him as he went. The ducks gathered about their feet, and the sheep too in a little crowd, and looked between the pales. The sun, not yet very high, struck right in among the bare trees, finding out the bright watery green of the trunks, and unlocking all the distances. The wind, moving strongly through the wood, filled it with sliding shadows, as if the air bore light upon its back as a running river bears ripples. So he went up and out of sight, under the great branches that bowed and swung, while the little twigs seemed to clap themselves together for joy.

A cloud covered the sun. He had gone, and Malle and Wat came back to the bare hillside among the boulders, where now the wind brought only chill. But for Malle it was golden harvest weather; the ears of corn were full, wrought four-square, firm as a rope, exact as goldsmiths' work; like rope ends they struck her thighs as she moved through them, loaded with goodness.

She plumped down on the ground, and caught Wat by his knees so that he tumbled against her. Then they sat together, rocking to and fro, and Malle kept on babbling, "We shall brast, Wat, we shall brast," while Wat made shocking faces and groaned in his throat; it hurt them so, the joy that was far too big for them, and the dread. For God, that was too great to be holden even of everywhere and forever, had bound himself into the narrow room of here and now. He that was in all things had, for pity, prisoned himself in flesh and in simple bread. He that thought winds, waters, and stars, had made of himself a dying man.

But at last, as if it were a great head of water that had poured itself with noise, and splashing, and white foam leaping into a pool, and now, rising higher, covered its own inflow, and so ran silent, though no less strong—now they were lifted up and borne lightly as a fisherman's floats, and as stilly.

They crouched on the hillside, looking toward God, feeling God under their spread palms on the grass, and through the soles of their feet. Beyond, beyond, beyond, and beyond again, yet always that which went still beyond—God. And here, with only a low wooden gate between, that thing which man could never of himself have thought, and would never come to the depth of for all his thinking, here that thing impossible was true as daylight, here was God in man, here All in a point.

April 3

Robert Aske went shopping that morning, before the courts were open. It was chilly in the streets, though the sky was bright above, so he and Will walked smartly along Distaff Lane stopping only to buy a new lute string at the sign of the Cock and Hen, and at the Mermaid a sugar loaf, and a pot of treacle, because in the last letter from home Jack had one of his great colds, and there was no treacle to be had in York. Nell, Jack's wife, wrote also to know the cost of all sorts of spices, because she thought the York shopman cheated her. Robert stopped at the corner of Friday Street, in the swimming warm sunlight, to read again—"Pepper, cloves, mace, ginger, almonds, rice, saffron—!" He groaned—"Mass! We must ask the price of all those, and yet buy none." When they came to the sign—"Do you go in!" he said to Will. But Will made way. "After you, master." They came out not only with the prices all neatly written, but also with some oranges and a jar of green ginger, "Because we are two great cowards," said Aske. "It's only women can so brave shopmen," said Will.

After that they went back up Friday Street and into the Cheap, to buy stuff for a new coat for Aske. The street was wide here, so that they came suddenly out into sunshine. All the gilding and painting along the front of Goldsmiths' Row caught the light, and already the busy chinking of the craftsmen's hammers could be heard from within, as well as the voices and laughter of the prentice boys and maids standing about the conduit with their pitchers and pails, waiting to draw water.

"There, master," Will said, plucking Aske's sleeve and pointing across the road to a shop where the wife, in a red gown and fine white kerchief, was setting out bales of cloth, with a brave scarlet on top.

"Not scarlet, Will."

"No. But the murrey."

They crossed the road. The woman smiled at them; she had gray hair and only two teeth in front, but her look was kind and her eyes merry. Aske leaned against the front of the booth, pushed his cap back on his head and prepared for pleasantry.

"Fie, sir!" the woman cried, after they had talked of the fair day, and the dame's good cloth, and Aske's need—so he said—of a new coat to go wooing in—"Fie on the smooth tongue you have! It's God's mercy I'm not a young maid, or you'd have the heart out of me following at your heels."

"Will," says Aske, "take me home, or I'll be plighted to this fair gentlewoman before I know it."

At that she pretended to fetch him a box on the ear, and vowed she'd call her husband.

"Don't vex the good man. Let's speak of the murrey cloth. What's it an ell?"

They settled to a brisk haggle; the price went down from eight shillings to five, and then stuck.

"Four and a kiss," Aske offered.

"God bless the man! Is he always so saucy?" she asked Will, but he glowered at her, and turned his back. He did not like his master to be so familiar with the common people.

In the end Aske paid five shillings an ell for fifteen ells. "And it's good width, two ells and a half," said she, as she rolled it out with soft heavy bumps, while the cloth billowed like the waves of the sea. "You can call the meter to measure it. Will you so, or trust me?"

Aske did not call the meter, but when the cloth was cut and folded gave it to Will to carry back with the rest of the stuff, while he himself made for Westminster.

At the corner of the street he turned to wave his hand and kiss his fingers to the cloth merchant's wife; she threw up both hands and laughed at him, and went inside to give her husband the money and to tell him about the merry gentleman—"a lawyer by his filed tongue and inked fingers"—and what he had said to her and she to him.

"And I said—'Call the meter if you will.' And he says, 'Not I,' says he, 'I know who'll cheat me, and who I can trust,' says he. And I says, 'Well, you can trust me,' I says, and he says, 'I can well see that,' and he laughs at me out of his one bright eye. Our Lady! It was bright too, and gamesome. And he says, 'I know who I can trust,' says he."

Her husband ran his finger down the pages of his ledger. "If he thinks he knows that he's a fool," he murmured.

"Fie!" she told him, "Fie! And he's no fool."

He did not argue the matter.

April 7

It was early, the sun not yet up over the opposite side of the dale, but already Gib sat reading, close to the window, and tilting his book to get all the light. It was safer to read thus early the book that he was reading, when no one was likely to come in and ask questions. Only the old mother was about, muttering as she moved to and fro in the house, and out to the cow shed to the milking. She was telling herself, and Gib, if he cared to listen, what a hiding she would give that useless idle brat, that had slipped out the devil knew where, when there was fire to light, and beasts to tend, and water to fetch.

Gib was reading, with great satisfaction and a cordial anger, the Epistle of Paul to the Colossians.

> Beware lest any man come and spoil you thorowe philoso-
> phy and disceitful vanitie, thorowe the traditions of men and
> ordinations after the world and not after Christ. For in him
> dwelleth all the fulness of the godhead.

He turned the page and by accident dropped the book, and as he stooped for it heard his mother screeching outside once more for "Wat! Wat!" She passed the window next moment, her mouth working with anger, the yoke across her shoulders, and the empty buckets swinging.

Gib opened the book again at random and his eye, running down the page, caught here and there a phrase—

And he came to Nazareth where he was nursed . . .

and then—

> To preach the gospel to the poor he hath sent me. And to heal
> them which are troubled in their hearts. To preach deliver-
> ance to the captive. And sight to the blind. And freely to set
> at liberty them that are bruised. And to preach the acceptable
> year of the lord.

After that he did not turn on to find Colossians again, but
instead sat thinking, with the book on his knee and triumph
mounting in his brain, because this very year surely was the
acceptable year of the lord. The power of the pope was minished
in England; soon it might be done quite away and the pure truth
of the gospel preached. The King was as valiant for truth as
King David (a good similitude, for Gib felt a qualm when he
thought of the King's love. But even so had David lusted after a
fair woman, and yet David was God's servant).

Gib got up. There were wheels that went turning in his head
like the interlocking wheels of a mill, but instead of soft, white,
silent flour, they ground out arguments. He had begun to write
them down two days ago; now the mood was hot in him again.
First he would put away the English Gospels, but because of his
impatience the old hiding place must serve. So he went to the
corner where was the loose flagstone, and knelt to prise it up
with his knife and lay the book again in its hiding place.

It was then that Wat came in, most untimely for both. Gib beat him, both for coming in at that moment, and for not coming earlier; only after Wat had run out again whimpering did Gib remember that the knave could not speak, and therefore could hardly betray.

But one beating more or less did not much signify. Spare the rod, spoil the child. He put the book away and swept the dust and scanty rushes over the stone again with his hand, got his ink and pen from the shelf and the last sheet of his paper, and sat down to write till it was time to go to the church.

The wheels in his brain worked, spinning this way and that. Some would have said that what came out of it was confusion, but Gib knew better. There was something higher and more terrible than ordinary reason, and the cold logic of the schools. His pen spluttered and squeaked as he drove it fast along the page. He dealt with the pope and turned his attention to the bishops.

> And that a subject can hold no land by no righteousness of God under the sun, but it be measured and meted by the King's standard right of God's law above the sun. The King knoweth not his own right of his head office; he hath given his head right to his subjects, which by his own laws hath robbed his kingly image by his sufferance to their wills; hath given it away from him to the Spiritualty, holden contrary to God's laws.

He stopped there, looked out of the window to see how the light had grown, and realized that time had run on while he wrote, so that now he must go at once to church. Besides, he was at the bottom of his last page. He scrawled hastily, "Here I made an end for lack of paper," bundled the sheets together and hid them away.

Though he had made an end of writing his thoughts did not break off, but, as he went he was full of excitement and triumph. "To preach the gospel to the poor he hath sent me . . . the acceptable year of the lord." He was an instrument in a mighty hand. He walked so fast that his breath came short, and he took great gulps of the clean morning air. Had the prophet Elisha, he asked the trees of the wood, spared the forty and two ribald children who mocked him? And—No—he muttered in defiance.

As he came to the corner of the churchyard wall something that stirred and rustled made him glance aside, and he saw Malle's face bob up. It was as easy to see from her look that she spied out for someone, as that Gib was not that one she spied for. At once she ducked down again, and when he came close tried to hide behind the big holly bush that grew in the corner.

"What are you at? Come out!" he told her, and when she came, rueful and dumb, "What are you at?" he asked again.

She mumbled that she wanted—she thought—she hoped— "Lest he should come again this way," she said.

He frowned his harshest at her. She had not even youth as excuse for wantonness, yet she was woman enough, with her large, sagging breasts, and broad haunches, to throw him into a fury of disgust.

"Off you go!" he cried. "Off to your work, or the Lady shall know, and you shall be soundly beat."

He watched her as she went, ungainly and slow, and with many backward glances toward the wood, till she turned in under the priory gatehouse.

April 8

Tomorrow was Palm Sunday, but the weather had turned back to bitter cold. Every one of the ladies at Marrick Priory had a cough, and not one would take any remedy more efficient and less agreeable than honey. Some indeed talked of lemon juice mixed with honey as being very sovereign, but since there were no lemons nearer, at the best, than York, their eagerness to undergo such a cure was of little immediate use. The prioress therefore, having endured the combined, indeed, she fancied, the competitive, coughing of the house for three days in church and in chapter, descended this morning to the stillroom, carrying with her a rushlight, because the shelf where the simples were kept was in a dark corner.

And there, as so often happened, she found that where her eye had not been, old chaos reigned. For one thing none of the jars was labeled; for another, when she laboriously began to take off the bladders that covered the jars, she found things that ought never to have been on this shelf at all—that is to say, distilled water of primroses, and the dried violets which would be made into sugar comfits at Christmas.

So, revolving in her mind just what she would say to Dame Margery, she set to work to look through jar after jar. First came the dried lime flowers; then the coltsfoot, gray-green and soft, which rustled as she stirred it with her fingers; next two jars full

of the light brown chips of the bark of wild cherry. And here—
she lifted first one and then another down and set them by the
rushlight on the table—here were the wrinkled black stems of
comfrey, and here the faded pins of juniper. These, efficacious if
unpalatable, should be the lot of every lady who was heard even
to clear her throat.

It was just then that she heard the clack of pattens and recognized Dame Margery's quick, scuttering walk.

The prioress had been minded to call her by name, to receive
the prepared rebuke, but there was no need. The door opened and
in burst the chambress, and came hastily over to the table where
the rushlight, shaken by the sudden draft, streamed aside with
a lazy tail of fume. She had come in as though on some urgent
errand, yet now she stood still, staring at the prioress; the flame of
the rush, steadying, swam brightly in her eyes, and shining from
below threw strange, distorted shadows upon her face.

"Madame," she began, and again, "madame."

"What is it?" In the old days the prioress would have been
proof against the infection of her excitement, but the times were
too precarious now for her to remain unshaken. She blanched,
but managed to preserve her calm.

"Madame, the Mermaid—she hath seen a vision."

So it was not that the King had sent to drive them all from
Marrick out of hand. The prioress found herself extremely angry,
the more so because her hand shook on the jar of comfrey it
held. Worse than that, she felt her mouth also shake.

"I thought," she cried furiously, "I thought—" and she
turned away, but not quite in time.

"Madame!" Dame Margery was quite at a loss.

"It is," said the prioress, away in the darkest corner, and rummaging among the jars so that they clashed together, "it is," she said on a high, unnatural note, "my many fears for the house."

Dame Margery knew those fears too. All the ladies knew them. But she and some others differed from the prioress as to the means that should be taken to save Marrick. Up till now they had only muttered together in corners of "the arm of flesh which shall not help us," or of "God and his saints to our warranty," lacking courage both to brave the Lady by protest, and, should she yield to their protest, to shoulder responsibility for the consequences.

But now, crimson and tearful, and caught in a strong flow of emotion, Dame Margery cried—

"But if, madame, if this be a sign that God is on our side—if this be a showing of God—"

The prioress stood, turned away, silent and wooden. Dame Margery's eloquence died.

"*Peccavi*! *Peccavi*!" said the prioress, and knocked on her chest with her fist.

But she meant, "I have been a fool! A fool!" That first vision—O that she had trusted her instinct and put her eggs into that basket! Instead she had taken Cromwell for her savior, and he had failed her. Now it was too late to turn back. No, not too late, for of course God was merciful. And perhaps it would work; at least it was worth trying. "*Miserere mei Domine*," she cried, meaning, "God! God! Do *thou* what the King's vicar general will not. Save the house of Marrick!" She turned back to Dame Margery.

"What—what was the showing?"

The chambress told her, tumbling it out as if spilling dried peas from a jar.

"The pear tree on the cloister wall, that storm two nights ago—there's a big branch broke loose. She—Malle—went to Grinton to buy nails; Cook sent her, for he says there'll be no pears if that branch goes on thrashing at the wall like it has—"

"Tchk!" said the prioress.

"And there was the peddler's donkey, she saw it, tied to the door of the wool store by Master Blackburn's house." Dame Margery gulped. "Just as it says in the Office book, where two roads meet. And they came and fetched it away, and Malle went after them and she saw him ride—"

"Well?"

Dame Margery whispered the rest.

"And she saw him ride on it across Grinton Bridge."

The prioress kept her eyes upon the candle flame for so long that when she looked up she could see nothing for the floating light that still dazzled them.

"Where is the woman?"

Dame Margery began to explain how Malle had been along the river bank gathering pussy willow for the Palm cross tomorrow, but the prioress cut her short.

"Where is she now?"

"Up the daleside after primroses." Dame Margery pointed up toward the hill behind the priory, and found herself alone in the stillroom.

The prioress came out of the gatehouse, and looked upward. At the top of the open steep slope, under the edge of the woods, a woman in a brown gown moved and stooped; a little lad was with her. That was Malle, and the lad was the priest's bastard.

Only when she began to climb the hill did the prioress remember that she had not asked why Dame Margery was so sure that it was a vision sent from heaven. "But that," she thought, "I'll find out better for myself."

When she had gone some way up she stopped for breath. As soon as she had it she called Malle by name. The two above turned and looked down; then the lad slipped away into the woods. The prioress beckoned with her hand and waited for Malle to come down to her. She did not watch her as she came, but instead looked down to where the whole priory lay spread out below her, the great court, the nuns' court, the orchard, all the farm buildings, and the church—like the picture of a priory. The servants were busy in the great court; a woman came out with buckets swinging on a yoke, and went into the nuns' court where the well was. Behind the stables a man in a red hood was carting dung.

She knew that Malle stood beside her, and turned. She looked, stared, then lowered her eyes from the creature's face. Never had she supposed that such a look could be. It was not a smile. It was not a light.

"What . . . ?" the prioress began, and must stop to clear her throat. It came to her with a shock that now she feared to be told what the woman had seen. She would have been glad to go away without another word said. But she drove off the fear; what else but good should God, Our Lady, and Saint Andrew intend to their servants? Yet she knew that of that good she was as much afraid as if God were her enemy.

"Come," she said, and heard her own voice harsh, weak, and strange. "What is this thing I hear? What have you seen?"

With a wrench, as it were, she took her eyes from Malle's face. When she did that, and looked down again at the priory, her mind steadied.

"Mad as a goose," she thought. "That look is of her folly. I shall say to her, 'Fie! fool, hold your tongue of these things!'"

But when she looked at Malle she could not say it.

Malle said:

"There was a great wind of light blowing, and sore pain."

The prioress shivered. A tide of air, snow-cold, steady and strong, rushed by them. The morning's blue was now threatened by a cloud that rose and darkened across half the sky. With her eyes on Malle's face the prioress began, fumbling her words in a way that the convent did not know—

"If it is— If you saw— If it was shown— I pray you," she got it out at last, "what in your mind is God's meaning to us in this showing?"

While she waited the wind shifted and rustled among the grass at their feet. Against the deepening darkness of the whelming cloud the frail green mist on the elm trees was visible as it had not been against the bright sky, and far away along the fringes of the wood the bare ash branches showed white like clean bone. Suddenly the cloud broke in a snowy shower, so that looking up the prioress saw a thousand thousand flakes spinning down, sharp white against the looming gray above, and so hard frozen that they rattled among the oak leaves in the grass.

"Marrick?" the prioress cried, coming to the heart of the matter. "Was it shown to you of our house? Shall it fall? Not our house, and the church that's hallowed to God and his Mother and Saint Andrew? Not Grinton Church?" she pleaded, though she cared not a button for Grinton Church.

But Malle did not answer and at last the prioress turned away and went slowly down the hill.

By the time she came back to the great court the sky was clear again, and the clouds sailing in it light and bright as suds. The tower of the nuns' church took the sun bravely. It was of stone, and built upon stone, but as the prioress looked at it, it seemed to totter, and her heart failed. "Jesu!" she cried under her breath. Then she realized that only the fast-driven cloud behind it moved; the tower stood firm.

"And shall stand," she muttered, and ground her teeth together, while her fists clenched at her sides in the folds of her gown.

April 12

The roof of Master Cromwell's new house beside the Church of the Augustines in Broad Street was not yet tiled, though the rafters were all in place, and threw down sharp bars of shade upon the sawdust and butt ends of wood, upon the carpenter's benches and tools that were below.

Master Cromwell stood with his backside hitched on to the edge of one of these benches as he talked to my Lord Darcy in the empty, bright skeleton of his house. The carpenters were at work laying battens for the roof tiles; they whistled, sang, or shouted to one another up against the blue, where fat white clouds sailed. Now and again someone would drop the end of a plank with a clanging noise and a hollow bursting echo.

"The horse," said my Lord Darcy, "is a good horse. He hath a fair pace and easy, and the harness will be worth a hundred marks."

He did not know if Cromwell was attending to him, or to the workmen; for the chief secretary's eyes went sharply about, watching what the men did on the springing ladders, or flat on their stomachs upon the roof timbers.

"But," my lord said, "if I may have leave of the King to go home I shall have no need of the horse, and would beg you take him for the sake of friendship and in token of kindness. And," he added, "in Yorkshire I could be of service to the King's Grace upon the Commission of Peace that is appointed."

"So you could," said Cromwell, not as though it were a new idea, but merely confirming Darcy's words. Then he said it again, fingering a palmful of sawdust as though there might be something hidden in it. After a pause he said, "And I thank you for your gift, my lord, and your good will to me."

Darcy said that the gift was naught compared to the love he bore to Master Cromwell. "And shall I have the King's leave in writing?"

"You shall." Cromwell reached up and clapped him on the shoulder, and kept his hand there as he led him about the house, showing him where the kitchens would be, and where the great hearth, and how choice a prospect there would be of a little privy garden from the window of a closet behind the hall.

In that closet they stood a while at the empty window frame looking into the garden. Nearby there were piles of slates, and nails dropped about in the grass so that there was nothing but disorder, but beyond, a pear tree, loaded with its snow, stood remote in beauty as a ship far off at sea. Perhaps because the door had swung to behind them the two gentlemen, leaning at the window in the sunshine, began to talk of matters of greater moment, and calling for greater privacy than the plans of the new house.

They spoke of the Queen's late miscarriage, and the sorrow of His Grace at the loss of this hope of male issue.

Then Cromwell said, with his eyes on the heap of tiles under the window, "His Grace takes comfort from going down to Greenwich."

"It's a fair palace," Darcy's face was decorously grave, but Cromwell hid a small glinting smile by again lowering his eyelids, and covering his mouth with his hand.

"And a fair flower grows there of late," said Master Secretary.

"You mean Mistress Jane Seymour."

Cromwell laughed out and called Darcy a right North Countryman with his free tongue.

Then he said, rubbing his back up and down upon the window frame—"a fair flower, but discreet too as any gray-beard. Did you hear how His Grace sent her a crimson velvet purse full of sovereigns, with a letter begging her to spend them for her disport, and calling her—well no matter."

"I've heard the like before," Darcy said.

Cromwell caught him by the shoulder again, laughing and as if much pleased.

"Yet this is not Mistress Anne," said he. "I told you this lady was discreet. Down she goes on her knees, kisses the letter, and then gives that and the pretty, plump purse back into the hands of the messenger, begging him to pray the King consider that she was a gentlewoman of good and honorable parents, who had no greater treasure in the world than her honor, and that if he would give her such a costly gift it might not be till her parents had made for her some honorable match."

Darcy shrugged, and muttered something about women knowing how to hold a man off so as to keep him on.

"You think it's her own wit devised the answer?" Cromwell asked quickly, and Darcy met that quick stabbing glance, and began to have an inkling of what Master Secretary was angling for. So he only shrugged, and let the other go on.

"So," said Cromwell, "the King's love waxes at the sight of so delicate a virtue, wherefore that she should know he loved her honorably, he sent to her a promise that he would never try to speak with her except in the presence of one or other of her kin. And," he laughed ruefully, "to that end was I bundled out of my chambers at Greenwich, and Sir Edward Seymour there planted in my stead, because there's a privy way thither from the King's apartments."

He moved from the window and taking Darcy by the arm led him to the door, but stayed before he opened it.

"You think it's but a maid's modesty? Yet it would not be strange if she were instructed by her friends, so as to bring His Grace hookwise crookwise to marriage. As indeed I think she hath been instructed by some, perhaps not so much her friends, to persuade the King against his present marriage, because these same friends, or sinister back friends let's call 'em, want to bring back the old ways, and the power of the bishop of Rome."

He had his hand on the door and turned so that the two looked at each other. Now Darcy was sure of what he was after, and according to his custom he replied with a something that was as much true as it was beside the point. He said that in his fantasy the King would not, for any woman, easily give up that power which he had taken into his hand.

"I think as you. I think as you," Cromwell said, but still held Darcy a second longer, trying to read his face before he opened the door and led my lord out, and to his litter, parting with him with the greatest pleasantness and courtesy.

In the litter Darcy let himself smile. He did not think that the chief secretary was any the wiser for that talk of theirs in the little closet looking on the garden. Cromwell might guess that my lord knew from M. Eustache Chapuys how carefully and earnestly certain persons had advised Mistress Jane Seymour to speak to the King. He might guess that my lord was one of those who liked the new ways little. But of neither of these suppositions was he anymore sure than he had been before.

As my lord smiled—a sharp smile with his handsome old head high—he was dusting his shoulder and his arm where Cromwell's hand had rested. "The place is full of sawdust," he said, catching the eye of one of his gentlemen who went along-side; but there had been no sawdust to be seen upon his coat.

April 20

My Lord Darcy's company came from under the arch of St. Mary's Gate and on over the five-arched bridge. When the way no longer rang hollow under the hoofs, they had left Doncaster behind, had crossed the Don, and were, at last, in Yorkshire.

Darcy dragged the leather curtains of the litter aside and leaned out. "Hi! lads! Halt at the first ale house. There's one a mile or so beyond. We'll drink there to the North Country and homecoming."

The gawky pages yelled, the gentlemen smiled, and the serving men's brown faces split with grins from ear to ear. Darcy smiled too, leaning back in the litter. It was good to be coming home, whatever was lost and whatever time had swallowed up.

Darcy remembered the little ale house from the first time that he had come riding with his father to London, when he was ten years old. Since that day he had never stopped at it, for it was a poor place. But today, because they came home after so long a time, and because that once he had halted there—today they should stop and drink.

The servants riding ahead turned off the road; the rest followed along the bank of a little brook where half a dozen children, naked as fishes, were wading and wallowing; these stood to stare at the riders, then turned their attention again to the minnows and the rat holes.

In front of the ale house there were three horse-chestnut trees, and a little green. Darcy sat down on the ale bench, stretched his long legs, and looked up into the young leaves, through which the sun thrust swimming shafts of white light. The serving men had gone away to the kitchen door; the pages had flung themselves down on the grass like puppies, and now like puppies began to fight and scramble together; the gentlemen stood about, their riding hats pushed off and dangling down their backs by the laces; several of them had peeled off hoods too, so warm the morning was for April.

The innkeeper came out with his wife and a man carrying horn cups, and one pewter pot, "for my Lord Darcy," says he.

"You know me." Darcy was pleased.

"I've known the Buck's head since I've known aught," and the fellow began to talk about what his father had told him of my lord's father.

"Draw for yourself," said Darcy, when he had come to an end, and, "Thank ye," said the man, curt and rough in good North Country fashion, and went off. Darcy smiled up into the deep, lit green of the big tree; such as this man would not be easily bent to new ways. "By God's Passion," he said to himself, "the King doth not know the Northern parts nor the men that here bide. Yet one day, maybe, he'll learn that heart and stomach they are of."

When my lord was in his litter and on the road again Tom Strangways the steward came up alongside. He had all the news of the North from the ale house keeper, and he retailed it as they went along, including that story of a deal that the abbot of

Jervaulx had carried through with the Earl of Northumberland over some horses; they both chuckled over it, then Strangways grew grave, and seemed to Darcy to be casting at him looks that were curious and probing. "Well, Tom," said he, "out with it," and laughed to see Strangways start.

"It is," he said after a slight hesitation, "more of that same tale I told you a while ago. There's talk again of the serving woman of Marrick in Swaledale."

"Serving woman? At Marrick?" Darcy could remember nothing about it.

"Of whom they say that she hath seen visions."

"Oh that!" said Darcy, as something of it came back to him, and he remarked that doubtless the priory had made a pretty profit of such a woman.

"Not in these days," Strangways reminded him, with anger in his voice. "It's said the prioress will not suffer the woman to speak of what she sees, lest it embroil the priory in greater troubles than those that are laid upon all by this late act."

"Hah!" said Darcy, softly and slowly. "Is it so?" After a moment he said, still speaking low, though the trampling hoofs and creak of harness drowned their voices, "Then in these visions the King's proceedings are in some manner condemned?"

"Jesu!" Strangways snorted, "and it would be strange if they were not, unless it be that heaven is deaf."

"But what do they say of her visions?"

"That she saw our Savior bodily as when he rode into Jerusalem on Palm Sunday."

"*Laus Deo!*" Darcy muttered, crossing himself. As he leaned back in the litter, easing himself into the best position to endure the joggle of it, he was thinking that one day, if the times did not mend, this woman and her visions might be of value. Things were now at such a pass that he and others must even use whatever lay to their hands. No hope now to be too finicking. But not yet, he thought, not yet. It might be that this new love of the King's would bring him back to the old ways, though Darcy himself had little hope of it. And anyway, just now there was no help to be looked for from the Emperor, who, by all seeming, would have a war with France upon his hands before autumn, and who, besides, was not like readily to mell himself in English matters now, with Queen Katherine dead, when he had so long refrained while she was alive.

So my lord reflected, but in silence, because Strangways, he knew, was impatient of policy, and loved things to be plain yea or nay, right or wrong. When he put his head out of the litter it was to say, "It might be well to seek the wench and question her."

This time Strangways said that he thought it would be well.

May 2

The groom porter went first down the stair in the White Tower, with the keys he carried lightly chiming one against the other. Then came Mr. Lieutenant of the Tower, Sir William Kingston, and after him Queen Anne, with her ladies, scared and white, following close. But at the low round arch of the stair, that burrowed both up and down through the huge walls, the Queen seemed to stumble, and stayed, laying her hand upon the rough cold skin of the stone, while her ladies bunched together behind her.

"Down?" she cried.

Sir William, already going down, said over his shoulder, "If you please, Madame."

But the Queen still stood, clutching at the wall, and looking down into the twilight of the stair.

"Shall I go into a dungeon?"

Sir William's voice came hollowly from below them. "No, Madame. You shall go into the lodging you lay in at your coronation."

At that she let out a cry.

"It is too good for me," she said, and began to go down, but weeping now, and trembling, and crying, "Jesu have mercy on me."

In the great chamber where she had lain before her coronation there were ashes of a dead fire on the hearth, and candles that had guttered low before they had been blown out. For a moment she thought, as she stood in the doorway, "They have not touched it since that night," and that the candles were those that had then made a glancing golden haze, and the cold ashes the ashes of the fire that had hissed and spurted out sweetness to the room from the spices that were cast on it. She moved on a few paces into the room and then could hold herself up no longer, but went down on her knees, crying again and again, "Jesu have mercy on me!"

Sir William drove her women toward her. They took her hands and after dealing with her a little, quieted her. He, at the door, was for turning his back and going away, since this was now no chamber of audience; but the Queen cried to him, begging him to move the King's Highness to let her have the sacrament in the chamber with her. "That I may pray for mercy," said she, still shaking so that he could see her flesh tremble. "For I am clear from the company of man, as for sin, as I am clear from you, and am the King's true wedded wife."

Then she put aside the women, and came close to him, catching his wrist and peering into his face. "Mr. Kingston, do you know why I am here?"

"No," said he, lying.

She began to ask him of the King, of her father and of her brother, and Kingston did what he could to keep to the letter of truth and yet hide from her, what he knew well, that her brother, Lord Rochford, was already in the Tower. And, lest she should ask more, he tried to loosen her hand from his arm and begone, but she would not let him go.

"For," said she, "I hear say I shall be accused with three men. And I can say no more but nay. Without I shall open my body," and at that she tore at the breast of her gown, and, as she met his eyes, huddled it together again, turning her head aside and crying, "Oh! Norris, hast thou accused me? Thou art in the Tower with me, and thou and I shall die together," and then, all in a jumble, spoke of Mark Smeton the spinet player, and my Lady of Worcester, and of the child that had never seen the light.

"Mr. Kingston," she cried at last, "shall I have justice?"

"The poorest subject the King hath," he told her, "hath justice."

At that she threw up her arms and began to laugh, so that he thought it best to leave her, with however little courtesy. When he had shut the door behind him he could not hear the voices of her women, trying to compose her, but her laughter only.

May 16

Robert Aske knocked at the door of Master Snow's room at Gray's Inn. His finger was on the latch when he heard Snow's voice cry sharply from inside, "Who's that?" and then, in a different tone, "Come in! Come in!" So he went in, and found not only Snow but Clifton and Hatfield and another gentleman whom he knew by sight for a man of Lincoln's Inn.

"Come in," said Snow again to Aske, with great cordiality, and to the other gentleman, "You may speak before him."

Aske shook his head at the stool that Snow shoved toward him with his foot. "I come but a-borrowing," and named a Year Book he needed.

"You shall have it. But sit down now."

"Not craving company. I'll come again for the book."

He was going out when Clifton called to him, "Robin! Robin! come back."

Aske came back. "Well?"

Snow said, "Shut the door," and Aske, after a sharp, hard look at him, shut it, frowning.

"Master Stonor," said Clifton then, waving a hand toward the stranger, "is telling us of this trial of the Queen," and again Snow pushed forward the stool. Aske did not take it; instead he set his shoulders against the door, and shoved his hands through his belt, and so listened, while Master Stonor told all he knew, and that was much and on good testimony, for he had it of a Sergeant-at-Law of Clifford's Inn, who had been present at the trial of the Queen and her brother in the Tower.

When he had finished not one of them spoke or moved till Hal got up from the bed with a sort of laugh.

"And meanwhile," he said, going over to the door, "they say that the King goes junketing on the river all these sweet, fair evenings, with minstrels playing, as if he rejoiced to be a cuckold. And you should rejoice too at her fall," he said, looking down into Aske's face, which was grim. "You have been always set against this Queen." And then, "Let me out, Robin," he said, because Aske had not budged.

"You said," Aske spoke to Stonor as though he had not heard Hal, "you said there were no witnesses called?"

"Never a one."

"And that though the Queen and Lord Rochford both denied the charges?"

Stonor bowed his head.

"It is done so in the King's courts?" Aske looked around at them all, and Clifton grumbled, "By the Rood! No!" but Hal cried out, "Let be! Let be!" putting his hand on Aske's shoulder again, to let him pass out.

This time Aske opened the door for him, and when it was shut again said, as if there had been no interruption, "And of all these accusations, save that great one of cohabitation with those three men, there is naught but what would make men laugh in a Twelfth-tide play. God's Death! She and Rochford made mock of the King and his clothes! She showed openly she loved His Grace no longer. They two laughed at the King's ballads. Well then, bundle up all those charges together with that which you cannot prove, hand a man a written accusation, forbidding him to read it aloud, frown heavily on the jury—and then, by God's Passion, law and justice being fairly kept, pass sentence of death."

Clifton growled, "You've said it," and Stonor tightened his mouth and nodded his head, but Snow got up and began to fidget about the room, protesting that it was unmeet to say such things.

"For why?" said Aske.

"For that—"

Aske caught him up. "For that they are not true?" and Snow began to say, "No, but—"

"I'll tell you for why," Aske interrupted. "For that it's come to this, that not one of us dares lay his hand on the latch to lift it and cry aloud, for any man to hear, that in this trial neither law nor justice is done, but only the King's will, and Cromwell's."

He looked round at them again, and they were silent.

"Each of us," he said, "knows that it is so. But none knows to what pass we shall be brought before the end."

He opened the door then and went away, with Wat Clifton following close behind.

May 18

The ladies had sung Lauds and gone back to bed some time before, and all the house had fallen silent again for the short hours till dawn. But my Lord Darcy was waking in the guest chamber that was above the gatehouse; he lay on his side with his face toward the westward window, through which looked in an orange moon with two large stars beside it, standing clear in the ashen sky of this hour before dawn.

The first cock crew, but sleepily; and faintly out of the distance another answered it.

"Tom," said my lord, "Tom!" and Thomas Strangways sat up on his pallet rubbing sleep from his eyes. "The servants will be stirring soon," said my lord, and Strangways, groaning and yawning, got out of bed, dressed himself, and then helped his master to dress.

By the time that was done there were footsteps and voices below; a latch lifted, a door banged, the dogs barked, and there came the jingle of harness and stamping of horses led out to plow.

Strangways said, "I'll find and bring her to you," and went out.

My lord sat down on his bed, with his back to the old, round-headed window that looked eastward down the dale. This guest room, which was the oldest part of the priory, ran right across the upper floor of the gatehouse, with a window at each end and an open hearth in the midst with a louvre above. It was still dark in the room, because of the smallness of the windows, so Strangways had lit two rushlights and set them on the bench. But outside the sky was paling slowly, as all but the greater stars withdrew before the coming day.

Darcy sat absently fingering his beard and considering this venture on which he had set out. He could not be sure that the prioress, that woman with the keen eyes and deep voice, believed that he and Strangways were, as they said, merchants going over into Wensleydale to buy horses. Yet even if she doubted, it was no matter, so long as she did not know, and did not discover, who indeed he was. And if she did know or discover—God's Passion! he did not greatly care, now that he was once again in the North Country. Yet, he thought, in coming here he might prove to have been a fool for his pains. It was not probable that a serving wench of a small, poor house like Marrick should have anything to tell that would serve in so great a matter as that would be if it came to raising the realm against Cromwell and the King.

Strangways came up the ladder into the room, saying over his shoulder to someone below, "Come up! Come up! None'll hurt you. And you shall have a groat for your trouble for lighting of the fire. But my—my friend is of a humor that cannot suffer these cold mornings."

Then Malle came up into the room with her apron full of sticks and dried bracken for kindling, and having bobbed to my lord upon the bed went down on her knees and began to blow upon the pale ashes of last night's fire, and paused a moment sitting back on her heels to say that for all it was May it was shivering weather; then she crouched again, puffing noisily.

While she was at it Darcy looked at her, and looked at Strangways. He lifted an eyebrow and shook his head, and Strangways shook his too. The woman had a patient, cheerful face, but she looked to have as much wit as the handle of my lord's walking staff.

"Well," said Darcy, when she had done, and the flame licked up and the smoke swayed and crawled and curled along the hearth, "here's for your labor," and he held out a groat.

Malle came near and he put it into her hand, but she held it so slackly that it fell between them.

"Are you she," he asked—because having come here he would at least put the question—"Are you she of whom they say that you have seen in a vision or dream holy things?"

He looked down quickly at the groat which she had dropped, and again at her face; then he got up quickly from the bed; the two rushlights were behind her; no gleam of their flames shone on her face, nor was it, when he looked again, any light at all that he saw there, only something which might be to light as man's thought to his spoken word.

"I pray you," Darcy urged, when she was silent, "to tell me what it is that you have seen."

Malle said: "There was a great wind of light blowing, and sore pain."

He waited for her to say more, not looking at her now, but turned toward the window beyond which the eastern sky showed pale, cold and strange, not colored yet, but flecked with small dark cloud. He had to make an effort to recall what it was he had hoped to get from this woman; something that could be passed from mouth to mouth among common men and gentle too; something that showed it was God's will they should resist the King's proceedings in religion; something that promised the downfall of Master Cromwell, chief secretary.

"But," he said, having fished all this up from the bottom of his mind, as if these were things long forgotten and now become unfamiliar and unreal, "was it told you that God is angry with them that have counseled the King against holy church? And that he will have them brought low?" When she said nothing he persisted. "In these days there are deeds done—there are wicked men—" He glanced at Strangways for help, but Strangway's eyes were fixed on the woman.

"In times past," Darcy urged, "when his birthplace and his sepulchre were in the hands of the heathen, he spoke by the mouths of popes and saints to call on men to take arms and guard his honor. Is it not so now? Is not this the meaning of what you saw?"

He tried to see her face again, but she had turned aside, and the torn and crumpled kerchief she wore hid all but the tip of her blunt nose. He lifted his hand and beat with one clenched fist on the palm of the other.

"He would not resist his enemies. That I know. But for us it is different. Shall we stand by and see—and not—"

But, though he waited, Malle made no answer.

He moved at last and went from her down the length of the room to the window that looked up the dale. For a moment he stayed there, looking out to where, above the humped back of Calva, the moon hung in the sky, pale and round as a white cheese. When he came back Malle was gone and Strangways stood at the top of the ladder, staring down after her. Darcy went by him restlessly to the other window, as if there he might learn something that he needed to know; as if what was not to be found in the dim west might be written upon the brightening east. And upon this side the dawn had come. Harsh thin flame had lit all the small clouds, and, even as he looked out, the light changed, grew warmer and softer, till the cold fire had turned to rose color against a heavenly blue.

"Tom!" cried Darcy. "If all honest men were to hold their hands would not knaves rule all?" He knew he had said that before, and then knew that he had said it to his wife, and the remembrance cut him, and joined with this woman's silence to condemn him. But he cried, "Surely God would not have us stand by while his enemies work their will?"

"Surely not," Strangways said confidently; but then the weight of the decision did not fall upon his shoulders.

And Darcy said never a word more of using the woman's vision to hearten men to resist the King's doings.

June 15

The sun was shining into the upstairs room in which Master William Ibgrave, the old embroiderer, sat with his three workmen. It was from the hands of these cunning craftsmen that those sumptuous garments came that the King and his Queens—one or another—wore at high feasts of the church or on other solemn occasions. Round about the walls hung doublets and kirtles, mantles and petticoats, and among them, hardly more glorious, was stuff for the King's chapel—copes, orfreys, chasubles, and frontals.

Master William had, laid across his knees, a doublet of white and green satin of Bruges, with the pattern faintly traced upon it, which was to be embroidered for the King; and now one of the men brought to him a little locked coffer from the carved chest by the window. Master William took the key from his pouch, unlocked the coffer and lifted from it two packages of soft leather. He unrolled them upon the bench beside him; in one there were eighteen emeralds set in gold; in the other twenty-nine little things like brooches, but without the pin, of pearls set in gold in the shape of the letter I, for the initial of the new Queen Jane's name. Master William and his men were to stitch them upon the green and white satin doublet, the pearl letters on the green, the emeralds upon the white, and all in an intricate mesh of embroidery in silks and gold thread.

Of the three other men who sat in the sunny room one was stitching small pearls upon a pair of crimson sleeves; another was busy with gold thread upon a black damask girdle; and the third, who had brought the coffer to his master, and who was to help with the green and white doublet, sat with his hands on his knees and his eyes cast down; he was a mournful man of Lutheran belief, tormented by fears of damnation, but he was the best workman that Master William had.

He who was sewing at the crimson sleeves paused to let his needle hang twirling at the end of the thread till the twisted silk ran sweetly again. But then, instead of stooping once more to his work, he lifted his head.

"Surely it is that they come," he said, and nodded toward the window. There had been a good deal of noise in the street all morning, of voices, footsteps, and the tread of horses. But now a sound of shouting was growing in the distance, and flowing nearer.

"Tcha!" said the Lutheran, as his two fellows got up and hurried to the window, to hang out, straining to see farthest. Master William, however, only shook his head gently. Though he disapproved of such interruptions, being himself tirelessly industrious, he did not rebuke his men, for he was of a very patient and pacific humor, and willing to suffer the infirmity of more frivolous minds. So he went on, delicately tacking the emeralds and the pearl and gold letters upon the doublet while the road below filled with a moving flood of velvet and satin, jewels, steel and feathers, as noblemen, bishops, ladies, knights and gentlemen, and the King and Queen went by to the Corpus Christi Day Mass at Westminster.

When all had passed the two men came back to their work, and were perhaps the brisker at it for the interlude. Now, as they sat stitching, they told Master Ibgrave how very fairly the embroidery of the Queen's kirtle had showed; they all knew that kirtle by heart, for between them they had embroidered the gray satin with gold, and among the gold had set on no less than 1,562 pearls which, in today's sunshine, had given the whole a sort of milky radiance. They commented too, upon the new Queen's fair face and gentle demeanor, comparing her favorably with her predecessor. The Lutheran, on the other hand, defended Queen Anne, declaring her to have been a great favorer of the gospel, and, in his mind, to have been done to death, innocent, by those who were enemies of the true light. Master William through it all sat contently stitching with his knotted deft fingers, and on the eaves of the roof above the windows the swallows, with the sun on their breasts, kept up a tuneless, ecstatic twittering.

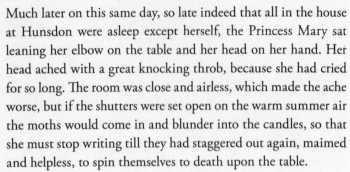

Much later on this same day, so late indeed that all in the house at Hunsdon were asleep except herself, the Princess Mary sat leaning her elbow on the table and her head on her hand. Her head ached with a great knocking throb, because she had cried for so long. The room was close and airless, which made the ache worse, but if the shutters were set open on the warm summer air the moths would come in and blunder into the candles, so that she must stop writing till they had staggered out again, maimed and helpless, to spin themselves to death upon the table.

Yet she was not writing; and now because her fingers were clammy with heat she laid down the pen and wiped them on her gown, and afterward sat looking at the pen, and not looking at the piece of paper beside which it lay. All she had to do—but she had sat here for hours, and it was yet undone—was to sign her name three times upon that piece of paper. If she did that she would declare the King her father to be the Head of Christ's Church, his laws good and just, and herself to be born of a marriage "by God's law and man's incestuous and unlawful."

"Oh!" she whispered, "I shall be sick. I shall be sick," and then crammed her knuckles against her mouth to stifle the word that had come to her lips. She could not cry "Mother!" because she knew that she was going to sign the paper.

And she must do it quickly, before the heavy hammers began to beat again in her head, hammering out arguments, for and against, as they had hammered them out for days. It was wrong.

The Emperor's ambassador said it was right. They would kill her. Then she would be a martyr. It was right to obey a father. It was horribly wrong to deny the truth.

She snatched up the pen and set her name to each of the three articles, then folded and sealed the paper, but clumsily and spilling the wax because of the trembling of her fingers.

When it was done and the thing lay there, signed and sealed, she sat looking at it. It was done, and for a few moments her mind was quite empty except for a dull and heavy sense of relief. She did not remember the dwindling hope of the last week, the growing fears, the letters she had written, submitting, praying for pardon always more abjectly, yet always stopping short of that which now she had done. She did not remember how a couple of days ago she had sat in this chair while two of the King's Privy Council, the Duke of Norfolk and the Earl of Sussex, had stood over her shouting that if she had been the daughter of either of them her head should have been beaten against the wall till it was soft as a rotten apple. She remembered and thought of nothing now except that now the thing was done.

She stood up clinging to the chair for a minute to keep herself steady, and then went crookedly toward the door. Behind her, upon the table between the two candles, lay the sealed paper. She did not turn her head to see it, but it filled her mind, because that small square of white with the clumsy botched seal on it, was that by which she had cut herself off from her mother, from the Church Catholic, from God. Even now she might have gone back to the table and set the paper to one of the candle flames; but she did not.

When she came to the door her fingers fumbled for the latch. She was muttering to herself.

"So it's done. I can sleep now. I must sleep."

June 29

The rain caught them again as they were approaching the priory, so Dame Nan Bulmer sent the two men servants on to the manor, and herself, with little Doll and her younger waiting gentlewoman, who was Julian Savage, and the servant behind whom July rode, turned into the priory gate. Dame Nan and Mistress Doll were brought up to the prioress's chamber, and at once there was calling for wine and wafers, strawberries, and a dish of cherries. The servant went off to the kitchen where he greatly enlivened a dull and disagreeable morning for the cook, his boy, and as many of the wenches who could find excuse to pretend business in that direction. July slipped away to the cloister, and, finding that empty, to the parlor.

There the ladies were, all but Dame Anne Ladyman who was with the prioress, and Dame Joan Barningham who was now so old that for the most part she kept her bed.

"Lord!" they cried, "it's July!" and shook Dame Eleanor Maxwell by the shoulder to rouse her, shouting in her ear that it was July, and pointing to where the girl stood by the door in a gray gown with a red petticoat. It was a moment before the old lady recognized her in this guise, but then she lumbered up, very slowly, while all the rest were crowding round July, crying out that she's grown and was now quite a woman, asking her why she had never yet been to see them till this day, bidding her tell them if she'd rather be at the manor or here, and then never listening to a word she said, but pouring out all that had happened at the priory since she left. Dame Margaret's little dog was dead, and Dame Bet's brother promised her one of those talking popinjay birds but it never came, and Dame Joan had had all her teeth out, and had a very great cough even though it was summer.

Then they made way for Dame Eleanor, who, leaning heavily on her stick, leaned also on July's shoulder as she bent and kissed her, saying in her flat toneless voice that it was good to see her. July, who did not like to be kissed or touched, stood stiff, and then, looking into Dame Eleanor's face, forgot everything but the change she saw there; in these weeks Dame Eleanor's firm, freshly colored fat had sagged and paled; her eyes, which had been cheerful, now seemed to be bleared with tears, and her big mouth trembled.

So, all the time July sat with the ladies and they talked and showed her their new embroidery works and plied her with cherries and strawberries ("but we can't give you wine for the Lady hath the keys"), she kept stealing a look at Dame Eleanor. When Dame Bet Singleton would have her come upstairs to look at a murrey cloth gown that had been left to her in a sister's will, and they were alone together, July began to say, "Dame Eleanor—" and then did not know how to go on.

But Dame Bet understood.

"Alas! You saw? Even we who are with her can see how she's changed."

Dame Bet laid her hand on the lid of the coffer, where the murrey gown lay, but did not open it. Instead she sighed, "I do think that when—that if—they turn us out from Marrick, that day will be her death."

July could make no sound in answer, and Dame Bet said in a different tone, "All well! You are gone forth into the world. It cannot be the same to you as to us." Then she opened the coffer, and in displaying the gown became more cheerful.

But when they sat together on the top of the coffer with the gown across their knees, Dame Bet seemed to remember that all this time she had learned nothing of how July was getting on at the manor, and began to question her. Was it merry among all those folk? Wasn't Mistress Doll a sweet little maid? Was Dame Nan kind? July said, "Yes," to all, because that was safest, but she spoke with so little spirit that perhaps Dame Bet guessed how often the truth would have been, "No," for she heaved a sigh and said inconsequently, "Alas! now we may prove in ourselves the mutability of things temporal," and from that went on to tell July that the prioress, being of so stout a heart as she was, maintained that all would yet be well with the priory, though monks and nuns in the South were even now turned out. "But the rest of us are sore afraid. Only one—" she obviously had difficulty in swallowing back the name—"*one* would not be unwilling to be put forth, I do think. She has a gown of carnation color in her coffer and she embroiders a pair of gray sleeves as if she were a maid preparing for a bridal." Dame Bet looked down on the murrey-colored cloth that she was stroking with one hand and added as if it needed some explanation, "This is of a sad color, and, besides, will be only for a petticoat, and the gown over it open but a little way."

July, whose eyes had wandered to the window, got up hastily. "The rain has stopped. I shall be chidden. I must go."

They were indeed calling for her below, and she got sharp words from Dame Nan when she came. What made it worse was that the rain began again before they had gone far, and Doll began to cry, and Sir Rafe, hearing her grizzling as they came into the Manor, rebuked his wife for not having more care of the child. All this, July knew, would like curses come home to roost with her. And then she thought of Dame Eleanor Maxwell, shrinking and dwindling to a helpless, wretched old woman, and all the ladies except the prioress and Dame Anne Ladyman, dreading the day when they would be put out of the priory, leaving behind them the kind, quiet life, to live as July had come to live, in some crowded house in which they had no place.

She was at table now, and listening to all the chatter and shouting, laughter and bickering, she thought of the priory as a place of peace. Those tiffs which from time to time divided the ladies were no more than ripples on the placid surface of their life. Here—July looked along the table—here this lad was quarrelsome because a wench would not look at him, and there that wench was cock-a-hoop and giggling because the lad she liked had handled her in a dark corner. From behind the shut doors of the summer parlor came the sound of Sir Rafe's voice raised and harsh. You would never hear Dame Nan speak loud in anger, but July knew just how she would be answering, cold and bitter and cruel as she could be in the fewest words; July did not love Dame Nan, but she knew, without having thought about it all, that here was another who was unhappy, and whose security had been taken from her as it had been taken from July, and would be taken from the ladies of Marrick Priory.

Just before supper July was sent to the stillroom to turn the green walnuts in their pickle. On her way back instead of coming at once to the parlor, she slipped across the little yard and out into the dripping garden, for the rain had at last taken off after a drenching day, and now the clouds were parting and showing in the west a hint of the sun. She heard footsteps, and looking down at the road below the little stone terrace she saw Malle coming along carrying a bolt of homespun linen that one of the Marrick women had woven for the priory.

July let her pass, and then, in a great hurry, ran down the steps to the little gate; the key was in the lock; she pulled open the door. "Malle! Malle !" she called.

Malle stopped, turned, and came back. July wished that she had not called her. "No matter," she began to say, and then remembered how much it did matter. If only the ladies might have peace. If only for them there might be still that quiet island in the troubles of the world. Even though July herself must be buffeted on the high seas it would be comfort to know that there were some safe in a sheltered haven.

"Malle," she said, "tell me. They say that the saints show you what shall come to pass. Malle, what of the ladies? Shall they be turned out?"

Malle said nothing.

"Oh, Malle, tell me. I'll give you my brooch. They say that our Savior appeared to you, riding over Grinton bridge. Tell me what it meant." She was busy unfastening it, but it caught in a thread of her gown, and looking up she saw Malle's face, and after that forgot about the brooch, and was pierced through by a sudden sharpness of hope.

"Malle," she cried. "*Is* it well? Is it? Oh! what did you see that you look so—so—"

Malle said:

"There was a great wind of light blowing, and sore pain."

July flinched. She still had her hand on the latch of the gate, and her fingers grew cold on the cold iron, though she could feel warmth on her cheek from the sun which now shone through the scattering clouds, edging them with flame. She stood waiting, then glanced again at Malle's face, and saw that there lingered on it still that shining that was not from the brightening west.

"You say 'pain' and you smile. What do you mean?" July cried out, though Malle's look was no smile either. Malle did not answer. She went slowly away along the wall of the garden, and July watched her till something moving on the road below the big gate of the manor caught her eye. It was one of the hinds toiling up with an oak beam on his shoulder for mending the hall roof; he was coming up from the saw pit. Beyond him lay the depth of the dale, now so brimmed with sunshine that it seemed to be full at once of drenched green air and fiery gold; it was as though July looked down into the deep sea, and saw there a great fire lit and burning below the green water, with flames at once glorious and fatal.

"They hanged him on the cross," she thought, and in the furthest corner of her mind cringed away from sight and sound of the big round-headed iron nails biting through flesh as the hammer drove them. Malle's look of light meant nothing. There was always, round about the whole world, an ocean of pain. It crept toward the ladies of Marrick; it lapped to the feet of the one she could least bear to have suffer. "But he's well, and in no danger," she assured herself. Then—

"Oh!" she cried, wringing her hands together. "You are a fool!" she cried after Malle's broad lumpish shoulders and bent head, "A fool!"

She went back into the garden, slamming the gate so that a branch of sweet briar above it, smelling like paradise after the rain, shook down on her cold drops that struck as sudden as little knives.

July 24

There was a posy of clove-scented pinks, white and fringed and each with a deep crimson eye, on the sill of the open window by which the King leaned. The Lady Mary, his daughter, standing before him with her hands clasped upon the velvet brocade petticoat of her gown, looked no higher than the stems of the flowers which showed, lean and jointed, through the Venice glass; little shining bubbles clung to the stems.

"Therefore," the King said, "I charge you tell me if from your heart, and truly, you have submitted yourself." He paused, but not long enough for an answer. "I tell you," said he, "I hate nothing more than a dissembler. My Lord of Norfolk, or Master Cromwell—Lord Privy Seal—" he corrected himself, for such was Cromwell now and baron too, "either of those, and other of my council, would often have me dissemble with ambassadors of foreign Princes. But I'll never do so. Now, good daughter, will you in this show yourself my daughter indeed?"

He laid his hand, warm and heavy, on her shoulder, and she knew she must meet his eyes.

She did it, curtseying to the ground, and taking his hand to kiss it. She said that most truly, most humbly, as his bounden subject and penitent, unworthy child, she submitted herself with unfeigned heart to his will, "such as has been and shall be declared unto me for my obedience to—to—" She stumbled and the sentence trailed away, because his eyes were still on her. "Oh truly, truly, sir," she cried.

He nodded then, and smiled before he turned away. But he said over his shoulder that she would want to write to her kinsman the Emperor, and to the bishop of Rome, how freely and of a good conscience she renounced her mother's marriage as incestuous, and took her father as Supreme Head of the Church in England.

She stood there for a long time after he had gone, looking again at the posy of pinks, and wondering whether, with practice, lying came more easily.

She gave a great jump as someone came up behind her. It was one of the King's gentlemen.

He held out a little green silk purse. The King's Grace had sent it to her for a token of his love and favor. There was a ring with a fine diamond inside the purse. She thought, "So I'm to be paid for lying." That made it worse.

August 23

July was glad not to find Jankin at the gate when she and little Ned, the Bulmers's new page, came into the priory. Neither she nor Ned had any good reason for coming here, and July had been trying all the way down the hill to think of a good excuse, but the wind and the rain seemed to make it impossible to think, so another moment or two was welcome. Once inside the gate she edged Ned quickly to the right, and when he asked, "Where are we going? What's in here? Why do we go in here?" she told him truly, "To look at the horses."

But as they came to the door of the stable kept for the horses of guests, they found Malle, sitting on the ground with a great wet pile of rushes beside her, that ran water to meet the water that was blowing in from outside. The reeds had all been cut in summer, as time served, and had since then lain in the river, tied up into bundles, and each bundle moored to a big stone. Now Malle was peeling them for rushlights; all about her feet the curled peel lay green and sopping, and on one side there was a pile of thin lengths of white pith, each with its rib of green; these were the lights.

"See," said July, "there are the horses."

There was a sorrel horse, and beyond it a bay.

"Is that all?" Ned objected. "My father has far more. My father has ten horses, twenty horses. My father has forty horses."

"Has he?" July laughed at the child's brag because she was so happy. It was true, what they had said at the manor last night. Master Aske had come to the priory. The sorrel horse must be his, and the bay his servant's. But still she had not thought what she should say to explain why she and Ned had come here. She could not say, "I had to know." Still less, "I thought I might see him."

"Come on," said Ned, and tried to drag her to the door. But when they had reached it it was he who hung back to make a dive for one of the fine curls of green peel from the rushes. July let herself be checked, and stood in the doorway of the stable looking out into the rain that rushed down out of a lowering, somber sky, filling the empty great court with noises of gurgling, splashing, dripping, all overlaid by the great steady swish of its fall.

As she stood there Master Aske came through the gatehouse. He carried a straw basket, and a fishing rod over his shoulder; as he tilted it up again, clear of the gateway arch, the thin end danced high above him. He came straight to the stable door, his head down against the rain. July slipped back, and he pulled up abruptly with an apology that he left unfinished.

"Why," said he, peering into the dark stable, "it's—it's little Mistress July, grown big!"

He came in, laid down his basket, and set the rod against the wall.

"I suppose," he said, "the fishes I left behind me in the Swale aren't wetter than I," and he bent his head down to peel off his soaked hood, and wrung out his hair, and laughed at July, his face wet with rain and his eye very bright and gay.

"Sir," Ned asked, not waiting for an introduction, "have you caught any?"

"Would you see?" Aske picked up the basket and opened it, and Ned and he stopped together, their heads close, but July drew back; she had no wish to look at the gasping, wretched things flapping about in the hay there.

"Marry!" Ned piped in his clear voice. "It's a great catch—three big fellows and two, three small ones."

"That's no mastery," said Master Aske, "on such a day as this," but July could see he was pleased, and he took Ned and tossed him up on the back of the sorrel horse. When they came again to July, still standing beside the door, Ned had Master Aske by the hand and was wanting to know all about what Malle was doing.

"Why does she peel them all wet?"

"Because they won't peel else."

"And what will she do next?"

"Lay them out in the dew a few nights, then dry them in the sun."

"Then the ladies will burn them to read their books by?"

"They will—when Cook has dipped them in the scum from the bacon pot."

"Oh," said Ned, and stood with his feet wide, staring at Malle, and putting away in his head all this information.

But Master Aske came over to July. He smiled at her, swinging his wet hood, and then she saw his thick straight brows knot together in a frown.

"Mistress," he began, and then with a hesitation unusual for him, "I thought—you wore a novice's habit when I was here last year."

July nodded.

"And now?"

"I'm waiting gentlewoman to Dame Anne," and July nodded toward Marrick up the hill.

"Did you choose so?"

She shook her head and he continued to look at her, very hard and intent. He had not seen till now that pinched, defensive, east-wind look, which others knew so well; but now he saw it.

She said, in a flat matter-of-fact voice, "Sir John would not pay my dower till I was professed, and that cannot be now, the visitors said, till I should be twenty-two. So the Lady would not keep me."

He turned away from her, biting his lips and frowning. This—an unhappy, frightened little wench—was one tiny fragment of the destruction that the King and Cromwell were making.

He said, continuing his thought aloud, "And there's my kinswoman, Dame Eleanor." Those two, July and the old lady, were present and painful in his mind, and beyond them all the others, known or unknown, now turned out. "Some," he went on, arguing it out, "some will go to the greater abbeys, but old folk—such as Dame Eleanor—that's not for them. But you—" He hesitated.

"By the time I am old enough there'll be no abbeys."

"God's Cross!" He turned to her. "Who told you? It's not possible. Our King cannot change all that has been for a thousand years, and in all Christendom. Who said it to you?"

She said, "No one," and he rebuked her for putting about such a word, and went on to show her at length how impossible it was that such a thing should be. "I cannot think how you should suppose it," he said; and she, dumb because he was angry, could not tell him the reason, which was indeed no reason at all—but a conviction that just because the fragile peace of the little house at Marrick was the only peace she had known, therefore it would surely be destroyed.

"If it should come to that—" he said, "if it should come to that—" She heard him grind his teeth together, and she clutched at his sleeve.

"Oh! do not—do not— What would you do?"

He put his hand on hers and lifted it from his arm, but gently, and for a second he held it in his. Yet she knew that if he was not angry with her neither was he thinking of her at all.

"There's nothing a man may do now," he muttered. "Not rightly do."

Then he left her and went across the court to the outer stairway up to the guesthouse. She took Ned with her into the parlor, for he had become clamorous to know why they had come to the priory. She counted, and rightly, that so young and plump a small boy, with his comical parade of manhood, would wile sufficient sweetmeats out of the good ladies to satisfy him as to why.

But she would not let him stay long, and the ladies found her fidgety, inattentive, and abrupt. They did not realize how she was looking at them with eyes which were almost, if not quite, hostile. But it was so, because now the King's dealings with the abbeys meant to her nothing more nor less than danger to Master Aske. If the quick, utter, and unresisted suppression of every abbey in the country could have been procured by July nodding her head she would have nodded, lest otherwise Master

Aske should somehow be dragged into the quarrel. "There's nothing a man could do," she told herself, repeating his words for comfort. Since, however, he was different from every other man in the world, the words, though so obviously true, did not comfort her much.

August 27

Will came unsteadily into the room, tripped over a stool, and dropped the saddlebag he had brought upstairs; this morning his master and he had come up from the priory to the manor, because Aske was to spend a few days there, being kinsman to Dame Nan, though distant.

"Mass!" Aske cried. "Already! Could you not wait even an hour before you must drink yourself sodden?"

Will stooped to grope for what he had dropped, but the floor was tipped too dangerously for him. He stood up again and laughed.

"By Cock! but a temperate man'd be tempted, so many pretty trulls there are below stairs. There's one called Cis, and another—called—called— Well I can't mind her name now, but there's *thy* old trull here, master; Mistress Meg No-better-than-should-be Bulmer."

Aske got up then and struck Will a blow which knocked him flat, and the fellow turned tearful and penitent and would kiss Aske's hand. He swore he'd never take such a word on his tongue again, nor never drink no more than he could carry. "And God knows I know you are as clean from sin for her as it's sure I'm a sinful man and an evil-tongued, graceless servant."

Aske left him, disgusted with himself, angry with Will, and put out too at the knowledge that Meg Bulmer was here. He'd not have come if he'd known, and now that he knew he thought of staying but one night, and then making an excuse to go. But he had met that little July in the gateway as they came in, and he had seen her face kindle as purely as the wick of a candle taking light. He had thought of her more than once, since they had talked in the stable, with compunction and great gentleness, wishing that there was something that he could do to amend what it seemed could not be amended. Now he thought, "Why! it is that she lacks friends in this strange place, and she takes me for an old friend. Poor little wench!" he said to himself, "I'll be as true friend to her as I may." So he could not have found it in his heart to go away at once, guessing just how the light in her face would be quenched if he were to tell her, "I'm for Aughton tomorrow."

August 28

Sir John Bulmer came into the room while Margaret's woman Bet was lacing her mistress into the leather corset, busked with wood, and with side pads at the waist to hold out the over-petticoat and the gown. Sir John had been out hawking early with some of the other guests, but rain had come on heavily when they were far up the valley, and had blown in their teeth all the way home. He was very wet and out of temper, and began at once casting off hood and coat and doublet, and pulling down his hosen. Margaret said he'd make Bet blush, and Bet pretended to hide her eyes, but peeped at him from behind her hand, laughing. He said if she was going to be married she'd best get used to the sight of a man. "Oh fie, sir!" cried Bet, but she went by him with a look that was anything but coy.

When she came back she had Margaret's bodice and petticoats on her arm. She slipped on the bodice and tied the points, then the petticoats, and asked which gown and sleeves. Margaret said, "The blue, and the damask sleeves."

Sir John was sitting on the bed, rubbing his wet legs with a towel. He told Bet to fetch him a pair of hosen and a gown from the trussing coffer. Margaret nodded, so Bet left her mistress to get the things and tie his points for him. Then she came back to Margaret, and he lolled on the bed, warm and comfortable again, watching Margaret turn or stand still, raise her arms or thrust them into the wide sleeves that Bet laced up to the bodice. Whatever she did she was lovely, and once he came from the bed, pushed Bet away, and lifting Meg's hair kissed her neck.

Bet was fastening the last petticoat which was of crane-colored damask like the sleeves. Then Meg dived her head into the gown, and came out with her bright hair tumbled.

"How much longer?" he cried.

"Not long," she told him, "Not long. Bet has to do my hair. Are you hungry?"

"You'd be hungry if you'd ridden as I have through the rain."

Margaret had sat down in front of the mirror and Bet began fastening up her hair; neither of them had any intention of being hurried, but Meg leaned forward so that she could keep an eye upon his face in the glass, in case he grew too impatient.

"Who went with you?" she said to him; and to Bet, "Draw out that pin again. There's a hair pulls. That's better."

He was naming the other guests; Aske's name came last, and Sir John chuckled, but sourly. "He's lost his hawk. I told him he would. She's not yet fully reclaimed, though she's a handsome enough eyas. He cast her off after a couple of mallard and she flew wild, and got into the trees at the top of Gill Beck. He's riding a young mare too, that's but half-managed. I told him so, but he's a man that thinks he knows better than any, though he was very sorry to lose his hawk, and acknowledged I had been right."

Margaret had met her own eyes in the mirror at the mention of Aske's name. Now she smiled and murmured, half aloud, "Poor Robin!" and because she was smiling at herself did not see Sir John lift his head. She took a long look at her own lovely face thinking, "Jesu! no! It was because he loved me too much that he never came again. And that is why he remains a bachelor." Then she glanced at the reflection of Sir John. He was drumming with his fingers on his knee. He looked up suddenly and said to Bet, "You can go. Yes, go. No—leave that alone." Bet went hastily, but for a full minute he said nothing, and Margaret sat, with her hands in her lap and eyes lowered, in her pose as still and easy as a fish in a quiet pool, and as ready to flash into life.

"I marvel," said Sir John, still frowning at his knuckles, "that Robin Aske has never married."

That chimed so exactly with her thoughts that Meg turned about on the stool, to look at him with a new respect. Could it be that the slow ox had hid such perception behind his dull face all these years? At the thought that there might be some smolder of anger under his sluggish devotion she brightened visibly like a flame.

"I have marveled too," she said sweetly.

"You have?" He looked up and was aware of the brilliance of her beauty. He stared at her, and she saw anger, pain, and a hungry worship trouble the dullness of his inexpressive face. She said, on a sudden inspiration, "Shall we marry him to July?" and watched him, all wifely submission outwardly, and with her spirit dancing and daring him within. Laughter bubbled up in her too as she saw him trying to work out how this might relate to that which he suspected.

He dropped his eyes and muttered that July was well enough here with Dame Nan.

"This," she told him, "was but for a time. I'm her sister. I must see the child provided for. We cannot keep her dower forever. Robin Aske—or another—but as she hath small looks, it were well soon rather than late."

She stood up and moved to the door. Let him puzzle his head as to whether or no she cared whom Robin Aske married. He got up heavily and followed her. "I must think on it," he said.

August 29

Robert Aske was very pleased with himself when he marked his lost hawk rather high up in one of the trees near the top of Grinton Beck. "It's well," he thought, "that I came." Sir John Bulmer had been positive he'd never find her.

He got down from the saddle and slipped the bridle over a low bough; the young mare was a joy to ride, footed like a fairy, and would soon lose her whimsies. "There, there, my sweeting!" he said, smoothing his hand down her neck, before he started to climb the tree.

About two minutes later, with a great crack of a breaking bough, he came down, rushing through the leaves with a prodigious and startling commotion. When he had picked himself up he sat down again hastily, and began to assess the damage. He had torn his doublet; something was very wrong with one ankle; the mare, taking fright at his sudden and noisy descent, had dragged the bridle from the bough and was away; he could hear her go clattering down the beck, slipping and stumbling and churning through the water in one of the pools—he could only hope she would not break a leg.

It is tempting, but it is unwise, for a man whose ankle is swelling inside his boot to try a shortcut. Before long Aske knew that it was so, but because he was obstinate he would not turn back. When he came to the road running from Grinton up the dale below Harkerside he was going very halt. He had thought to find someone on horseback who would take him up behind, but, as luck would have it, only those on foot were going his way, and these were children and women; those on horseback going toward Keld he would not ask to turn for him.

So he went slowly, and in pain, and had made up his mind to go in to the manor, though the bailiff and a few servants would be the only people there, when Gib Dawe, coming briskly up from behind, drew level, stopped, and asked what was to do.

Aske told him what had happened, and Gib, in a stiff, harsh way, offered his help. Aske hesitated, then accepted; it had long been in his mind to speak a word to the Marrick priest, and perhaps this was as good an opportunity as another; he did not reckon that the pain he was in would make it difficult to keep his temper. They went on together then, but with some embarrassment, and, for Aske, a good deal of discomfort, since Gib was by so much the taller that to lean on his shoulder was difficult, and besides that Gib did little to moderate his pace in order to make it easy for a limping man.

So it was abruptly that Aske opened his matter.

"Sir Gilbert, from all I can hear you are one of those who teach heresy to the simple poor folk."

"Sir," said Gib, very harsh, "that you call heresy I call the true word of God."

"That I call heresy general councils of the church have called heresy."

"As what?"

Aske bit his lip as his foot turned on a stone. "I'll not dispute it with you," he said shortly. "You know well enough what things are contrary to that which the church has always taught."

"Ha!" cried Gib triumphantly. "But now it is all to be reformed. The King and the vicar general—"

Aske cried, "Out on Thomas Cromwell! Was he to make and unmake what men should believe?"

"Yea. He and the King. Because that is the work to which God hath sent them. You have seen what is done already—superstitious practices forbidden, the pope's authority broken; carnal ill-living monks and nuns driven like conies out from their buries—"

Aske stopped and took his arm from Gib's shoulder and faced him on the road.

"I'll hear no more of this—" he began, but Gib did not wait for him to finish.

"Aye, but you shall hear more of it. The work's only now begun. But the field shall be reaped clean, and it is the King that has laid his hand to the sickle."

He gave a sort of laugh, but cut it short at the sound of Aske's voice when he spoke.

"Sir Priest," said he, "the King will do what he will. But here in the North the time for these things is not yet, and I swear to you I shall some way let you from this preaching. I'll be loath to bring a man into trouble, but you shall not so deceive the simple commons. I shall see to it."

"Against the King's will?" Gib said, and was angrier almost with himself than with the other, because his own voice lacked that ring of sureness that Mr. Aske's had.

"I've told you. I shall see to it."

They measured each other, eye to eye, then Gib's dropped; he shrugged his shoulders and turned away. But when he had gone a step or two he came back.

"Lean on my shoulder," he said.

"I shall make shift well enough without."

So when Gib went on again alone each of them was much out of temper—Gib because he had not been able to outface Master Aske, but Aske for a deeper and more grievous reason. What Gib had said of the King and of the work yet to be done was only too true. And though he himself should be able to have one preacher silenced what would that avail? As he limped on downhill toward the mill and the yew trees in the churchyard he contemplated a prospect of such total ruin that he could hardly yet believe it possible. Then he remembered a story that was going about, of a simple fellow who had come to the churchyard of a village, nearby a monastery to which the King's commissioners were come to suppress it. This fellow had a spade and mattock on his shoulder and when he was asked why, "Marry," quod he, "because I am here to bury Jesus Christ." "Fie," quod they, "on such a word!" "Marry!" quod he, "but it is sure he must be dead. Whoever heard of a man's goods being appraised while he was still alive."

The church clock struck, leisurely and sweet, the hour of seven. Aske, abreast of the gate, stopped, hesitated, and turned in. "Indeed," he thought, "I can't go farther." There was a bench under the south wall where folks sat who came to Mass on Sundays from far up the dale, bringing their bread and cheese, pork and beer, to eat and drink in the churchyard. He got that far and plumped down on it, and then, taking out his knife, began to slit away the boot from his leg. It took long, for the pain increased as he jagged at the leather, so that he must go gingerly. A small child came and stood close to watch, but Aske had no attention for him; his hands were shaking now and there was a darkness in his eye, and roaring, as if the Swale were in flood, in his ears. He heard someone say, "You've dropped the knife," and he muttered crossly, "I know that," not connecting the voice with the child, because it seemed to come from so far away; but though he groped for the knife he could not lay his hand on it.

Then he knew that someone was lifting his foot from the ground. There was a wrench that spun blackness and noise together into one, and then relief; the roaring died to no more than a rustling, and the blackness to flying spots that cleared and let in the brightness of the day. He saw that Malle, the priory serving wench, had his knife in her hand; she had got his boot off and was slitting away the lacing of the gusset of his hosen at the ankle. He wiped his forehead clumsily with the back of his hand, and said "That's better. Thank you," smiling at her, and she smiled back with her dull, indeterminate smile.

He did not speak to her again till she had bound up his ankle with a strip of linen borrowed from the miller's wife, who would have come to attend the gentleman, she told Malle, who told Aske, but that she was baking, and her husband should have the cob saddled for him so that he might ride at his ease back to the manor. Malle had soaked the rag in well water, deliciously chill, and Aske sat, enjoying with a vacant mind mere physical sensations, the warmth of the sun on his hand, and face, ease after pain, and the simple but primary pleasure of light.

While Malle stooped over his foot he looked about the churchyard where the long, low hummocks of the graves made soft shadows in the grass. There were three yew trees along the wall, two to one side of the gate, one to the other. The rumble and splash of the millwheel filled the air with comfortable sound, and now and again came voices, speaking or singing, from the village beyond the wall. Up the dale there was the great heather-red flank of Harkerside; looking down, past the roofs of

Grinton, he could see the steep woods behind Marrick Priory. It was always a strange thing for him, a fenland man, to find himself so deep among the hills, which, like great silent beasts, lay to this side and that of the quick flowing river. Sometimes he felt stifled by the depth of the dale, but today the fells, steeped in sunshine, stood up as if to shelter this quiet place.

"Montes in circuitu ejus, et Dominus in circuitu populi sui; ex hoc nunc usque in saeculum."

The well-known words slipped into his mind so aptly that it was as if someone had heard and answered the thought in his mind, and answering had led him out into a great peace.

As the hills about Jerusalem, and as the hills about the dale, even so God stood round about his people.

Malle sat back on her heels. "There, master," said she, "I'll help you stand and bring you to the gate."

"No. No. Wait a minute."

He had never, except that first time when Jack had spoken of them, taken much account of what he had heard of her dreams, or visions, or whatever they were, having heard at the same time that she was but a crazy creature, and knowing how poor folk will make a marvel out of nothing. It was, he had thought, a gold chain to a duck's egg that whatever she had seen was but part of her madness. But now, having talked with her, he knew that though she might be simple she was certainly not crazed; and if simple might not God have spoken to her simplicity?

Suddenly, with relief, he felt his own littleness, as he had felt a few moments ago the greatness of that which stood round about to shelter.

He said aloud—but it was to himself that he spoke—"It is sure that God must prevail." And he leaned forward, laying a hand on her shoulder.

"Tell me," he said, "has there been word given to you, or a sign shown, that God will come to our help?"

Malle said:

"There was a great wind of light blowing, and sore pain."

She lifted her head, so that now he could see her face.

He got up hurriedly from the bench; she got up too and stood; it was he who went down on his knees and knelt in front of her on the grass.

After a moment he uncovered his eyes, and drawing a deep breath let it out with, "*Deo gratias*! Then it's true. You saw him. Tell me."

When she said nothing he instead began to tell her, but as if she knew all about it already, how he needed—"How we all need, we that fear—that think—" He broke off. "I have needed the comfort of that blessed sight which was shown you."

But when she still was silent he cried, as if in anger, "Him that the Jews crucified, you saw ride in triumph. It was in triumph?" He caught at her gown and shook it.

But Malle made no answer. He joined his two hands together and bit at his knuckles, and in a minute got to his feet and without looking at her went heavily toward the gate of the churchyard. She had tried to help him, but he put her by, though gently, so she stood and watched him limp away. He checked once and half turned, for he had remembered that he had given her nothing for her service to him, but he knew that now he could not give her money, so he went on, and found a boy in a red coat and ragged hosen standing looking in at the gate, the bridle of the miller's white pony over his arm, and his eyes like two round O's. When Aske had got into the saddle and was riding off he looked back, and saw the boy speak to a man passing by with a sack of meal on his shoulder. The man dumped the meal, and together they stood staring into the churchyard. When Aske turned again there was a little crowd there, all looking toward the place where he had knelt before the priory wench, Malle.

August 31

Gib Dawe was wakened just before daylight by a knocking on the door. When he opened he found Perkin a' Court standing outside with a lantern; Perkin was an old man who lived in a hut up Cogden Beck in a very lonely place. He said that his wife was dying and asked Gib to come.

So Gib dressed, and came down again. As he went out of the door the old goodwife, his mother, called sharply, "Gib! Gib!" and he answered her that he was going out. He heard her call again as he shut the door.

The sun was up, but hidden from the dale in a white, weeping mist when he came back. He took a shortcut along the side of one of the hay closes where the aftermath stood pretty tall, and crossed the Swale below the stepping-stones, then up past the nuns' fishponds with his wet gown slapping uncomfortably against the calves of his legs. He intended to go straight home, break his fast, and only later to return the oil and the pyx to church. Let any that saw him disapprove if they chose.

Such things to him were superstition, and often his conscience pricked him that for the sake of quiet, and lest the prioress should deprive him of his benefice, he ever performed such rites.

When he came to the door of the parsonage it was open. He shouted for Wat, but there was no answer. He called to his mother, but got no answer from her either.

When he went in he found her body, wizened, twisted, shrunk, sprawled half out of bed, but she was not in her body any longer. Wat did not come back till suppertime, having an animal's dislike of death.

September 2

Sir John Bulmer and Robert Aske were playing chess in the window of the summer parlor. It was evening and the sharp fierce gold of sunset, pouring through the trees, turned all the leaves to a burning green, while the flies shone gold as they jigged in the light. Through the open casement came the voices of Dame Nan and others of the ladies who sat together under the apple trees: farther off some of the village children were playing a singing game that went to a sweet plaintive tune. Aske sat astride of the bench, very still; when it was not his turn to play he kept his hands on his knees; when he should make a move he bent his head a little lower, and sometimes, if the game went badly, sucked in his cheeks; then he lifted one hand from his knee, made his move, and sat still again. Sir John, on the other hand, was both indecisive and fidgety; he would keep his fingers on a piece, push it this way, set it back, and begin all over again with another; when it was not his turn to play he drummed tunes on the edge of the board. Yet for all that he was a wily opponent, and it was long before Aske murmured softly, "Ah!" and, having moved a rook, "Check." Ten minutes later he said, "Mate," and raised his arms to stretch them over his head; it was like seeing a bent bow slacked to see the intent look pass from his face.

"You are too good for me," said Sir John.

Aske smiled, "Nay—nay," but then he turned his head to the window; just outside, Sir Rafe and one of the older guests walked up and down along the terrace. They spoke of great matters, and, Aske thought, rashly, making no bones but that they were much discontented with the King's doings. But then, Aske remembered, it was not in the North Country as it was in London, that a man must guard his tongue every minute. He turned back to the room, for Sir John was speaking.

"Anon?" said he.

"Have you ever thought of marrying?"

"Marrying?" Aske was vague.

"They say," and Sir John stared at him as if to read it written upon him, "they say you have a manor in the South for which you pay your brother eight pounds a year."

"So I have."

"For life?"

Aske said yes, for life.

"And land in Yorkshire—worth twenty pounds a year they say."

"They say too much. But why all this?"

"If you thought to marry—Do you think?"

"I might."

"What would you say to a dower of two hundred marks?"

Aske picked up one of the pieces from the board, and began to rub his finger over it. He had not thought of marriage lately, but the idea was not unpleasant. It had a good settled sound in these unsettled times. "Maid or widow?" he asked.

"Maid," Sir John said.

"And the dower in money or land?"

"Money."

"Who is she?"

"Meg's sister."

"Little July? Surely she's not of an age to be married?"

Sir John said she was fifteen or sixteen at the least. "It's only that she's so lean and small," he said.

Aske looked down at the chess piece in his hand. Such a thing he had never thought of, yet after all why not? He'd promised himself to be good friend to her, and in this manner he would be. He began to smile, partly with amusement, because still the notion seemed comical, but partly also for gentleness.

Sir Rafe and the old man he walked with had come back and were standing just outside the window. The older man was speaking.

"Throgmorton himself told me so. They had spoken in the King's presence how His Grace was troubled in his conscience for his marriage to his brother's wife. And Throgmorton said he feared that if His Grace married Queen Anne his conscience would be more troubled at the length, 'for that it is thought,' said he, speaking to the King's Grace himself, 'that ye have meddled with both the mother and the sister of her.' To the

which His Grace replied, 'Never with the mother.' From which
it is manifest that His Grace had first the one sister and then
the other."

Sir Rafe gave a snort.

"And that if the first marriage was incest, so was the second."

"First the one sister, and then the other . . ." Aske felt his
face reddening. He set down the chess piece upon the board and
said to Sir John, "No." But then, realizing that he could not let
the blank flat negative stand alone, he added, "She is too young
for me."

Sir John got up. He stooped over Aske, thrusting his face
close. He was a slow man, but he had been on the watch, and he
had missed nothing.

"Is that all your reason?" he said, and Aske knew that he was
dangerous, and why. As they faced each other eye to eye, Aske
had time to marvel that suspicion should have lain working in
Sir John's mind for so long. But he must think of an answer that
would put an end to the business, and yet not be the truth.

He said, with a hard look, "No. If you will have it, I'll not
marry with a bastard," and he thought, "How long will it take to
work through his thick skull that that is what he has done? And
will he then strike me?" He saw in his mind the two of them
scrapping together on the floor like a couple of pages. Or would
Sir John take his dagger out?

None of that happened. Relief, rather than anger, and some
perplexity, perturbed the other's face.

He said vaguely, "Well. Well. If you will not . . ." and went
away, leaving Aske to sit alone with the disordered chess board,

and to feel reviving within him a deep disgust and anger against himself. It was not that he wished with any vehemence to marry poor little Julian Savage, even now when he knew it impossible, but it went clean against all the grain of his pride that he should be let from marrying her for such a reason.

July was stooping and gathering among the raspberry canes in the dusk. She and several of the servants had been at it all evening since supper, because tomorrow, guests or no guests, Dame Nan was determined to preserve the fruit. July was alone now, the servants having gone in; she intended to fill her basket and then follow them. It was while she was working down the last of the rows that Meg Bulmer came by with Bet. July saw them, but took care that they did not see her. She bent lower and kept very still as they passed by, and as they passed she heard Meg tell Bet that Sir John was speaking to Master Aske of marriage with "that ill-favored sister of mine," and then Meg laughed and said something else that July did not catch.

After that it took July long to fill her basket, because at first, when Meg had gone, she stood still in a sort of maze, and even when she went to work again she kept forgetting what it was that she was doing, and would come to herself and realize that she was letting the raspberries drop on the ground instead of into the basket.

At first she could hardly take it in. Then she could not imagine that for her such a thing should ever be. Then just because it would be a thing so absolute, so like the perfection and certitude of a completed circle, so contrary to anything which she had ever thought of, like a voice speaking from heaven, she began to contemplate it as a thing which, by its very incredibility, might come true.

She was glad when it was time to go to bed, where she could be private, and lie awake, playing delicately with little imaginings of how it would be if she were Master Aske's wife. She would have a puppy dog. She would make for Master Aske rishaws such as they used to make at the priory. He and she would take a boat out on the Thames in summer evenings, with green and flowering branches to deck it, and a fiddler and a singing boy to make music. She would walk beside him through London, while he talked and looked down upon her with his bright, laughing eye.

It was late when she went to sleep, and then she dreamed that she and some others, Meg and Dame Nan and Sir Rafe Bulmer among them, sat together in the prioress's chamber down in the dale, looking out at Calva. One of them asked, where was Gray's Inn? And then Robert Aske was standing close behind her. He laid his arm on her shoulder and pointed out through the window saying, "That way it lies."

That was all. She woke, and lay in a sureness and peace far more profound and potent than any bliss, because among that company she and he had belonged one to the other, and the circle was indeed closed, complete, and of a perfection infinite.

September 7

Rain had washed the sky as clean as if it were made new, and the sun was warm on the wall where the flies basked. Master Aske stood on the terrace below the window of the summer parlor, dressed for riding, with a hood on his head and a cap over that, and the stirrup cup in his hand, for he was leaving this morning. Now as he waited for Will Wall to bring out the horses he talked to Dame Nan and Sir Rafe inside the room.

Dame Nan was teasing him. She was very cheerful with him always, and far more easy than with most others, as if his cheerfulness and ease gave her confidence. It had even, for the moment at least, given her back confidence toward Sir Rafe, and she looked at her husband laughing, as she called Aske "good-for-nothing knave," and then she stretched out her hand and flipped Aske's ear with her finger.

He was just raising the pot of ale to his mouth, and, in trying to dodge, he jogged his elbow on the wall and the ale slopped out. He clapped the pot down on the sill and began to shake the drops from his cuff.

"Now I shall smell like an ale house. And what a waste of good ale too," he said.

She told him it served him right, and went away laughing, but Sir Rafe said there was no lack of ale at least, and called to July, who was going round among the other guests filling their cups from a pitcher. But the pitcher was just now empty, so, "Go and draw some more for Master Aske," he told her.

She had drawn the ale and was crossing the passage on the way back to the parlor when she saw, through the open door at the end, that Master Aske had left the terrace and was standing under one of the apple trees. Doll was with him and he was reaching down an apple for her, for those on that tree were the earliest of all to ripen. July went out of the door and across the grass to him. He glanced toward her and smiled, but with some constraint, and he affected to be watching Doll who had run off with her apple, so that he was half turned from July as she filled his can again, and only murmured thanks when it was done, without again looking at her.

July stepped back, and then stood still. He was going away. Certainly he must have refused Sir John's offer of her marriage, of which indeed no one had spoken to her from first to last. She did not hope anything now, yet to let him go away without a word was to drown and not cry out for a line to be thrown.

She jerked out, "Sir," and as he turned, stretched a hand toward him, because she wanted so much to have it taken and held, and besides she was unable now to think of anything that she could say.

He looked at her, but did not, or would not, see her hand. Only he smiled again and said, "Good-bye, little July—and thanks for the ale."

She knew that he was trying to put her off, and had never seen him so ill at ease. It gave her courage. "Sir," she said, though in a very small voice, "Sir, they—they—offered you me—to marry?"

He nodded.

"But you will not?"

He said, "No, July," and grew red and went on hurriedly, "I have no thought just now to marry. These are evil times."

That was so far from the reason which she had guessed that she began almost to hope. "Sir," she urged, coming closer, "could you not? I would cost you very little. There's not as much stuff in my gowns by two ells as Alice needs' (that was Dame Nan's elder gentlewoman). "And I can sew and spin; Dame Anne says I spin well when I try. I would try."

To that he could only shake his head.

"I—I can make rishaws. I would make them for you."

At such a child's plea he almost smiled, but, to her, rishaws had brought back the brief hours of that happy night when her castle in Spain had been a house in London with a kitchen in which she herself would make rishaws for him. She cried, "Oh, why will you not? If you would tell me why not. Is it me—me myself?" If he had looked at her—but he would not look—he would have seen on her face more than a child's misery.

"No," he said. "No." And his voice was so angry and troubled that she whispered, "It does not matter, never mind."

He took no notice of the words, if indeed he heard them. "See here, July," he said. "Let's have a token between us that we are friends and shall be always." He clapped his hand on his pouch as if to find a token there, then looked round, and with a sort of laugh reached up and plucked an apple. "And you shall eat one half and I the other," he said, taking out his knife and splitting the apple. "And we'll plant two seeds, and when next I come to Marrick you shall show me where our two little apple trees grow." He thought he was talking to a child, and smiled down at her, and was glad when she smiled.

They ate the apple standing there under the tree, and when only the core was left he asked, "Where'll we plant the seeds?" She said, "By the bee hives," and took him there, and knelt to plant them, because she said he must not soil his hands.

So he stood looking down at her while she dug with her fingers into the wet, warm earth, planted the seeds, and patted the place smooth again. When she had done that she still knelt, her hand cupped above where they were buried, while her eyes were on his feet as he stood by her; he had on riding boots of brownish red leather, and there was a patch on one of them; she knew, as she looked, that she loved all of him, from his head to his feet; not that Meg would have recognized it for love, though Will Wall might have. And he was going away; the apple wasn't a token of anything more than that, and the seeds that she had buried in a grave would never live; that was only a foolishness. She crouched there in the sunshine, with a light soft wind touching her face, and with the pleasant murmur of the hives in her ears, but it was on the edges of the world that she knelt, looking over into the naked, lifeless, sunless places.

"July," said Aske suddenly, "there's nothing amiss here, is there? Nan—my kinswoman—your mistress—she's kind?"

She had never before armored herself against him, but now, in her extremity, she looked up at him with a little smile that cost a huge effort.

"Nothing much amiss. My lady's often out of temper, but what's that? At least she is easy to take in."

"What?"

"She believes whatever we tell her."

July found that what had seemed as bad as it could be was now worse, much worse. A moment ago she had not cared that she should displease him, but now she did care, yet it could not be undone.

He said, "July, you must not tell lies. Never. To no one. Promise me!"

She cried out, "You don't know what you are talking about." Then they heard Dame Nan calling "Robin!" and Sir Rafe also, "Robin! Robin!" and he went away from her quickly, with no more than a muttered word that might have been farewell or anything.

September 8

It was just dark when Aske and Will Wall got home to Aughton. Supper was long over, and the tables taken down in the hall, but Will went off to the kitchen for his supper, and Mistress Nell had the servants bring cold beef and salad, beer and a dish of apples to the summer parlor for his master.

So Robert Aske sat eating by candlelight, while Dame Nell sewed, Hob, Jack's eldest boy, read and yawned over a book of law, and Julian, his youngest girl, between spurts of sewing, watched her uncle; Julian, fourteen years old now, so unlike her father or mother, being stocky and solid, with a square, dark-browed face, might easily have passed as her uncle's daughter.

Jack Aske sat at the table facing Robert, and told him of all that had happened at Aughton—small beer it would have been for anyone but an Aske, but not for Jack, and not for Robert, though his life had taken him out from Aughton; when he came home again he felt that he and Aughton were no stranger to each other than buckle is to thong. So he munched lettuce and listened, and nodded, putting in a word here and there, or stopped eating and gave his advice at length, whether asked for or not, or teased Jack with the old crusted jokes that went back through many years, and were always the better for keeping. He was very happy to be at home.

But when Julian had been sent off to bed with Mistress Nell's gentlewoman, Jack fell silent, and began to fidget. It was clear that his attention was not on what Robert was saying, though it was in answer to a question he had asked about Rafe Bulmer's sheep.

Then he turned his face to his wife.

"I shall shew him the letter," he said.

"I do not see need," said she.

"I am not of your mind in the matter," said Jack, and got up. While he went to the little old coffer in the corner and unlocked it, Nell bent her head over her sewing, tightening her lips, and Robert fiddled with the core of an apple on his plate, spinning it about by the stalk, and wishing that Jack would either keep his wife out of his affairs, or not try to bring his brothers in.

Jack came back to the table, and threw down a letter in front of his brother. He leaned over him as he read, a hand on his shoulder.

When he had finished reading Robert laid the letter down on the table, and then flipped it from him with one finger. "Well?" said he.

"Uncle," Hob broke in suddenly, and Robert turned to him. Hob had been christened Robert after old Sir Robert and himself, though, to distinguish, he was never called by his proper name. He was eighteen now and in October the two of them would go up to London together, as the young man was to read law.

"Uncle!" said the lad again, and then, red and stammering a little, "Oh! isn't it shameful this fellow Cromwell should be able to write to whom he will to let him have this or the other for his servants."

"Well," said Robert Aske pleasantly, "he may write—"

"You think I should refuse?" Jack cried, and Mistress Nell in the same breath, "No! No! I told you he would say so. But do not listen."

Jack bade her hush, and repeated, "You think I should refuse, Robin?"

"I did not say so."

"No, but you mean it," cried Hob triumphantly, and his father bade him also be silent.

"Come, Robin," he said, "what's your counsel?"

"You will have it?"

Jack said, "Yea," and Dame Nell got up suddenly and went out. Jack picked up the sewing she had dropped, and flung it on her chair. He looked troubled and sorry, but he said: "Well now—"

So Robert gave his counsel, at length, and with many good reasons, and when he had finished they were all silent. This request of my Lord Privy Seal—that a servant of his should have the farm of the 300 acres of the Askes' saltmarsh, near Pevensey—was a small thing, but as a straw which is a small thing, it showed which way the wind blew.

"I said it was a shame," Hob muttered, with his eyes moving between his father and his uncle.

"I shall say nay." Jack stood up. He went close to Robert again, and again laid a hand on his shoulder. "You're right, and Hob's right, saying it's a shame this man should rule over us, changing and breaking, and doing as he will. And," said he, "I see now clearly for the first time, since you have showed us, how greatly and grievously our freedoms have been minished by all these acts lately passed. Whoever heard before that a man's word should be counted treason?" He looked about the candle-lit room frowning, as though something was in it to disturb and threaten its quiet. Then he said; "Who knows but that the time may come when we must take dreadful measures to amend what has been done amiss."

"God forbid!" Robert Aske muttered.

Hob asked him what he meant, but he only shook his head, and Jack Aske took no notice of what he had said, but repeated, "I shall say him nay."

He got out pen and paper and wrote and sealed it while they sat watching him. Then he put it in his pouch. "Now to bed," said he, "and that's a thing well done."

September 9

Marrick Manor was almost empty of guests now, but not quite. Two remained—if you did not count as guests Sir John Bulmer and his lady—the elderly man who had walked with Rafe on the terrace when Aske and John Bulmer were playing chess, and his wife. Old Sir Christopher might have stayed forever without putting anyone out, but his lady was a different matter; she talked.

All Yorkshire knew how she talked, and Dame Nan, teasing Aske one day, had proposed the question whether Cousin Robin or the lady had the longest tongue. "By the Rood!" said Aske at that, "if there's a doubt I see I must tie knots in mine."

Now, with all the other guests gone, she was more difficult to avoid, while the penalty for being caught was more prolonged, since it was likely that only the horn blown for the next meal-time would bring release. It was for this reason that Sir Rafe had dodged into the shed where the gardener kept his tools and baskets and twine, to lurk there in the brown twilight that smelt of dust and potting soil and dung, and it was for this same reason that Dame Nan, lifting the latch with caution, slid quietly in and as quietly shut the door. They saw each other then, and they laughed.

"What are you doing here?" he asked. "And what are you?" said she. They laughed again, and standing close listened for foot-steps. Sir Rafe put his hand to his wife's waist, and she laid hers on it, moving slightly so that she almost leaned on him, though not quite. She turned her head and they smiled at each other.

"Hark!" he whispered.

"What'll we say if—" she murmured, and then came closer yet. In that moment, with all of it unsaid, she was able to renounce the unanswerable, unforgivable words that had burned and swelled in her for months about the woman that he kept at Richmond; nor would she think on the creature again, but things should be as they had once been. And Sir Rafe, also without a word spoken, swore to himself that he'd go no more to that trull. He had, in fact, been tired of her for some time, but it was pleasant to be able to make a virtue of it. He and his wife stood close as boy and girl shyly approaching love, like them wishing to dare more, yet exquisitely content.

When it was safe for them to come out of hiding they went together to look at the new cow-shippon that Sir Rafe was building. Dame Nan had not seen it before, but they must ignore that, because now everything was to be as it used to be. At first she praised all, then was silent, remembering that she had been used to no such insincerities, and at last, forgetting that anything had ever been different, said roundly that this or the other seemed to her to be wrong. And once more, as he had used to listen, Sir Rafe listened to her advice.

So they were at a very sweet accord when they came again into the sunshine, and lingered, willing to prolong their companionship. It was then that she said, "Rafe, I shall tell your brother's—I shall tell Dame Meg to take her sister from here."

"Well," said he, "I never liked her much."

Dame Nan seemed to think more explanation was needed. She was sorry for the girl, she said, a bastard, and with such a sister, and she glanced a little apprehensively at Sir Rafe, whose brother had married that sister.

"Speak not to me of her," said he, in a tone that told his wife she could say what she liked.

"It is my fault. I should not have brought the girl here. She cannot help herself that she is come of such blood. Yet though she is young I doubt she is not as a young maid should be."

"Oh!" Sir Rafe narrowly avoided the mistake of reminding his wife how positively she had proclaimed July's virtue.

"I saw her go up to Robin just before he left. She would not leave him. She stood by him and stretched out a hand to him."

Sir Rafe would have liked to inquire if Aske had taken it, but had sense to see that the question would be untimely. He tried to look shocked, but, disabled by a sudden recollection of his dealings with the trull at Richmond, succeeded only in looking sheepish.

"The way she stood," Dame Nan said disgustedly. "It was pure invitation. Thus—" She showed him how July had stood. Sir Rafe shook his head. It was no use reminding Nan that the girl was too plain to be likely to attract a man, unless one with a very strange taste.

"Is that," he asked, "why you spoke privily to Robin just before he got to saddle?"

She flushed a little.

"He first spoke to me of her. He meant nothing but kindness. He thinks of her still as a child."

"And did you—"

"I said nothing of what I'd seen. But I told him the girl's a liar in grain, and that's a thing he hates worse than any other. 'And,' said I, 'after all, she's Meg Cheyne's sister.' He said, 'I know that.' He was angry but perhaps he'll think of it."

"Well—" Sir Rafe had been going to say, "it's none of our business," but changed it hastily to, "Well, let Meg Bulmer take her sister away."

"When will they go?"

"God knows!" said Sir Rafe.

That evening Meg's woman Bet had the colic, so Dame Nan sent July to help her sister to bed. Meg did not talk about anything in particular while July undressed her and brushed out her hair, except to make fun of Dame Nan, and a little also of Sir Rafe, though she admitted he was a fine figure of a man. "Not so like a well-stuffed sausage as my blossom," she said, and made a face at the curtains of the bed as if Sir John lay there already.

When she was between the sheets she began to talk about Sir John, saying things that would have sent Bet into squeals of delight. July heard them alright, but said nothing, and moved about the room, doing what was necessary, with her black scowling look. At last, as she passed the bed, Meg flung out an arm and caught the skirt of her gown, and then sat up, dragging her nearer, and shaking her a little, angry, but still laughing.

"And you need not behave like a nun now, mistress," she cried. "For if I can I'll have you married before the month's out, and you'll learn such things for yourself, though I doubt your husband will not be so hungry for you as mine is for me."

She felt July stiffen in her hand, and smiled into her face, a malicious, pointed smile.

"Why shouldn't I stay here?" said July.

"Because Dame Nan is sick of you, and will have me take you away. And it is by good fortune that I hear of a bridegroom for you in London, so you shall ride there with Sir John when he goes thither two days hence, on his affairs." When

July said nothing Meg asked did she not want to know her bridegroom's name.

"It does not matter," said July.

"Fie!" cried Meg, "and that and a scowl is all the thanks I get for trouble enough. Here am I, doing a sister's part, with Sir John grudging all the time to lift his hand from your dowry." Then she laughed and said, "It's as well you don't care to know his name, for by the Mass! I've forgotten it. But he's a man of substance— a widower. It is his dead wife's brother that has writ to me so timely, asking could I help his brother-in-law to a good sober wife. He says he remembers me well, but I can call neither of them to mind, though he says he is one of William Cheyne's friends."

"Oh!" cried July.

"Well, you must be content. I'd have done better for you if I could. Aye, and you know not what, nor how well I would have done. Far above your deservings I'd have set you, with one I myself might have matched with had he not been a younger son with little gold in the kist. If it does not matter who it shall be, will you know who it should have been, only that he would not take you?"

July did not speak, but Meg told her, "Robin Aske! There! And now will you thank me for that, though, for no fault of mine, he would not." When July stood silent Meg flung her away with a push. "There's gratitude for you," she said.

"I know," said July, "why he would not."

Meg gave her a sharp look and then began to laugh very much.

"God's Mother, that you do not."

"By God!" July said, and for once the proud Stafford spoke in her, "I do. It is because I am your sister."

Meg was silent, staring at her.

"Who told you then? Did he? No, for he said he never had nor would tell any. Mother Judde? Did she tell you he came to me one night when Sir John was away?"

"I'll not believe it."

At the shrinking horror in July's face Meg stared again.

"How then? You did not know. Then what did you mean when you said he would not because you're my sister?"

She saw how July shook, and began to nod her head and to laugh. "Lord! You thought that it was because your sister's a wicked wanton he'd have none of you. But, you see, you're wrong, for I was good enough for him. Good enough? I was his bliss and his heaven."

She grabbed July again, and peered at her closely. "Jealous, sister?" she whispered.

July was not jealous, because what Meg had had from Robert Aske she nor knew nor thought anything of. But she saw the candle flames reflected, bright and trembling, in Meg's eyes; she could smell her bare, warm flesh, and the perfume of orris that she used, and she shut her own eyes because she felt sick.

Meg smiled at her blind face and shook her gently to and fro.

"Nay," said she, "but I think I know indeed why he would not have you. He said to me it was because it would be incest, after he had had me. But I think the truth is that he would not because he wants me still, and fears he could not command himself were he too often near me. Poor Robin! Poor fool!" she purred, and smiled and sighed.

July opened her eyes.

"He hates you," she said. Watching him as she did, and having by heart every expression of his face and tone of his voice, she knew that.

"Hate lies close to love, they say," said Meg lightly.

July said, "*I* know it doth not."

Then Meg began to shake her, crying, "Take your eyes from me, little black-faced witch that you are."

Outside the door July lingered a few moments on the dark stair before she went to serve Dame Nan, for her knees were shaking.

It was no wonder, she thought, that he hated Meg. But he did not need to hate so perfectly, with such a deadly killing hate as July. If Meg had not caught him in that way that July had seen her catch other men—and yet she, July, did not know how—"If Meg had not caught him," she thought, "he might have taken me. He might."

It was a while later that she remembered she was to marry one of Master Cheyne's friends.

September 10

When Gib drew near the churchyard he paused. In the woods the highest branches of the trees swung in the wind, but below they hung still and heavy, burdened with rain; and there was quiet, except for the sound of fat drops falling. But from ahead there came the noise of shouting and hallooing, with barking of dogs; it might have been that the last of the corn was being cut, and the boys and dogs setting on after rabbits, had the day been one of harvest weather.

Yet when he reached the stile to the churchyard and looked in he saw that it was indeed some of the reapers who shouted and laughed—strangers these were who came from over the hills to work for hire, and who were keeping about the priory now, waiting for the weather to clear so that they could finish the barley.

They and their dogs were after game too, though the game was not rabbits but the woman Malle, who stood in the angle of a buttress, threshing about her with a rake to keep the curs off, while the men threw sticks and small stones at her shouting, "Hue! Hue! Run, wench, run!"

A few of the Marrick hinds had been watching it all from the shelter of the wall. They came out as Gib climbed the stile, looking at once surly and sheepish. The Lady, they said, had bid the bailiff turn off Malle, and when she would not go the bailiff had set the strangers and their dogs on her.

As they spoke Gib's eye was drawn, by a slight movement there, to the window of the prioress's chamber which looked out this way. Dame Anne Ladyman, scared and truly shocked, had peeped out and as quickly withdrawn. But Gib thought that the Lady was looking out upon her handiwork—though furtively—and the obliquity and tyranny of women, running together in his mind, were not to be endured.

"God's Passion! The Lady!" he cried. Here was rule. Here was power. Here was one of the worldly rulers of the darkness of this world. Then her he would defy. Against her he would wrestle manfully.

He ran forward shouting. One man he caught with a buffet on the ear; the other he tripped up, more by chance than design, as the fellow backed away. No more than that was needed. Gib was left alone with Malle; behind him the Marrick hinds saw the reapers off; they were glad to have the poor wench ridded, though they had not liked to risk the Lady's anger by doing it themselves.

"Now," said Gib, well pleased with himself, "you may go safe." But she did not move.

"Go," he said again, and waved his hand toward the gate.

"Whither?" she asked him, as if he could tell her.

Half Gib's mind remembered the shifts and discomforts that there had been at the parsonage since the old woman, his mother, had died; the other half chewed triumphant upon the rich iniquity of prioresses, who drove out poor wretches to starve.

"If you will," said he, "you shall come home with me. I need a servant to tend the house." He looked up toward the Lady's window and shook his fist that way, then wished that he had used a gesture more suitable to an ecclesiastic. He nodded to Malle with a stern look and went into the church. Let her wait for him or go otherwise as she chose.

While he said his Office he heard a sound at the door which was not one of the sounds of the rising wind outside. He turned to look over his shoulder, and frowned, seeing Malle come in and peer about. She came no nearer though. A little after this it struck him that he did not know why the prioress had turned her away. If it was for thieving—well—he'd find that out from her; he would shelter no thieves, no, nor a loose woman, if that had been the trouble. So he went on with the Office, while the wind snored in the tower and whistled shrilly through a broken pane in the vestry; when he paused for a moment he could hear the turmoil of the beaten woods outside.

He found Malle sitting by the door. She stood up and bobbed to him.

"Now," he said, speaking sternly, "tell me this. Why are you turned out?"

"For that which I saw."

"For that which you saw? What did you see?" he asked her, though he knew well all the talk of her seeing our Lord himself riding the peddler's donkey over Grinton Bridge. He had sworn to himself that he would never speak to her of it, telling himself that if he heard her speak the words, presumptuous, blasphemous, he would come near to striking her down for her wicked folly. But the fact was he dared not take the risk of finding that so poor an ignorant creature as she, had in truth seen this wonder. Now, suddenly, because of the pride of the prioress, and because he had routed the fellows she had set on, he dared take the risk. And if the thing were true he would make it ring in all men's ears; they should not silence him. They—

"Come!" he said.

She was silent, standing with her hands hanging and head bent.

"Come!" he said more sharply, and brought his face close to hers, for it had grown very dark in the church.

He drew back, blinking. It was not that there was any brightness in her face, seen dimly in the dusk. Rather it was as if, peering at her, he had looked into some shadowed secret place in the woods, and there found the scent of violets, or heard water running sweetly.

Malle said:

"There was a great wind of light blowing, and sore pain."

Gib found himself bumping against the sharp corner of the Founder's tomb, and only then knew how he had turned from her and moved blindly away. He gripped the edge of the chiseled stone while his thoughts ran this way and that in confusion. He was hugely angry, and glad. He was angry because she had seen this thing; he was glad of the thing which she had seen. He was far more angry with the rich and great whom Christ in his righteousness had come to judge. "Now," he thought, "we shall see the day of wrath for those who turn their faces from the gospel. Now the Lord comes once more, wearing a poor man's coat, and poor men will follow him."

He came back to Malle.

"This means that the hour is come. In this vision God speaks through you to me. It is time I lay my hand to the plow. It is time I go out from the dale to proclaim the day of the Lord. This was the meaning of that other showing."

He saw himself, gaunt and fierce as one of the ancient prophets, preaching and exhorting endlong and overthwart all England. "I shall be greater than Trudgeover," he thought. "I shall be a new Forerunner. I shall tell them of the crowd of poor men that went along the road, jostling and thrutching, tearing down of branches, throwing down of coats, crying 'Osanna.'"

"That is the meaning of what you saw," he said to Malle again, and more urgently.

"The day of the Lord. Osanna," he almost shouted at her. But Malle made no answer.

He caught his hand to his breast like a man who has run on steel. "Osanna!" he said again, but in a faint and shaken voice, and laying his finger on the door latch lifted it.

At that the wind burst into the church, snatching the door from his hand and sending it clattering back against the wall. The flames of the lamps on the screen of the Founder's Chapel rocked and streamed aside; even the light on the rood-loft of the nuns' church leapt up, so that the dimness was filled with the noise of wind and the pulsations of living light.

Gib stepped out, his head down against the wind. "Osanna," he had cried at Malle, and had remembered that that was the word by which the children greeted the Son of David in the Temple of God. All those children crying "Osanna" in Jerusalem, and one child here, the dumb half savage brat who was Gib's son. Not for Gib to guide the plow or sow the seed for Christ's harvest. It was not Gib's voice which should sound through the King's realm, nor his name that should be feared by the wicked and the great. He must stay in Marrick, shackled, like any grazing beast on the sykes, to the clog that kept it from straying. Wat was the clog, the child that Gib might not leave, and could not come anywhere near to loving.

He looked over his shoulder. Malle followed slowly after him, unquestioning as any dog; the wind beat at her skirts and flapped her kerchief across her face.

"She saw nothing!" he told himself. "Nothing! Nothing!"

But as his feet squelched on through the deep mire of the road it was to the tune of other words that repeated themselves in his mind against his will—

"Depart from me! Depart from me! If any should offend against the least of these little ones—"

September 14

Kit Aske had come home today from the Earl of Cumberland's household, and directly after dinner he must go out and see how the new church tower was getting on. The tower was his tower; it had been his idea to rebuild it, and stone, timber, and work were being paid for by him. He was passionate for it, as if it were a living creature and his child.

So he was all in a fidget to be off and see how it had grown, and wanted Jack to go with him. But Jack had a great cold, and Dame Nell would not let him out, so instead Robin must come. They went off together through the orchard and across the bridge over the moat. Kit, though he went nowadays a little bent and limping, was ahead all the way and kept on saying, "Come, Robin! Come on!"

At the churchyard wall they stood back to get a good view, and to be clear of all the masons' and carpenters' stuff that lay about. It was a fine stalwart tower, not high but strong; broad based, with splayed buttresses at the corners. It looked as though it had strode out of the very verge of the marsh, and there stood, defying the waters.

"Your tower'll last, Kit," said Robert Aske. "We shall not see him come tumbling down in a gale." That had been the end, three years ago now, of the old tower.

Kit was pleased.

"And look," he pointed up, "my name in stone to tell who was the builder." High up on the wall there were shields of arms carved, and the words, "*Christopher second fils Robert Aske Chevalier. Oublier ne doy. Anno Domini 1536.*"

They went nearer, through the piled sand and lime and the stacks of clean planks, meaning to go about the church to look at the new work from the other side. But just under the tower they met the master mason, with a bit of oily rag in one hand and a chisel in the other. So they stayed talking to him with the wind whipping the skirts of their coats while the sun went behind heavier cloud, and a few driven spatters of rain flew by them.

The master mason, who was a sad-looking little man with a rare smile that gave him, while it lasted, the look of an old and wise child, was very deferential to Kit, promising that the work should be finished in a few weeks now, and taking Kit's chiding for the slowness of it with a chastened air. But just as the brothers were going on he looked to Robert and smiled.

"And have you found your aske, master, that you bade me carve you on a stone?"

"I?" said Robert. "Did I so?"

"That you did. For you said if there was the name of one Aske carved up there, so should there be an aske out of the fen carved for to remember you by. So there I carved him for you," and he pointed behind them, where low down on the west wall of the tower an aske, as the fen-men called a newt, wriggled his tail across a stone.

"Why," Robert cried, "so I did. I remember it now," and he began to laugh, and then, seeing Kit's face, checked himself.

Kit was very angry. "God's Death! To deface my tower with such foolishness!" His passion startled the master mason, who stepped back before him. Kit even had his fist raised, but Robert stepped in between, hastily, so that his shoulder jogged Kit's chest.

"Easy, Kit," said he.

"Easy!" cried Kit in a high, furious voice.

Robert heard the mason clicking his tongue soothingly in the background.

"If there's blame it's mine," he said. "But indeed—" he shrugged because really it was so small a thing, and one he had never intended, his words to the mason having been of the idlest.

"'Indeed?' Yea indeed. Indeed it is you, always, all the time, spoiling my works, making mock of me behind my back."

"Dear, dear, dear!" the master mason lamented softly and distressfully as Kit went limping away from them. "Would I had not done it, but I thought—"

"Think no more of it. It is nothing," Robert said in a loud and cheerful voice, so that Kit should hear.

For he was angry too, and that which he called "nothing" was to him, as to Kit, all the past rolled into a ball—all their bickerings, emulations, angers, grudgings—present with them again; for these, like wood lice under a stone, needed only a touch to wake and set them squirming and busy.

After he had talked a while, to hearten and console the master mason, he went off, not to the house, being too sorely out of temper for that, but round about to the workshops. He was thinking that all the sins that Kit must be hoarding against him, and he could remember quite a string of them, going back and forth through the years—a broken bow, a page torn in a book, a gold button borrowed and lost—all these, he thought to himself, don't amount to the price of a man's eye.

He found Will Wall at work in the carpenter's shop sharpening a knife on the grindstone. He nodded to him, then went over to a corner where there was an iron pot containing an ill-looking black mixture; he croodled down on his heels by it, to see the better, and picking up a chip of wood from the floor, lifted the lock of hair, taken from Jack Aske's white horse's tail, out of the mixture of strong ale and soot in which it was steeping. It had lain in soak for a day and a night but yet it was not dark enough to twist into a line fit for fishing in the black cloudy waters of the marsh land.

He was staring at it moodily, when the slithering, petulant hiss of the grindstone ceased, and Will spoke.

"Master," said he, "I was over to Thicket yesterday."

Aske did not turn his head nor answer.

"They've been stripping the lead off the nuns' church, and the rain's come through something cruel.

"There's puddles all about the altar," he said.

Aske got up and went over to the bench. He began to root about in the litter there.

"Where's that whoreson quarrel needle?" he muttered, and having found it began to work the bellows of the little fire till the soft ash flew about.

"God's Body!" he cried suddenly, and let the bellows die on a long breath. "What of it then? So I suppose will it be in many a church these days."

Will came over to him, and taking the horn-tipped handle of the bellows began to blow gently and persuasively, till the tiny heart of red in the fire had spread through the whole. Aske gave him a quick glance, and then set the quarrel needle between the tongs and thrust it into the fire. They watched in silence while the little black thing changed and brightened till it was indistinguishable from the glowing charcoal. Aske drew it out and began to work on it with a knife. "I want a small fishhook," he said gruffly to Will, and left him, to temper the quarrel in a pail of water.

It was not till it was again glowing and sparkling, and Aske was bending it to a hook, that he spoke again.

"Why do you say this to me?"

"Because—is it—master, in your conscience, do you think it is right?"

Aske stopped his work with the hammer. He took a long while to answer. Then he said, "In my conscience, I think it is not right."

"Then—"

This time Aske did not give Will time to finish.

"It is the great lords temporal that must bear the blame. It was for them to take such order that this should not have come to pass. It's for them to amend it."

"But, master, will they amend it?"

Aske laughed shortly. "God knows what they will do."

"And if they do not?" Will watched him with an under-look, then said, "They're saying that if none else dare, then the gentlemen and the poor commons must amend it."

Aske tossed down the hammer on the bench and stood staring out of the window, but knowing nothing of what he saw.

"That," said he at last, "would be rebellion against the King."

"But." Will mumbled, "there's the King's King, master, to think on."

Aske turned to him with a look that seemed startled, and went away out of the workshop as if he had not heard.

But it was this chiefly, of all that Will had said, which was in his mind that evening when Jack, Kit, and he were standing about with Nell and Master Thomas Rudston and his wife, who were staying at Aughton. They had their wine cups in their hands, and the candles stood lit and ready on the sideboard to carry up to bed. But there they stood disputing, as they had disputed for the past hour, and, like dogs in a fight, not one of them would break away for long enough to let the dispute stop.

What they were arguing was all the same that Will had meant, and yet was totally different. For on the one side they spoke of the poverty of the North, and how the King's taxes were too heavy and might not be paid, and how much of the relief of the poor commons was in the abbeys, who would suffer sorely by their suppression—such was the line which Jack, Master Rudston, and Robert Aske took. But Kit spoke of how the King's will must be done or the realm fall into confusion, and that there was much to be reformed among the spiritual men, and that heretics would before long be put down, and nothing but the lordship of the pope broken in England, and that perhaps only for a time. Of the two ladies Mistress Rudston said nothing, but Nell Aske cried Kit on, and now and again gave Robert glances of fury.

"Furthermore," said Mr. Rudston, "there is this statute by which the King may bequeath the crown to whom he will. That's no good thing," and he turned to Aske as to another lawyer, for they were both men of Gray's Inn. Aske shook his head.

"And on the other hand," Mr. Rudston continued, "there's a statute to forbid us willing our lands to any but our heirs, which is injustice manifest."

"Aye," said Robert Aske, seduced once more into the argument by the fascinating complexities of the law—"Aye, but, as I think, as there are now more ways than there were before this statute to defeat the King of his right—" and he plunged into a subtle and ingenious exposition to which even Nell Aske listened with respect, and all the others, saving Kit, with approbation. But Kit broke into it.

"Lord!" he cried, "Hark to Mr. Justice Aske declaring the law," and he slammed his wine cup down on the sideboard and snatched up his candle and went away upstairs.

In a few minutes the rest came after, Nell first with her chin high and a stiff, flushed look on her face, the Rudstons next, and Jack and Robert last. Robert, stealing a glance at his eldest brother, could smile, though sourly, to think that the Rudstons alone would find peace in their bed, for Jack must go to Nell, and he and Kit were sharing a room together.

Kit was already in shirt and hosen when Robert came into the room. He said he'd sent away Mat, his servant, "And that's a pity," thought Robert, setting his candle down.

"I always think," Kit said behind him, in a soft, unpleasant voice, "that with you, Robin, it matters little what's right, or wrong, what's good or ill, so that you can play on it to show your wit."

Robert swung round.

"Oh! That's what you think?"

"So you will egg on Jack and others to talk treason enough to hang us all."

"God's Blood!" Robert threw back at him, with equal unpleasantness.

"And if any hang it will be that you have informed against them. For, but yourself, there was none that thought other than as I said."

And then they were standing in the middle of the room shouting at each other, while their shadows crawled up the walls and shrank down as the flames of the candles were flung by their furious gestures.

At last Robert tried to get a hold on himself—

"Mass!" he said, "Kit, let's leave it at that."

"Aye," Kit sneered, "because you can't deny but it is treason against the King you have been saying."

Robert threw his hands wide, as if to ask an invisible witness to hear him out that he had tried to disengage from the quarrel.

"But I can deny it. And if it were true there's a worse thing than treason. Hark you, Kit, it was a poor man of the commons said to me but today, 'There's the King's King, master, to think on.'"

"A poor man of the commons?" cried Kit. "You give such fellows leave to come and grudge and mutter to you? Why? Shall they rise, and choose you to be their leader forsooth?"

Robert had his fist clenched. He was glad indeed to find that Will had come into the room and was standing behind them. How much Will had heard he did not know, and anyway it did not matter. The great thing was that the interruption had come in time to prevent him striking Kit.

"Be off with you, Will," said he, and, turning from Kit, sat down on the bed and began to take off his shoes and unlace the gussets of his hosen. Kit went on talking, but Robert kept his face like wood, and after a while Kit gave it up and they got to bed in silence.

September 17

Four men, Will Wall, the miller from Ellerton, an Aughton yeoman, and a stranger, a man out of Lincolnshire, were hanging with their elbows over the gate of Goose Green Close where a dozen of the Askes' horses were grazing; these had been brought up out of the ings earlier in the day, because all three Aske brothers, and Master Hob too, were leaving tomorrow, early, for Ellerker, to get a fortnight's cub hunting with the cousins there before Robert Aske, and his nephews, Hob Aske and young Jack Ellerker, started for London to keep the law term.

As the four leaned on the gate it was the Lincolnshire man who was talking. He was a thin fellow, red as a fox, with quick eyes, and quick wits in his narrow head. He had come, he said, from Louth (they'd heard of Louth?) and he came to Yorkshire, said he, because brothers and neighbors should help each other. "For now there be things devised against the commons too grievous to be borne, as that every man shall be sworn what goods he hath, and if he have more than so much all his goods shall be taken away. Likewise there is a statute made that none shall eat white bread, goose, nor capon, but if he pay pennies to the King. Likewise another that none shall be christened, wedded, nor buried but at the price of a noble. For these days there is a sort of Lollards and traitors that rule about the King, and have brought him to such a covetous mind that if the Thames flowed with gold and silver it would not quench his thirst."

The miller and the Aughton yeoman could only murmur approval, but Will Wall, as one who knew London, and moved in learned circles there, was more forward. He had, he said, heard his master declare that the statute of the King's supremacy was an evil statute because by it came division from the Church Catholic, and that no king before this king had had the cure of souls. "And I have heard other gentlemen too—"

The Lincolnshire man interrupted impatiently, "Fie on your gentlemen! For what will they do but talk? I'd have none of them. There are in Lincolnshire who say 'We must have gentlemen to lead us.' But I say 'Nay.' For if they would lead us it should be for no longer than serves their own purses and purposes, and then they will fall away, betraying us so that they can save their necks while ours stretch in a halter."

Will cried, "That's not my master!" and the miller and the yeoman backed him up, and they began to tell the Lincolnshire man stories about Master Robin, all trifling, but to them these trifles had significance. He listened, fidgeting, and waiting to take up the word again. But it was Will who interrupted by jerking the miller in the ribs and muttering, "Here he comes."

They all turned at that. Robert Aske was coming toward them over the sharp, springing stubbles that showed yellow and shining in the new deep green of the reaped fields; he had a capful of corn in his hand. He nodded to them as they made way for him, cast a sharp glance on the Lincolnshire man, and opened the gate. They watched him in silence, and as though he were a strange sight, and because he gave them no second look, and no word at all, they felt that somehow, though he could not have heard what they said, he must know the subject of the Lincolnshire man's discourse. They let him go halfway across the field toward the horses and then slunk away along the hedge.

It was not that, however, which had made Aske keep his mouth shut, and pass them with only a nod. It was because he saw that the Lincolnshire man was a stranger and of no stranger did he want to ask, "What news?" since in these days all was bad news. So he went on to where the young mare moved slowly, switching her tail against flies as she cropped, and keeping a soft, wild eye on him as he drew near. When he reached her she lifted and shook her pretty head, whinnying, and then nuzzled in his cap for the corn. He stood for quite a long time, smoothing his hand down her neck till his fingers were dusty and sticky from the warm, dusty hide. When he looked back to the gate there was no one there. He was relieved; then he thought, with a sharp misgiving, "Had that fellow news?" and then, "Mass! I shall put it all by for this fortnight at the least."

When the Aughton men and the stranger left the gate of Goose Green Close one of them suggested that they should drink together before they set the man from Lincolnshire on his way. But as they went they began to jangle, so that they parted before the door of the ale house was reached. The cause of their disagreement was that Will had begun again on the subject of Master Robin.

"And if you had him to your leader," said he, "in the stead of this one you call the Cobbler—"

"Pooh!" the stranger interrupted. "Him! A little man like that with but one eye, and too proud withal to speak to common men!"

The miller put him right on the last point. "It's not his way to pass without a word. Most times he'd have come and set his shoulder to the bar of the gate and stood among us to talk. But if he'd wind of your business—"

"Fie then—" the Lincolnshire man began, but thought best to leave the rest unsaid. "Well," said he, "by your leave I may say he's a man of no great station nor worship, and of a name unknown."

They told him, angrily, that if Master Aske were not known in his country, "yet there's many in Yorkshire knows him; all this countryside, and by Wressel to Beverley and south to Humber. And in Swaledale too."

"Aye," says Will grandly, "and further north yet, to the Border itself, and wherever the Percy's name runs. For in his young years my master was of the Earl's council, and for all he was young the old Earl leant much on him."

"So," the miller summed it all up, "though he's a little man, and one-eyed, a lawyer and no knight, we'd sooner go out behind his back than any other's, and we'd know that he'd die with us if it came to the pass."

"How'd ye know that?" the Louth man sneered.

They could not say how they knew, only that they did know.

"And," said one of them, "it's my belief you could hack Master Robin into gobbets, and every one of them'd tell the same tale, and that'd be the truth. And you couldn't make them gobbets hold their tongues neither."

September 24

There was a sharp knocking on the door of the prioress's chamber and one that she did not know, though she knew the manner in which every one of the ladies, or of the servants, would knock. When she cried out to come in, in came Piers, Sir Rafe's elder page. He pulled his cap off, shut the door behind him and stood against it, his eyes and cheeks very bright; it was plain that he had been running.

"I could not steal the pony. So—I ran," he said with gasps, and she stood up, crying out, "What is it? Is it news?"

He nodded.

"I heard Sir Rafe say it to my lady when he had read the letter. He'll send a message to you but I came out to tell you quick."

"What was it you overheard?" Now she would know whether Marrick should stand or fall.

"I was waiting upon them. I did not overhear it. They knew I was there," he corrected her.

She did not care for that, although he did. "What?" she cried.

"Sir Rafe said, 'Here's from my brother. He hath done the Lady's business for her. The King hath given license that Marrick shall continue. There's his seal.'"

"Ah," cried the prioress on a deep breath, and then, "The King's seal? You're sure?"

"Sure!" said the lad, and he grinned at her, friendly and impudent, and the bearer of these tidings. For a second she thought to kiss him, and he knew it. She saw how he stiffened and flushed, and instead she held out her hand. "No. Not to kiss, but to take you by the hand for a good true friend," she said, as he ducked his head with an awkward bob to kiss it. So they shook hands together, smiling at each other, and she smiled inwardly with amusement and with pleasure.

"I am glad," he said, out of his young simplicity. "I'm all for the monasteries to stand, and I think it shame that the King should be in the hands of such a rascal as Cromwell. They say, and indeed I think it's full likely, that there'll be rebellion soon if he should continue about the King. The great lords, they say, will take up arms to compel the King to put him away. That would be a thing to see," and he looked at her, gaily as a robin.

"Aye," said the prioress. She did not want rebellion, since Marrick was to continue, but she was not going to damp the boy's anticipations. She let him talk, in a very grown-up strain, and with his eyes dancing, of how this lord and that was said to have harnessed men ready in his lands. She said, very gravely from time to time, "Truly?" and, "You think even so?"

At last he remembered how time was passing, and gave a whistle, and said he'd get a box on the ear if he didn't get back quick. She kept him while she got out from the coffer a bag of money, and putting two angels into her own little silk purse gave it to him—"For bringing me good news."

He kissed her hand this time, and went out. She heard him go whooping down the outer stair in two bounds.

After a little while she followed him. The evening was coming in still and overcast, with the fells showing damson-blue through the rainy air. Summer had gone by. There was over all a sense of returning, of withdrawing, of coming home, so that even the poached mud of the great court seemed to speak of quiet. Winter was to come, but the world was ready; like a dormouse it was curling itself up. And the little world of the priory would light its fires, bar its shutters, and snuggle down safe at home. Even though gales tore through the gaping doors and empty rooms of other less fortunate houses of religious, Marrick would snuggle down, safe and permanent.

She went toward the gatehouse, meaning to look out and along the dale—much as the dormouse may look out, to taste more sweetly the comfort of his security. One of the women was feeding the hens. She tossed the good corn out in handfuls, then emptied out the last of it from the wooden measure; it rattled on the stiff wing feathers of the nearer birds. They were all dipping and dabbing at it on the ground; fussing, quarreling, clucking, gobbling as quick as they might. Among the hens a few pigeons sidled, swinging their tails.

The prioress came to the gatehouse arch and saw, striding along outside on his way back from Grinton, with a full poke slung from a stick on his shoulder, Sir Gilbert Dawe.

Because, if she spoke to him, it must be to rebuke him for letting the altar linen get dirty and also spotted with damp; and because tonight all should be peace, she turned hastily back as if she had not seen him and went in and up to her chamber.

But Gib knew she had seen him, and snorted aloud with indignant laughter. Had she let him come up with her he would have denounced her: her tyranny, her love of money, her easy living, her cruelty to the poor creature Malle. But she feared him. She had fled from him.

The triumph of that thought warmed him. He refused to consider what the presence of Malle in his house did indeed mean. It meant that there was a woman to do the woman's work, but it meant a woman's tongue too. It had never entered his head— even if he had stayed to think it never would have entered his head—that the woman would speak except to answer him when he chose to speak to her.

But she talked to Wat, cheerfully, foolishly, endlessly.

September 26

On the evening before his wedding Master Laurence Machyn dressed himself in his best doublet of yellow cloth faced with gray sarcenet, and taking with him the brother of his late wife, he went to greet his bride, who had been brought to London by

Sir John Bulmer, and left in the charge of Sir John Uvedale and his lady.

It was Laurence's brother-in-law who shouted to the servants at the Cardinal's Hat to find Sir John Uvedale; and his brother-in-law who so took the lead in conversation with Sir John's lady, that she thought for several minutes that he was the groom. Even when she learned that he was not she tended to address to him all the complexity of her explanations—how her husband and Sir Rafe Bulmer were acquainted because both had been in the household of the poor little Duke of Richmond, that sweet child, alas too early taken—and so Sir John Bulmer had entrusted the young gentlewoman to her, but, alas! today is the poor young maid sick—

"Sick!" Laurence's brother-in-law boomed, so that both Laurence and the lady jumped; and she explained hastily that it was no contagious sickness, but merely a disordered stomach, "but she retches so sore I would not bid her come down to greet ye."

"No. No," said Laurence hastily, speaking almost for the first time.

"Jesu!" the lady ran on, "it is but the weariness of the journey and her fears maybe, and time will mend all. Yet perhaps it was enough to scare the child, to be brought so suddenly to her marriage. But Sir John could not wait, and there was but two days for her to prepare, and so here she is with no more than six good shifts of her own, and a bundle of her sister's gowns that's far too big for her, but that was all there was time to provide, and they can be cut down. Not that the shifts aren't good and fine, and I told her a husband loved better that his wife should bring to her marriage good shifts that he alone should see, rather than great plenty of outward gear that other men should admire, and nothing but patches and rents beneath. So I said to comfort her, but—"

She had to stop there because Laurence's brother so slapped his thigh and roared out a laugh crying, "Marry! but that's good counsel for a bride. Marry! but that's good."

They did not stay long after that, and Master Laurence's brother-in-law was still laughing as they took their leave; his laughter and his big voice filled the courtyard of the Cardinal's Hat, so that men and maids turned from their work to look at him. Sir John Uvedale's lady gentlewoman looked too, peeping out from the window of the room upstairs where July lay limp and abject.

"Hark, there he goes, your groom," she cried, and opened the casement to watch the better. "Such a big man," she told July, "with black hair that bristles on his head. And that's his voice—great as a bull's. Do you hear it?"

July said faintly, yes, she heard it.

"But who is it goes with him? Is he a widower? Hath he a son?"

July murmured that she had been told that he was a widower, but of a son she knew nothing.

"Well," said the woman, shutting the window, "you must rest you now, and sleep well while you may, for such a man will give you no rest tomorrow's night."

July shut her eyes. She felt ill enough to die, but had no hope to be so lucky. It was a few moments later that she drove herself to ask, "What manner of man is he?"

"Big. Black—as I told you."

"But of countenance and favor?"

The gentlewoman had not seen more than his back so could not say. July was left to picture an ogre, huge as a bull, and black-bristled, yet with the gleaming, thin malevolence of a friend of William Cheyne.

September 28

Master Laurence Machyn lived in Knightrider Street, almost next door to the Church of St. Andrew in the Wardrobe. The house from the front looked very small, because Laurence's grandfather, who had built it, had squeezed it in between a fishmonger's house on one side and on the other a much older house of stone, which had belonged to the Black Prince, but which now had a shoemaker's sign—the Cow & Garland—hung over its stately but half ruinous gate.

Inside, the Machyns' house was larger than it looked. You came, by the door from the street, to the passage beside the screens, with the great chamber opening off on the right. There had been no room to build the kitchen and offices opposite the screens in the usual way, so these—a kitchen, a little buttery, and a pantry—lay at the back of the house through a door opposite the street door. Upstairs there was quite a big solar over the great chamber, and leading off that the bedroom in which Laurence Machyn had been born, and in which last night he and his bride had been bedded. Above there were smaller rooms where two of Laurence's men and three serving women slept, and one little empty attic where an old chest and a couple of trussing coffers were stored.

Behind the house, opposite the kitchen, stood the long workshop where the men made the coffins, for Laurence, who belonged to the Guild of the Merchant Taylors, furnished forth burials. A woodstore opened out of it, and above was a dark loft, where the candles, big and little, were stacked, some as stout as flails, some no thicker than ash twigs. In presses there, kept under lock and key, there were palls of rich stuff which Laurence hired out; being for rich dead men they were very fine, woven with gold among the colors; lesser folk would hire a pall from their parish church, but those, of course, were not so splendid. Sometimes the loft was gay with the painted buckram shields that Laurence had had painted to be carried after the dead, and always, hanging on pegs, there were black gowns worn by poor men who followed the dead, carrying the lighted candles and banners.

Pinched in between the buttery and the workshop, and enclosing a little yard where there were flowers, mixed up with parsley, thyme, sage, pennyroyal and other kitchen stuff, there was a brew house, and if you went past that by a covered passage you came to a little garden. Most of it was taken up by an old mulberry tree, but along one wall there was an alley built with poles and planted with honeysuckle and with a vine that bore tiny grapes like green beads.

July wakened in the big bed in the room off the solar. The curtains were drawn close but she could see that there was daylight beyond them. She started up, then, because of a sick faintness, lay down again, and buried her face in the pillow and cried.

Yet that she could cry at all meant that the worst had not come upon her. If it had been as she had feared she must have hardened herself to stone or to cold iron. As it was she could cry. For when they had brought her to church and she had made as if to give her hand to the big, black-bristled man, it had been taken by another, not indeed very attractive to look at, since he was lean and light, with pale brown sparse hair, and a thin face with a ridiculously large mouth. When he smiled his smile was more gentle than merry, and he showed very black and bad teeth, which made his breath unpleasant to her when he kissed her. But at least he was not alarming like the other, and nothing at all like William Cheyne.

Yet even so, and though during the feasting and the dancing she caught him sometimes looking at her with a kind look, the day had been a nightmare of fears and sickness, and then came the night. Now she lay with her face hidden. She did not realize how great his forbearance had been, but, as she thought of that night, she believed she had not slept at all till the light came, for even when he slept she had lain awake hearing the bells from the Black Friars' Church ring so loud that they might have been in the room.

Now they rang again, and other bells, more distant, on this side and that, with a sweet, wandering music. But since the hour was so late she must get up quickly. Why had he not roused her? He—they all—would be angry. Where were her clothes? And what must she do when she had them on? Call the women? Go to look for him?

Trembling and clumsy she began to dress. But she could not put on the gown she had worn yesterday; that was for feasts only. She had to tumble out all Meg's gay stuff upon the floor to find one of her own, and at last was ready to go down, in her old brown gown and gray petticoat.

It was absurd, and also acutely embarrassing, to be creeping about the house like this, an intruder, and yet one who might not go away. And she began to know that she was terribly, achingly hungry. She thought that if she found the kitchen one of the women might give her bread and perhaps a drink of ale. She came down into the great chamber. It was yet in disarray after yesterday's company: dishes and cans on the table, and a cat crunching delicately at a chop bone under a bench. It occurred to her that she too might find something to eat fallen among the rushes, and so stay her stomach. But if they caught her so employed, or asked her after how she had breakfasted—? She could not risk it.

Yet where were the kitchens? Confused, she opened a door, and found herself looking out upon the street. She came to the other door opposite, and had her hand on the latch to open it when it swung in suddenly, so that she had to spring back as her husband came in hastily.

He stepped back too, and they stared at each other, in an equal embarrassment. "Where are you going?" he asked, not being able to think of anything to say, and at that she began to stammer excuses in so palpable a fright that it helped him to recover himself.

He looked down at her, small, thin, and dressed as meekly as any night-flying moth in gray and brown. And she feared him. For a moment he thought to take her hand and say, "Sweetheart, I left you to sleep." But no. He must be sure of his foothold before he encouraged her to take liberties. He looked grave.

"No matter, wife," he said; and then, "Shall I—I shall call Marget to show you the house."

"If you will, sir."

She looked utterly miserable. "But you've not breakfasted," he cried, and, forgetting that he must at all costs make himself master in these early days, he left her hurriedly to call on the women in the kitchen to be quick—"Be quick and bring your mistress breakfast."

When one came in with it he came back too, and pushed aside the cups and platters from the end of the table in the great chamber by which July had sat herself down forlornly. While she ate he sat opposite her, not saying much and keeping, when he remembered, a solemn and even a frowning countenance, and when he did not remember, looking at her with gentleness, pity, curiosity, and lessening apprehension.

On the whole he felt greatly reassured by her appearance and behavior. He thought that it was impossible she should prove to be such another wife as his first. The late Mistress Machyn had been five years older than he, and a widow when he took her. She was, besides, a great hearty creature, with a complexion like a farmer's wife, and a voice like an usher in the courts. You would have thought that she would have outlasted half-a-dozen such as Laurence Machyn, and when she died of the sweating sickness he had been so amazed that he had quite forgotten to fear that he might die of it himself.

So he watched July, noting with approval that she ate most daintily. But, he thought, if she's too dainty how shall I ensure that she well orders the house? And he began to foresee troubles other than those which he had already suffered.

But when, having finished eating, she looked up at him with a little color in her cheeks and life in her eyes, he smiled at her and began to fumble in his pouch.

"See, sweeting," he said, "there's four angels for you to spend as you will," and then he coughed, and told her sternly that the women must be set to clear out the chamber before dinner time—"And that's not long," said he, "for it must be near ten of the clock, and look at all this!" He swept his hand about to direct her attention to the confusion on the tables, as though it was all her fault. "I shall send you old Marget," he said, and left her.

September 30

Will Wall said, as he held Aske's stirrup this morning, "You did ought to have let me take the mare to be shod. That off fore is working loose," And then, as though it were all part of the same reproach, "They're turning forth the canons from North Ferriby this morning."

"It'll last me today," Aske said cheerfully, as if he had heard only Will's warning about the loose shoe.

But when the mare dropped it, and Aske lost the rest of the hunt, instead of going back to the smith at Swanland he began to walk her downhill toward where the tower of North Ferriby stood up amongst the trees of the village.

The smith told him that all the canons had gone away early this morning—"except Dom Philip Cawood," said he, "and you'll find him, I doubt not, at the ale house." But Aske was only too glad to hear that he need not see any of those who were turned out; and if one of them were to seek solace in drinking himself silly Aske did not blame him. He left his horse at the smithy, and walked along the empty street of the village toward the priory: only the ducks and the hens were about, but already he could hear the sound of voices which told him where were all the absent villagers.

In front of the priory gatehouse a row of carts were drawn up; three men were already loading up a big ironbound coffer, and as Aske went past them another came out with a bundle of woven hangings on his back. Inside the first court a group of women stood close, peering in through the doorway that led into the canons' offices. They fell back when they saw Aske, and let him go by in silence; he looked over his shoulder, and they had come a few paces after him and then stood again, silent and staring.

But in the church itself there was no silence but a great noise of voices, and the shouts of children skylarking up and down the canons' night-stairs. There was a sound of hammering too, and wrenching of wood, as wainscoting was stripped from the walls of a vestry beyond. Now and again there came a louder outcry when one of the villagers was caught pilfering from among all that which was now the King's, and which the receiver's men were collecting in great piles in the church and cloister. Aske stuck his hands through his belt and stood watching it for a long time; until, in fact, the fellow in charge turned all out of the church and locked the door behind him. He gave Aske good day politely, and then looked curiously at him, before he went to his dinner. Aske took his horse again at the smith's and started off in the direction of Ellerker, but at the lane that led to the manor he did not turn; instead he rode on along the old Roman road northward.

It was dark when he came again to Ellerker, and so late that as he approached the house he could see no light at all. Yet he had hardly knocked when the gate was opened by Will.

Aske rode in and dismounted stiffly. The mare had had enough too. Will swept his lantern over her and then lifted it so that he could see his master's face.

"Have you—sir," he cried, "have you been over the water?"

"Over Humber? Why should you think I went over Humber?"

Will did not say, and Aske did not care enough to press him. Of all fruitless journeys and foolish, surely his had been the most fruitless, most foolish. "But at least," he thought, "I have seen with mine own eyes, what it is that is done." He had seen, as at Ferriby, so at Pocklington, and at York, the emptied shells of what had been houses of religious. He had even been so near home as Thicket, and in the last glimmer of dusk had felt his way into the little church where, Will had said, the rain was coming in upon the altar. It was too dark for him to see, but certainly the place smelt of damp, and already of decay.

Will brought him some supper now from the kitchen and put it down at the end of a table in the hall where Aske already sat, with a rushlight making only a small and faint island of light in the darkness.

"Master," said Will, "they do not guess where you have been."

Aske looked at him dully. How could they guess?

"I said you had sent word by a peddler that came. I said you had met one of the gentlemen from Gray's Inn that was going to Hull and that you had gone thither to dine with him."

Aske said, "Will, go to bed. What are you talking about?" but he did not in the least want to know, and Will went off without answering.

Aske sat on a long time in the hall, very weary, stupidly eating and staring at the rushlight, and as stupidly forgetting to eat. At last he pushed his plate away, took up the rushlight and started to go upstairs.

Outside the door of the room which he was sharing with Kit and young Hob he blew out the light and stood in the blank dark, hearing the night noises of the old house—a faint sigh, a creak, a tiny but sharp crack. It had not seemed to him that he was thinking while he sat alone below. But now two things were clear, which till now, had been clouded; or perhaps it was that they were isolated by the general dullness of his mind, and so seemed clear as the little flame of the rushlight had seemed bright in the dark and empty hall. The first he could put into words.

"If I move," he said in his mind, "I do wrong. If I move not, wrong is done."

The other, which was a dumb thing, was fear—the fear lest he should stand alone, a man disowned by kin and friends; there in the dark he knew in a foretaste the weight and desolation of that loneliness. His hand, groping, found the latch of the door; as it opened he heard Kit cry sleepily, "Who's there?"

He answered, "Robin."

October 1

Lord Darcy sat in the garden at Templehurst. In this sheltered place, under the lee of the house and the chapel, it was warm as summer, and the dogs lay flat on the stones, twitching when the flies teased them. Below, in a little strip of orchard, a gardener and his boy were gathering apples.

In front of Lord Darcy a fat man with a broad brown face sat on a small stool; he wore my lord's green coat, and the Buck's Head on his breast and back.

Darcy said, "This man who told you was truly what he said—a servant of the King's commissioners?"

The fat man could only say that he'd never doubted him. Darcy nodded; it was enough; the fat man, for all his pudding face, was no fool.

"He was riding in haste. He did but bait at York. He'd slept at Howden maybe, or even Lincoln."

"And he told you that the Austin Canons of Hexham have resisted the commissioners?"

"Aye. He said that when his masters came to Hexham there was a pretty crowd in the streets, with bows, bills, and leather jackets he said. And the town rang the common bell, and they in the priory rang the great bell there; it was tang-tang-bom-bom-bom, he said, like as it might be a day when the Scots are into England, he said. And when the commissioners came nigh the priory there were the gates shut against them, and one of the canons came up on the leads, harnessed he was too with a steel cap on his head. He hollers down to the commissioners saying that there were twenty brothers with him in the house would die or they should have it. So he showed them a writing, with the King's broad seal dangling, saying it was writing for writing and seal for seal against that which the commissioners had. And then he says, shouting between his two hands that all the town should hear, 'We think it not to the King's honor to give forth one seal contrary to another. And afore any of our lands, goods, or house be taken from us we shall all die, and there is our full answer!'"

"Hah!" said Darcy, and nothing else for some time, till he asked, "Did this man tell you of any stirring in the North, other than these canons of Hexham?"

"No."

"Did you ask him?"

The fat man looked down for a moment, the comic parody of a coy girl. "I said to him, 'Though Northumberland's ever unruly, yet I'll think it strange if there be no more troubles here in the North with this suppressing of abbeys?' And he said, 'Well, there's none stirring yet.'"

Darcy nodded and sent him away to draw his livery of bread, beer, and mutton at the buttery and pantry. But my lord sat long after the servant had gone, letting his mind range back through dangerous old times, and forward through times that might be as dangerous; but then he did not think danger a very evil thing. While his narrowed eyes glanced about the sunny bit of garden, or followed the cruising bees, he was calculating chances. What would this man do if—and that man if instead—? Would Exeter make up his slow mind, or the Poles swallow their scruples? And if they should once move, would the Emperor—? He did not think so—not now—whatever it might have been three years ago. And then—?

He broke it all off. There was nothing stirring in the North parts but only these canons of Hexham.

He took up again that book of Lydgate's that he had been reading when the fat man came lightly along the path to him. But once he sighed.

October 4

Robert Aske drank the last of his ale, wiped his knife on a piece of bread and slipped it into its case.

All those at breakfast in the parlor at Ellerker looked at him as he stood up.

"Come on, Hob. Come, John," he said to his nephews, "or we'll miss the tide and the ferry."

The boys got up. Will Ellerker, John's father, half rose, then sat down again. One of the servants brought water and a towel, and Aske dipped and wiped his fingers and tossed the towel to Hob.

"You're set to go?" said Jack Aske.

"Since Rafe can't hunt, but must be about taking this cursed subsidy."

"Fie!" cried Kit. "That's no word for the King's will."

"By the Rood!" Robert answered in the cheerfully impudent tone that always enraged his brother, "I use no worse than that Rafe used."

Rafe Ellerker, Will's eldest brother, should have been with them these last few days for the hunting, but because he had been appointed one of the gentlemen to collect the subsidy he could not come. So yesterday Robert Aske had declared that next morning, and not the day after, he would set out for London, and that the two boys, John and Hob, who were both to begin their studies at law, must be ready to ride with him. "Because," he had said, "we shall ride the more easily with another day to spare before term begins."

But now Jack Aske said, "You'll not wait to know if it was true what that summoner out of Lincolnshire said? 'The commons all up about Louth,' he said."

"I don't go by Louth," Robert said obstinately.

"Mass, let him go. For he will go," cried Kit.

"I shall go," Robert answered him with a hard, hostile look, and then was sorry. It was not good to part from a brother in ill will. "The boys need not go," he said.

But John and Hob were not to be stopped. "What's a rabble of poor tradesmen and husbandmen?" cried John confidently. "Should we not have heard, sir—" Hob began to ask his uncle more soberly, but Robert Aske was already at the door and went out without looking back.

They were nearly halfway to North Ferriby when he said to the boys, "There's a word I must say to your Uncle Kit." He turned his horse about. "I'll be with you in time for the ferry," and he went back, riding hard.

He came again, only just in time. The servants and horses were all on board, and the boatmen waiting with the sweeps ready. Hob and John, however, stood on the staithes; they caught Robert's bridle as he swung out of the saddle.

"Sir," said Hob, and laid his hand on his uncle's arm as he was for stepping into the boat.

"Tide's turning, master!" the boatman cried, "I can't wait no longer."

Robert Aske said, "Come on," and went into the boat.

So they got his horse in, and pulled the gangway after them. When that was done, and the boatmen poling the big barge offshore, Aske left the boys and went forward. There was a coil of rope in the bows; he sat down on it as the boat swung slowly into the river. The men settled down to their oars and now they met the wind from off the sea, which, running against the first turn of the tide, cast up little waves that slapped and gurgled against the bows, and ran alongside hissing.

Aske sat with his chin on his fist and a dark look on his face. The nephews, watching him, could guess well enough that whatever word it was that he had ridden back to speak to Uncle Kit he wished now that it had been left unspoken. "But," said Hob, and squared his shoulders, "I shall tell him what they say. He might think we should turn back."

He came and stood near his uncle.

"Well?" said Aske shortly, without looking up.

"Sir, the boatmen say that all Lincolnshire is in a floughter, and ringing their bells awkward. As well as Louth, Caister is up, and Horncastle, they think. The commons are taking any gentlemen they can and swearing them to an oath. And they've killed the bishop's chancellor—dragged him from his horse and beat him to death with staves, and killed others too, they say."

When his uncle neither answered nor looked up, Hob touched him on the shoulder.

"Do you hear, sir?"

"Yes. There's no ferry back till tomorrow morning."

"Would you go back?"

"No."

"The ferrymen would not go about."

"No."

"Unless you should persuade them."

"You can try if you will."

Completely puzzled Hob went off. He spoke a while with John Ellerker, then with the master boatman. At last he came back to the bows.

"No. They will not."

"I thought not," said his uncle, and no more. When Hob had gone away he sat still, his eye upon the widening rift of palest blue above the dove-colored water, which showed where, far down the broadening river, the sea lay. Now he could not turn back.

They rode up from the ferry staithes toward Barton village, keeping pretty close; the boys and the servants were spying about them all the time, as though the dykes might be full of ambushed men. In the village itself, just as a touch of sun flooded over the flat land, they came on the first sign of trouble. Two men stepped out from the door of one of the tofts; they saw the riders, and went in again; one of them had a bow slung at his back and a long woodman's knife at his belt. The other carried a pike.

At the duck pond where, from the straight road to Lincoln, a little narrow lane branched off between a barn and an orchard, Robert Aske wheeled to the right. "We'll make for Sawcliffe," he told them over his shoulder. The others had been expecting that, since the ferrymen had told them that they'd never make Lincoln by the high road. At Sawcliffe lived Sir Thomas Portington, who had married Robert Aske's eldest sister Julian, and never married again since she died.

Aske had been riding always a little ahead; now the distance increased; when they came to Barton Windmill, whose sails were turning briskly with a whirring noise while the shadows of the sails raced upon the road with an endless quick flickering, they could see him a hundred yards ahead. But when they were quite clear of the village, and riding in the open with the wide river on their right, flashing now in sunshine, he was so far that even in that flat land they kept losing sight of him, as they had altogether lost sight of Will Wall and the Ellerker servant behind.

It was quite suddenly that they came up with their uncle again in the street of South Ferriby. He was in the midst of a small crowd of men, one, with a black coat and gray beard, on horseback; the others, close on a score of them, on foot, but armed. As Hob and John Ellerker came round the corner into the village they saw one of these shorten his pike and move in till the point of it was close to Aske's breastbone.

"Mass!" cried Hob, and spurred, then pulled in, his horse.

Their uncle's voice came clearly to them.

"Friend," said he, "that spit of yours is too long for a small fowl like me," and he put the blade aside with his arm, and, taking one foot from the stirrup, gave the fellow a gentle shove in the chest, so that he went backward. The boys heard some of the men laugh, and one of them cried that here was a little cock but it crowed gamely.

"But," said the gray-bearded man, "you shall take the oath or not pass undamaged."

"The oath, or you shall die," they began to shout, and then someone said, "What of these others?" and pointed back along the road.

Aske turned and saw the boys. He lifted his hand and they thought he meant to wave them back, but he must have changed his mind, for he called them to come on.

"Well," said he, as if now they were all friends together, "and what is your oath?"

"To be true to God, the King, and the Commonwealth."

"There is no treason in that," said Aske, "but it stands well with that oath I took before."

"The easier then," said they, "for you to take it. Nor shall you pass otherwise."

So he took it, laying his hand upon the book they had. But when they would have had the lads take it he would not, but began to argue with them, till Hob pulled him by the sleeve.

"Sir, I'll take it so that we may pass."

"You shall not," he told him angrily. "You are minors at law. Come on. No, no! They shall not."

He put his horse forward at the group of men, and they must use force to keep him, or let him go through them. They let him go, and the boys followed after him a little way behind, until they heard him say, but without looking round, "Range up on either side of me."

When they had done that he said, "Lean down, Hob, as if you looked at your gelding's feet, and tell me do they follow us."

"No," said Hob; only a woman with a pitcher of water and a child at her skirts was watching them.

"Well," Aske said, "that's well." He laughed suddenly. "There it is, and it is done."

After that he did not ride forward alone, but went with them and talked a lot, merrily and learnedly, and sometimes listened to what they said.

When they came to Sawcliffe the big gates were shut. From within the court they could hear oxen lowing and the bleating of sheep, as if market were being held there.

"Hammer on the gate, someone," said Aske, and Will, who had caught up with them by now, got down and beat on the doors with the handle of his knife. After a little while the shuttered window above the gatehouse was opened, and Hal Portington and his younger brother Tom looked out. "Oh! It's you!" they cried, and seemed very glad of it. "The commons are up all about," they said.

"We know that," Aske told them.

"And they've taken my father," said Hal. "The girls fear lest—"

"Well," said Aske, "let us in."

They were indeed very glad to have him in. Hal and Tom put such a face on it as if they could have done well enough without him, but Sir John Portington's sister wept on his shoulder, and little Meg flung her arms about his knees and wept into the skirts of his coat. When he had comforted them with a grave face, and a twinkle in his eye to the lads over the lady's head, he went away to the kitchen. They heard his voice rating the servants, they heard the sound of someone getting a drubbing, and then they heard his voice again, not angry now, but laughing. After a while he came back with a big dish of eggs and told them that he thought a wooden spoon was as good as a stick for beating a lad's backside, "and better perhaps, for it covers more ground, and also the noise it makes is more ghastful."

Then the servants came in with the rest of a hastily prepared dinner, and when they sat down to it, they all felt more cheerful. "And," he told them, "there's no need to fear harm to your father, who hath in nothing offended the commons. They'll but have taken him, as they took me, and made him swear the oath. And if they keep him it is because he has land in Lincolnshire, and they need his counsel."

So the rest of the day was cheerful, if strange and disorganized, and they sang in the evening to Hob's lute. When bedtime came Hal Portington took John Ellerker to sleep with him and Tom; Hob went off to Sir Thomas's own bed with his uncle; it did not take him long to get to sleep, and if Robert Aske watched, Hob did not know it.

He did not know either what time it was when Aske wakened him. When the boy sat up, mazed with sleep, he saw that his uncle was dressed and ready to ride. He sat down on the bed by Hob, saying, "Wake up, sluggard. Now listen." Then he said that he was going to try to cross over from Wintringham back into Yorkshire.

"Back?" Hob was confounded both by such a sudden change of purpose and by an uncertainty and haste in his uncle's manner that was altogether strange.

"God's Death!" cried Aske in a sudden flame of anger. Then he began to argue. For if, he said, the oath he had taken stood well with his first oath to the King, then so, semblable, did that oath stand with this, and in keeping of the first he could not but observe the second. "Therefore," he summed it all up at length, "I'll get back if I may." He got up and stood biting his knuckles, then said, "Nor is this my country that I should take hand in this matter," and turned away to the door.

Hob flung out of bed. "I'll come with you." "No." "Then I'll call Will." Aske turned on him, causelessly angry again. "But you shall help me saddle and lock the door on me," he said, and put his hand a moment on the boy's shoulder.

When he had gone Hob got back into bed and thought that, for listening to sounds, he would never sleep. And the next thing he knew was that a handful of pebbles was rattling against the shutters. He looked out and saw his uncle below.

"Well," said Aske, when he was back again in the room, "here I am and here I'll bide, as the cat said when she fell into the milk pail." His cheek was raw, and the knuckles of one hand, and his thumb was swelling prettily. He said that they had caught him even at the riverside, for their watch was good. "One of them," said he, "will have to bite apples with the side of his face, for his front teeth aren't there where God planted them. But they got me down and sat on my head as though I were a horse. Then the fools let me get into the saddle again."

He stood listening, but there was no sound but that of the wind in the chimney, and the ticking of the cool embers on the hearth.

"It must be close on midnight. Let's sleep while we may," he said.

October 5

It was still dark when the family at Sawcliffe, half-dressed, cold, and miserable, came together around the embers of the hall fire. Robert Aske was not with them, nor Will Wall, because half an hour ago a big band of the commons had come knocking at the gate and calling for "Master Aske of Aughton. And you shall not deny him to us, for we know he's here." He had spoken to them out of the gatehouse window, and in the end had ridden away with them into the dark.

Between the time when the great knocking on the gate had set all the dogs barking and the cattle in the court lowing and the women screaming in the house, and the time when the men servants barred the gate behind him, there had been leisure for almost no words between the three young men and their uncle. Only, he had told Hob and John Ellerker to get them back over Humber early next morning. "For it seems," said he, "that the commons will be drawing to the southward. And if so be you find the way clear and safe, send back a servant to Hal here. Then shall you, Hal, follow after with the women and the little ones."

That had been while he was dressing, and Will Wall trussing up a suit of harness for him, borrowed from among those of Sir John Portington. And a few moments after he had gone, with no word more, but only a gesture of his hand and a hard glance that seemed to pass them by as if he had already forgotten them.

Now, when the women and children had gone again to bed, the three had time to talk it over, and at first they could make nothing of it—how their uncle had taken the oath that afternoon, and tried to make his way back over Humber last night, and this morning had gone off with the commons. Hal argued that it was not strange the commons should say they knew him, and that therefore he must go with them, because Kit Aske's lands lay close over Trent in Marshland. But Hob doubted that there was something in it that needed to be bolted out, and, growing sharper in argument, cried out at last, "My mother says she will never trust him, but that he will bring himself and others into trouble by his tongue. There is one thing mine uncle has never learned to do—you know the song—" and he quoted it sententiously—

Whatsoever be in thy thought
Hear and see and say right naught:
Then shall men say thou art well taught.
To hear a horn and blow it not.

"But now," he said, "I do fear he is confederate with the commons."

"Fie!" cried Hal and John Ellerker together, and John said, "No gentleman could be. Surely, it cannot be so." Then he frowned and said, "But it appeared that they let themselves be ruled by him in that they consented that we should return to Yorkshire." Before they concluded the discussion Hob and John thought very gravely of their uncle's behavior, and if Hal argued for him it seemed to be more for cussedness than from conviction.

Meanwhile Robert Aske rode southward knowing in the darkness only that there was a great company both before and behind upon the road, and that most of them were on foot, though he could hear some horses. Only when the darkness thinned could he see their numbers, and their arms, which to a Yorkshireman, used to the harnessed men who would turn out to fight off the Scots, seemed wretched indeed, for their harness was mostly no more than a leather coat, and their arms very often only quarterstaves and clubs.

Daylight came, but a murk daylight deadened by heavy mist, just as they reached Appleby. They were still in Appleby when, several hours later, the fog was shredding into a light, shining mist. Aske sat on his horse in a yeoman's stackyard. All through the little town and out into the fields the commons were crowded, shaggy-haired, dirty fellows many of them, and with a pale sick look, for Lincolnshire was a poor country and aguish.

Round about him they were mostly of the better sort—that is to say, the horsemen, and such as had bows or bills, or here and there a broadsword. He had come in here half an hour ago to chivvy off two or three ragged fellows who were set to rob the yeoman's hen houses, and these others had followed him, much as dogs follow a man, from a habit grown so strong that it has become a need. So far as he could see there was no other gentleman in all that host, though he guessed there must be pretty near two thousand of the commons.

All about him he could hear them talking of what had been done—"Aye, Cock's bones! and it was well done," at Louth and Caistor and Horncastle. They talked also of what should be done next, and, as they talked they would break off and look to him, and wait an instant, as if that he might speak. But Aske had not spoken.

And still they did not move. The fog had quite cleared: it was not now even a mist, but only gave a delicate bloom and sparkle to the sunshine. The yellow straw of the stacks was a shining silky gold against the blue air; a red cock and his hens picked about between the feet of the horses; the cock jerked the fringed feathers of his neck petulantly, and the light wind blew the arched, cascading feathers of his tail about him, like a woman's veil; he sloped his head and stared up at Aske with a fierce round stare as he stepped under the horse's belly.

It was only when the cock, clucking fiercely, hustled out on the other side and made off with a furious pounding stride, that Aske knew he had shifted his heel and put his horse forward.

As he moved all the talking round about him ceased, all heads turned in his direction. The men on the green beyond the stackyard turned too, and came nearer. When he spoke he lifted his voice, meaning that they also should hear.

"Masters," said he, "what will you do? The day's passing. There's no gain in staying here forever. Where next?"

After a pause someone said that Aske had already heard many times that morning, that Lord Brough had sent to raise the men of Kirton in Lindsay and all the Soke. "But they'll not move against us," another cried. "We'll call them up to join us instead."

"Well," said Aske, "let us set about it then. Let some go to Kirton, and some about the Soke, calling on all to join the commons."

They said that would be a good thing to do, a very good thing, and then began asking each other who would go where. They stopped at last because Aske spoke.

"Let the Sokemen go to Kirton. I will raise the Soke."

The Sokemen came from out of the rest like the salt beads of water out of butter. Then Aske stood up in his stirrups, put his hands to his mouth and shouted—

"Two score men to ride with me along Humberside to raise the commons there!"

He had them very soon, and was riding out of Appleby toward the Humber, saying to himself, "This is treason."

It was between one and two in the afternoon that he and his two score came to Kirton in Lindsay to rejoin the Sokemen. He had seen enough that morning of the poverty and simplicity and indiscipline of these poor commons of Lincolnshire to give his face a very grim look. Now, as he rode into the township, he glanced around at the scattered mob of footmen who, having eaten, lounged about in groups or lay asleep; a few of them shouted to him as he rode by. "And that's about all they're good for," he muttered to Will beside him. Will pretended not to hear.

The Sokemen were sitting about in the churchyard round the foot of the cross. But that they were all awake he could not see that they were doing more than the poor footmen outside. He pushed between them till he came to the step of the cross, set his foot on it, and looked down on them. They looked up at him, waiting.

"God help us," he thought. "Sheep. Very sheep." He said— "And what now?"

They told him that they planned to go toward Caistor, to meet the host of Caistor, which was mustering.

"So Jake said," one of them put in.

"He saw many riding thither," said another.

"But when Will came by Briggs no one knew if Caistor were up or no."

"God's Bones! Of course they're up!"

"If they're not up—" someone began, in a voice that sounded scared.

Aske did not let him finish.

"Is there any man who can tell me surely whether there's a host of Caistor or no?"

They stopped arguing it and looked one to the other for the answer. At last an old man with watery eyes said, "No, but they thought it was so, for so the talk went in the country. But they knew it not for truth."

Aske turned from them. He laid one hand flat on the stone shaft of the cross. The stone was warm, but his heart was cold and very heavy. He said:

"Who will go and see whether it is true or not?"

He kept his eye on his hand for what seemed an age. No one spoke out loud, though he could hear them whispering together. He took his hand from the cross and looked at them again.

"Well then, if none will go, I will go."

He went out of the churchyard to where Will waited in the saddle, as he had been bidden, holding Aske's horse. "To Caistor, Will," he said. As he picked up the reins some of the Sokemen called to him to stay till he had dined. He laughed at them, too angry to answer. Three of those that had ridden with him that morning came running after him, stuffing hunks of bread and bacon into their faces. He did not wait, but they scrambled into the saddle and beat their horses till they drew level with him beyond the village.

"What about your dinner?" he threw at them.

They grinned, shamefaced.

"Those fellows," said one of them, "would make a pig sick."

But Aske's heart was lightened.

Late in the afternoon the host was still at Kirton. They had lit fires about the green and were cooking supper now. The Sokemen were all together in a farm, at table still, having well eaten.

Aske came in to them with Will and the three men who had gone after him. He stood at the end of the board, setting his hands on it because he was so stiff with riding that he did not well know where his legs were.

"Caistor host," he said, "will be at Downham Meadow tomorrow, and there you shall meet them."

"And you, master," cried one of them, "you're going to Caistor with us."

"No. I'm for Sawcliffe and then Yorkshire."

"No, by God, you're not," someone shouted.

Aske looked at him. "Why not?"

"By cause we know you gentlemen. You'd all skulk and hang back while we commons bear the brunt."

Aske looked over his shoulder to the Lincoln men who had ridden with him about Kirton Soke, to Kirton, to Caistor, and back to Kirton. They laughed aloud angrily.

"Where hast thou been today, Tom?" cried one of them.

"Ah," said another, "Tom's the nose that must smell out ale houses for the host. He's a great man at that, he is. He can't be spared to ride about on errands."

There was some laughter from the other Sokemen, but Aske said—

"I can make Sawcliffe tonight before dark. I'll cross into Marshland tomorrow where my brother has manors, and men know me; then to Howden, where also I am known, being a Yorkshireman. For it's not one county that will bring so great a matter as ours to a good end, but all the North must rise, yea, poor commons, gentlemen, and noblemen too, if they know their duty to God. So I will make a beginning of raising those parts, and return. And now, shove along, shove along. We're hungry."

"How do we know that you'll return?" someone jeered.

Aske gave him no answer: but one of the men who had ridden with him did, bidding him in a fierce whisper to shut his face for a fool. "He's said he'll return, and, by God's Nails! so he will."

October 6

The Burton Staithes ferryboat ran silently aground on the soft mud by the landing, and Aske and Will Wall led their horses out of it. The hoofs made a great noise on the hollow timbers of the Staithes, and then suddenly none at all on the wet meadow grass. They rode off, past the shuttered inn, for it was so early that the light was barely come; but before they had gone a hundred yards they turned at a noise behind them; the ferryman was beating upon the door of the inn. Aske consigned him to the devil. The Marshland men knew paths that a horseman could not take, which cut miles out of a journey. "By the time we come anywhere," he said, "all but the rabbits and the waterfowl will know as much as we do."

He was right. It was daylight when they came to Reedness, but there were no men in the fields, and yet the village street was full. The steward, with his ox horn slung at his back, was making no attempt to call them to the plowing; it was he who caught Aske's bridle, crying, "Master, shall we ring our bells and muster?"

Aske did not answer for a minute. Then he said,—

"Wait till you hear the bells of Howdenshire ring over the water."

He told the same to every village along the river, where, as at Reedness, the commons thronged the street, and so they came to the ferry across to Howden town itself. The place was like market day for crowds, only today the shops were shut because the journeymen were all out in the streets, and would not go in for anything that their masters would do. Aske pushed his horse as fast as he could through the throng, answering questions over his shoulder, but never staying. When they cried out to know if they should ring their bells awkward, and muster, he said, "Wait till you hear them ring in Marshland."

When they were clear of the town he turned, frowning, to Will's puzzled face.

"But, master, I thought—" said Will.

"What did you think?"

"Why did you bid Marshland men wait for Howden bells, and here in Howdenshire you say they shall wait for Marshland? Will you have none rise?"

Aske looked at him as if he were an enemy.

"Do you think I'm in this for my pleasure?" he asked bitterly. "I'd give my right hand to be clear of it. Lincolnshire has sent articles to the King. If he should give a gracious answer shall Yorkshiremen rise? And shall I put a halter round my own neck? If," he muttered, "I have not already."

"Master!" cried Will, but Aske said, "Now, ride!" and spurred so fiercely that it was a little while before Will could come up with him to ask whither.

"Home. Aughton. Fool!"

But when they had ridden at that furious pace for some while Aske slackened, and turned again to Will, who had come up beside him.

"My brother Kit," he said—and his eye seemed to search Will's face—"My brother Kit and I do not agree over these things. Perhaps I cannot even now make him see—but the master" (he meant Jack) "he and I think semblable in this. He said that himself when we spoke of how he should make answer to a letter of Cromwell's.

"So," he concluded, watching Will all the time, "so I do not doubt, though he may at the first think it strange I should so mell in insurrection, being a man of peace as I am . . ."

When he left that unfinished, Will said, fervently, "You will be able to show him why it is right, Master Robin."

"Yes, that is what I think," said Aske.

They came between the thin, wind-torn woods to Aughton crossroads, and turned away westward. The track dipped down to an arm of the Fen, grew heavy and boggy, and crossed a sluggish course of dark water lined with browning reeds by a little wooden bridge. When they came up again to the level they could see, beyond the village, Kit's new church tower. Aske said, "Come on. We'll not stop to answer any," and so they went through the village with the wind whistling past their ears, hearing the shouts of those who ran out and ran after them drop quickly behind.

The gate of the house was open. They rode into the court, and Aske was out of the saddle and up the steps to the hall door while the servants were running out from the offices and from the stackyard beyond.

The hall, though now it was getting on for dinnertime, was still littered with the men's pallets, and the tables with last night's supper; as he came in two of the young dogs leapt down from among the plates and slunk away.

He went on to the parlor, though indeed he knew now that he would find no one there. He opened the door and stood for a while, staring stupidly at a pot of dead flowers on the window sill; the hearth was cold, the sideboard was empty of the silver cups, salts, and flagons that should stand there, and there was dust everywhere. Beside what had been old Sir Robert's chair a book lay upon the floor, with a straw to mark the reader's place, who had laid it down beside him. On the table, at the very place where Jack had sat to write his letter to Master Cromwell almost exactly a month ago, lay a quill pen, as though that letter had been written yesterday, or as though time had run back through all the days between. Aske looked about at it all, then went away.

The key of the church door hung in its place upon the nail in the screens passage just beyond the pantry. He took it, and let himself out of the house by the little old door into the orchard.

When he came out of the church Will Wall jumped up from the bench in the porch, and, taking the key from Aske's hand, made a great business of locking the door.

"Master, they have all gone away," he said, as though that were news. "Master Kit went first. He had money of my Lord of Cumberland's. He swore he'd get through, and that a rabble of lousy commons should not stop him."

"He'll get through," Aske said, wishing he could have told Kit (only he never could) how well he knew the measure of his brother's intrepid and impetuous spirit. "And—Jack?" he asked.

"Master Jack sent Mistress Nell and the children to Master Monkton's."

Aske took that for an answer. It made no difference whither Jack had gone, since he was gone.

"The court's full of folk, master," said Will. "They wait for you to tell them what to do."

As they went together into the house Aske said that he would name Shipworth Moor as the place where, if the bells rang, they should muster; it was a place just over the river Derwent from Aughton. "For thence," he said, "they can pass over the river at Bubwith to go eastward, if the commons are rising on that hand, or northward toward York, or to Selby, or south to Howden."

"Yes, master," said Will. While Aske spoke to the men in the court, telling them to be ready, to see to the buckles of their harness, their swords, bills, and bows, to have their good wives boil bacon for them to carry in their pokes, Will watched him with the eyes of a dog.

The rest of that day was most busy. Aske wore out the quill pen that he had seen lying on the table in the parlor, and another after it, and Aughton servants and men from the villages round about were riding off this way and that way all the time with the letters he wrote. Then there were the arrows and bows to count in the church tower, and harness both for master and men to find, and clean, and pack.

When at last he and Will left Aughton it was evening. A strong, clean wind blew out of the west, and as they took the road through the village, the clouds behind them drew up in a great pomp of purple and gold about the golden sunset.

Sir George Darcy and his score of riders did not get back to Templehurst till about an hour before midnight, but the porter who let them in had word for him from my lord to go up at

once. As he spoke the porter's eyes were wandering beyond Sir
George to watch the rest of the riders come in under the gate
lantern, for all in Templehurst knew what business it was that
had taken Sir George off just after dark, with a coil of rope
hanging at the saddle of one of the horses. But when the horsemen were in it was clear that the rope had been useless, for there
was no prisoner trussed up behind any of the riders.

My lord's voice, clear as ever for all his age, cried, "Come in,"
as Sir George knocked. When he went in the same young voice,
and this time with a sort of laugh in it, asked, "Well, and have
you him safe by the heels?"

Sir George came round the high-backed settle and found,
sitting side by side upon it, his father and Sir Robert Constable,
each in his velvet and fur-lined nightgown, and each toasting his
bare, hairy shins before the fire. There was a dice-board between
them, and even now my lord threw and cried out in triumph at
a double six. George, who was already ill-tempered from failure,
took such levity much to heart.

He paused just long enough for his silence to be significant,
then said: "I have him not, for he was warned, and fled."

"God's Bones!" said Darcy, "and that's a pity."

"How could I help—" cried George, and began to tell how
coming near to Howden he had sent scouts this way and that, to
hold the roads—"Aye, and to the ferry to keep that. There was no
way but I had it stopped. But when we came to that house where
it was told us he lay—he was gone, though the bed was warm."

"By the gardens no doubt, to lie snug in some other toft till
you were away."

Again—"How could I help?" Sir George protested angrily, and much more till my lord told him sternly, "not to speak so to me." "And it's likely that if you'd used less guile, and ridden straight ways, you'd have caught our man. Na! Na!" he added sharply, and held up his hand, "If you will be so het, son George, then leave us. But if you can command yourself, sit beside Sir Robert, and let's take counsel what next."

After a pause Sir George plumped down on the settle, though he could not bring himself to speak for a few moments, but listened to his father and Sir Robert discussing what were best to do next.

"Where will he lie tonight?" Darcy asked his son, and George answered gruffly that it was said he was going to Lincoln, "because it is bruited that the King has sent answer to the rebels' articles."

"If that be a fair answer—" Sir Robert began, but Darcy laughed.

"That answer will be such as may set the whole North on flame, if I know the King's Grace, and if the commons can find them leaders."

"That was why," Constable said, "I came in such haste as soon as I heard at Holme that Robert Aske was in it. I heard yesterday that there was in Lincolnshire one gentleman was very active for the commons. And then today, when I knew how Aske was at Aughton, and how the people flowed to him—"

"Why do they so?" Darcy was interested. "You know what manner of man he is. Tell us."

Constable tweaked at the hairs of his shin, frowning into the fire. "I'd not have thought him, mind you, of such ill condition as to meddle in treason. But once in, he's a man of such obstinacy and audacity as to be very dangerous. And he hath a very pregnant wit too."

"A very pestilent traitor!" cried Sir George, and getting up announced that he was for bed. "A vile villain," he said. "Even the commons speak of him as they could of no gentleman. When he left Howden they were singing in the streets a song—'Then came a worm, an Aske with one eye!'" He pulled open the door with a jerk, grinding his teeth as he remembered how, as well as singing, there had been laughter in Howden streets as they came away, and though Sir George was spared hearing his own name in a song, yet people had called from the upper windows words that showed no due respect to their Sheriff.

When he had gone Lord Darcy sat in silence for a little, stroking his nightgown over his knee.

"Robert," said he at last with a little laugh, "by what you say of this man Aske you show me such a bold, ready man, as, were he not a traitor, I could love."

"God's Cross!" cried Sir Robert, "I do not love him. In the Percy's Council we were always at odds. For a more positive, opinionated, obstinate fellow does not live than he."

"And if," thought Darcy, with an inward smile, "he excels in those qualities the man beside me, then indeed—" but he knew better than to hint at such a thought. And besides, there were matters of urgency to speak of. He said, "We must lay for him again, to take him whenever he shall come again into Yorkshire. For with one or two such taken and hanged incontinent, it's not like the commons will stir."

Sir Robert nodded, but with a glum look. He stretched out his fist, clenching it so that the muscles of his forearm stood up. "We must needs take him," he said, and then, with a jerk, "I do not say that he is not a man of very open and honest manner of dealing."

"He should ha' kept out of treason," said Darcy cheerfully.

October 7

July was in the kitchen, and her fingers were all bloody from gutting the smelts that Arnold the journeyman had brought in. Laurence came through, wanting hot water for a glue pot, just as she was laying them in the pan. He put the glue pot down and laid hands on her to kiss her. She turned her face from him, and pushed him away, leaving red stains on his green doublet, so he let her go and she went to the table to fetch the board on which were set out the sliced lemon, the little piles of nutmeg, ginger, mace, and chopped bay leaves.

She knew he was watching her but she kept her eyes down. She was always expecting him to be angry with her, though as yet he had been patient. "I have no wine vinegar," she said.

"Then send out."

"But, sir, I know there are some dregs of red wine souring in a pot, ready to use."

"Well," he began, and then remembered that he kept the keys. The late Mistress Machyn had been a most abundant housekeeper when it came to feasting friends, and, to make up, the diet of days in between had often been lean. Laurence had a little grudged at that, but far more at the noise and jollity which seemed almost perpetual in the house. So, he had thought, this new wife should be curbed from the start.

That had seemed easy enough, and July had made no objection, no comment even, but usually asked him for the keys whenever she needed them. But now, because she would not let him kiss her, and because she had not asked, he was smitten through with a pang of fear. He had offended her. She was shutting him away because she knew he distrusted her (though God knows he'd never thought whether he trusted her or no, nor thought indeed at all, only had floundered deeper and deeper in love, till he feared his feet would soon lose the bottom).

He pulled the keys out of his pouch. They still were attached to the fine broad lace of blue and yellow that he remembered well swinging against the first Mistress Machyn's gown. That gave him warning. He must pull himself up. He must not be a weak fool—or must not let this wife see that he was a weak fool. He said shortly, "Here they are."

July came to take them. She saw where she had smudged his coat with blood, and raised her eyes no higher than that, but held out her hand for the keys. She thought he would surely be angry when he saw the stains.

He said suddenly, "Sweetheart, would it please you to keep the keys? Do not be displeased with me that I did not at first—it was because she—I feared—I did not know—"

July took the keys and he gave up trying to find a suitable explanation.

"Give me a kiss, sweeting," he said, and when she allowed it kissed her very gently, and went away, not sure if she were pleased or displeased, willing or unwilling, but sure that to deal with her, withdrawn, fugitive, almost hostile, and yet so dear, was as delicate a business as to walk on egg shells.

When the smelts were in their bath of pickle, July tied on a hat over her hood, and, taking one of the women with her, went out shopping. The keys swung from her waist, and she found the occasional jingle they made quite pleasant. She was still only playing at being Mistress Machyn, but it was a pleasant enough game for all its drawbacks. Laurence she could make little of, and their relationship was a puzzle to her, though one on which she had not spent much thought. When the serving woman said with a little laugh, "Anyone can see you are able to twist the master about your finger," she cried, "How can you be so foolish?" Such a thing was to her too new and too foreign to all her experience to be easily believed.

They were going along toward the stocks market to buy meat when July's heart jumped suddenly up into her throat. Further along, going in their direction, she saw in the crowd a man with dark hair, a dull red coat, and black hosen. "He's back to London," she thought, and then saw that it was not Master Aske, nor even very like him. She went on feeling light and shaken, like a cloth drying on a line on a breezy day. After that it was not of the meat for tomorrow's dinner, nor of the chink of the keys at her girdle, nor of playing at being Mrs. Machyn, nor of her husband that she thought. All those had become unimportant to her as thistledown drifting.

October 10

The ferryman at Burton Staithes was weary of Mr. Aske's demands to be put across into Marshland again. Surly and unwilling he came down once more to the swollen river and swung his lantern over the dark edge of the water. It still swirled by above drowned grass, but between their feet and the lip of the water there was a couple of feet of meadow, sodden, muddied, and strewn with sticks and water weeds.

"See how the river has fallen since dusk," said Aske.

"See how it has risen since last week," said the ferryman, and pointed to the mooring post of the barge, feet away from them across the hurrying water.

"It has not rained since noon. I have listened." At Sawcliffe Aske had indeed listened and watched, all afternoon, ever since sunset, and ever since, in the first dark, he and Will had come to the ferryman's door, urging him to put them over—but he would not.

Nor would he this time. At last Aske gave it up, and went slowly over to where Will held the horses. They got to saddle and rode up the steep, brief hill, which rises above Trent here, facing west across the marshy flats opposite, and in daytime even commanding parts of the northern shore of Ouse and Humber.

Aske was cursing the ferryman under his breath. Will, to comfort him, said there was no harm done, and he was sure that none knew where they were biding.

"God's Passion!" cried Aske. "We left Lincoln yesterday morning. Tomorrow is Tuesday. Another night, and another day, lying listening and waiting, and not knowing what—not knowing—"

They came at the top of the hill to Burton Staithes village, and turned at the church to take the lane to Thealby. The night was very still, with a smell of sodden ground after the great rain that had fallen since Saturday, filling all the rivers and turning every road to deep mire. But overhead the clouds were beginning to break; here and there stars showed. In the sky to the northeast there was a red-golden star that grew huge in the hollow gulf of night; it spread to a smudgy flame. Further to the west another red star sprang and trembled.

Aske pulled up his horse. They both sat staring. "They've lit the beacons," said Will. "That's Yorkswold over that way." But Aske had swung his horse round, and was floundering back through the quaggy lane, so Will followed him.

The ferryman, just warm in bed, stuck his head out of the window and swore at them. Aske's face, a blur of white in the darkness, was all he could see, a little way below him.

"I'll not put ye over. And so I told you before, and a murrain on you!"

Aske said, "They've lit the beacons along Yorkswold. If you'll not put us over, by God! I'll break your door down and take you out and throw you in the river."

Afterward the ferryman remembered that Master Aske, though so fierce, was but a little man, his servant a mere weed, and the bar of the door amply strong to have withstood anything that they might have done. Now, however, grumbling and cursing, he turned out and led them down to the ferry; the big sweeps over his shoulder, and the lantern swinging from his hand.

"I'll take one," said Aske, and sat down on the thwart beside the ferryman. Will had the horses in and shoved off. "Ye'll have to pull hard," said the ferryman.

But in a minute he said, "Steady! Ye'll jerk the guts out of you if you tug at the oar like that, besides swinging her across the river." Aske only grunted, but pulled less violently; above the whine of the oarlocks and the swash and hiss of angry unseen water his ears were straining to catch the sound of bells. But beyond the river noises there was only a great silence, and silence when they landed in Marshland.

They went through Aldingfleet and Ousefleet without a check, but this side Whitgift Aske eased his horse to a walk.

He said suddenly, "There's a poor man, a fowler, that lives aside from the road by a clump of alders. You turn by a long pool."

They went on a few yards. A faint looming in the darkness at the side of the road hinted at water. Aske pulled up his horse.

"This is the place," he said, and then sat still.

"But, master—"

Aske cried out suddenly, "I said I would go back, and I went. And they tried to kill me in Lincoln; whether it were gentlemen or commons matters not. You know how they would have taken me in my bed if the host of the Angel had not warned me. They would have killed me because I went back to Yorkshire to do what I might there. When I had returned, keeping my promise to them, they would have killed me."

When he had said that he was silent again, and Will dared not speak.

"And," his master went on after a minute, not violently now but earnestly, as if appealing to a judge, "And you know how I bid Marshland wait on Howden, and Howden on Marshland. Now, when Lincolnshire is breaking to flinders like a faggot of dead wood, they light their beacons. They'll ring their bells next. But in it I've no part, no word."

"Why do you say nothing?" he cried, and then thrust his horse across Will's, and took the little sludgy track beside the long pool, toward a darker patch in the darkness which was a clump of alders, and a cottage beside it.

He said, as Will came up behind, "You shall take off the harness and hide it in the house. The man will show you a place to turn out the horses, that they be not seen. We can lie here till—till—"

"Master," Will cried, when that seemed to be all that Aske would say, "but, master, will you not— Will you not—"

He got no answer till they stood at the door of the little, lonely, tumbledown toft. Then Aske for an instant interrupted his gentle, insistent knocking to say—

"I must sleep. Four nights I have not slept. I must sleep."

But between his teeth, and to the door, he said, "I must have time."

The poor man, the fowler, let them in. He showed Will where to lead the horses into the fen so that they could graze unnoticed. When they came back Aske was not where they had left him, sitting beside the hearth with his head between his hands, but they heard his voice from the loft above telling them he would lie there, and none should disturb him. "And see to it that you tell no man where I am. D'ye hear?"

"Yes, Master Robin," said the fowler, who remembered Aske as a lad at Wressel, for he was a man of the Percy's.

"And you, Will?" Aske cried sharply.

Will said, "Aye, master."

But for Will it was a long day, and glum. The fowler went out with his net, and did not come back. At what he guessed to be about noon Will went off softly up the ladder with a bowl of pottage, a spoon and a piece of black bread. He could just see Aske lie, with his hands behind his head, on a pile of bracken.

"Put it down," said he, and Will put it down and went back to the fireside, to listen for the sound of his master going across the boards to take up the bowl. There was, however, no sound at all, so perhaps he slept.

It was late afternoon, and the light waning, when Will got up at last, stood listening, and then, with infinite caution, let himself out of the toft. He would, he thought, go toward the fen to look for the fowler, but instead he turned along the track that led to the road. It could do no harm, he thought, to walk that way, if he did not go so far as the road.

But in the end he came to Whitgift village, and found it very busy, and the smith busiest of all, for besides those men the rivets of whose harness the smith was fettling, or whose horses the smith's man was shoeing, there was a crowd of others, hanging about the side doorway and talking to the tune of the gulping bellows and the dan-dan-dan-trinkety-dan of the hammers.

Will, a small man, and not of any noticeable or distinguishing appearance, slipped quietly in among them to listen.

But when he had had enough, and was for dodging back out of the press, someone cried out, "Hi! I know you," and laid his hand on his shoulder, crying loudly, "Here's Master Aske's man."

Then they all crowded round, clamoring, "Where is he? Is he here? Has he sent you to us?"

"No," said Will, lying stoutly. "But he went to Lincoln, and left me at Sawcliffe."

"By Cock! Let him be," cried a big yeoman. "We'll not need such as Master Aske if we follow the Buck's Head and the popinjay green coats," and he jerked his head toward the road beyond the crowded smithy.

"What's that?" Will, being so small a man, could not see what he saw.

"Aye," said the yeoman, "Lord Darcy's own servant here, in his master's livery, bringing the articles out of Lincolnshire to us of Marshland." And he cried, laughing a little, "A Darcy!" The press in the smithy broke a little just then, and Will could see, going by, two gentleman's servants, one in a tawny coat, the other in green like young leaves in spring. This man waved his hand. "Na! Na!" he said, but he laughed.

The thoughts were running round in Will's brain like a mouse in a cage. If my Lord Darcy were in it other lords would be in it too, and the King would have to be gracious; no one would be hanged. Master Robin forsake the commons? Never! Not he! He had only turned in to the fowler's toft so that he might sleep.

He grabbed at the yeoman's great arm.

"Hark ye!" The yeoman leaned down his ear that sprouted bristled red hair. "My Lord Darcy sent to take my master at Howden." The yeoman nodded. He had heard that before. "Now you say my lord's servant brings the commons' articles. It's no treachery?"

The yeoman said, "He saith my lord was never pleased that the abbeys should fall. He saith he knows, though my lord may not declare himself yet, that he's for us."

"Then," said Will, "if there's no treachery I'll bring you to my master. And bring you my Lord Darcy's men, with the articles of Lincolnshire."

"Ho!" cried the yeoman, clapping his big hand on Will's back. "That's a better song to sing." He shouted, in a bull's bellow, "Here is Master Aske come. His man will bring us to him."

While Will was still coughing the smithy emptied and he was on the road with them, going back toward the fowler's toft. When they had gone a little way someone cried, "We should ring our bells. It means that we should ring, now that he is come again." By that time Will was very frightened at what he had done. When the cracked jangle of Whitgift bell began behind them his heart gave a great throb in his chest. Master Robin had said Lincolnshire was a faggot of dead wood breaking. He'd told Marshland and Howden to ring no bells till he bade them. And if he would lie hid—safe—and have Yorkshire also to keep quiet, that was not to forsake the commons. Will would have liked to turn back, but, "Where does he lie?" they asked him, and when he told them—"Why did he not show himself?"

"Because he's foredone for lack of sleep," said Will, and tried to hang back, but they said, "He'll have slept enough by now."

Aske had not, however, slept. Not sleep but time to think was what he must have, though all the hasty ride from Lincoln and all the two days and a night and half a night at Sawcliffe, waiting for the water of Trent to fall, he had been thinking, and thinking.

He thought now how crookedly, how almost, as it were, backward, he had come into the rising; so that now, it seemed to him, he was less resolved than he had been that night at Ellerker to do whatever should be laid upon him.

He thought—"Even yet I do not know what I shall do," not understanding that the drift of a man's will can persist under many eddies of hesitation, to carry him at the last either with his conscience or against it, as he had once chosen. For indeed, though he thought the choice not made, he had chosen long before. Yet now he muttered to himself, "I must have even a little time longer to be sure what I will do."

For he was sure now that the Lincolnshire men were as he had said to Will, no better than a rotten faggot, so easy it was to see how gentlemen hated commons, and commons mistrusted gentlemen. Therefore, if the Yorkshiremen rose, they were like to stand alone. And if one county stood against the King that meant failure, and failure meant— He clenched his teeth, and lay stiff in the darkness of the loft. It would be no worse for him than for any man to suffer the shocking outrage of a traitor's death. "Yet," he thought, "as not all will be hanged, so not a leader will be spared," and one of his hands went down to draw upon his own body that line which he had seen the executioner mark on the bodies of the Carthusians, before he began his bloody work. He snatched his hand back and thrust it under his head; if he could by no means rid himself of that fear at least he could trample on it.

But he thought of Aughton then. He had come home, and found himself alone, like a leper from whom his brothers fled. At that it seemed that indeed the weight of this thing that they would lay upon him was too great for him to endure, and he must even now resolve to lay it down.

"I have laid it down," he thought. "They sought to kill me. So I have laid down."

And then, as if he had not yet laid it down, a sharp and trembling qualm ran through his mind. If to rebel were truly against the will of God, as it was against the law of man—

He sat up, and groaned aloud, *"Miserere mei Domine!"* he muttered, and then was silent, but with his soul at a stretch to reach help.

When he got up from the bracken he was stiff, and very cold, so that he stumbled as he made for the ladder. But there was quiet in his mind, and, so it seemed to him, enlightenment. A year ago, against his conscience, he had sworn an oath; now he must take on his conscience, another sin to set right the first. The chain of his own sin bound him, and he must suffer the bond. "And do thou," he said, just aloud, "forgive me in the one as in the other, for now I can no other than this."

He groped his way down the ladder. The houseplace was quite dark because the fire had died down to ash. When he opened the door the gray soft light of late afternoon surprised and almost dazzled him; he stood, leaning against the side-post of the door. The fowler's tethered goat gave him an intolerant, pallid glare from one protruding eye, and bent again to its grazing; nothing else in the wide, empty country was alive, except the flop-winged plovers; a few of them went by overhead, but toward the north the whole sky was full of their wide wheeling drifts. He stayed there for a long time, mind as well as body lapped in a great quiet.

The sound came to him, sweetened by distance, of church bells ringing. Almost before he knew that he heard them his hand tightened on the doorpost. Each note was sweet, but, like a rising scream, the ascending instead of the descending peal meant alarm. He listened, his ears straining, his back growing cold under his shirt. From farther away to the west he heard other bells, but again in that undue order, and from the southward, more. They were ringing awkward to arm and muster. Then while he still tried to doubt, he heard, dull and distant, the note, which he could not mistake, of Howden great bell.

October 12

It was just after noon on a bright day, with a light, whisking wind, when the mounted men of Howdenshire and the East Riding came to Market Weighton. Among the first of them rode a big, elderly yeoman from near Wressel, and in the stirrup beside his foot was set the foot of the great cross from Howden Church; as his horse moved the brightness of the sun flowed in waves down the gilt shaft, like light ripples upon water, and shot out colored sparkles and uncolored blazes from the jewels set in the gold; all about and behind the cross the sunshine blinked and flickered more coldly on the pikes and spears of the horsemen that filled the road.

The host was very orderly. Men went into Market Weighton asking for leave to sleep in barns and garners, or in the kitchens and outhouses. But when, in the afternoon, the footmen came up, there was more trouble, for these were the poorer folk, and some of them already hungry, and not knowing whether to be angry or scared. As well as these footmen, to add to the crowding and confusion, there came in also the men from Beverley and Holderness; so now it was not all neighbors together, but there were strangers about a man whom he had never seen before.

As it was in the host, so it was among the captains, who sat around on the tossed piles of yellow straw in a rickyard, eating bread and cheese and drinking ale. There were the Howdenshire people who knew each other, whether gentlemen like Sir Thomas Metham, and Master Saltmarsh, or men of the commons like the miller of Snaith with his flour-whitened hair, and flour in the wrinkles of his big, fleshy face. But besides these there were townsmen and yeomen from Beverley and Yorkswold, strangers to the others; as yet the two groups did not mingle, but eyed each other across their ale cans.

Then, as they sat in comfort of sun and ease of the yielding straw, a Weighton man came running to say that certain footmen—of what party he knew not—were driving away Weighton cattle to kill for supper.

There was silence among the captains for a minute, except that Sir Thomas Metham murmured, "Let the commons' own fellows

call them off," and he looked toward the miller of Snaith. But Aske
lodged his can carefully in a pocket of straw, and got up.

"We must stop all spoil," he said, and went toward the horses;
then he paused, and looked about at the Beverley men, searching their faces for a moment. Among them was a big fellow with
a broad, brown face, eyes of a windy blue, and hair that curled
lightly over his head. "Come you with me," said Aske, and the
big yeoman stood up. The miller had got up too, and the three
of them took their horses and rode away.

It was not very long before they came back; those in the rickyard saw them ride among the paling, and get down at the gate
where Will Wall was waiting to take the horses. The big yeoman and the miller came in after Aske. When he stopped they
stopped too, standing on each side of him but a little behind.

"I have given order," Aske spoke so that all in the rickyard
should hear, "I have given order that there shall be no spoiling
of cattle, no rifling of farmyards. The man who makes spoil
shall hang."

No one spoke as he sat down and took up his can again. The
miller and the yeoman went back to their places too, and those
about the yeoman plucked him by the sleeve and rowned him
in the ear, and he and they muttered together, looking across at
Aske, and at the other Howdenshire gentlemen.

It was this yeoman who, when they had finished eating,
stood up in the midst and said: "Masters, when the host is gathered, what do we next?"

He caught Aske's eye, then looked from one to another, then
again to Aske, who, when no one else spoke, said that in his

mind the host should divide, part to move on Hull, the other part on York.

But then Sir Thomas Metham cried out that this was folly. "York has walls, and Hull too, and we have no engines for assault."

"What then," said Aske, "would you have us do?"

Mr. Saltmarsh, who sat beside Sir Thomas, said that they should wait till the host was greater, for that men were coming in every hour.

"That's my counsel too," said Sir Thomas.

"And then?"

"Why, then—" Sir Thomas waved a hand, "then we can see."

A sort of growl came from the big yeoman, and Aske spoke hastily. He had seen this thing before in Lincolnshire (and God, he alone knew to what end it would bring them there): gentlemen against commons and commons against gentlemen, each fearing and distrusting the other. "We cannot wait to see. My Lord of Shrewsbury is already at Nottingham, and the Duke of Norfolk gathers men and is named the King's Lieutenant against us." He looked round at them, and those who felt dismay at those names and at the thought of the King's power behind the names, did what they could, at his look, to keep dismay out of their faces.

"Besides," he said, "if we wait, doing nothing, for one man who comes in to us, three will go home."

"Aye, aye," came from several of the yeomen there who thought of their fields lying unplowed.

"But," cried Mr. Saltmarsh in a sharp voice, "it's treason to march in arms against the King's Lieutenant."

Aske did not answer that. He said again that his counsel was they should first make sure of York and Hull. "Then when the King's host draws nigh we can go to meet with them, and, by the King's lieutenant, send unto the King's Grace our petition for the remedy of our grievances. But York and Hull we must have first."

Sir Thomas Metham and Mr. Saltmarsh began to protest. "It's treason." "We have no siege train." "York will shut its gates." Others joined with them.

The big yeoman with blue eyes broke in. He spoke for all to hear, but to Aske alone.

"I'll answer for the commons, master. They'll go to York or to Hull with you. Which first?"

Aske said, "There's nine thousand of us, and all lies in speed. Give me half, and tomorrow I'll go toward York; the rest to Hull."

Sir Thomas Metham jumped up, and swore by God's Nails he would know why a man who was no knight should set himself over them all in that matter.

"I'll tell you," said the big yeoman. "It's because the commons will follow Master Aske. That's why."

It was after dark that the commons who had taken Will Monkton and Hob Aske in Monkton's house brought them to Market Weighton, and to the farm where the captains were.

Monkton, always a silent man, had ridden in silence, but Hob had fallen back to join those of the commons who came behind; he found them very ready to talk; one and all they wanted to tell him of what Master Aske had been doing; they also wanted him to tell them about his uncle. That Hob found to be difficult, since the conclusion that he and Jack Ellerker had reached on that night at Sawcliffe was clearly not to be mentioned here. If he had told the truth Hob must have said that until a week ago he had never really considered his uncle at all, but taken him for granted, as he took his bed and his breakfast for granted, and the house and fields at Aughton— all things necessary to sustain or to form a background for Master Hob Aske. So he could only think to tell them that Uncle Robert liked much mustard with his meat, and that he wrote in a book whatever tombs of noblemen and gentlemen were to be found in any church he saw.

But this was not the kind of thing that they wanted to know, so they fell back on talking among themselves about Captain Aske while Hob listened. It might have been a stranger that they spoke of, so much they saw in Uncle Robin which Hob had never noticed; he began to feel himself not a little important to be his nephew.

They got down from the saddle in a farmyard, by the faint light of a clouded moon, and as they came to the door of the farm it opened and a man stepped out with the light behind him. Hob went back so smartly that he trod on Will Monkton's toe. The man coming out stopped too.

"Ah!" he said. "You are come. Are you come willingly?"

They knew him then by his voice, and Hob cried, "Uncle! By the Cross, right willingly." He felt that needed something to back it up and added, "You know I would have taken the oath that day at Ferriby, if you'd have suffered me."

Aske said, "Yea," and thought, "Would it had been Jack—or Kit—instead!" But he turned the thought from his mind, and kissed the young man heartily. Will, from behind Hob, said: "Nan would have had me come to you when you were at Aughton, but I would not. For one thing I had Nell and the children on my hands. But now I am glad to be here."

"And, oh Will!" Aske cried, and kissed him too, "I'm glad to have you." Then he said sharply, "Listen!"

As they stood listening they heard a sound, no greater than the click of knitting needles, but they knew it for the sound of a horse's hoofs, ridden hard, far off, but coming nearer.

"Go in," said Aske, and they went in, but he shut the door on them and did not follow.

It was not very long before he came into the room, walking lightly with his chin high. Monkton and Hob were at the fire talking, rather uneasily, with others there, some gentlemen, some men of the commons, under the big hams hanging from the beams, and the bunches of dried herbs.

Aske said, "There is a messenger come from Lincolnshire. He brings news."

"Good news then!" cried Hob, watching his uncle's face.

"No. Not good," said he, answering Hob's question, but he spoke to Will Monkton. Then he told them what the news was—that the Lincolnshire men would surrender themselves, without terms made, to the King's mercy.

Sir Thomas Metham started up from the seat in the chimney corner. "Then—" he cried, "then what shall we do?"

"Go forward," said Aske.

The big yeoman, who was called John Hallom of the Wold, got up too. He eased his sword belt round, so that the hilt was more ready to his hand.

"I never did think much," said he, "of them as lives across Humber. It's better as it is. Now we shall know where we are."

His blue eyes met Aske's eye with a reckless dancing look, and Aske looked back at him steadily. Each had the same thought in his mind, "This is a man to have at a man's back."

October 13

Even in the great chamber at Pomfret, where Lord Darcy sat at dinner, there was an air of disarray; a pile of cloaks and a riding whip cast down on the carpet in a window, and paper, ink, and pens pushed aside but not taken away from the board when the table was laid. My Lord sat on an elm seat with carved ends, with his back to the fire; on his left side was Sir Robert Constable, on his right an empty place. There was another table in the room, but not near enough for those who sat there to hear what my lord and Sir Robert might say if they spoke low.

"Well," my lord said, taking up his spoon, "you have seen what provision is here against a siege. Not one gun ready to shoot, arrows and bows few and bad, money and gunners none, and of powder—" He pointed to a dish of nuts before them— "enough to fill a walnut shell. And this" (he leaned his head closer), "this is the King's strong castle of Pomfret, even the most simply furnished that ever, I think, was any man to defend."

"Tchk!" said Sir Robert sympathetically, and then saw a sort of spark leap in Darcy's eye as the door opened and an old man came into the chamber, leaning on the arm of a young priest. The old man wore a long violet gown with silver buttons down the front of it; from under the violet velvet cap that covered his head his silver hair waved delicately back from a face that was handsome, dignified, and petulant.

"I fear," said the archbishop of York, "that I am late." He dipped his fingers in the water that a page brought and wiped them on the napkin from the lad's shoulder. "I had forgot time in my devotions." He sighed. "And in sad thoughts of these sad times."

"It is no matter unless you will grudge at your pottage being cold," said Darcy, just on the hither side of discourtesy.

"Pottage?" says the archbishop, and sniffed at the plate. "Leek pottage again?"

"The leeks grow in the garden," said Darcy. "When they are at an end maybe we'll sup pottage without even leeks to flavor it. For if it comes to a siege there'll be little to eat."

The archbishop turned in his chair. "Do you not take victuals into the castle?" he asked.

"And did your grandmother not know how to suck eggs? I would take in victuals if I could get them. But what the townsmen will bring in is naught, and these rebels are taking up all about."

"Have you then," the archbishop asked, with a slight shake in his voice, "written to the King's Grace to send help?"

"Once, and had no answer. And again today," said Darcy, and helped himself to a handful of nuts and began to crack them between his teeth. He glanced again at Constable, and again the spark of anger and angry laughter was in his eyes.

"But," said Sir Robert, whose sense of propriety was a little troubled by my lord's baiting of so reverend a spiritual personage, "but it is not to be thought that a rout of poor commons and husbandmen will assault such a castle as Pomfret."

"No," said the archbishop.

"No?" said Darcy. "If I thought that I should sleep the easier. But I think they will, and shall I tell you for why?"

The archbishop took out the spoon from his pottage and laid it on his tranche of bread. He waved his hand to show that they should take away the pottage, and his gesture conveyed by its delicate languor that worn though he might be by the cares of his high station, and in need of sustenance, yet to set leek pottage before him was not so much a stupidity as an irreverence.

"Shall I, my Lord Archbishop," said Darcy again, "tell you for why?" and leaned toward him and said, nailing his words, as it were, to the wood of the table with a stiff forefinger. "Because you, my lord, are come into the castle, therefore the commons will not pass it by."

"I?" said the archbishop haughtily. "What have I done against them?" He looked at the plate of cold rabbit pie set before him with a pained disgust. "I have done nothing against them," he muttered, with a trace of anxiety in his voice.

"It is not what you have done against them, but what you shall do for them," said Darcy.

"For them? I'll do nothing for them."

Sir Robert asked what should my lord do for them, and Darcy turned to him to say, "Why, write the articles of their grievances that they shall send to the King."

"No," cried the archbishop from his other hand. "Never! Never! I will die first before I should give aid or counsel to traitors."

"But see, my lord," Darcy turned to him, "see what they do for you—periling their necks to save the privilege of the spiritual men, and defend the faith of the church! Meetly—as it seems to me—might they ask of your counsel, and think to have you go along with them." He turned again to Sir Robert. "You'll have heard how they call this their 'pilgrimage,' so it is seen that in their eyes it is all for the sake of the church, and of the spiritual men."

"They are mistook. The faith is in no peril. The King hath so provided by his late book. It is rebellion. I would see them all hanged, every one. You hear me say it."

"Then let us pray," said Darcy, "that it cometh not to that pass that I must surrender the castle to them."

The archbishop's mouth opened as though to breathe, "Surrender?" but he shut it again. Then he said hastily and softly, "I am not well," and got up from the board and went out.

Darcy gave a sharp laugh and stood up. "Come on, Robert," he said, "let's take view of the well, and the offices. And I told the carpenters to look to the timbers of the bridge and tell me how they stand."

They had seen to all these things, and found all in bad state, and were on their way back to the great chamber; my lord said he would write a letter to the Earl of Shrewsbury, who lay at Nottingham, gathering men. "But they come in slowly," said Sir Robert, who had this very morning come from there. They opened the door of the brewhouse yard, and came on a little space of garden beside an old pear tree on a wall, where great tits, handsome and bold, swung and sported. There were leeks growing here, proudly fountaining their dagger-pointed leaves, which from the plait pattern in the center sprang up and out, to drop with a sudden stately fall.

"Pottage for the archbishop," said Darcy grimly, and laughed.

"What," asked Sir Robert, "was the news that fellow brought you just now?" A man in a homespun coat and clouted shoes, but with a sharper face than a poor country hind was like to have, had whispered with my lord in the wood yard.

"He? Oh! he saith that the Howdenshire men and those beyond Derwent were yesterday at Weighton. That means Howdenshire has joined itself with Beverley and Holderness."

Sir Robert looked grave at that, and stood frowning along the ranks of leeks. At last he said: "And yet it sticks, like a crumb in my throat, that what we hold for the King we hold to keep that hound Cromwell in place, and others as great heretics as he." He glanced at Darcy and then added, "Yet we can do no other."

Darcy looked down at him, and the corners of his mouth twitched. Constable, when he would be indirect, was so transparent.

"Ask me outright, Robert, 'Will you surrender Pomfret?' But first answer me this. Do you conceive me a man lightly to surrender such a castle to such an enemy?"

"No," Sir Robert muttered, a little red, "that I do not."

"But," cried Darcy, "our most reverend father in God, the archbishop, by God's Passion I am sick to hear him!" and he laughed a little. "I like to make him quake, now for fear of the King, and now of the commons."

October 15

Julian was in bed already, and Laurence was just pulling his shirt off over his head. She let her eyes slide away from his thin shanks, and looked beyond him to the press, which had the story of Deborah, Jael, and Sisera carved on it; July did not know it, but Deborah, a stalwart lady in a wide starched veil, always reminded Laurence of the first Mistress Machyn.

"They say," said Laurence, through his shirt, "that this rebellion in Lincolnshire is worse than was thought."

"I supposed," July murmured, "that it had been put down." After a great scare, when she had first heard of "trouble in the North," she had ceased to take any interest in the business. Lincolnshire was not Yorkshire.

Laurence folded his shirt neatly and padded across the rushes to the bed where his nightshirt lay. "The Lincolnshire traitors are put down. But now they rise in Yorkshire, under one Aske. What he is, I know not—some low fellow."

July sat up in bed. Laurence, slipping the nightshirt over his head, did not see her wide, frightened eyes, nor the hand which covered her open mouth. He turned and blew out the candle. When he groped his way into bed he put his hands out to draw her to him.

But she pushed him stiffly away, and he knew she was shaking all over.

"What is it, sweet?" he asked hastily, thinking her to be ill.

For a minute she could only hold him off, saying nothing. Then she muttered, "Who? Where?"

At first he did not know what she was asking. But she said, "Who—leads this—this new insurrection?" and he told her again, "It is one Aske, so they say. But you do not know him?"

"No," she said. "No."

Laurence heard her teeth chatter together as she spoke. He thought, "She is as scared as a bird," and his heart melted, as if it laughed and cried over her at once.

He said, "Peace, peace, my sweeting. They shall not come here." He might have been soothing a child wakened out of a nightmare.

Not because of his words, but because his hands ceased to constrain her, she suddenly flung herself toward him in the bed, clutching him by the wrists.

"It's not that. It—it is—it is—" She stopped, and then made herself speak. "It is what is done to traitors."

He did his best to soothe her then, using all the gentleness he knew, and, at last, when he thought she slept, he lay long awake, pondering upon her, upon her terrors, and upon the frightened child, the frightened lass, whose life, fugitive as any wild, hunted thing, these terrors seemed to betray.

"But," he thought, "if God would give us a child— Then it would be well with her. For," he said to himself, "she should see it grow and thrive, God of His grace permitting, like a flower. And nor it, nor would I, do anything that might frighten her. And so she would forget to be afraid."

October 16

Robert Aske rode, the first of all the host, through Walmgate
Bar into York. Under the ringing hollow of the arch the sound
of his own horse's hoofs swelled so that it overmastered even the
tramp of all the horsemen behind him. Then he came out into
the street beyond, and was met by the shouting of a great crowd.
And while the people still shouted the bells began to peal, from
all the church towers in York, and among them the bells of the
minster, dancing up and down unseen stairways of sound, till
the air was wild with their flying feet, running after each other,
overtaking, clanging together.

The long procession of horsemen came out from Petergate into
the great space before the west door of the cathedral. There had
been rain that day, and a high wind which had only dropped toward
sunset, leaving the air very clear, and the sky swept and blue. There
were pools in the paving, and great leaves blown from the chestnut
trees lay scattered there. The chestnut leaves were bright gold, and
the pools reflected all the colors of the riders' cloaks, in flashes and
gleams of scarlet, green, sanguine, murrey, and blue.

When they had got down from their horses the minster bells
stopped ringing, leaving a great silence troubled only by little
and near noises, and by the dancing of more distant bells. Then
those who stood close to the west doors heard the great bolts run
back; the doors groaned as they swung inward, and at that same
moment the choir began to sing just inside, boys and men, sweet
and deep, high and low, while beyond the organ pealed and
rumbled. So they went in, the choir leading, then the priests,
vested in cloth of gold and silver, in satin and velvet, spangled

with jewels and stiff with gold embroideries, a paradise garden of color, toward the high altar. The captains followed the priests, Aske first, and after him the other captains, and after them the host, till the great church was crammed.

Through all the solemnity of Vespers Aske knelt, stood, knelt again, and knew no meaning in what he did. Trifles possessed his mind; the miller of Snaith's cloak had a long darn on one shoulder; there was a priest in a blue velvet vestment who was very like old Dom Henry at Ellerton, but with a wart on his nose. And a foolish anxiety beset him—lest he should miss the signal which would call him from his stall to make his offering upon the high altar. He did not miss the signal, and in a few moments he was back again, and a blue velvet purse fringed with silver lay on the altar; now his thoughts strayed to the farm at Bubwith which he had pledged to raise the money in the purse; there was the rickyard stuffed for winter, the oxen were coming slowly home from plowing in the last light, and hens were scratching round the kitchen door.

They knelt again. The priest at the altar raised his hand for the blessing, and in a moment the voices of the choir flowered again in the silence. Aske, in the darkness that his hands made before his face, tried to collect his thoughts. But he could not do it; the most he could reach was a confusion of words as empty of meaning as chaff is of the winnowed grain. "*Deo gratias! Miserere mei Domine!*" he muttered, and did not know whether he gave thanks or prayed for mercy.

Close on midnight Will Wall knocked at the door of the chamber in Sir George Lawson's house where his master was to sleep.

But he was not sleeping yet. His voice called out to come in, and, when Will went in, there he sat at the table, with Master Monkton on one hand and Master Rudston on the other, and the three of them busy writing. Gervase Gawood, a man from Howden and a captain in the host, was on the settle by the fire notching tallies with his knife as they called out numbers to him.

Will shut the door before he said that there was one come in secret.

"He says he is my Lord Darcy's steward."

"Ha!" cried Master Rudston, and clapped his hand down open on the table. "So my lord would be with us!"

Aske said, "Bring him in. And keep the door, Will."

So Will brought him in—a big, gaunt, gray-haired man with a red face.

Will kept the door for perhaps half an hour, and then out came Rudston, Monkton, Gervase Cawood, and my Lord Darcy's steward. So after they had been gone downstairs a little while Will went in to his master, and found him sitting at the table with pen in his hand and paper before him, but staring at the page as if he did not see it.

Will went softly about the room for a while, glancing at Aske from time to time, but he did not move.

At last Will said, "Master, will you not sleep?" And then, "Oh, Master Robin, this is a blessed day. Listen yonder!" From the streets, which should have been quiet hours ago, came a distant sound of pipes, tabrets, and fiddles. Just below the window a boy went by singing very sweetly, "Salve Regina." "The commons," said Will, "are putting in the monks that have been turned out. They will do it, late as it is, and this night God shall be worshipped again," and he ran to Aske and knelt and would have kissed his hand.

"Will! Will!" said Aske, touched, but more displeased. If only this strange, unaccountable creature that was his serving man would cease to swing between moods of devotion and beastly drunkenness, "then," thought Aske, "it would be the better for both of us."

"No, master," Will cried, mistaking Aske's tone, "I've not drunk. Not tonight I would not touch the ale tonight," and he fell to crying wildly.

"Tchk!" said Aske under his breath, and patted Will on the shoulder, and, to quiet him, began to talk about Lord Darcy's steward. My lord, it seems, had sent him to bring away a copy of the commons' oath, and of their articles, "And he asked to know whether we would agree to a head captain, if the articles should please my lord."

"God's Passion!" cried Will hotly. "You're our chief captain."

"I told him," Aske said, as if Will had not spoken, "that a nobleman of the King's Council was more like to send a spy than a true messenger to know the purpose of the commons. This man, Strangways, promised us we should have Pomfret if we came there. Would God that we might. But my lord would never yield up the King's strong castle."

"Would he not? Why not?"

"No man would," said Aske, but he meant, "I would not," and then, he got rid of Will by sending him, late as it was, with the copy of the Oath of Lincolnshire. "And bid Master Strangways be forth out of York before daybreak, for I'll not have my Lord Darcy's man see the muster," said he, "when it is held."

After Will had gone he sat awhile, thinking of my lord—of all that he knew of him in the past, and of what Darcy's steward had said of his master—and there was little of it that pleased him, for he said to himself, "He's a man of deep counsels, wily, full of statecraft. That which we have entered on is not for such as him."

And suddenly he knew clearly what it was that they were entered on. He took a fresh quill, and a fresh sheet, and wrote—

The Oath of the Honorable Men,

and under that—

Ye shall not enter into this our Pilgrimage of Grace for the Commonwealth, but only for the love that ye do bear unto Almighty God, his faith, and to holy church militant and the maintenance thereof, to the preservation of the King's person and issue, to the purifying of the nobility, and to expulse all villain blood and evil councilors against the Commonwealth from His Grace and his Privy Council of the same. And that ye shall not enter into our said Pilgrimage for no particular profit to yourself, nor to do displeasure to any private person, but by counsel of the Commonwealth, nor slay nor murder for no envy, but in your hearts put away all fear and dread,

and take afore you the cross of Christ, and in your hearts
his faith.

Will came in. Aske said, "I have nearly done." After a moment
more he laid down his pen.

"Here is the oath that we shall swear tomorrow," he said, and
read it aloud.

October 17

Thomas Strangways found Sir Robert Constable in the great
chamber at Pomfret; it was crowded, but Sir Robert sat in a corner bent over a chessboard upon which he had set out a random
number of pieces; he was plotting subtle moves and dark ser-
pentine approaches against an imaginary opponent, and his face
when he looked up wore an expression of pure, blissful absorp-
tion. But as he saw Strangways it changed.

"Ah!" he cried. "You! You are to go in. My lord's in his bath,
but he will not care for that."

So they went in together to the smaller privy chamber
beyond where my lord simmered, pink and sweating, in his tub,
with one soaping his back. The room smelt damp and sweet
from the steam and the sweet herbs strewed on the water.

"You!" said my lord, as Sir Robert had done, and told the
servant to put a towel round his shoulders and then go away.
"Well," said he, when they were alone, "and what treason have
you been pledging me to, you old whoreson?" and he laughed.

But Strangways was solemn.

"I've the copy of their oath, and the articles that you bade me bring," said he, and my lord beckoned and bade him hold it for him to read, "For my hands are wet," he said.

So they were silent while my lord read the two papers, making little dabbling noises in the water under the towel as he read, and sometimes swearing and sometimes laughing below his breath.

Then he said, waving Strangways away: "What are the numbers of their muster?"

Strangways said he could not tell, for he had come to York long after dark, "And their captains said I must forth before daybreak that I might not see them. But York seemed stuffed with men, as for an expedition against the Scots."

"Tcha!" cried Darcy. "A rabble of poor commons."

"And I saw Lord Lumley's banner hang out," said Strangways with a stubborn look, "and Lord Latimer's. And the rest that are not gentlemen are yeomen of Yorkshire, harnessed and horsed every man. The poor commons that go on foot lie outside the city. And order is kept as good as in the King's palace at Westminster."

"You hear?" Darcy turned to Constable. "The fellow's as full of treason as an egg of meat. And did you say," he asked lightly, as if the matter was nothing but a jest, "that I would lead them if they would go the way I will?"

"I said as you bade me," Strangways answered, and shut his mouth like a trap.

"And no further?" Darcy teased him.

"I spoke for myself what was the truth."

"And was rank treason, I'll be bound. Well, and what did they answer?"

"One of the captains said it was more like you would send a spy among them than a true messenger."

"Which of them was that?" Darcy rapped out.

"Master Aske—I knew him by his one eye."

"Well," said Darcy, and laughed softly, "he may have but one eye, but it seems he can see as far through a wall as another man."

After that he questioned Strangways sharply about many things, and at last bade him and Sir Robert go and let him get dressed.

Strangways, once they were out of the privy chamber, would have gone away to find breakfast, but Constable laid hold on his arm.

"What does he mean?" He tipped his head toward the room they had just left. Strangways shook his head.

"But what will he do?" cried Sir Robert.

"I'll tell you one thing he will not do. He'll not hold Pomfret."

Constable cried out at that, "God's Wounds! But he will!"

"If the commons come this way to knock on the gate no man in Pomfret, save the gentlemen only, will fight."

"God's Wounds!" said Sir Robert again between his teeth, thinking it to be only too true.

Then he said: "But will he yield with a good heart? Does he approve their purposes? I—" he hesitated, "I like it ill that we who stand against the commons stand between them and that rascal Cromwell and those that he has set on to spoil the church."

Strangways looked at him searchingly. "So that is your conscience in the matter?" He took his arm from under Sir Robert's hand, and lifted the latch of the farther door. But before he opened he said: "What my lord means now, nor I nor any man can know. He has a deep, working brain, and more wit and wisdom than all of us. But I know this, that since the commons' cause is the right cause, and the cause of all true men, my lord will be with them one day. For there's no man truer nor he."

Then he went out, and left Sir Robert not much less puzzled than before.

A tramping tinker told the news to the yeoman at Oxcue, who told it to a Marrick hind, who brought it to the smithy at Marrick, quite early on a fine morning. The smith was busy over a plow, which two improvident fellows had brought in to have the coulter reset; they said it was leaving a rest-balk between the ridges which would breed thistles next year, and so it might, but any good husbandman would have seen to it long ago, not left it till the very plowing season itself.

So those two lounged and leaned at one side of the smithy doors, and the nuns' shepherd stood at the other; the bag of his pipes was under his arm, and now and again he would set his lips to the mouthpiece and blow a low and thoughtful note, which was, for the most part, his only contribution to the conversation. His life made him a very silent man, and set him, as it were, always at a distance: even when the Marrick hind told the news of how the commons had taken York the shepherd did not watch the face of the speaker, but seemed to measure with his eyes the long shadows which the bright morning laid across the fields.

The owners of the plow were jubilant at the news, their nature being to take pleasure in trouble. The smith, stooping over the coulter, said little, but by his silence managed to convey doubt of the truth of the hind's story; he did not want to believe it, since, being all for the new ways, he had been very cock-a-hoop about the pulling down of the abbeys. The hind, however, was positive. "Sure it was truth," he protested, and the two others rammed it home by every means they could, calling upon Shepherd to agree with them how good news it was. All he would say was, however, "Marry, that such things should be! What a coil in the country! What'll come of it?"

Then—"Here's Priest!" cried the hind, and as Gib Dawe came by, bent under a load of bracken for winter bedding, the two Marrick men hailed him, telling him the news, which, they guessed rightly, would please him as little as it pleased the smith.

Gib halted, holding his pikel with one hand, and with the other wiping the sweat from his face.

"So," cried one of the two, "Master Cromwell and his heretic bishops shall down," and he began to sing a song that was going about in those days—

Much ill cometh of a small mote
As a Crumwell set in a man's throat,
That shall put many other to pain, God wot!
But when Crumwell is brought alow—

"Yea, yea," said the other, cocking a snook, neither exactly in the direction of Gib, nor yet far off. "Our valiant North countrymen that have gone forth for the sake of Christ Crucified shall knock on the King his doors—"

"Aye!" cried Gib, "and you're valiant men too. And yet I would have you wait a while till you have seen the King his doors; namely, the great gates of his Tower of London, and the guns therein, very many; aye, and that which may sooner cool you—the gates of London Bridge, where the flies buzz about the meat of traitors thicker than round the butchers' stalls. And what will a lousy pack of countrymen do against the King's high nobility with their men-at-arms and the King's—tcha!" he broke off, "I'll answer you no further," and he tramped on, leaving them, for the moment, silenced.

But he himself was ill-satisfied with what he had said, having, as it were, conjured up the great and the rich to set down poor men. Yet those poor men, fools and blind, were such as spurned the pure new light of the gospel; and among them as leaders were proud, overweening men such as Master Robert Aske.

"'Christ Crucified!'" He spat out the words. "They'll cry on Christ Crucified when the hangman's hand is on them!" Yet it was all awry, to have poor men rise for such a cause, and also to prosper in it. He was angry, but his anger could find no sure aim. He came, panting because of his wrathful hurried pace, to the gate of the parsonage, and pushed through it, his wide burden of dry bracken hissing against the posts of the gate.

❧

Dame Nan Bulmer brought the news to the ladies at the priory, coming hastily into the prioress's chamber, handsome more than ordinary in her untidy, hungry-looking way.

She interrupted Dame Christabel at mixtum, would not shut the door, would not sit down, would not eat, yet, as she stood talking took up from the table and broke and munched the fresh manchet bread, and then reached for the prioress's plate of quails, and ate from this small choice morsels casually yet delicately.

None of these things pleased the prioress, who had a sore cold, and for whom, alone of the ladies, there were quails, a present from her sister. Nor did the news please her.

"And so," Dame Nan concluded, "before them all my kinsman went into the minster, and before them all laid his gift upon the altar. They say," she declared, "that there are forty thousand men to follow him, gentlemen and commons. And in the South Country will be many more to rise with our people. So you need not fear," said she, "that this house shall be brought to an end."

She was holding out her fingers vaguely, as if she expected the prioress to hand her the water to dip them in. Dame Christabel did not move, so she wiped them on the cloth. Dame Christabel looked at the greasy marks and said, "I did not fear it. We have my Lord Privy Seal's promise for our continuance, and the King's."

"Mass!" Dame Nan laughed. "You trust to your bribes to bind such a rascal as that fellow Cromwell?"

"Fie! To speak so of the King's servants!"

"Fie on such a servant of the King!" and Dame Nan turned away. "I must on to tell the ladies of St. Bernard this good, great news," said she, and went, leaving the door open with the fresh morning wind flapping the tablecloth, and scattering light wood ash from the hearth over plates and dishes. Dame Christabel did not, even for courtesy's sake, follow her across the great court to see her away. Instead she shut the door with an angry, quiet care, and, going back to the fire, stood looking at the bright sparks running along a blackened log, and one hand jagging at the beads at her girdle.

"Ill," she said, half aloud, "will come of it. Ill will come of it." She did not know how; she did not fear any ill in particular, but because Master Aske and these others had blundered in where they were not needed, she would be ready to blame them if ill should come. And then she remembered Dame Nan's last words—she would away to tell the ladies of St. Bernard the news. The prioress heard the beads, the string of which a sharper unconscious jerk of her hand had snapped, begin to patter on the hearth, and into the rushes. It had been indeed these last words that pricked her most nearly. Should the rebels succeed in their purpose not only Marrick, but all abbeys should stand. For long now, hardly recognized but dearly cherished, there had lain at the bottom of her mind the thought of Marrick continuing secure, thrifty, prosperous in barn and byre; while in the house of St. Bernard's nuns, down the river, the wind would blow through the unshuttered, empty rooms, where no more were there any ladies in the white gowns of the Cistercians.

"But," she said to herself, as she stooped to search for the beads, which were of pretty carved boxwood, "rebellion doth not prosper, because God hateth it."

She had to endure much that day from the ladies, to whom Dame Nan had managed to scatter the news on her way across the great court, as though it were corn, and they a company of clucking hens.

And clucking hens the prioress found them, assembled as they were, a noisy excited company in the warmest corner of the cloister. Dame Margery Conyers, her face crimson and eyes streaming, had her hands clasped, and was crying: *"Deo gratias! Deo gratias!* Our house is saved! Our house is saved!" (As if Christabel Cowper, prioress, had not already saved it.) And there was Dame Anne Ladyman, shaking her head, and casting her eyes this way and that in the very manner of a brainless hen, and declaiming upon "that sweet noble gentleman Master Aske. Jesu! he hath all our hearts at his feet."

The prioress came near them and the tumult a little hushed, but then Dame Margery cried out, demanding that they should send money to the commons to help the cause. "And if not money," said she, with surprising common sense, "then we have cattle that can be driven thither for their meat, and none of us will grudge to go a little hungry this winter for those men that are our defenders."

The prioress only looked at her, but she spoke to Dame Anne Ladyman.

"How old are you? How old?" They all knew as well as Dame Anne herself, which was not precisely, but dismally near enough.

"And you talk of your heart, and of sweet noble gentlemen! Oh!" she cried, "if you had committed fornication I could better forgive it than such very foolishness. Yet that you never did, but only and always cackle of it, cackle, cackle!"

There was, however, one who, in the prioress's opinion, spoke with propriety of this unlawful scurry of the commons. In chapter that morning Dame Margery's suggestion was debated by the ladies, but, by the force of the prioress's resistance, defeated. In the charged silence that followed, Dame Eleanor Maxwell slowly rose. They all turned to her, staring. Not one could remember when it was that she had last spoken in chapter, but they thought they could be sure enough of what she would say concerning this great news of her kinsman, which someone had shouted into her ear.

And then she began, in her faint, light, toneless voice, to tell them that though she could not herself well recall the evil times when men fought for the two Roses, yet she had very often heard her father speak of them. "And evil times they were, though you think not of them, nor does that rash boy. Nor can he nor any other serve God by moving war against his Prince when the realm is in peace." And she sat down again, her face trembling, and her hand shaking on her stick.

One of the manor plowmen told the news to Malle. He was an old Aske servant, and so he took great pride in what Master Robin had done, since Aske was Aske to him, whether of the older or younger branch.

Malle had come out with her spindle to drive Gib's cow to pasture on the grass along the verges of the road. The sun was still not yet high, and the shadows were long. In a neighbor's croft a man was digging; as he drew the spade out the earth-scoured iron flashed white; the new-turned earth of the plow furrows glittered too, sticky wet, and the polished quarters of the two horses shone dark, yet bright.

"Hi! mad Malle!" cried the plowman. "Have ye heard this good news?"

Malle stopped, letting the spindle run down and hang still at her knee. But when he told her she did not seem to make much of it, only mumbling, "What will they be at?" Then she moved on, after the slowly moving cow. The plowman shrugged, slapped the rope rein against the horses' flanks to start them again, and tramped away with a good heart, looking forward to the drinking and talking there would be at the alehouse, when dusk brought all home from the fields.

That night, when the door and shutters were barred, Malle was cutting bread for Wat's supper and hers; bread and lard was their supper; Gib had had his, and gone up to bed with the rushlight to read there, so they groped by the last light of the fire and must speak only in whispers. But it was pleasant here and friendly; Wat had his bare feet in the ashes that had a touch soft as silk, and warm. Before Gib went he had told them, sharply and angrily, the news from York. Wat was rubbing his belly over it now, as if he had eaten something very good. He was always pleased at things which displeased his father. But Malle mumbled to herself over the loaf.

"So there *is* news," said she suddenly, in as loud a whisper as she dared. "A marvel is the news. God is here comen to us. That is the news!" She flapped her left hand in the air as though Gib's news was a fly which she drove away.

"How can he put on," she said, "such a homespun coat, and not burn all up with the touch of him? If he shouldered down the sun, and quenched light with his coming, it would be no marvel."

Wat scrambled up, and catching a handful of her gown shook it impatiently, being hungry. Malle shoved into his hands two thick slabs of bread with lard between, and he went back to the hearth. But she lingered at the table. "Instead," she murmured, "He came stilly as rain, and even now cometh into the darkness of our bellies—God in a bit of bread, to bring morning to our souls. *There* is news."

Gib called angrily from the room above. Wat looked up with a glare, but shrank away from the fire and into the safer shadows. Malle cried that they two would not be long. She laid her finger on her lips, and laughed silently at Wat, to wipe away his seared look.

October 18

All the captains except Robert Aske stood in a wide, deep window in the house of Master Collins, the treasurer, in York. The window was open, and the late afternoon sunshine and mild air came pleasantly in. The captains had put on what they had with them of best clothes to sup with Master Collins; some had bought a new cloak or doublet or a finer sword since they came to York, so that they made a cheerful show. They talked cheerfully too, for Master Collins was known to keep a good table, and the smells that they had met on coming in had promised well.

They heard someone come pounding up the stairs, and then Aske burst into the room. He had a quill pen stuck behind his ear, inky fingers, and a smudge of ink on his cheek.

"Master Collins," he said, "I pray thee have me excused, but here's no time to sup today." He turned to the others. "The vicar of Brayton has come to me. He says that Strangways, my Lord Darcy's steward—you know him, Cawood, Rudston—" He looked to them and they nodded. "The parson says Strangways has shown him a way to enter into the castle. What castle? Marry, Pomfret. But whether that word of Strangways be truth or trick the parson says this is sure—that the servants and even my lord's men will not stand up against us. Which of you will come with me? How soon can we muster to ride?"

"Wait a moment." Mr. Saltmarsh pushed his way forward. "Where is this vicar of Brayton? Let's have him in to question him."

"He's gone. I sent him back forthwith. He'll have ways to—"

Sir Thomas Metham's sharp voice came from the midst of the group.

"God's Death! You sent him? And now you'd send us?" and he laughed in a silence.

"Aye, Mr. Aske," Saltmarsh said, with more courtesy, but no less malice in his voice. "It seems to me also that the messenger should have come to all the captains, and if he came to one, that one should have brought him to the rest."

"Mass!" Aske began, and had been about to say the truth, that indeed he had never thought of it, and now was sorry. But Sir Thomas snickered again, and—"Mass!" said Aske instead, "what does it matter? There's the news. Now—"

"Yet," Mr. Saltmarsh objected in his smooth voice, "yet tarry."

"I'll not tarry. Pomfret we must have. I tell you—"

"You tell us too much, Master Aske." Mr. Saltmarsh looked round about for approval. "Are you head captain over us?"

"Aye," cried Sir Thomas, "are you?"

"I tell you—" Aske said again, his voice easily overmastering their voices, and thereafter for a few minutes the servants below, and passersby outside, could hear the clamor and sometimes the words of a very pretty quarrel.

At last—"We cannot," Aske cried, "wait on further news from Lincolnshire. We hear news enough."

"Yet no sure news."

"Enough. And so ill news that I am sick to hear it."

"Then the better to wait."

Aske caught at his temper.

"If," he said slowly, "if they have yielded already in Lincolnshire there is nothing we should wait for. If they have not yielded, and we hold Pomfret, they may take courage from it."

"Then," Mr. Saltmarsh dropped the words one by one, provocatively, "then, if Pomfret must be taken, a' God's Name go and take it."

"A' God's Name I'll go if I go alone," Aske cried, in such a voice and with such a blaze of anger in his eye that till he slammed the door on them not one of those left behind spoke or moved.

But then Lord Latimer drew toward Lord Scrope, and they put their heads close. Master Collins came up beside Lord Lumley; he, pleasant good man, was distressed to think of the good dinner so interrupted and left spoiling, for already two or three of the Howdenshire captains had gone hurrying after Captain Aske.

Metham and Saltmarsh had come together at the open window. Metham leaned out; he laughed, then pointed his finger:

"There he goes. And in what a fume!"

Saltmarsh leaned out too, and together they watched Aske, a little man, very angry, and in a great hurry; they saw him snatch the quill from behind his ear, stare at it as if it were strange to him, and throw it down.

"Let him go," Saltmarsh said; he was still much huffed, and red about the ears. "He is," said he, "of too rude and tyrannical a humor to be borne."

Aske came to his lodging still angry, and still very much in a hurry. As he ran up the stairs he was calling for the men to turn out, and for "Ned! Ned!" to come and arm him; and he was thinking it was well Ned should do it, because he was a quick handy lad, and always cheerful; but if Will Wall had been on his feet, instead of ill in bed, Ned would have been driven off for Will to fumble and bungle, and, besides that, to start a bickering with his master. "For he's a difficult fellow these days," thought Aske, "or else I am," as he flung open the door of his chamber.

Will stood up from the bed. His face was like paper, and he looked about as sturdy as a rag in the wind.

"What! Are you here?" Aske cried, and added hastily, "I'm glad of it. You're better?" But already he had seen Will's face fall and his mouth shake. Then he saw beside Will's feet, neatly laid out in order, all the pieces of Sir Robert Aske's armor, which he had brought from Aughton. They were ready for him to put on, and Will, stooping slowly, was lifting the padded coat that went on first. Aske ripped open the buttons of his doublet, and threw it and his coat together on the bed. He must even suffer Will; he could do no other. When Ned put his bright, smiling face round the door Aske bade him to see to the horses.

So while Will armed him he stood very still, helping when he might, as unobtrusively as possible. But often Will would push his hands away, and then fiddle over a catch or a buckle that might have been righted in an instant. One thing there was to the good; he did not talk; but that, Aske supposed, was because he needed all his strength; sometimes when Will's hands came down on his shoulders he thought it was only thus that the man managed to keep himself upright.

When at last it was done, and Will stooped over the buckle of the sword belt, Aske struck him lightly on the shoulder in place of farewell, and thanks, and all that was not to be said.

"And now off you pack to bed again, and lie snug till I come back from Pomfret," he told him cheerfully.

But Will, straightening himself, showed a face tragical and quivering.

"And," said he, "if I was not the sot that I am, I'd be beside you, to die there. For here you go to the assault of a strong castle, and there over the water of Humber—they have—they have—"

Aske turned his eye away from Will's face. He could hear the horses stamp on the cobbles of the yard; it must be much longer than the half hour he had given the others to be ready at Micklegate Bar.

"Have they surrendered then, in Lincolnshire?"

"You know it?" Will cried. "They told you as you came in."

"It was easy to guess." Aske gave a little laugh, and then was silent for a moment. "Well, I must not fail of Pomfret, let Lord Darcy shut his gates or no."

He touched Will on the shoulder again, but absently, as if already his mind was on the road, and went out. Will blundered back to the bed, flopped down there, and cried shamelessly for a while. But in the end he took comfort, seeing, in his mind, Master Robin stand, and hearing him laugh. Will remembered the hero called Samson, who had plucked up posts, gates, bars and all from some Jewish city, and carried them away on his shoulders. Master Robin looked, Will thought, like as if he could carry away the world on his shoulders, if he should resolve to carry it.

There were about three hundred men waiting at the bar, Howdenshire men mostly, with some from Beverley. It was few enough; but Aske hid his chagrin; and anyway, speed was more than force in this, he told himself. Besides, though few, they were of the best sort of yeomen, and there were Aughton fellows grinning at him in the front ranks, and Will Monkton with them.

They made such good speed that in order not to reach Pomfret in daylight, and so betray their little strength, they must lie up somewhere for a while. So for an hour of twilight they waited in the cold whispering shadows of a little wood just across the Aire.

Aske and Monkton tramped up and down together to keep warm, while the wind flapped the hem of their cloaks against their steel back and breast pieces with a hollow sound. Monkton glanced aside more than once at Aske, but he plodded in silence, and with a grim face. At last Monkton spoke:

"Robin!"

"Anon?"

"You did not well to rate Metham and Saltmarsh with so rough a tongue."

"Did I not? Oh? I did not well?"

"Now, Robin," Monkton began, but Aske bore him down.

"No, I'll not hold my tongue, neither for you nor no man. Why would you all have me whisper, cog, speak smooth?"

Certainly he was not whispering. The men stared at them, and Monkton wished with fervor that Robin's voice were less powerful, or his patience longer. "Robin," he thought, "used to be a good-humored fellow," but not seldom in these days he had felt that he did not know this brother-in-law of his, whom, for so many years, he would have said he knew.

He declared, with more than his usual doggedness, that such language as Aske held toward the others might estrange them from the commons' cause.

That brought Aske's anger to blow against himself. What! did he think there were any such in the host? "No, by God's Passion! for I think there are none with us but are willing to go forward in their hearts," and Monkton could see, even in the dusk, how his face had turned darkly red. "There are none," said he again, as if by vehemence he could make it be so.

Yet after he seemed to wait, as if he knew that that was not all.

"And listen," said Monkton, "to what I heard. For those two were at the window when you were gone, but I stood below in the doorway. Saltmarsh said you should break your teeth against the walls of Pomfret. And Metham said—let you go and have your will, so as, if our pilgrimage miscarried, you should be clearly seen to be ringleader, and so come under the King's vengeance in especial."

Aske flung away, laughing loudly. "Shall I listen or care to hear such talk as this?"

He stood apart, biting at his knuckles. The long, impatient sighing of the wind went through the wood, and there were incessant small noises like water trickling, but it was dry leaves that fell spindling past branches, and past other dry leaves not yet fallen.

He came back to Monkton. "It'll be full dark by we make Pomfret now," said he, and shouted to the men to make ready.

He became suddenly cheerful, and Monkton could not see that his words had been at all heeded. Yet what he had said was there in Aske's mind, unregarded as a thorn in a man's thumb, which he will feel only when there is pressure put on it.

October 19

Aske, having waited at the gate of Pomfret Castle in a heavy cold rain till the hostage for him (it was George Darcy's eldest son) was brought out, now had to wait again in the great hall, while the gentleman went up to announce him to Lord Darcy and the great men above. There were a few young gentlemen, none of whom he knew, standing at the hearth; they looked over their shoulders, drew themselves closer together, and went on with their guarded talking. The servants who were clearing away the tables after dinner had, he could see, one eye on the gentlemen and one eye on him. But he would not look at them; he guessed that if he gave them half a chance they would be all about him, and shouting for the commons. Even as it was, when the gentleman who brought him in came back to bid him in to my lord, one of the women at the screens cried out shrilly, "God save you, sir, in your pilgrimage!" Aske turned and raised his hand, but he neither smiled nor spoke, and went on upstairs.

In the great chamber there were many lights, which, after the dark afternoon outside, dazzled his eye. For a minute he could see only lights—firelight, candlelight, torchlight—and among these the forms and faces of many men, but none of them clearly. Then, as his vision steadied, he could see my Lord Darcy on a high-backed settle beside the hearth, and beside him, haughty and beautiful in his violet velvet, the archbishop. Sir Robert Constable sat on my lord's other hand upon a stool; his sword trailed out behind him like a long, black, silver-tipped tail. On the hither side of the archbishop was another priest with a clever, ugly, inscrutable frog's face. Beyond, and behind these, there were faces he half knew or did not know at all. He bowed to them and some of them did the same to him, but all watched him, in silence, waiting to see what he would do.

He went, his wet cloak dripping, to the hearth, set his foot on the edge of it and stretched out his hands to the warmth, not looking at any but keeping his eye on the flames, because he was thinking of what he should say, when he must speak. It mattered very much, he considered, what he should say.

Lord Darcy bade someone, "Take his cloak," and a gentleman came near, to whom he slung off the heavy wet fustian, and who then went away out of the room with it.

"What is that you carry?" Darcy asked.

"What? This?" Aske touched the white rod which he had tucked under his arm, then told them, what my lord already knew, that it was the rod of his captainship of the commons.

"And you carry it here—within the King's castle?"

"It was given me," Aske said, his eye still on the fire, and his thoughts on the words he should speak, "so I carry it."

Constable muttered under his breath that this was the same Robin Aske as ever! He glanced at Darcy, but could make nothing of his face, except that he was watching Aske closely. The archbishop ceaselessly twirled a ring upon his finger without raising his eyes.

In a moment Aske said:

"My lord, shall I speak?"

Darcy bowed his head in a very stately fashion.

"Speak freely!"

"Freely?" said Aske, but half to himself, as if he were still within his thoughts. "Surely I shall speak freely." But still for a little longer he was silent, and to more than one of them as they sat watching him it seemed that he gathered up some strength that was in him, before he lifted his head and spoke.

When he had done he looked round about at them, and then only at my lord. "And now," said he, "it is for you to answer me."

Lord Darcy said that he must take counsel, so Aske was led away into the privy chamber beyond. When he had gone each man waited for his neighbor to speak.

"Well," said my lord to the archbishop, who had flushed to his silver hair. "It was to you he spoke first. Let us first have your counsel then."

"Fie!" cried the archbishop, "that such a man should so rebuke the lords spiritual who have the cure of souls of all laypersons, saying we have failed of our duty in that we have not been plain with the King's Highness—" He stopped there, because Lord Darcy laughed shortly, remarking that, well, surely this man Aske had been plain.

"Plain!" the archbishop repeated, heightening the word by his tone of outrage. "But for us—for me—I vow before God I would have stood against the King's Grace's will in—er— certain things—to the death, if I could have prevailed. But it would have served nothing. To have resisted would have been

death, and," he added hastily, "death profitless," and then went
on to say that perhaps on the other hand this man Aske spoke
not much amiss with regard to the temporal lords, who should
have warned the King.

"Enough!" Darcy interrupted him, and turned to Sir Robert
Constable because he felt him fidgeting alongside.

"And you?" he asked sharply.

Sir Robert gave up fretting with his feet among the rushes;
he planted them squarely, and tugged his sword round so that it
was near to his hand.

"I think," he said, "that he speaks as an honest man."

George Darcy sprang up with such amazement, incredulity,
and disgust written upon his face that his father laughed aloud.
But my lord said, before George could speak, "Come now, here's
little to the purpose. You all heard him say that he and his would
assault tonight. How shall we answer him?"

"But," cried the archbishop, "he cannot so soon. And my
Lord of Shrewsbury will be here—"

He looked round, much less confident than his words, and
caught Constable's eye, who growled that to his knowledge
Master Aske was a man who acted with speed.

"By the Rood!" Sir George Darcy said with bitter disdain.
"Let the commons assault! What then? Here's the King's strong
castle to be held."

"Mother of God!" cried Darcy, "to be held by whom, son
George, and held by what? Here are we few, two of us spiritual men, and there are a parcel of gentlemen of ours that will
fight. And what of the rest?" He looked all about and no one

answered. They had heard enough of the muttering that went on in corners, and seen the unwilling service that was done by servants and soldiers alike. "And," my lord concluded, "with what shall we hold Pomfret? Marry, with quarter-staves and fleshing knives, for of munitions of war there be none."

"Yet," the archbishop protested, obstinately, but with a quaver in his voice, "so great a castle—do we but shut the gates—"

"Mother of God!" Darcy broke in. "Can you no better counsel than that?" and there was a silence broken by Constable, who asked, "Shall you then surrender the castle, and, as he saith, take their oath?"

Darcy gave him an angry look and answered that if the castle had been well furnished "nor he nor any should have had neither the one nor the other but to his pain." Then he said: "Well, here's my counsel. Call him in and say we must have till Saturday eve. If he will tarry till Saturday maybe he'll tarry till Monday, and by Monday, who knows?"

So Aske was fetched in again, and my lord said, speaking haughtily and roughly:

"Well, here's your answer. I neither can nor will give up the King's castle."

"Nor join us," said Aske slowly, "in our pilgrimage?"

"That's a fine new name for an unlawful scurry against the King's Grace and the peace of the realm."

It came to Aske then, like a great blow, that he had failed. He had spoken as well as he knew, plainly and truly, and they looked at him still with unbending, wooden hostility.

It was more difficult now to meet their eyes, knowing that he had failed, but he made himself do it lest there should be one among them who would be of the commons' fellowship; he found himself looking first, and also last, at Sir Robert Constable, but he would not raise his head, and Aske thought—"Why should I think it? Always he would be set against me."

He said: "Then we shall assault you, by every means whenever we will. You cannot hold the castle. Not one of your servants, nor of the soldiers neither, but is on our side." Then he struck his hands together, being much moved by failure and a sort of bewilderment it had brought him into, that they should not understand, or should not believe what was so plain to him.

"Yet," he said, "I had looked for more than to have Pomfret in our hand. I thought to have had you with me in our high cause; some of you at least. You, my lord," he looked at the archbishop, "you in especial."

The archbishop caught the changed tone of his voice and grew haughty.

"And what would you have had of me?"

When Aske said, "To have your counsel, and that you should be mediator for us with the King," the archbishop took him up.

"Then it were not well I should be joined with you, for a mediator should be neither of the one party nor of t'other."

Aske looked at him, saying nothing, and he went on, with an offer to come on a safe conduct and declare his mind to the commons, as to the righteousness of their cause.

Still Aske was silent, and the archbishop, growing bolder, said, with the judicial air of one teaching logic in the schools, that, as for giving counsel, first it must be considered whether their enterprise were lawful, "for," said he, with a noble and lofty look, "you may have my body by constraint, yet never not my heart in the cause unless—"

"No, my lord," Aske interrupted him, speaking softly, "I shall not give you safe conduct to come out to speak to the commons." Then he cried, in a voice that startled them all, "Oh! you churchmen, archbishops and bishops, and all the sort of you, will you never deal plainly with a man? Did you stay to speak with the commons when they came to you at Cawood? By God's Wounds! I have heard how you fled away. And you did well, for there are men among them would be without mercy, should you fall into their hands. Safe conduct? God's Bones! That you may so snarl up a plain thread that none can disentangle it. For you archbishops and bishops are able to find wherewith to justify yourselves that ye let not out the squeak of a mouse against the King's doings. But we that have taken arms can see—" He stamped his foot, and then, ashamed to have let himself be so mastered by anger, turned back to my lord. "So there's no more to be said."

But Darcy, looking proud and disdainful, bade him wait a while. "Give us," said he (this being Thursday), "till Saturday before you assault."

"Till tomorrow morning," said Aske; and when my lord pressed him, "Till tomorrow morning at eight of the clock. For I know what is in your thought and it is in mine too—that my

Lord of Shrewsbury may come; but I, as I deal plainly, I do not fear to speak of that I fear."

He swung round and went to the door. Lord Darcy waved his hand to Mr. Bapthorpe, who got up quickly and followed him. But Aske turned back. For a moment he stood looking at the ground and even now he thought, "No use to say more. No use." Then he lifted his head and spoke.

"Whether that I have said be true I put to your conscience. But if you fight against us, and win, you put both us, and you, and your heirs, and ours, in bondage forever; for if you will not come with us, be sure we will fight against you, and against all that stop us. And we trust, by the Grace of God, that ye shall have small speed."

He put by Master Bapthorpe's hand, stretched out to unlatch the door, and opened it himself.

After he had gone there was a deal of talking, but few could find much that was new to say, the facts were so baldly plain. Lord Darcy lamented to the archbishop how little hope there was that my Lord Steward (that was the Earl of Shrewsbury) should come in time. He beat his fist on his knee and cried that had he but munitions he would hold the castle till all the food was gone—"and that would give us eight days, or ten, or more if we should endure awhile the extremity of hunger," and he looked searchingly into the face of the archbishop, who replied, but faintly, that indeed they would all be ready to suffer to the death, in their service to the King's Grace.

"Aye," said Darcy solemnly, "so would each man of us," and turned to lay his hand on Constable's shoulder who stood beside them. "Come, Robert, since these lousels are all about us, and may make assault any time—"

"But he granted us truce," cried Constable.

"Tush! Will you trust them? We'll make sure. Safe bind, safe find," he said, and pushed Constable toward the door.

They went out and about the castle, each noticing, but in silence, how indifferently watch was kept, and how surly were the looks of those whom they passed. At last, in the still, uncolored air that the rain had left very keen and clear, they stood on the top of the keep, looking toward Micklegate and the town above. The commons were busy there, and, it seemed, cheerful about their work. The two on the tower saw the quick cold flash of axes above the heads of a little knot of men; the choked ringing note of the steel came to them just after each white flicker.

"What are they at?" Darcy muttered, and then answered himself. "Hah! a ram to bring down our gates." He looked down at Constable, and then said: "And what's amiss with you, Robert?"

Constable continued to scowl at the stones of the breastwork, which he was kicking with his foot. He said: "Will you send a message to Shrewsbury?"

"No. I will not. For he cannot reach us now. Nor can we get a message through to him."

"Then why—why this truce? A' God's Name if we must yield, let's yield."

Darcy looked at him, but he would not look up.

"And take their oath? And join us with the commons?"

Constable was silent. Then he blurted out, angrily and in a hurry, that for himself he would be ready to take their oath— "By cause that what he spoke was truth," said he, and met Darcy's eyes.

That my lord was smiling a little made him angrier and he cried out that surely such was his opinion, and he'd not hide it. "But what yours is, Tom, in all these windings and turnings that you make—God alone knoweth it."

Darcy laughed at him again, and began to explain, very calmly and reasonably, that he had spoken as he had spoken, and done as he had done, so that men should report him to the King not as one who flung away a great castle lightly, and lightly joined with rebels.

"And who shall report you?" Constable grumbled.

"My lord archbishop." Darcy laughed again at Constable's expression. "Or any other." But on that he ceased to laugh, for like a flaw in crackled ice the thought struck through both their minds of George Darcy, with his look of pregnant disapproval. "By God's Cross, Robert," said Darcy, throwing off that thought, "you too may be glad if things go ill, that by these same windings and turnings of mine it is made clear that we are forced to their oath and to their company."

"Oh!" Sir Robert groaned. "Here's policy! But—"

Darcy clapped him on the shoulder. "And why not policy? But—what?"

"But—Mass! But did you not in your conscience think that he spoke the truth to us?"

"So you and Strangways are of a sort in this!" Darcy pulled a face, then, catching Sir Robert's glowering look, said that none could deny but Aske had spoken boldly.

"And—truly?"

Darcy looked away into the town, where the smoke trails from evening fires were going up, straight in the stillness, with only the slightest pulsation from the living heat below to trouble them. "I wish," he muttered, "I knew how many he brought with him from York." Then he said, "Nor I'll not deny that to me he seemed, in the main, to speak the truth. More especially with regard to the spiritual men."

"Then," cried Sir Robert, "shall we that are gentlemen dread to take a good cause in hand, when the poor commons dread not?"

"And be hanged with them for traitors?" Darcy mocked.

"This pilgrimage of theirs," Sir Robert went on doggedly, "I'll undertake it with a good will."

"Well," said Darcy, "it seems we'll all undertake it, will we nill we. But," he added, unexpectedly, "what plagues me is I cannot for the life of me remember where I saw the man before. 'Twas in a great sunlight. But where?"

October 21

Lancaster Herald waved his hand to the commons, whom he had been haranguing, and rode on toward Pomfret more briskly than they could go, tied as they were to the pace of the wain that was loaded up with certain carcasses of salt beef, three sides of bacon, five sacks of flour, and two barrels of beer.

He rode cheerfully as well as briskly, for it was a cheerful day, with sunshine and a fine galloping wind that swept down from the west over the wide, mounting fells that lay that way. Besides, after his persuasions, those fellows, who had sweated much to bring the wain safely over a small but swollen stream, had told him that indeed they were weary of the life they were in, since this business began, and would gladly go to their houses. So that it seemed to him that he had done very well already in his errand, for these last had been a great band, and he had spoken in the same vein, showing them how little reason they had to rise against their gracious Prince, to many others on the way. Therefore he jogged along merrily, with two servants in green and white behind him, and the golden leopards and lilies of the King's arms on his breast glowing bravely in the sun. It was well, however, for his good cheer, that he did not overhear the disputing with which those same commons, coming slowly after, wiled away the time beside the slow trudging oxen. For at first telling each other how true it was, that that the Herald had said, and indeed never in words contradicting it, they had, by about the third milestone after he left them, returned contentedly to their conviction that this business of the pilgrimage was a main good thing, and that the commonalty should set all right again in the realm, as the great captain said, and should be thanked of all men, even of the King's Grace, for what they were doing. That Lord Darcy had so soon surrendered Pomfret Castle, and that he and all the gentlemen with him had taken the pilgrims' oath, these were stronger arguments than any words Herald Lancaster could use.

The streets of Pomfret Lancaster found to be crowded with men and horses. In place of last summer's pea-sticks, bundles of pikes and halberds were stacked up against walls, and the smiths were far busier with steel caps and rivets on steel breast and back plates, than ever they were with shoeing horses, even on Fair days.

When the people saw Lancaster they ran along to see him better, some shouting that the King had sent to answer their griefs, and some just shouting, so that very soon he moved in a great crowd, and slowly, till he came to the market cross. There he stopped, and bade that one of his servants who was not incommoded by his master's trussed-up gear, to blow his trumpet, and cry "Oyez! Oyez! Oyez!" But while the last of the proud mounting notes of the trumpet was dying among the chimney stacks of the houses and the servant was drawing his breath to shout, and Lancaster was unlacing the thongs of his purse to get at his proclamation, the faces of his audience, so unanimous in their attention, began to turn this way and that, as a murmur went through the crowd. Men craned their necks, not to see Lancaster in his bravery of blue, scarlet, and gold, beside the cross, but to learn what it was that caused a stir in the crowd beyond. "It's the grand captain. No—it's Captain Monkton," someone cried, and Lancaster found that a big man in leather hosen, and a padded privy coat of fence, had a hand on the bridle of his horse, and was inviting him to come to the castle.

"Gladly, when I have read the proclamation that I am charged withal," said Lancaster, and snatched at his reins, for Monkton was already leading him away.

"The grand captain said you should read no proclamation," said Monkton, "at the least, not yet," and went on. The half dozen pikemen who had come with him formed up alongside, and Lancaster saw no possibility but to sit in the saddle and go where he was led. Once he said, "So you have Lord Darcy now to your grand captain. I trust I shall persuade him and others—" He stopped then. "Why should you laugh?" he rebuked one of the pikemen.

"By cause Lord Darcy is not our grand captain."

"Then who?"

"Captain Aske."

"Chosen," said the pikeman, stepping closer, with an ugly upward look at Lancaster, "chosen by all the nobles, gentles, *and* the commonalty of the pilgrims. And why should *you* laugh?"

"Sim!" Will Monkton threw over his shoulder, and Sim fell into line again.

Lancaster had preserved his temper and his dignity through this episode. He was able to glance sharply about as he was led through the three wards of the castle, noting, for report, the many harnessed men, and the porters, one for each ward gate, and each with a white staff of office, as had been proper if this had been the palace of a great Prince. In the hall they left him awhile, with only two pikemen to keep a space about him in a great crowd of what seemed to him mainly the better sort of yeomen and lesser gentlemen. Here, he thought, was his opportunity, and with a vague word to his guards he pushed his way toward the upper end of the hall and stepped up beside the high table. The pikemen followed him, but did no more. For lack of

a servant he cried his own, "Oyez," and began to speak. But
he had hardly opened to them the cause of his coming when a
hand was laid on his arm, and the big man Monkton stood by
him, saying that the grand captain had sent for him. That did
upset Lancaster. "Had it been Lord Darcy—" he thought, "But
this fellow Aske—" He tried to wrench his arm from Monkton's
hand, then desisted and went along, but wrathfully. "God's
Bones!" he said to himself, "I shall show him. He shall have
from me so much courtesy as a vile traitor should."

The great chamber was pleasant with both firelight and sunlight. Lord Darcy sat in his chair by the fire, his knees wrapped
in a gown of velvet and marten skins. The archbishop and the
archdeacon were side by side on the settle; these two Lancaster
knew, but he looked quickly about among the half dozen or
so gentlemen who stood or sat nearby, to find the traitor Aske,
without being able to pitch on any that should certainly be the
grand captain. Since he was determined, when he did see this
Aske, to pay him no respect, he would spare only that hasty
glance, and then with great, indeed with exaggerated, courtesy,
singled out the archbishop and Lord Darcy for his salutation. To
them he took off his cap, made a leg, and began to declare his
business—how he came from the Right Honorable Lord, the
Earl of Shrewsbury, lord steward of the King's most honorable
household, and lieutenant general from the Trent northward,
and the Right Honorable Earls of Rutland and Huntingdon, of
the King's most honorable council, bearing a proclamation to be
read amongst the traitorous and rebellious persons assembled at
Pomfret, contrary to the King's laws.

He had got so far when someone behind him said, "Herald Lancaster!" and partly because everyone was now looking beyond, to the man who had spoken, but more because the voice was such that he could not ignore it, he turned half about, also to look.

Along the whole of that side of the room ran the dais of two degrees, on which the high table stood, still littered with plates and cups from breakfast, and besides these with pens and sheets of paper. At the far end, beyond the table, there was a window, through the glass of which great shafts of colored light struck down, in which the motes danced. A gentleman leaned there, as if he had been sunning himself, a short, black-haired man in a scarlet coat and doublet. He came from the window now, yawning and stretching: when the bright sunshine was no longer behind him Lancaster could see that he had only one eye. He came and stood before the table, his feet set wide apart, his hands thrust into his belt, and from there he looked down into Lancaster Herald's face. He had heavy brows that drew into a straight black line, and a big mouth that shut very firmly. Lancaster took an instant and vehement dislike to him—"Keeping thus," he thought, "his port and countenance as though he had been a great prince!"

"Since," said this gentleman, "I am chosen great captain of these same traitorous and rebellious persons, it is to me, Master Herald, that you shall do your errand."

It only needed that Lancaster should meet his eye with a casual, scornful glance, and then turn his back, and continue to address my lord and the archbishop. Nothing could have been simpler; nothing, the Herald would have thought, easier, but now he found it to be impossible. Instead, hot with anger, and the hotter as he felt himself growing flustered, he turned his back, not on the great captain, but upon my Lord Darcy, and began his recital again, from the beginning, gabbling it a little.

When Aske stopped him, saying shortly, "Show me the proclamation you say you carry," Lancaster fumbled his purse open, and gave him the folded paper.

"Well," said Aske, "now I will read it." And he read it steadily through, loud enough for all to hear, and gave it back to Lancaster, who took it with a snatch.

"In this," said Aske, "is no cure at all for our griefs, nor even pardon offered, so it shall not need to call no counsel for the answer of it, but I will of my own wit give you the answer." Then he said:

"Herald, as a messenger you are welcome to me and all my company, who intend as I do. But as for this proclamation, sent from the lords from whence you come, it shall not be read at the market cross nor in any place among my people, which be all under my guiding: it doth not enter into our hearts to fear loss of life, lands nor goods, nor the power that is against us, but we are all of one accord, with the points of our articles, clearly intending to see a reformation or die in these causes."

"And what," Lancaster asked, "are these articles?"

"I shall tell you," said the great captain, and he rehearsed those words of the pilgrims' oath which he had written down that night at York. At the end he said: "And you may trust to this, for it shall be done, or I will die for it," and shut his mouth so hard that the Herald could see the muscles tighten over the jaw bone.

When he thought over his mission afterward Lancaster knew it was at this moment that he had begun to feel sure that however boldly the grand captain spoke of "my company" and "my people," and however true it might be that the ignorant commons would follow him, yet he had no certainty that those others—my lord, the archbishop, and the knights and gentlemen whom he had taken yesterday in Pomfret, and who now listened in silence—were, in their hearts, anything but pressed men on whom no certain dependence could be put. And with that there came into the Herald's mind a way to reward this proud and traitorous captain's insensate pride.

"Sir," said he, in a tone at once more courteous and more easy than he had yet used, "I would ye should give me these articles in writing, for my capacity will not serve to bear away the whole tenor of them."

"With a good will," said the grand captain, and, "Who has a copy of the oath? For," he explained to Lancaster, "the articles are comprehended therein," and he turned to the table behind and began hunting among the papers there. As his back was turned Lancaster could smile; it was a pretty thing to see the fellow walking into a trap that a wiser and a humbler man would have shunned. But he was properly grave when he took the paper from the grand captain's hand, and asked:

"Will you, sir, set your hand to this bill?"

For an instant then he doubted whether indeed the man was not aware of the trap, so sharp and scornful was his look.

Lancaster tried, but could not continue, to meet his eye, as the great captain, stooping, twitched the paper from his hands and turned away to shove aside some of the clutter on the table, take up a pen, and bend over the writing; in the silence they could hear how hard he drove the quill.

"And," said he when he had done, in a great voice that rang in the vaulting of the room, "this is mine act, whoever shall say to the contrary."

Lancaster made himself glance up; but the grand captain's eye was not on him. Once more he was looking beyond the Herald, with a dark, hard stare, and a set mouth, to where my Lord Darcy and the others sat.

When the grand captain had gone out of the room, himself leading Lancaster Herald by the arm to see him safely out of the gate, the others melted away too, leaving alone the archbishop, Lord Darcy, and Sir Robert Constable. It was the archbishop who spoke first, crying out that it was not well that Master Aske—"the grand captain," Darcy put in, and no one could tell against whom the irony of his voice was directed—"the grand captain, as he calls himself," said the archbishop. "He doth not well to speak rebellion so openly, saying that he will see a reformation or die in these causes. And saying that the commons shall to London to the King's Grace. It's treason against the King's person."

"He said," Constable broke in, "that we meant no harm to the King's person, but to see reformation."

"So say all rebels," the archbishop answered him fretfully.

"And so say I," Constable affirmed stoutly.

"Well," said Darcy, "since we were willing to take him for captain, we must e'en abide by it." He gave a little laugh. "We cannot say we knew not what manner of man he was."

The archbishop thought that he was a man of an ungentle and rude port, and said so. He also said that in his mind it was great pity that when Master Aske would have laid down the white rod and the head captainship my lord would not take it up.

Darcy interrupted. "You heard what I said. There are other lords in this business now. They would grudge were one of their own fellows set over them. Besides," he smiled into the archbishop's face, "how if I, no more than you, most Reverend Father, wish not to appear to the King's Grace to be the foremost in this pilgrimage."

The archbishop got up rather hurriedly, and went out, saying something to the effect that he was the King's most loyal subject and so it should appear.

"And sworn to this pilgrimage," my lord threw after him; but the archbishop shut the door on that and did not answer.

Darcy looked at Constable smiling, with dancing lights in his eyes that gave him the look of a lad in mischief. But Constable was jagging at the tongue of his belt and scowling into the fire.

"Tom," said he with a jerk, "is that the true reason why you refused to be great captain?"

"Must I tell the truth to the archbishop? It were a waste of good coin."

"Then it wasn't the truth?" Constable met Darcy's smile with an angry, obstinate look.

"Well, would you have me, like Master Aske, to dash my name on to paper at the foot of a list of treasons?"

Constable muttered, "He should not ha' done it. Why did he do it?"

"Because he's a man that drives his furrow as straight as a stone falls."

Constable looked up sharply. "You think that of him?" He considered it a moment and then said, "Mass, it was even so. But yet," he said, "I had supposed you should find him too proud and unreverent."

Darcy reached out his staff, and lifted back to the fire a log that had rolled off.

"The salmon, Robert," he said, "is a great fish, strong and courageous, so that it pleases a man well to take him."

"What's this talk of salmon?" asked Constable crossly, and added, not without malice, that if one of those two, my lord or the great captain, were a salmon, it was not the great captain that was taken with a hook in his jaw.

Darcy laughed at him. But then he said, not laughing, "The salmon is Master Aske. My thought was that a man might be as glad to have him for a friend as to take the biggest salmon of them all."

That same afternoon those in the castle heard the sound of cheering run like a March dust storm through the streets of Pomfret. When some ran up to the top of the keep to look, they saw the Percy crimson and black filling the streets among the cold broken gleams of pikes and halberts. They could see now the silver crescent of the Percys' on the banner, and the man who rode beside, in half-armor, with a red cap and red feathers, a long leggy man on a tall bay gelding.

"That's Sir Thomas Percy," they cried on the top of the keep, and cheered him so that he looked up and waved his hand. For all Sir Thomas and Sir Ingram Percy had been disinherited by their brother, poor sick Earl Henry, no one in the North but took them for the true Percy heirs, for what the Earl had done was, they were confident, only by the contrivance of that minion Reynold Carnaby with Thomas Cromwell himself.

Thomas Percy came late into the great chamber, so that it was already full of men standing about while the boys and servants went round with water and towels for washing of hands. Percy stood for a moment with his back to the door, and craned his neck to see over the heads of the rest, which he was able to do because of his length. Then he elbowed his way through the crowd till he was close behind Sir Robert Constable and Master Robert Aske, who stood in front of the fire; they had been all afternoon on St. Thomas's Hill together, outside the town, taking musters of the commons who came in every hour, more and more. Now they talked together as they warmed themselves.

Percy put his elbow on the great captain's shoulder and leaned heavily on it. "Ha! my little Robin," he said, "you've not grown any taller for all your greatness."

Aske turned about. He and Sir Thomas had gone fowling together in the days when Aske was a lad in Earl Henry the Magnificent's household; they had learned their Latin and the lute playing together, and known the sting of the same birch.

"No," said Aske, "but you've sprouted feathers," and he put up a hand and flipped the end of the crimson feathers in Sir Thomas's cap, at which Sir Thomas laughed his wild shouting laugh, showing all his fine teeth.

"Behold me," he turned himself about, "and admire, for it has not cost me a penny, coat, doublet, feathers, and all. But Master Collins the treasurer has gone surety for it."

"Mind you pay him then."

"Or will you hang me?" Percy asked, lightly but dangerously.

"I'll have no spoil taken."

Percy eyed the grand captain for a moment, then laughed again, and thrust his arm through his, swinging him round toward the high table.

"Get me and Ingram our rights again," he said, "and we're with you to the death."

October 24

Gib chose the way down alongside the river, though it was a little longer, because he did not wish to go up through the village, where it might be remarked on that he was carrying a bundle tied on his staff. "Whither goest thou, priest?" He could hear them so calling to him, and himself lying, along with the truth—"To Richmond. To Richmond only, with some of the wench's homespun to sell."

Last night had been one of stormy wind and rain; indeed, it was while he lay awake hearing the pelting rattle of the driven showers that he had at last resolved, after the thing had lain long working in his mind like yeast, to do what this morning he was setting forth upon.

The woods, as he went through them, seemed strange to his eyes, and being so intent upon his own resolve he thought they were so because he was leaving them forever, since a man sees a place, as it were, newly when he knows he will never see it again; yet the truth was simpler than that; rain and wind had brought down most of the leaves during the night, stripping the boughs bare; brightness had fallen from the air, and now lay in drifts of copper, gold, or golden green to be trodden underfoot.

Now the sky had cleared to blue; at the foot of the hillside the river ran, shallow and quick, winking back the sunshine into Gib's eyes with every flicker of its ripples. He walked fast, feeling, as the distance lengthened between him and Marrick, a growing sense of freedom and relief. He saw only one man as he went and that was the Marrick swineherd, but him Gib could not avoid, for he stood under a tree watching the swine that thronged all the road, trampling and shoving, squealing and rootling in the mud for the acorns which the wind had brought down. Gib must wait till the swineherd saw him and cleared a way, with much shouting and many blows that sounded dully on the tough, dusty quarters of the swine. Then the fellow would walk along a piece with Gib, chewing a beechnut and spitting it out, and talking, with an intolerable slow pertinacity, of a diseased pig, of its long, mysterious illness, of its death.

At last Gib shook him off and settled down to his own brisk pace again. Almost he had been driven, as he had walked beside the swineherd, to grit his teeth together to contain this impatience. Yet now, alone again, the very sharpness of his relief promised so well for the future that he was glad he had not passed the man by with a word. "Lord!" he thought, and drew a deep breath, "in London I shall not suffer from such fellows, but there wits be keen."

In the street at Marske the Conyers' priest hailed him, and would have had him in to breakfast. Gib refused, but since it was the last time he should have to suffer this fool also (for he conceived the Marske priest to be a garrulous, and also an idolatrous fool) he consented to drink a cup of ale at the garden fence.

So, in the pleasant sunshine, they drank a can of ale together, while the women and pretty young girls went by to the well, the pails swinging on the yokes, and now and again a long plaintive chirrup sounding from the creaking well wheel. Now that the sun was warm a white steam went up from the thatch, and smoke went up too, trembling, hyacinth blue against the hillside, but a stain upon the brighter blue of the air.

When the ale was finished Gib went on. As he had expected, the Marske priest had talked a great deal, and, whether it were of old Perkin or of young Hodge's little brat, or of how the King should take heed to his kingdom—"but give him an apple and a pretty wench to play withal and he'll not stir from the fireside, but leave it all to these rogues of heretics"—whether it were of this or that it was all foolishness.

"Surely," he found himself saying again as he climbed the hill out of Marske, "such shall I not need to suffer in London," and he kicked out fiercely at the stones of the road. Here was he—a man of learning, though that learning might, from his sojourn among want-wits, be a little rusted over—here was he, a man (as he knew) whose thought moved quicker and stronger and more vehement than other men's slow, turbid thoughts, as Swale ran brighter than a marshland stream—here was he, lit and burning with eagerness to render to God his due service— "No! No!" he cried aloud suddenly, quite scaring two horses that hung their heads over the gate of a little close. "No! No!" he said to himself. It could not be that God meant him to bide in Marrick, only to drone the idolatrous Mass to a few ignorant blocks, and to harbor in his house a simpleton and a lad that was less human, he thought, than a monkey that he had once watched in the window of a great house in London, scratching and picking at itself.

He switched his thoughts quickly from Marrick parsonage, where perhaps even now Malle was halloing to him to come in to breakfast. Instead he would chew upon one of those grudges and resentments that lay so thickly scattered on the floor of his mind. If there had been any in these barbarously ignorant Northern parts that could have recognized of what quality the man was behind the harsh and hungry looks of the Marrick parson, then, thought Gib, I might have endured to stay. But there was none that had the penetration to see it. Sir Rafe? An ignorant, careless, proud gentleman. His dame? More ignorant, and prouder than he. Trudgeover? A coarse, unlettered fellow, though eloquent, and if he were coarse and unlettered what might be said of the "known men" that were in Marrick, of whom the smith was the best instructed? So, there was none.

Yea, but there was one who came and went, one who knew London and London wits, one who might have recognized what manner of man was Sir Gilbert Dawe, priest. For the rest of the way to Richmond his thoughts circled, angrily yet with a bitter satisfaction, about the oblivious, confident, victorious Master Aske. Never once would Gib let them slink back to the parsonage at Marrick.

Richmond was full, for it was market day. He saw Sir Rafe Bulmer's bailiff, and turned hastily down Friars' Wynd to avoid him. Well, this way lay his road, so why linger where the wall of the Grey Friars began? He said to himself: "Because I'll go the better if I break my fast here, and keep that I have in my poke for dinner. Besides, if I wait awhile there may be those going from the fair with a spare nag that I can ride. So shall I make much better speed."

With such good reasons he turned back into the big marketplace, and bought a piece of hot mutton pie, and ate it sitting on a doorstep. From here he could see, about five houses along, the round jutting window with which Will Cowper had improved the small, frowning face of old Andrew Cowper's house. The stonework of this window was new and white; one of the glass casements stood open, so that Gib could see right through to the upper light of the window on the far side, which was filled with golden colored glass upon which was a white lily, the whole very pretty and bright in the sunshine. A plump woman came to the open window and looked out for a moment; her sleeve that hung over the sill was turned back with sapphire velvet. Gib dropped his eyes and bit into his mutton pie. He greatly and bitterly disliked all Cowpers, and with them all those who had so much money that they could spend it upon new round windows, upon golden colored glass, and sapphire velvet.

But it was not this which now blackened away the sunshine, and kept his eyes upon the cobbles, where bits of straw and cabbage stalk and all manner of household rubbish lay scattered. The sight of Will Cowper's house had brought him up with a round turn and he must perforce remember first the prioress, and then the parsonage at Marrick. It seemed now that his mind (or else it was his conscience) had never forgotten it.

Someone stopped in front of him; he saw a pair of boots, gray hosen, a brown coat. The Bulmers' bailiff cried his name; he was already a little drunk or he would not have bidden Gib to an ale house. "And you shall ride back after behind one of the men. If you've done your business." Gib said he had done his business, and went, and drank, silently and savagely. As the drink worked on him, and his thoughts grew nimbler, and more lightsome, he was chasing one question, yet could not resolve it. Was it God who drove him back, or the devil who wiled him? Had he determined to go back because (God have mercy!) Malle's angel and Wat's angel beheld always the face of the Father in heaven? Or had he determined to go back so that the prioress should stand condemned, because she had thrust out the poor creature Malle, whom he had saved? He could not tell, for the two thoughts were twined in his mind like strands of a rope, and his head by now was ringing.

It was black dark when the horses stopped and the servant said: "Here y'are, parson," and with his hand rather spilt than helped Gib down from behind him. They rode on, cackling, and then their laughter and slurred words died in the deep silence. He found the gate, and his thought was only, "Well, here I can lie down and sleep. Here's home."

His hand, groping, touched the door, which yielded; it was neither barred nor latched. He pushed it open, and saw the little houseplace by the dullest red glow of a dying fire, but after the total dark it was bright enough to his eyes.

Wat lay sprawling just clear of the ashes, his shirt was wide open over his thin, ridged ribs. He was wriggling, wildly throwing arms and legs about, his mouth wide open, and the gurgles that with him passed for laughter came thickly from his dumb throat. Malle knelt beside him; she was laughing too, and tickling his bare skin with a peacock's feather.

She looked up first and saw Gib.

"Jesu Mercy!" she cried.

Wat sprang up with one quick move, and slipped away so that he stood with his back to the wall. Neither laughed now.

Gib said: "Bar the door," and went past them without more words, and up to bed. He pulled off his clothes in the dark, and pitched into the corner the bundle which he had carried all day. It fell with a thud, for there was in it, besides Gib's best gown and hosen, and two shirts, his copy of the Gospels Englished.

Well, here he was home again, shackled by conscience; he was where duty sent him, but that tender loving kindness which was all God's service—he could as well render it, as with his fingers make one of the light flashes on the ripples of the Swale.

October 25

July propped herself against the edge of the table in Mistress Holland's kitchen, and nibbled at an almond wafer. She did not want the wafer, having little appetite these days. She did not want to be in the kitchen either, though it was a pleasant room into which this morning the sun came. It smelt pleasantly too of Mistress Holland's baking, of the herbs that hung in neat bunches from the beams, and of several little birds now turning on the spit against dinnertime. It was a far pleasanter kitchen than July's own, for which she took no care, and which therefore showed accordingly.

Mistress Holland talked with one of her maid servants, earnestly, as two speak who are concerned with grave matters; their communication was of mincemeat. A big woman, twenty years and more older than July, with a plain face and contented, shrewd eyes, Mistress Holland found young Mistress Machyn rather a trying guest—"shy" she tried to think, though "proud" she feared shot nearer to the mark; but whether the one or the other it would do no harm to leave her for a few minutes to herself. So July sat, and nibbled the sweet crisp wafer, and felt sick, and felt the panic of waiting for disaster rise again into her throat. Since she had always known that what she waited for must happen, why must it be waited for so long? Then—"Jesu Mercy!" she cried inside her mind, since she had caught herself wishing to hasten the cruelty that dogged Master Aske's footsteps.

Mistress Holland came and sat upon the edge of the table by her. She also began to eat a wafer, but with a hearty appetite and critical appreciation.

"It was the ladies of St. Helen's told me how to make these," she said, more because she felt it to be courteous to talk to a guest than because she hoped to interest July. "St. Helen's for almond wafers, St. John Baptist of Holywell for crispey. Every house of religious, I dare say, has its own choice dish."

"It was rishaws at the house at Marrick," said July.

"Marrick? Is that where you had your schooling?" Mistress Holland took with both hands this first voluntary remark of her guest.

"I was a novice. I should have been a nun," July said, looking straight in front of her at Mistress Holland's scrubbed board, and at the cupboard where the slipware cooking bowls and crocks stood with light winking on their brown sides through the latticed doors. But she saw the great court at Marrick, under a hot afternoon sky, and Master Aske leaning his hand against the gatehouse arch, and talking to Jankin the porter.

"Then why—"

July gave her a glance, dark and sullen seeming.

"Because my sister would not let me bide."

Mistress Holland remembered Margaret Cheyne, since the good Master Holland was merchant of that same worshipful company of vintners as William Cheyne; her remembrance of Margaret had indeed weighed heavy in the scale against July, although Mistress Holland was too honest a creature not to own to herself that there seemed to be nothing in this sister of the other, except it were her pride—which might be shyness.

So now, knowing by July's tone that there was one subject on which they agreed, she put her arm quickly about the girl's waist, hugging her, and at once letting her go. The less the young wench liked her sister, the better would Mistress Holland like her.

"Yet," she said, answering July's words and speaking as became a good wife, and a happy one, "now you are wedded you would not be a nun there."

"I would. I would I were there. I would I might have bided there always."

Mistress Holland was startled by her vehemence. She could not know that Marrick, in July's mind, was a place enclosed, protected, inviolate. There, forever, Master Aske went about, carrying his fishing rod through the rain, loitering at ease across Grinton Bridge. Mistress Holland, not knowing this, must suppose that Laurence Machyn's wife had either a cruel, unfeeling husband, or a great devotion to the holy state of chastity. Mistress Holland knew Laurence too well to think the first. Therefore it must be the second. She looked at July, still gazing straight before her with a pinched mouth, and was filled with a sudden almost awed compassion. This was enough to account for the girl's distance, silence, strangeness. Mistress Holland, who was very devout, put July at once into the category of those holy and religious women who long for no earthly bridegroom.

So she shook her head, and was silent. Beside her July brooded, passing and repassing, light as air and quick as thought, through the fields, ways, and chambers of Marrick. The woman with whom Mistress Holland had conferred went off to fetch onions from the larder; the other opened the door on the street and stepped outside to look for the men who, every morning, came selling water from the conduit. Mistress Holland and July were alone.

"And to think," said Mistress Holland, "that the King, following the counsel of that man Cromwell—no, I'll not call him lord nor nothing but his unchancy name—that the King would have pulled down and destroyed all such houses of religious, had not these brave commons of the North letted him."

"But," July turned on her with a look so startled as to be almost wild, "but I hear them say that the Northern men are surrendered, and that now there will be—be an end." She could not say the words she had heard spoken, "That now there will be hanging of the wretches that led them, and there an end."

Mistress Holland tossed up her chin.

"*Benedicite!*" she said, "let them wait till they have sure news before they say so much. For my husband saith" (she brought her mouth near to July's headkerchief, and murmured softly), "he saith there is other news; that the King must send the Duke of Norfolk to treat with them," so great an host as they are, being all the North parts, gentlemen, lords, and commons, in arms for the sake of the church."

July, staring at her, could only whisper, "Is it so?"

"And besides that and better," said Mistress Holland, "I say that God will be their surety, who venture their lives in his service. He will be found at the last to be beside them in need."

July looked at her again, with caution this time; almost with suspicion. But Mistress Holland did not speak defensively, hardily, but almost, as it were, comfortably. It was not as if she clung with toes and fingers on the face of the naked scar at Fremington Edge, desperate and trembling like the boy who fell from there when he was taking an eagle's nest. July had dreamed, waking, of that boy many and many a time, feeling as he felt when his hand slipped, and the air rushed up past him, and he knew he was falling. No—when Mistress Holland spoke it was as if she sat on the warm turf of the sunny fellside, leaning, at ease, upon the safe kind bosom of the wide earth. Suddenly, unbelievably, July's heart, for a time at least, laid down its load.

"Where is this place Marrick?" Mistress Holland asked idly.

"In Yorkshire."

"Nay then, have you acquaintance with any of these noble gentlemen?"

"No," said July. "No."

Mistress Holland glanced at her and saw a smile shining, gentle, rapt.

October 26

Malle and Wat were burning garden rubbish; the heap was crackling merrily; below the busy flames were sliding their quick fingers about the dry wizened stalks, feeling along, licking up; above smoke, reeking of rottenness, poured out, leaned sideways, swirled wide and swept over half the garden. Malle and Wat, casting down fork and rake, fled out of it to the clear air to breathe, and leaned together upon the wall.

"Wat," said Malle, "have you thought that he has stained himself, soiled himself, being not only with men, but himself a man. What's that, to be man? Look at me. Look at you."

They looked at each other, and one saw a dusty wretched dumb lad, and the other saw a heavy slatternly woman.

Malle said: "It's to be that which shoots down the birds out of the free air, and slaughters dumb beasts, and kills his own kind in wars."

She looked away up the dale toward Calva, rust-red with dead bracken, smoldering under the cold sky.

"And it wasn't that he put on man like a jacket to take off at night, or to bathe or to play. But man he was, as man is man, the Maker made himself the made; God was un-Godded by his own hand."

She put her hands to her face, and was silent, till Wat pulled them away.

"He was God," she said, "from before the beginning, and now never to be clean God again. Never again. Alas!" she said, and then, "Osanna!"

October 27

The whole host of the commons lay on the north bank of the Don, the King's on the other side of the river, and Doncaster between them. Early this morning thirty of the King's lords and thirty of the commons' leaders had come together upon the bridge on the north side of the town, the commons to speak their grievances, the lords to answer them, that, in the end, some appointment might be made between them.

It was growing dusk now, and still the conference on the bridge went on. Earlier it had been possible for the commons to see, from where their ranks were drawn up, the crowd on the bridge, thirty lords and gentlemen from their party, and thirty from the King's host. But now, though lights were pricking out in the town beyond, the bridge was drowned from them in the twilight.

Robert Aske had half turned his horse, to ride again across the front line of the commons' host. This was what he and other captains had been doing at intervals since late afternoon, and he knew only too well how necessary it was, and how increasingly the commons were breaking line to clog into companies that muttered with their heads together, and only fell apart when one of the captains drew near. By now it was almost a good sign if any man of them would call angrily to know, "When will they on the bridge be done with talking?"

He heard a horseman coming up fast behind him; so he did not turn, but waited. Will Monkton ranged alongside.

"The bishopric men are saying 'Treason.' They say, 'Let's run upon them that are betraying us to the King's lords, and kill them.'"

Aske swung his horse about. "No—slowly, Will," he said, so they rode slowly across the face of the host, till they came to the midst where the banner of St. Cuthbert stood, the crimson dulled to shadow in the dusk, the white velvet and the gold of the embroidery still faintly bright. But the banner was now the center of a jam of men who shouted at each other, waving their arms. Aske said: "One is better than two here. Stay, unless I raise my hand." Then he rode into the crowd.

It was longer than Monkton liked that he had to wait, but after a while the voices dropped; there were times, and more times, when only Aske was speaking; at last he came back and together the two continued to ride along the line.

"Phew!" said Monkton, and then, "We'll not hold them much longer."

"But if we must, we shall."

Monkton shook his head. Then he said, leaning over to speak low:

"Robin, would they betray the commons?"

He could only see Aske's face dimly as he turned, but he knew all the same that he was angry.

"Would I? Would you? If it had been our part to go to the parley?"

The clock struck six from the friars' church, and at last the appointment between my Lords of Norfolk and Shrewsbury on the one side, and the leaders of the commons on the other, was concluded. Now the servants brought torches, and the men began to move about, stamping their cold feet.

Lord Darcy found himself for a moment alone in the diminishing crowd by the side of the bridge; then someone pressed his arm and he turned.

"Ha! Talbot!" he cried, and the two stood in a momentary silence till Shrewsbury said he was sorry to see my Lord Darcy on that side which he had chosen.

Darcy turned to lean on the bridge. Shrewsbury leaned beside him; in the torchlight Darcy could see his face, thin, long, infinitely wrinkled, and set on a neck as lank as that of a plucked chicken. Beyond Shrewsbury's head he saw also two of the gentlemen who had spoken for the pilgrims. So he chose his words carefully.

"All the world knows (if there is justice) why I am of that party." He bent his head as if to peer over the bridge to where the current made a slight lisping sound against the piers; farther off flames of the torches showed on the dark water in smooth oily undulations, becoming there wavering peacocks' feathers of gold, each with a dimpled eye of darkness.

"I must needs join with them to save my life," he said softly; Shrewsbury, he knew, was not one to be easy with words of double meaning.

As it was the earl frowned for a moment before he said doubtfully, "Yet you will not now join yourself with us."

"Talbot," Darcy with his forefinger tapped the back of the earl's hand as it lay on the stonework of the bridge—"Talbot, hold up thy long claw and promise me that I shall have the King's favor, and my case be indifferently heard, and I will come back with you to Doncaster this night."

Shrewsbury pulled at his ear for a minute; at last he shook his head: "Well then, my Lord Darcy, you shall not come."

Darcy laughed softly and scornfully.

"And so I thought. He that will lay his head on the block may have it soon stricken off." He held out his hand, and Shrewsbury took it; they had known each other many years and had always been good friends.

October 30

Robert Aske was sitting on a stool beside the great bed of the Earl of Northumberland at Wressel Castle. He looked not at the earl, but at the embroidered curtains of the bed, rich old embroidery in silks and silver thread, but the silver was tarnished and the silks fraying. His clenched hands were thrust between his knees; he looked down at them now, and, as he unclasped them, learned by the stiffness of his fingers what a pressure he had put on them. He drew a deep breath, meaning to let it out in a sigh, but Earl Henry mistook the significance of the sound.

"No," he cried, "it's no use to say more. You shall not move me. My brothers shall have nothing of me. And I care not to die. I can die but once. Strike off my head, and you will but rid me of much pain."

He was crying by now, and Aske jumped up. "Sir!" he said, "Sir! I pray you—have done. I'll speak no more of it." He went over to the window and stood there, trying not to hear the earl's whimpering, and wishing he might be able to recall some of the words he had flung at the wretched man in the bed—words that should have stormed him, or scourged or mocked him into consent. Yet for all the force and bitterness, aye—and cruelty, he had put into it, Earl Henry had not consented, but had answered over and over, wretchedly and obstinately, that his word was given unto the King; so Aske, who had begun long before this to be ashamed, was now very much ashamed indeed.

He heard a noise from the bed that was not a whimper. There was a silence, and then Earl Henry groaned again. Aske went quickly back and stood close to him; the earl turned his head, but very stiffly and cautiously, and as if all his mind was waiting, watching, listening for something which should arrive. Aske saw his face change and could not take his eye away from it, though he wished to look away; yet he knew that the earl did not care whether he looked or no, being now quite cut off from him in the privacy of extreme pain.

It lasted but a few minutes. When it was over Aske sat down again till he saw the earl lift his face a little from the pillow, looking for him. Then he asked, speaking almost in a whisper—

"Is it like this?"

"Sometimes bad, as now, and longer. Sometimes not so bad."

Aske said, "I should not have spoken. Yet—" He checked himself abruptly and said, "Forgive me."

Earl Henry gave him a little smile. "You are very earnest in this business, Robin."

It was a long time before Aske spoke. Then he said—

"Sir, I have thought of myself sometimes in this as a horse set to lug timber in the woods in deep mire of winter. There's the weight to move, that's one thing, and for another the wheels will not turn. So the horses must haul as to break their hearts, if they will shift the tree. But," he said, "I shall shift it."

The earl said softly, "It'd be a great load, Robin, that you did not shift."

"Surely," said Aske, "I shall see reformation done, or I shall die for it. But," he muttered too low and hastily for the earl to be certain of his words, "but I'll not be taken and judged as a traitor. I'll die on the field."

Then he began to tell of the course of the negotiations, and how at Doncaster it had been appointed that Robert Bowes and Rafe Ellerker should go with the Duke of Norfolk to Windsor, to carry to the King's Grace the grievances of the North, while both hosts should disperse until the King's answer came. "But surely," his face and voice kindled, "surely I think that if we would have chosen battle rather than to send our petition we should have had the better of them. For those gentlemen and commons that went with them went unwilling; but in our host I saw neither gentleman nor commons willing to depart, but to proceed in the quarrel, yea, and that to the death," and he drove his clenched hand down on his knee. And then, speaking in a hurry, "I would with all my heart, sir, that you were with us, for before God I do know our cause is just. How can a secular Prince—"

He broke off because the earl had moved sharply, and certainly this was to begin all over again. So they were silent until the earl began to talk about that stuff of his which the commons had seized, and Aske had saved from spoil. "You shall have it," said he, "and I would it were of more worth," and then he said, "And—yea, you shall have my great spice plate that lies in the keeping of the brethren at Watton."

So, as the spice plate was worth £40, and money was needed by the commons, Aske kissed the earl's hand and thanked him. Then he made up the fire, pressed and strained the juice of some oranges that were in the livery cupboard, and sprinkled rose water about the room to sweeten the staleness of the air. It pleased them both that he should do this old accustomed, long-discontinued service.

After the close, scented room the air in the dark court tasted strangely clean. Aske stood for a few minutes letting the wind stir his hair and looking round about at the lights in the windows. From the tower where the kitchens were came not only light but noise, for the servants were washing dishes after supper. He could hear them shouting to one another. "Yet they always shout," he thought, "even when they stand side by side at the same kneading trough." A woman in wooden shoes went clattering down the flagged passage to the dairy; he knew the way she went, and how the great bowls of cream would stand all along the stone benches; many a time he had stolen in to ladle out cream for himself, and come skulking out wiping his mouth with the back of his hand.

Through an arched passage just beside him lay the herb garden of the castle; if it had been light he could have seen from where he now stood the trim beds of herbs edged with clipped box; but it did not need daylight for him to see it all quite clearly in his mind. And as he saw it, so he remembered how angry the old earl had been when he found out that the cooks had been buying herbs at Howden and Hemmingburgh. He had started off into the garden to see for himself if there were not herbs enough, with the sulky chief cook on one side of him, and on the other a gardener to show him where every herb grew that a cook might need. When they found the herb the cook got a rating, and when they found it not, the gardener, so neither could crow over the other. When he had seen all the earl came back and had it written down in the Great Book of the Household:

"That from henceforth that there be no herbs bought seeing that the Cooks may have herb enow in my Lord's Gardens."

Aske smiled as he remembered it, and he remembered it well, for he himself had written it, being just then in the office of the clerk of the kitchen in the earl's household.

He went across the court, loitering, as his mind was loitering through past times. Then he turned into the spicery, and calling a servant asked for a pricket of wax; he had a mind to go up to the chamber that was called Paradise because in that pleasant, peaceful, sunny room the old earl kept his books; there they stood about in their presses, and in the midst of the room for convenience in reading, there were the hinged, latticed desks, which he had been so proud of. "For a little while," Aske thought, "I'll read there." But the truth was that he did not want to meet Sir Thomas Percy just yet, to tell him that the earl had utterly refused, and to hear what he would say about his brother.

But when he had shut the door of Paradise behind him he found that there was a light already in the room, and the very man he had hoped to avoid was flipping over the pages of a book with an impatient hand.

"Well?" cried Thomas Percy.

"He will not."

Then Thomas began, and Aske, having tried to soothe him, was caught into an argument. Both were angry, and Aske was angry with himself too, because there was much in what Thomas Percy said that he himself had said to Earl Henry, and as Thomas now stormed at him, so had he stormed at the earl, as he lay tossing miserably in bed. So it was manifestly unfair that he should take the contrary part now; and yet he must, for Thomas wanted to break into the earl's chamber, "and then see will he still refuse. And I can do it," he cried, "with my folk and those you have with you, maugre any men of his here that will withstand us." But Aske would not have it so.

As they grew hotter the argument ranged wider. Thomas said Aske cared nothing for his old friends but only for the new. Aske told him not to talk so like a shrewish chiding woman. Thomas cried, "Friends? Sinister back friends I'll call them that'll do you a shrewd turn one day," and began to rail on Lord Darcy, raking back over the old lord's past years, into what was hearsay for both of them—how it had been said that he had tricked old Lord Monteagle, and wasted the heir's wealth when the lad was his ward and Hussey's. "And here is this same man, but older, and you take him in Pomfret like a bird in a gin, and he swears an oath perforce, and you think that he will stand to it, and not escape away to the King if he might."

"Fie!" Aske shouted then. "God's Blood! Say that to his face, for I'll not hear it of him!" And he went out slamming the door, and only remembered when he stood in the black dark of the stairway that he had left behind him his candle standing on the desk.

So he began to feel his way down, and, as if by the touch of the cold stone against his fingers, his anger began to cool. He had not gone halfway when he stopped to argue with himself whether he should go up again. Just then he heard the latch of the room above lift with a click, and saw the stair and the newel and the curve of the wall swing unsteadily in the light of the candle which Thomas Percy carried.

"Tom," he cried, speaking on an impulse, "tomorrow I'll speak again with the earl. Perhaps I may move him."

Sir Thomas answered only by a grunt. But in a moment he said: "Here, take your candle that you left behind you." So Aske waited for him on the stair, and they went down together, in silence but with dwindling enmity.

November 2

The Duke of Norfolk, Sir Rafe Ellerker, and Master Robert Bowes waited together in a window at Windsor. Close to them gentlemen and yeomen of the King's Guard stood at the door of the King's privy chamber. This end of the long room was almost empty except for the Guard, the three gentlemen, and a few grave pacing couples, who looked soberly with frowning faces and spoke quietly to each other. Farther away the crowd talked more cheerfully and louder; among the men's voices could be heard women's too, and their light sweet laughter above the deeper hum of talk.

The duke was discoursing well and wittily. The two younger men listened, or seemed to listen, and tried to think collectedly of what they must say to the King when they had their audience. Sir Rafe kept his long, pale, placid face bent; yet it was neither so placid as usual, nor so pale, but a little flushed and frowning. Robert Bowes's heavy features and half-shut, guarded eyes did not easily betray either his feelings or the keen brain behind them, but even he was restless, shifting his shoulders inside his dark blue doublet that looked far less fine here, in spite of all its gold buttons, than it did at home in the North. Only Norfolk was, it seemed, at ease, chatting on about horses.

Somewhere beyond the room a little bell jangled softly. The duke, leaving a favorite and much vaunted black gelding in the midst of one of its most remarkable jumps, stopped speaking, and turned his head over his shoulder to listen.

A quiet-stepping, round man in gray velvet came out of the King's chamber; he was carrying a great many papers in a red leather pouch. He went away down the room, with pursed lips, and absent, calculating eyes; yet to Bowes it seemed that he had taken in the three of them in one sliding glance.

"Who is that?" he asked, and Norfolk told him, "Privy Seal."

Bowes nodded. He had never seen Cromwell before, yet he had hardly needed to ask the question. One of the gentlemen was coming toward them.

"If you show yourself humble and penitent I make no doubt His Grace will use you with mercy and his customary benignity," Norfolk said, speaking hastily. "But if you stand stiffly—"

He moved to meet the gentleman usher who drew near.

"His Grace hath sent for me?" His voice was cheerful, and he went briskly toward the door of the King's chamber. The two Yorkshire gentlemen envied his confidence; they had been too preoccupied with their own apprehensions to notice how, at the pretty silver note of the bell, the duke's chin had jerked, and his voice died.

Inside the privy chamber the King stood before the fire; he wore velvet the color of flame, his feet were set wide apart, his head was bent and his chin sank into roll upon roll of bristled fat above the gold-stitched collar. His bulk, blocking out the firelight on that darkly overcast forenoon, seemed enormous; Norfolk could hear something—perhaps it was the King's belt—which lightly creaked every time he breathed. Himself a man of a very spare habit of body, he felt a qualm both of disgust and dread at the physical grossness of the King. He knelt; he kissed the King's hand, and, as the King did not raise him, he continued to kneel.

"Well?"

This, and no better was the sort of welcome that Norfolk was prepared for. To meet it he had already resolved to use a cheerful, soldierly frankness.

"By the Mass," said he, "here am I a true loyal man imploring pardon for that which was no fault of mine, since neither for ease nor danger have I spared this little poor carcass that you see. Yet with a good will I would be prisoner in Turkey rather than to have had the matter at the point it is now. Fie! Fie! upon the Lord Darcy, the most arrant traitor living."

The King did not speak, but he moved sharply, and that shook Norfolk from his cheerful vein.

"Woe! woe worth the time!" he cried, "that my Lord of Shrewsbury went so far forth. An he had not done, you should have had other news."

"Cousin," said the King, and from his quiet voice the duke knew that this was going to be an audience of the worst sort; for the King was at his cruelest when he spoke like that—"Cousin, we have called to our remembrance the whole discourse and progress of this matter, with your advertisements made in the time of the same; which we find so repugnant and contrarious, the one and the other, that we cannot forbear frankly to make a recapitulation of the same; to the only intent, that you shall perceive that you have not therein observed that gravity and circumspection that in your person toward Us was requisite."

"Sir," cried the duke, but the King held up his hand. He went away from Norfolk and sat down on a big velvet gold-fringed chair beside the hearth and from there continued his rebuke. So the duke was left kneeling before the fire, ridiculous, humiliated; what with anger, fear, and the heat of the flames, now no longer masked from him by the King's person, the veins of his temples began to throb as if they would burst.

"Alas," he cried, in his agitation interrupting the King. "Alas! for I have served Your Highness many times without reproach, and now, having been enforced to appoint with the rebels, my heart is near broken!" And he felt that indeed it was, and wrung his hands together.

"Suffer me," said the King, with a yet more deadly gentleness, "to speak my whole mind," and he continued to speak it.

"And now," he said at last, and paused to shift one leg over the other, "now We have uttered unto you, as to him that We love and trust, Our whole stomach, which if you do, in your person, weigh toward Us, as We do utter Our love in the declaration thereof to you, We doubt not but you will both humbly thank Us for the same, and with your deeds give Us cause to thank you accordingly."

Norfolk could not raise his eyes; for one thing he dared not; for another, if he did, the King would see in them that anguish of rage that shook him in time with his heart beats; so that again he dared not. Looking only upon the King's broad black velvet shoe, he mumbled that surely he was thankful, and if the King's Gracious Highness of His benignity—

He looked up, saw that the King was raking his face with a slant, secret look, and found that words died on his tongue.

"There is," said the King, "another matter which must be touched on."

Norfolk waited.

"You said that in Our service you would esteem no promise you made to the rebels. Was that truth?"

"Very truth."

"Saying also that you would not think your honor touched in the breach and violation of any such promise. Are ye yet in that same mind?"

Norfolk cried that surely, and God help him, he was in that very mind, "and most humbly I pray You, Sir, to take it in good part that I think and repute none oath nor promise can distain me, so that it be made for policy, and to serve You, mine only master and sovereign. For," he plucked at the breast of his doublet, cleared his throat, and declared, "I shall be torn into a million of pieces, rather than to show one point of cowardice or untruth to Your Majesty."

"Well!" said the King. "That is well," and he smiled. Norfolk, glancing up, caught the end of the smile, and it was the bitterest and most searching torment of all to see that look on the King's face, a look satisfied, contemptuous.

"And now," said the King, "as to that villain Aske. Have you used any means with Lord Latimer or other of those lords to induce them to contain the wretch?"

Norfolk protested that at Doncaster was no time; that the rebels stood so stiffly to their demands; that all policy was needed to persuade them to disperse. "And besides," said he, "this Aske was manifestly leader over them all, lords and commons alike."

It seemed to Norfolk that rage puffed the King out to a larger bulk than ever.

"So," he said, speaking with the utmost gentleness, "so you think it no marvel that the nobility of the North suffer such a vile villain to be ruler over them? What was he in Our courts but a common peddler of the law? Is it aught but his filed tongue hath brought him in such estimation?"

Norfolk muttered that indeed the North parts were mad in these days.

"Yet," said the King, "you have done nothing against this wretch, though We and all Our nobles that are here with Us think Our honor greatly touched in that he abideth free."

In the silence Norfolk heard the first gouts of a windy shower strike against the window panes. He cried, his hands straining upon the brim of his cap, that to know his gracious Prince so used by ungracious naughty subjects was death to him.

"If I have done nothing," he protested, "yet I have thought— if great policy should be used—if one of the lords might be brought to deliver him up by promise of favor—"

At that he saw the King lean forward.

"A way," said Norfolk, "might be found. If I wrote to—"

The King's hand checked him. "How, shall be your concern." And then—"Where are those two of the rebels that have come to ask Our pardon?"

Norfolk said that they were without, that he had brought them with him, that he had so wrought with them that they were, he conceived, most truly penitent.

"Go and fetch them."

The duke got up, in haste to do the office of an usher.

November 10

Lord Darcy was sitting in the little garden at Templehurst, which lay between the house, the jutting chapel wall, and the moat. Always a very sheltered place, except when the south wind blew, today—a day of St. Martin's little summer—it was so warm that even a bee or two worked among the last carnations. As well as Lord Darcy's gentlemen, strolling to and fro along the paved walk, and my lord, who, wrapped in a fur-lined cloak, sat at a table dictating to a clerk, there were half-a-dozen or so of yeomen or squires from round about Templehurst. They had heard that a messenger had reached Doncaster and had sent asking for a safe conduct. They meant to know what letters and what news that messenger brought, so they hung about in the lower part of the garden where it dipped to the moat, eating my lord's apples from his trees, and throwing the cores into the water, where the silly fish rose at them. Sometimes a few would come unobtrusively nearer, but if they hoped to catch any words of moment from my lord's lips they were disappointed, for all they heard was, "charcoal for the great chamber fire, because the smoke of sea-coal will hurt my Arras," or again, "Great wood for fires too, because coals will not burn without wood."

But at last the door at the top of the stairs leading down to the garden was opened, and servants in green coats came out, bringing with them a small gray man, who looked stupid, but who was only very weary with hard riding.

"Ha!" cried Darcy, and got up. "Welcome, Perce Creswell."

Creswell, who had been Lord Hussey's servant, and now was Norfolk's, came down the steps stiffly as though his legs were made of wood and not well jointed. He said, speaking hoarsely because his throat was dry, that he had a letter. He put one into Darcy's hand.

Darcy turned it over, looking at the seal. "The ermine and the bows," he said. "It is from Sir Robert Bowes?"

"And Sir Rafe Ellerker."

"And you bring news? And good news, I hope."

"Good enough, my lord, for I trust all will be well." Creswell added then so that only Darcy could hear, "I have a privy letter."

Darcy turned. He knew that his gentlemen had stopped their pacing and were listening; he knew that the commons were edging nearer, listening too.

"You hear that, my masters," he said loudly. "That all will be well." And then, "Who will bring the news to the great captain, and bring him here again?"

"I'll go." "And I." "And I." Three of the commons began to move away, then stopped and hung uncertain, when Darcy asked, "Where will you find him?"

Someone said, "Wressel." Someone else said, "Hull." "Or any other town or castle in all Yorkshire." They all laughed at that; it was well known that the great captain was apt not to be long in one place, and that he covered the ground quickly.

"Come, Perce," said Darcy, when they had gone, and put his hand on Creswell's shoulder, and led him into the house. All the rest followed, the clerk coming first, bearing the cushions my lord had used, the papers, rolls of accounts, bundle of pens and a pot of ink. In the way between the chandry and the boiling house, just before they came out upon the passage beside the screens, Lord Darcy half turned, and slipping the big fur-lined cloak from his shoulders, tossed it to the clerk, but so maladroitly that the skirt of it flapped paper, ink and pens, cushion and all, out of the man's hands.

"Tchk!" said Darcy, and went on with Creswell beside him, leaving the clerk and the others who came after to pick up what had been scattered. They could not know, when they came up again with my lord and the messenger going through the hall to the great chamber, that a letter sealed with the Duke of Norfolk's seal lay snug in the long hanging sleeve of Darcy's green damask velvet gown.

Alone in his own privy chamber Darcy lingered for a minute before he shut the door. He had left Perce Creswell outside in the great chamber, with the others, to ease his stiffness by the fire, and to drink a cup of wine. Now Darcy could hear them begin to question him of Thomas Cromwell, Lord Privy Seal, and now to say what they themselves thought of him; that, Darcy conceived, would keep them busy long enough; he shut the door, latched it, and went away to the deep window on the far side of the room. There were cushions there on the stone seat, and the sweet smell of the herbs strawed on the floor came to him as he stirred them with his feet. Outside the window the country stretched away, still and golden green, with blue above, and mist of a deeper blue lurking in the further trees. He opened the letter and read what Norfolk had written.

Not till he came near to the end could he guess why for the delivery of this letter such secretness had been needed. Then he understood.

He read the whole through not once, but three times, then laid it on his knee, upside down; yet he could not take his eyes off the duke's clerk's neat, pretty penmanship. At last, after a very long time, he picked it up, and looked it all over, most narrowly, examining the writing, seal, and all. Then he folded it, put it back into his sleeve, and opened the door into the great chamber.

Perce Creswell was sitting by the fire, dandling an empty wine cup in his hand. He looked a much nimbler man than when he had come in, and he swung round quickly as he heard the door open.

His quickness was a mistake. The commons jumped up, as when one dog wakes, all wake. They boggled that Darcy should speak with Creswell alone; they thought they should hear it too. Yet when Darcy told them he would but speak a while with an old friend, reminding them too how Lord Hussey, whose servant Perce had been, was now a prisoner for the Lincolnshire rising, they consented. "And you shall hear all anon," said Darcy, as Perce followed him in.

Darcy sat down again in the window seat. Perce Creswell took a stool.

Now, Darcy asked him, "what is your credence for this?" and he swung the end of his long sleeve between them.

"The same," said Creswell, "as is the effect of the letters. That my Lord of Norfolk, my master, bids you account him your true friend to follow his advice in this, that in order to declare yourself ye shall by your policy find the means to take, alive or dead, but specially alive if ye can, that most arrant traitor Aske. Which," said Creswell, "my lord my master doubts not by your wise policy ye shall well find the means to do."

Robert Aske was in the parlor of the Buck's Head at Selby. Will Wall, still as thin as a straw, but now not quite transparent, was writing to his dictation at the table by the window; Aske would not sit, but went up and down between the hearth and the table. He had come from Wressel this morning and would return before dinner. At Wressel was Kit, and they had quarreled before he left. And here at Selby a letter had reached him which said that the brethren of Watton would not hand over the Earl of Northumberland's spice plate; the letter said much more than that—such things that Aske had first crumpled it in his hands, then torn it into pieces and thrown them into the fire.

He swung about at the hearth. "Have you writ that?" Will, his pen still scurrying, nodded.

"Then write this," Aske said, tramping off in the other direction: "'For I will assure you that I will have nothing of no man, but that it may be lawful and reasonable done.'" He stopped, biting at his knuckles, said—"'Wherefore'"—Then, "No, it's enough. Conclude—'And therefore fare you well from Selby, the tenth day of November.'"

But though he had said it was enough, when he had read through what was written he twitched the pen out of Will's fingers, and, with one knee on the bench, began to write a postscriptum. "If you have the spice plate, send it me with haste." The pen flew over the paper. "It is pity apart from God's sake to do anything for that house that so unkindly doth order me." Will looked up to Aske's face with its black frown; these days, Will thought, his master was angry where he had been positive, bitter where he had been stubborn, and very seldom merry.

Then he saw that Master Robin had stopped writing to listen. "Open the window, Will," he said, but before it was open Will had heard the sound of a horse ridden very hard. Aske ran out into the street.

Yet, when he had stopped the messenger and almost hauled him out of the saddle, he came back in silence into the parlor with the fellow behind him, and sat down on the bench.

"Well," he said then, "what's your errand?"

"My Lord Darcy says, 'Come back to Templehurst. There's a letter from Sir Robert Bowes and Sir—'"

"Did he say no more?"

"He told us all in the garden, 'This messenger says all will be well.'"

Aske got slowly from the bench. He turned his back on them and went down on his knees with his head between his fists against the edge of the table. Will knelt too, and the messenger, after fidgeting with his belt a moment, did the same.

No more than two minutes after that, Aske set off for Templehurst, on the horse which the messenger had ridden. He would not have Will come; he must go back to Wressel. But he laid his arm for a minute across Will's shoulder and said, softly and quickly in his ear, "Oh! Will, I had forgotten that God might have mercy on us, and lay to His hand on our party."

Then he looked down at his knees. "See, I have knelt in a puddle of ale." He laughed, and Will heard him laughing as he went out and swung up into the saddle.

Lord Darcy and his people were at dinner when Aske reached Templehurst. He came up the length of the great chamber just behind a big ham and an apple pie; he laid his hands on the shoulders of two who sat opposite my lord. "Come, make room, make room," he bade them, and vaulted over the bench to the place between them.

Lord Darcy said: "Where did they find you?"

"At Selby."

"And the messenger? And your servants?"

"Oh! Somewhere behind." Aske waved his hand vaguely. But when he had eaten a little he looked up and around from one to another, and laid down his knife.

"Your messenger said, 'All will be well.' Is it well? What does Bowes write?"

"Well, there it is." Darcy threw the letter to him over the table.

When Aske had read it he slammed it down on the table and then gave it a great blow with his fist so that the dishes jumped.

"It's a lie that I moved war newly since we were at Doncaster. You all know that I have not. I have stayed the people wherever I could. And after Pomfret, God knows, I could stay them hardly."

"Good Master Aske," Darcy interrupted him, "we shall answer these letters, but after dinner."

"I shall answer them article by article," said Aske, and after that sat eating without lifting his head. After such hope as he had had this was too sore a trouble for him to take it lightly.

When dinner was over my lord said it would be well to send out messengers to fetch some of the other captains, because, besides Aske's answer, this letter should receive an answer from them all. So those of the commons who had come to Templehurst to hear the news went off, as well as certain servants of my lord. Darcy himself went into his privy chamber; Aske took pen and paper to the little chequer chamber where he could be undisturbed.

He had barely finished his answer when a lad came saying that my lord would speak with him, and so led him through the house. It was a great house, and crowded with servants, all in the green livery, besides gentlemen sitting talking, singing, or dicing round the fires, for evening was closing in, and within doors it was almost dusk. Every here and there, in little closets or at the wider parts of passages, there were barrels of arrows, or stacks of bow staves or of pikes. Aske thought to himself as he went after the lad, that my Lord Darcy was master of a big meiny, and well furnished; he remembered how he had, like every lawyer, condemned the bad old days when the lords had each an army of men in his own livery, to fight for one or other of the two Roses; but now it heartened him a little to see Lord Darcy's strength.

"And I need heartening," he thought, with an uncheerful smile, as he came to the privy chamber. Kit's words at Wressel, the letter he had answered at Selby, now this lying accusation which Bowes and Rafe Ellerker had believed—all these things together had borne him down.

He sat down by my lord upon the settle. Darcy put a letter into his hands, and then got up, and began to move about the room behind him. Aske leaned forward, holding the letter aslant to catch the light of the fire, and so read it to the end.

He did not stir when he had read it, and he knew that his face did not alter, whatever was the alteration in his mind. When he first took the meaning of what the duke bade Darcy do, he thought: "He would not do it," and then hearing how Darcy prowled restlessly behind him, and between him and the door, down went his confidence like a shot bird. He thought, "It was always what I feared," and he read again—

"In your life I think ye never did such service that both to His Majesty shall be more acceptable taken, nor that shall more redound to your honor and profit. My lord, the bearer, your old acquaintance, can show you how like a friend I have used me to you all this time."

"Like a friend." And the letter was signed—"Your loving friend, T. Norfolk."

So the Duke of Norfolk, who was Darcy's friend, expected him to do it.

Darcy had stopped moving about and now stood still. "Well," thought Aske, "I must say something." But he was thinking that there were five gentlemen and several of Darcy's servants in the room outside, and himself one man alone.

He said, in a flat voice without looking up: "They want me 'alive or dead, but better alive.'" He had been about to say, "I'll see it's not alive," when Darcy cried—

"Alive, or your head in a sack. He said that to me. God's Bones! but that he was mine old acquaintance, and besides came on a safe conduct—" He broke off, and coming to the settle leaned over, and snatched the letter from Aske's hand. "What I have answered to Thomas Howard," he said, "is between me and him. But there was need I should show you that letter. God's Bones!" he cried again, and Aske heard him rap out with his staff at the frame of the bed as he went by it. Then he stooped for a long time over a fine little coffer bound with steel and with five locks of steel, till he had put away the letter and locked it safely in.

Aske stayed where he was, his face burning, and not with the heat of the fire. He felt himself, for his suspicion, no better than a cur.

He said the same to Sir Robert Constable that night. They were sharing a bed; Sir Robert lay already between the sheets; Aske had sent away the servant, and now he sat down on the edge of the bed in his shirt and hosen.

"Did you conceive," cried Sir Robert, when Aske told him, "that Tom Darcy would act so?"

Aske hung his head without answering.

"It's well you did not say it. He could not have forgiven you, I think."

Aske muttered that he thought shame ever to have—but—

Constable, watching him, felt a spark of their old enmity kindle. But it was the last spark. He had never seen Aske utterly abashed before, never, in all his experience. To see it now tickled his vanity; the cause of it wakened his generosity; so the spark dwindled and was quenched.

"Never," he said, "would Tom betray a man. Though I grant you I myself find him overfond of policy and subtlety some-times. But then he hath a very busy working head. But this is a different matter."

"I did not know," said Aske, "what to think of him." He twitched his shirt out, and as he plucked it over his head he said: "I knew, and did not know, I think."

"Well, you know now."

"By God!" Aske turned his face, "Now I do know."

There was something so warm, and so moved, in his look that Constable was moved too. They faced each other for a short instant. Then Constable, drawing up his knees, drove with his feet at Aske's backside, hoisting him off the bed.

"A murrain on you!" Aske cried, rubbing himself. He was laughing, but each of them knew that a line had been passed.

November 14

It was a perfect hunting morning, blue above, lightly crusted
with hoar frost underfoot; the shadows of the bare trees, delicately penciled and perfect in every branch, lay stretched across
the clean ridged plow lands, as the King and his court went by
with noise of trampling hoofs, jingling of bells, and the tantara
of horns; above them the gulls, in from the sea, turned with a
flash, then flowered into golden white, sailing.

The King was in a good humor. The Duke of Norfolk, who
rode beside him on the one hand, and my Lord Privy Seal, who
rode on the other, got each a teasing that the King pitched loud
enough to be heard by those that came behind; so when the
King laughed, these laughed too; their laughter, which Lord
Privy Seal bore with apparent complacency, was to Norfolk a
hair shirt on his shoulders.

So when, within the forest, they waited for the huntsman's
horn to tell them of the game afoot, Norfolk let himself be
edged to the outside of the crowd, in the midst of which the
King's green velvet cap and white feather could be seen above
the rest, mounted as he was upon a tall black gelding. Norfolk
did not look that way, but downward and sidelong; winning for
the moment, in spite of the crowd, a fragile, narrow privacy.

There had been murder done just here, sometime this bright
morning; a scatter of feathers filled a little grassy hollow; a spot
of royal sanguine, on which the dogs pored and sniffed, lay upon

the dark, soft earth. The feathers were gray, and black and gray like mussel shells; Norfolk's eyes being on them he saw instead, in his mind, the long low shore opposite Orford, and the heaps of mussels there. It was lonely on Orford ness, lonely and quiet unless tides and winds were angry. At Orford and thereabouts, and at Framlingham, and in all those places where Howards were lords of the soil, Thomas Howard was a man different from the Duke of Norfolk who had ridden by the King's side, his ears burning, cackling with a sick and raging heart at the King's baiting. He wished now that he was there and not at court; he almost truly wished it.

One of the huntsmen came trotting by, circling the crowd, with the dogs after him; the hoofs of his horse trampled the spilt feathers, not with the brittle cracklings of mussel shells, but in the silence of a trodden cloud. Then a dog bayed, the horns blew, and the hunt crashed away down the glade, with the slipping, flickering shadows of the bare boughs racing over them. Norfolk rode light, and rode boldly, so he was soon able to choose his place. He came to the King's bridle hand, and clung there, not to be dislodged by any other, for the rest of the hunt.

When he came again into the chamber he had been given at Windsor, there was Perce Creswell waiting for him beside the fire. So Norfolk sent everyone away, and then Perce drew out of his doublet the letter which Lord Darcy had written three days ago at Templehurst. The duke took it, but before he opened it he asked:

"Will he do according to my counsel?"

Perce shook his head. "By no means could I prevail on him."

So Norfolk read the letter through, hurrying on to the part he least liked to read, and reading with a shrinking mind.

"Alas, my good lord," it was written in Darcy's bold, round, tumbling hand,—

> Alas that ever ye, being a man of so much honor, and great experience, should advise or choose me to be a man of any such sort or fashion, to betray or deceive any living man, French, Scot, yea or Turk. Of my faith! to get and win to me and my heirs four of the best duke's lands in France, or to be King there, I would not do it, to no living person.

About an hour later Perce Creswell stood before my Lord Privy Seal, looking down at the table which was heaped with papers; among them was a very dainty silver-studded leash for a hound; there was a little wrought coffer, too, of steel work overlaying some light colored horn; the coffer stood open, and from it trailed a pair of beads of ivory and cornelian; the room was warm and smelt heavily, though sweetly, of musk.

"What my Lord Darcy wrote to my master," Perce said, "I do not know."

"No?" Cromwell did not raise his eyes from his two plump hands, spread starfish wise, on the table before him. "But if there were words that you can remember—"

Perce said: "My Lord Darcy showed himself much displeased at my master's letter. He went about the room, halting on his staff, saying, 'I cannot do it. I cannot do it, in no wise, for I have made promise to the contrary.'"

"Ah!" Cromwell snatched at a word. "A promise?"

"So he said. And he said further—'It shall never be said that old Tom shall have one traitor's tooth in his head. Not the King nor none other alive shall make me do an unlawful act.'"

"Fie!" said Cromwell, but softly, "is it an unlawful act to take or kill a rebel?"

"I say what I heard," Perce mumbled, and Cromwell nodded for him to proceed. "Then he, leaning at a window and fretting at the catch thereof, said: 'My coat armor was never stained with any such blot.' And he said: 'My Lord's Grace, your master, knows well enough what a nobleman's promise is.' And again: 'For he that promiseth to be true to one and deceiveth him may be called a traitor, which shall never be said of me.'"

"Why," said Cromwell, "here's a great talk of promise, and promise again." He looked up, so that Perce saw his bland, quiet face, with the sharp pig's eyes. "And did my Lord Darcy seem to bear your master an ill will for his counsel?"

Perce looked down at his cap. "He believed not that it came of my lord's device."

"Then of whom did he conceive that it came?"

Perce shook his head. He wished he did not so clearly remember what my lord had said as to that man of whose device he conceived this thing had come.

Cromwell picked up the pair of beads, and began to run the pretty things through his fingers, but he was not praying. He smiled, thinking, "Surely my ears should have burned—" Then he stopped smiling. "Surely, God willing," he thought, "those words shall return home to roost."

"And was that all?" he asked.

Perce, greatly relieved, said: "That was all, bating sundry great oaths."

November 18

From the windows of Wressel Castle you could not see twenty yards across the flat deserted meadows, the mist lay so thick. It crept also into the house, filling the rooms with a clinging chill, for it was a fog that followed on frost. Kit Aske, waiting while the servant went up to inquire whether the grand captain would receive him, felt the ache of his back which came with such weather, and chewed the bitterness of having to wait on Robin's convenience, and of hearing Robin called "the grand captain."

When they brought him upstairs to the Earl's bedchamber—"No less," thought Kit, "will content his pride"—Robin was standing in doublet and hosen while Will Wall helped him into the velvet and steel brigandine.

He put Will by and crossed the room to Kit, shrugging himself into the coat as he came, and laying his hands on Kit's shoulders, kissed him lightly and went back to the fire. Kit was nothing softened by the greeting, nor by Robin's casual, "Well, Kit, you're welcome. Now about those fellows of Skipton—" Not even if Robin were in a hurry to be gone did that excuse his positive dictatorial brevity, the manner in which he interrupted, or contradicted, Kit; Kit did not even try to conceal his resentment; soon they were at it ding-dong, disputing whether or no, had the grand captain chosen to attack, he could have taken Skipton Castle.

Yet the quarrel, which might have eased Kit's mind, was constantly interrupted; a gentleman would knock and look in to ask a question; the clerk steadily writing at the corner of the room in a welter of papers would come forward with a pen for the grand captain to put his name to a letter; Robin must, for this that or t'other reason, take his attention from the argument, so that he only seemed to sustain his part in it for a pastime; and that was bitter to Kit.

So, at last, he himself broke it off, saying, "But whether it were Skipton or the King's Tower at London you would say you should take it. Yet it was not to speak of this that I came. Shall I speak with you alone?"

Aske looked at him. "You shall. But I may not stay long."

They were silent till Will, the clerk, and a boy who was trussing up such of Aske's harness as he was not to wear, went out of the room.

"Well," said Aske, "now what will you say?"

If ever there had been any motive of brotherly kindness which had brought Kit here, by now he had forgotten it; certainly he found a sour pleasure in the news he brought.

"There is," said he, "a general pardon offered, but ten are exempted therefrom, of whom, you, brother, are the first."

Robin had gone away across the room. On a stool between the windows there was a trussing coffer bound with iron. He tried the lid, and when he found it locked nodded to himself. Then, but as if Kit had only half his attention, he said:

"That I knew," and went to the bed and began to rummage among the stuff cast down there, muttering something about a key. Yet he did hear what Kit said, for when Kit had finished urging him—"for the sake of all us Askes that be loyal"—to sue for his pardon at the next meeting with the Duke of Norfolk at Doncaster, he answered sharply that he would do it only in so far as all the commons did, "And as the King shall grant our just demands. And now," said he, "if that be all you want with me, I can stay no longer," and, giving Kit barely time to reply, went out of the chamber.

Kit stood still where he was for one long minute. He had come, he told himself, to give a brother warning. Well, he would stay for another purpose, and it was Robin's own fault that he did so. But in order to accomplish that purpose Kit must appear to be good friends with the great captain. He went off, as quickly as he might, after his brother.

Robin was standing in the great court with the reins in his hand. Kit went near, and spoke in his ear.

"You'd best take care."

"How?"

"Not so loud." Kit tipped his head back toward the hall. "They are using ugly talk in there, grudging at you because you would make them ride in haste without their dinner. They say that a man is worth his meat, or else his service is but ill. And one said that you use them no better than slaves."

"Well?"

Kit said: "It is not well," but the talk of the commons had been balm to his sore mind. "The end," he said, "will be that either they'll kill you, or deliver you over as a traitor, like Jacques Dartnell, or William Wallace the Scot."

Robert Aske cried out suddenly, very loud, "Jesus! Will they?" and laughed in Kit's face. He left Kit standing by the horses and went running up the steps to the door of the hall. Kit lost sight of him then, but he could hear his voice, as he rated the men with a kind of cheerful ferocity and in very damaging terms; sow-bellied swill-bowls was the prettiest name he had for them.

Kit clenched his hands. "Now! Now! Will ye endure it?" He did not speak the words but something in him was crying after that fashion to the men in the hall.

"Come on you!" He heard Robin's voice again with a laugh in it. "Out you go first, since you are the smallest"; and the great captain came to the door again holding by the ear and one wrist a big, bearded fellow who yelled and swung his other arm like a flail, but aimlessly. At the top of the steps Aske loosed him with a shove that sent him sprawling down into the yard. There was a crowd of commons in the doorway now; one of them laughed, and then they all laughed with a great gust.

When the great captain had gone, and the men, for whom he would not wait, were scurrying to get horses saddled and away, Kit went back to the earl's chamber upstairs. Will Wall had been busy here. His master's coat and doublet were folded and laid on top of a chest at the bed foot. The litter of stuff on the bed was tidied away too; not a paper was to be seen anywhere; the clerk had gone, taking with him his little desk and all his writing gear. But the trussing coffer was still there.

The great house was very quiet now that all the men had gone clattering out after Aske. The fire was dying down; Will Wall, nor no one, Kit thought, cared for the comfort of the

great captain's brother. He listened. He went, stepping softly on
the rushes, to the door, to see that the latch had fallen home.
Then he came to the great bed, and, still listening, began to shift
the curtains along the tester rod; the old silk and velvet smelt
sharply of dust as he moved them.

Something fell with a little thud. He stooped and picked up
a dark green leather pouch; it had silver-gilt aglets on the ends of
the thongs that drew up the throat of it.

Kit, with his eyes on the door, undid the thongs, and felt
inside, and found the key that he had hoped for.

When he had at last put away again all the papers in the
little trussing coffer, and locked it, his hands were very cold,
but sweat was running down his back. He sat down by the fire,
and as he stirred the logs to get a blaze he ran over in his mind
the heads of all the matters that he had learned, especially the
plan for marching south in three hosts which should unite again
after Trent was passed.

Then he thought of Robin riding post to Lord Darcy at
Templehurst, and the men hammering along the road after him.
"But he hasn't my hands on a horse's mouth," he thought. He
warmed himself also with thinking how clever he had been to
find both the key, and that one writing among all the others
that was of such moment. "And it's not every man," he thought,
"could have got it all pat so soon. Robin couldn't—at least no
sooner." And Robin had done all he might to ruin the whole
Aske family, so it was but just if one of them did what he could
to save the house by discovering to the King the detestable, traitorous plans of the rebels.

Lord Darcy sat by the fire in the privy chamber at Templehurst. He said: "Thomas Cromwell was with the King before you came to him?"

Bowes nodded; he was sparing of words. Rafe Ellerker said that they'd seen him come out as they waited. "But," he added, "I think he's painted blacker than need be. After, when he spoke to us, he said he wishes well to the North Country and we should know it."

"He does, does he?"

Aske, speaking from beyond the group beside the fire, said it was time they came to the tenor of the messengers' charge, and Lord Darcy agreed. So they sat down much as they stood, my lord, Sir Robert Constable, Sir Rafe, Bowes, and Master Challoner at the fire—Aske astride of a bench beside the table; he drew a pile of clean paper to him and tried a pen on his nail. There would be letters to write after this news.

Sir Rafe and Master Bowes, one prompting the other, gave their account of their mission to the King. None of the others said a word while they spoke; Lord Darcy listened, resting his elbow on the arm of the chair and his head on his hand; Constable stared at his feet; Master Challoner teased at the pilgrim's badge on his breast, pulling and twirling at a loose thread between his fingers; Aske after a little threw his leg across the bench and sat with his back to them all, jabbing with the pen at the table.

When the messengers had finished there was a little silence, and then Aske said, without turning about:

"Why did you not tell the truth to the King?"

"The truth?" Rafe Ellerker cried sharply.

"You say you told him that the gentlemen were taken by the commons and forced to swear the oath."

"And we were. You were too. You told us so yourself."

Aske turned and looked at him. "Would you go down into the hall now, Rafe, and tell my fellows what you told the King? Well? Will you not answer?"

Bowes answered instead of Ellerker. "The King's Grace," he said, "was very angry. I think we only spoke what we dared. I know I dared not have spoken bolder."

"But," said Aske, "if none dare tell the King the truth how can he know it? It was your charge, to tell him, and you did not dare."

"Of course," put in Ellerker in a cold, unpleasant tone, "Robin would have dared."

Darcy lifted his hand.

"The captain is right. Let the King and Cromwell think that there is the thickness of a thumbnail between the gentlemen and the commons, and they'll go about to drive in a wedge will split a mill post."

Bowes stood up, and then Rafe Ellerker; it was Rafe who spoke.

"We have made our report to you. If there's no more ye would know, give us leave—" They moved toward the door, and none of the others bade them stay. But at the door Bowes hung back.

"Among other words of reproach His Grace said these, or near as I can remember—'Now the intent of your pilgrimage with the devotion of the pilgrims may appear, for who can reckon that foundation good which is contrary to God's commandment, or the executors to be good men, which contrary to their allegiance, presume to order their Prince, whom God,' said he, 'commanded them to obey, whatever he be, yea though he should not direct them justly.' The which hearing, no subject but must be troubled in his conscience, being in arms against his Prince."

"Ho!" cried Darcy, "and is your conscience even so?"

Bowes replied that yea, so it was, and went away with unshaken dignity.

When he had gone there was a silence, and then Darcy spoke:

"Well, Master Aske, and what do you think of this answer of the King's?"

"I think," said Aske, "that it is no answer at all."

November 19

When most people in the great house at Templehurst were asleep Aske still sat writing in Lord Darcy's chamber. The old lord was in bed, but awake, sitting propped up against pillows, in a fine embroidered linen nightshirt and cap, with a black velvet nightgown about his shoulders.

Aske got up, sighed, stretched, yawned, and went over to the fire. He threw on a couple of logs and dusted his hand on his hosen.

"Are you done?" my lord asked.

"Near done." He clapped his hands upon his backside and gave a little laugh. "You know, my lord, they say that a lawyer needs three things—an iron hand, a brazen face, and a leaden breach. But I have fallen out of the way of much sitting these last months."

He went back to the table and took up his pen again. "I've near done," he said again, and now he was not laughing. "I wish we were as near the end of our great affair."

Darcy said, by the Mass, he wished so too, and just then a servant knocked and let in Sir Robert Constable. He sat down on the settle, and let his gown fall away from his knees so that the fire should warm his bare shins.

"Have you opened it to him?" he asked of my lord, tipping his head toward Aske.

"No."

"Opened what? I've done now," Aske said, without looking round. He tipped the sand back off the last letter, folded it, and tossed it onto the pile of those that were ready for sealing. Then he came over to the fire. "Well?" he prompted Sir Robert.

But it was Darcy who said: "We all think alike of the King's answer. If I mistake not, we all think now that the matter shall come to battle."

He waited, and Aske, looking down into the fire, muttered that the North was ready. "And where erst we took up one man to go on our pilgrimage, if we go forward now, we shall take up seven."

Darcy said: "One trained man-at-arms is better than seven of your armed husbandmen. The Emperor has the best men-at-arms in Christendom."

Aske began to say, with some heat, that Yorkshire yeomen were as good as any—then he stopped short. "What do you mean?" he asked sharply.

"Look outside the door!" Darcy bade him. Aske raised his eyebrows, but did as he was told.

"Rawlyns is there?" Darcy asked when he came back.

Aske said: "At the stair foot."

"Good. You ask what I mean. Then this, in a word. We must send and ask help of the Emperor."

"No," said Aske quickly, but Darcy went on—"Two years ago Master Chapuys, the Emperor's ambassador, promised help. There were those then who thought that the King's proceedings would not be endured. Now, if we ask, and if the Emperor will send men, we have Hull for a port for their landing—"

"And we have the friar," Sir Robert broke in, leaning forward to look up into Aske's face, "for a messenger."

"What friar?"

"An old man, and honest. Waldby. You know him. He will go."

Aske went away to the table and stood quite a long time fiddling with the pens there. They watched him all the time. At last he came back.

"My lord," said he, "Sir Robert—this pilgrimage that we have set forth upon—it's God's business, though"—he dropped his voice and spoke so low and hurriedly that they hardly heard the words—"though it is done our way not His. But," he looked from one to the other of them, "let's finish it with His help, and without more treason than we need."

Sir Robert said in his plain way, "We knew you would not like it."

But Darcy began to argue. Just because it was God's business, they must bring it to a good end. "If we fail, the church and all our liberties will be quite overset. Cromwell, his servants, and these new bishops will pull all down. Would you have that?"

"No. No."

"And you would fight that it should not be?"

"Oh!" cried Aske. "But this is another matter."

"And it is yet another to suffer God's church in England to be rooted out, heretics to bear rule, and teach what they will. Why, in fifty years, if they have their way, there will be none, barring a few old men, who have heard anything but that which the King hath been pleased they shall learn."

Aske said, "I must think." He began to walk about the room, and they let him alone. At last he came back and stood looking down at Sir Robert.

"Are you for it?"

"I'm with Tom," Constable said. "Here's Cromwell making Bowes—even Bowes—believe he loves our commons well, and the same day he writes that letter we took, saying he'll make a fearful example of them, and of us, to all subjects while the world shall last. What will they else but trick us if they may?"

Aske gave a sort of groan. "So we shall trick them first. I think I know now what it means—'*Quicunque enim acceperint gladium, gladio peribunt.*' It's not only that a man shall be killed by the sword. But all he fights for perishes, while he fights, and it perishes by his own sword. Well—" He threw out his hands. "Since I am in I must wade on till I'm over. But God knows whether once there I'll find I have left Him behind me on the hither side."

"Then—you consent—" said Darcy.

Aske nodded. So Constable went to the door and bade Rawlyns to fetch the friar.

November 24

This was the last day of the council of the commons at York, and the stormiest. They disputed till the candles were lit, and the painted glass in the windows of the great chapter house showed only looming gloomy colors in which the flames were dully reflected. This day they spoke of their grievances, and men, growing angry, hammered with their fists on the arms of the monks' stalls, and the commons used the same oaths that they used for swearing at their sheepdogs and plow beasts.

It was against Cromwell that they spoke most freely, but they grew very bold also against the King, Sir Francis Bigod recalling how Rehoboam, by young foolish counsel, had so used the commons of Israel that they would no longer suffer him to reign over them. Then another of the gentlemen said it did not need Israel for a lesson, "For in this noble realm who reads the Chronicles of Edward II shall learn what jeopardy he was in by reason of Piers de Gaveston, and other such counselors."

"Aye," cried one of the commons from near the border, "and a Prince should rule by justice mixed with mercy and pity, and not by rigor to put men to death; for though it is said that our bodies be the King's, when he has killed a man he cannot make him live again."

Another asked, "What of the King's vices, which men may say truly have most need to be spoken on, to be reformed of all things, for if the head be sick, how can the body be whole?"

And then they came round to Cromwell again, calling him "the Loller and false flatterer." "He says," said Sir Richard Tempest, "that he will make the King the richest Prince in Christendom," and at that one of the rough fellows from the dales broke in—"But he can have no more of us than we have, and that he hath already, nor is not satisfied—as a man can have no more of a cat than to have its skin." They must have their laugh at that, before Sir Richard could go on. "Yet I think this Cromwell," said he, "goes about to make the King the poorest Prince in Christendom, for when by such pillage he has lost the hearts of his baronage and poor commons, the riches of the realm are spent."

Then a big man with a beard jumped up, a yeoman from beyond Beverley.

"If that traitor live," he cried, "none of us who are head yeomen or gentlemen can trust to any pardon. Some other device will be found whereby we shall lose our life, goods, and lands. It is better to try battle than to submit."

"Aye, and good to take time when time is fair," said another.

When they saw Sir Robert Constable on his feet they were all silent, for they knew that he was one of the chief leaders. He said his counsel was that as they had already broken one point with the King (he meant by taking and keeping a ship that had come into Hull), he for his part would break another. "Let's have no meeting with my Lord of Norfolk at Doncaster yet, but make all the country sure from Trent northward, and then I doubt not but all Lancashire, Cheshire, Derbyshire, and the parts thereabouts will join with us. Then" (and he laughed), "then I would condescend to a meeting."

But at that Aske got up slowly, leaning with his hands on the arms of his chair. He said surely the commons must go to Doncaster. "It's all our whole duty to declare our griefs to the King. If he refuses, then our cause is just. But first we shall ask for a free pardon and a free Parliament."

There was a great outcry then, one advising battle, and another to treat. When the noise died a little one of the captains, called Walker, a man with a voice like a bull's, cried to the great captain, "Look you well upon that matter, to have a free Parliament, for it is your charge. For if you do not you shall repent it."

Aske, who had sat down again, gave no more answer than to bow his head. It was Sir Robert and the other gentlemen who at last quieted the commons. After some more debate the meeting broke up, and all went away, excepting the great captain. He, when Constable asked was he coming, only shook his head; he had a paper in his hand, one of the many petitions of grievances, and seemed to be studying it. Sir Robert, who had thought just now that Aske had spoken too roundly in differing from a friend, was nettled by his silence, so, shrugging his shoulders, went off, leaving him there, with all the candles burning around him, in the empty chapter house. When once Aske was alone, and no one there to see, he leaned forward, letting his head hang down, as he hugged the great pain that wrung him.

Will Wall, who waited at the Silver Crescent with the other servants, took quite a long time to cover the short distance between the tavern and the chapter house, being, by the time the meeting broke up, pretty sodden with drink. When he reached the chapter house only the porter stood there, swinging his keys. Will leaned against the door jamb and looked into the high, vaulted place. He rumpled up his hair all over his head and said, in a blurred, reflective tone, "They've gone away. Where've they gone to?"

"The grand captain's there."

"By Cock! He is, is he?" said Will. "And what's he doing there? Cock's Bones! I'll go see."

Aske heard him coming and raised his head. He knew from the sound of Will's footsteps, before ever he saw him, what the fellow had been up to. And now Will was leaning over him, swaying and bleary. Aske gave him a push.

"Take your ugly face away. You stink of ale. I shall be sick." He got up heavily and began to go toward the door.

"Lord!" cried Will, with a cackle of laughter, when he saw Aske stumble, "if I'm drunk, you're drunk too."

Aske said through his teeth, the pain being very severe, "I'm not. It's the colic." But Will would have it that his master was drunken too, and linking arms rambled on beside him out of the chapter house and into the moonlit streets singing loudly. In spite of the pain Aske could not help an inward wry smile, so like to a pair of homing roysterers they must appear; the height of the dismal joke came when they two with one consent diverged in order to be vilely sick. "God's Mother!" said Aske to himself, wiping his forehead with a shaking hand and laughing feebly, "Like man, like master!"

They got back somehow, and after some time, and Aske called to Chris Clark to come and undress him. But Chris came up the stairs saying there was "a gentleman from the South," and he looked at Aske with a look that meant more than the words. So Aske sat down on the bed and the gentleman came in, and delivered his news, which was of moment, and urgent, and very secret; and then Aske must write a letter to my Lord Darcy, and Chris Clark must mount and take it. By this time Will was snoring, and all the others in the house off to bed, so Aske lay down, dressed as he was, to sweat and shiver, to fall dizzily to sleep, and to waken hearing a voice cry in his ear, "Look you well upon that matter, for it is your charge. For if you do not you shall repent it." In his dream it had been his charge to prop up with his two hands the tower of the church at Aughton, which was toppling over, and he had known that his hands could not avail.

November 30

Malle and Wat stood on the edge of the Swale just below the stepping-stones. Malle had the nuns' big mule, Black Thomas, by the bridle; the steward had lent him to Gib to take a sack of wheat and a sack of rye to the mill to be ground for maslin. Thomas stooped his gray velvet muzzle, soft as a night moth, down to the water, and began to draw in deep gurgling drafts.

Malle let him finish and then nudged him with her elbow and he began to go over. The water was biting cold so that Malle and Wat went trampling and splashing to be quick across, but Thomas trod as daintily as though he could walk upon eggs without cracking them, tossing his ears and switching his long tail.

When they were over Malle stopped to wring out the skirts of her gown, and Wat began to dance about to warm his feet again. Black Thomas tripped the bridle out of Malle's hand and went on along the track by himself.

Malle said, in a muffled voice, for her head was between her knees as she tried to reach the hem of her skirt behind—

"All's smitten through with Him. Love, frail as smoke, piercing as a needle—near—here. He that's light has come into the clod."

She stood up and for a minute seemed to listen to the unceasing voice of the Swale.

"So," she said, "yon brown cows, and the grass, and us, all things that's flesh, for that He is flesh, are brothers now to God."

Then, "Look," she cried, "look. There's Thomas rubbing off the rye sack against the tree. Run! Run!"

So they ran, while Malle cried out "Shoo! Tom. Shoo! Tom, wicked old whoreson!"

December 9

Robert Aske came home to Aughton in the dusk. The windows of the hall were lit, and he could see, as he crossed the court and the dogs met him, the arms of Aske, de la Haye, Clifford, and Bigod shining colored upon the colorless twilight. Inside the hall door there was a warm steamy smell, such as would always hang about the house once a month while the ale was brewing. A couple of servants were just coming out of the kitchens; they were carrying dishes of eels in broth; when they saw him they cried, "God's Mother!" and "It's Master Robin!" and "Hast 'a come home, master?" and one of them tipped his dish so that the broth ran over, as he turned to shout over his shoulder that Master Robin was come home. So Aske must stay a while in the hall while the servants crowded in, to tell them what had been concluded at Doncaster yesterday. When he stopped speaking there was a deal of shouting, and as he went down the passage to the parlor, a great burst of talking and laughter, and someone singing a song of the pilgrims that others took up.

He went into the parlor and shut the door behind him, and the noise outside was cut off. "Give you good evening," he said, but for a moment they all sat in silence round the table, staring at him, and saying not a word.

Then Jack cried, "Robin!" and started a fit of coughing that bent him double. Dame Nell turned her eyes from Jack to his brother, with a look as fiercely accusing as if Robin had been to blame for Jack's cough as well as for everything else. Beside Nell was a young girl, very pretty, whom Aske had never seen before. She half got up, and then sat down again. Jack's two younger boys, together on a bench, lifted their eyes from their trenchers and stared as they ate. But Julian, Jack's youngest daughter, came rushing across the room, oversetting a cup of ale on the table; she threw her arms about Aske's neck and kissed him.

"Julian!" said her mother, and the girl went back to her place, but with a smoldering, obstinate look.

Jack got up then and kissed his brother and asked, very husky, "Well, Robin, what news?" but Dame Nell cried, "No, I'll have no talk of these treasonous doings."

So Robert sat down, and since no one else spoke, asked, "Where's Hob?"

It was Nell answered him. "Hob's in London—safe."

"Good!" said he, in that same cheerful tone that always enraged Kit, and now had the same effect on Nell, who cried, "And no thanks to you for that."

But Jack said hastily, "This is Hob's wife," and Robin looked at the pretty girl, who smiled again at him, though dubiously, and with a sidelong glance at her mother-in-law.

As they ate their supper, talking disjointedly, and in a thorny, uneasy way, Robert wondered if Will Monkton were having such a cold homecoming as this. He thought also of my Lord Darcy, of Constable, of many other men both gentle and simple with whom he had been in company so lately. His heart felt hollow as a bucket and heavy as lead.

It was early yet when he stood up, and said now he'd take his candle and go to bed.

"Julian and the little ones," said Dame Nell, looking down at her sewing, "have the room you and Kit had. But there's a bed in the room over the buttery, and Will Wall can carry up a pallet from the hall."

The room over the buttery was an upper servant's room but Robert did not care for that. He said, "I'll tell Will," and then Julian jumped up.

"I'll see to it," she said, and went out in front of him with such a look over her shoulder at her mother as made Robert think, "Here's one that needs marrying, or there'll be bickering in this house." Jack certainly ought to have beaten her before things came to such a pitch that a maid could behave so to her mother.

But as they went side by side through the hall she tripped up his thoughts about her by suddenly coming very close, and taking his hand in hers. She gave it a hard, quick squeeze, with a sort of shake, and dropped it again, saying, "You shall sleep in your own room. No, you shall. Dickon and Jack will never wake at moving." So, as they went up after Will and a maid servant, Robert Aske was thinking not of her ill behavior to her mother, but of the way she had caught his hand, and how she alone of them all had welcomed him.

Upstairs, when the two little boys had been carried off sleeping, and the room put to rights, and Will had been sent off by Julian to fetch candle for his master, Aske took his niece by her two hands meaning to kiss her good night. But instead of letting herself be kissed she shoved him masterfully back toward the bed, sat down herself, and dragged him down beside her.

"Now," said she, "tell me what you stayed to tell the folk in the hall tonight. For I heard your voice before you came in."

He looked at her sitting beside him on the bed. She was at that stage of growth when a girl can change in a few months, and she had changed since he saw her last September. Then she had been a coltish creature, with abrupt, almost harsh, features, dark straight brows and a square face. Now she was ungainly no longer, though she was big, broad, and strongly built, being far more like in that to the Cliffords than she was either to Askes or to her mother's Rither kin. In face she had a likeness to old Sir Robert—and, Aske supposed, to himself—being a maid far from maidenly prettiness, with a dark line of hair upon her upper lip; yet she had a fine mantling flush at times, that gave her a sudden comeliness, and she wore it now.

"Tell me—everything," she urged.

"Do they know nothing at Aughton?" he asked, half teasing.

"Who would tell *me*?" she cried, rudely and scornfully. "You heard my mother tonight. And my father dare not—" His look checked her but she added obstinately, "The servants think that I am as my mother and my father."

Aske thought, "Surely she should be well beaten. Or should have been a lad."

"But," she said, as if she knew his thought, "if I'd been Hob, Uncle Robin, I'd not have left you."

"I sent Hob back," he told her sternly.

"You couldn't have stopped me from coming on."

He turned his face and looked at her. It was all wrong that she should speak so. She was a willful, saucy, unbroken wench, but to be with her was like warming his hands at a fire. He half smiled. "Truly, and I think I could not, neither. Well. What shall I tell you?"

"There was a great council at York. I know that but no more."

"Then we came to Pomfret—" He locked his hands about one knee and began to talk. As he talked he forgot the familiar room in which he knew by heart each knot and shake in the beams, every twist of the painted leafy trellis pattern on the walls; he forgot the single candle burning on the stool by them, and casting their shadows huge and distorted, across the floor and halfway up the door; he forgot his niece in her old rayed gown of blue and red, and white country kerchief. Instead of these he saw the crowded hall at Pomfret where my Lord Darcy, Constable, and all the rest, gentlemen and commons, sat on benches, like the King's Parliament at Westminster, a great, solemn and an earnest company of men.

"The best blood of the North," he told her, "was there, and that's not all noble blood, July, but also the yeomen and the poor commons of Yorkshire." He stopped and she saw his eye had kindled, but when he went on it was more lightly.

"We talked and talked. And when we did not talk, I wrote. We drew up articles that the duke should be given to carry to the King. We took three days over it, and the spiritual men over their articles took two more."

"And then?"

"Then ten of us went to Doncaster. No. Not I. But those ten carried the articles, and asked for safe conducts. Next day three hundred from our part rode into Doncaster. We lay at the Grey Friars and my Lord of Norfolk at the White Friars. Then we chose twenty, and those twenty of us went to him. And there, being chosen to speak for all, I argued the articles."

"You!" she cried with a bright flush, and a ring of pride in her voice that he could not miss. He put his arm round her, and felt her body, young, solid, yet supple, close against his.

"The duke read out to us the King's free pardon for us all, and declared His Grace's promise of a free Parliament, and pledged his own word that the abbeys should stand till that Parliament be met.

"When I got back to Pomfret that night it was too late to declare the same to the commons, but next morning early I sent the bellman round, and had them all to the Cross and told them. After, I went again to Doncaster, but then comes one riding in haste from Lord Lumley, saying that the commons would not be content but if they saw the King's Pardon and the Great Seal. They were crying again to fire the beacons, and that we gentlemen had betrayed them."

"Shame on them!" she cried.

He shook his head. "The commons," he told her, "are like dogs that have been scared when they were whelps. They'll trust a man, and then at a word or a look they'll remember what men once did to them, and, when they remember, they'll either run, or bite. And after they'll trust again.

"So back I went to Pomfret, by consent of all, and the rest of that day I talked. Mass! I marvel my tongue was not quite worn out talking to the commons there. Good men they are, niece, but obstinate, and some of them have skulls as thick as a clog sole, and it's as difficult to draw a notion out of their heads as to drive it in. But by evening I had contented them, and sent to Doncaster to have Herald Lancaster with the pardon; who came, after dark."

He looked at Julian, and gave a little laugh. "There were, among those gentlemen with me, I'll not say who, that would have had me turn all out once more that night to hear the herald's message, fearing, they said, that the commons should murder us in our beds. But I said, 'Well, if tonight I be murdered, in my bed it shall be, for nothing shall keep me out of it longer!'"

"So next morning, on St. Thomas's Hill, where Constable and I had used to take the musters, the King's Pardon was declared to the commons, and received of them, and then—"

He stopped abruptly, and looked at Julian as though he saw her again after being away at a great distance. "Then—they all went way—I watched them most of that morning, from the top of the keep. When they'd all gone, and the town was empty, except for us few gentlemen—I—I could have wept."

She asked, after a little silence, "Was that this morning?"

"No. Yesterday." But to him it seemed half a year ago already. He said, more to himself than to her, "And I should be on my knees to God for His grace to us, instead of talking so like a thankless fool."

"What then?"

He went on, after a moment, "Then we that were left rode back again to Doncaster, and there, in the White Friars' frater we all, kneeling on our knees, tore off our badges—look, you can see the mark." She looked, and saw where his finger touched the breast of his doublet, a line of stitching and a patch where the color seemed deeper than round about. "I prayed, and they granted me, that they would never call me captain anymore.

The white rod I carried I tried to break across my knee, but I could not."

"What did you do with it then?"

"Kicked it under the table. The poor friars will have a fine sweeping up to do with our badges and all."

He was smiling, but she stretched out her arms with the hands clenched, and letting out a deep breath cried, "So you did that which you set out to do."

"If God speed us. The duke will go to the King now, and the King must ratify the terms."

She started round, and stared at him.

"So it's not finished yet?"

"Our part is finished. And—yes—it is as good as finished."

She sat brooding with her chin on her fists, and after a while he answered her silence, almost as though she had been a man, not a chit of a girl.

"The duke," he said, "spoke in the King's name, knowing the King's mind. With a free pardon, and a free Parliament, we need fear nothing. The rest will be done by that free Parliament, held here in York."

"And the duke?" She turned to him with her obstinate, truculent look. "You will trust him? And the King?"

He rebuked her sternly, almost fiercely for that, saying that he marveled to hear her speak so. "For if," he said, confusedly but with vehemence, "if I may not trust—if such men—if—surely I would rather die." Then he was silent, for in the bottom of his mind there was a thought which he could not find words for, nor even plainly know its meaning. But like a dread in a dream it lay there nameless—if there could be such treachery as that she glanced at, he had rather not have been born, for God Himself could not prevail against it.

But he shook it off, and came back to the ordinary world.

Julian sat beside him, crimson and scowling after his rebuke. He put his hand on her shoulder.

"I thought once," he said, "much as you do about my Lord of Norfolk, because of a thing that was told me. He would have had one to—well, to betray me."

"But that one would not?"

"He would not. And now I see that the duke so dealt because of his loyalty to the King. So I count he shall be loyal also to us. He spoke long with me, Julian, most graciously and frankly too, standing in a window at the Grey Friars."

"I see. So it is well." She jumped up from the bed, then put her clenched fists against either of his cheeks, chafing them roughly.

"You great hoyden!" he said, laughing and catching her wrists.

"It is because I am so glad."

He got up and kissed her, bidding her "Good night, sweetheart."

December 18

Julian Aske slipped into the dairy, sure that no one had seen her. She dipped a canful of cream, and stood with it in her hand behind the door, spying through the crack between the hinges till Uncle Robin should come through the gate. From the

window upstairs she had seen him walking across the ings, so
there would not be long to wait. When he came she would walk
out, with the can of cream in her hand, meet him in the court
as if by chance, and give him warning. Then he had only to turn
and go out of the gate again, and to Aughton Landing where
already Will Wall and Uncle Will Monkton must be waiting
with the horses.

It was a beautiful plan, all her own in conception and execution, but it failed. She had not been in the dairy two minutes
when she heard her mother calling, "Julian! Julian!" She stood
still, making no answer. But one of the servants cried, "Mistress
July's in the dairy." "Send her to me," Mistress Nell answered.
Julian whisked out into the court. If she was quick enough it
might be possible to do her mother's bidding and be back in
time. But it was not possible. She had only lifted down from
its peg the big fat bank of woolen yarn for which her mother
sent her, when she heard her father's voice hailing, "Hey! Robin,
what have you been at?"

"I've been at missing every duck I aimed for between here
and Bubwith. All but this one, and he, I swear, ran on my bolt
for pure charity. And, for pure amazement to see him fall, I fell
into the bog."

Julian looking down from the little low window of the
weaving loft could see them below—her father, who must this
moment have returned from Selby, on horseback; her uncle,
mired to the waist, and drenched with rain beside, for there had
been sharp sleety showers driven on a northerly wind since sun-
rise. He had a crossbow on his shoulder, and the charitable duck

dangled from his hand. Now he waved its corpse in farewell, and went on to the hall.

Julian knew that in the hall waited Master Peter Mewtas, Gentleman of the King's Bedchamber, with the King's letter summoning Master Aske to London.

Too late to give him warning, but as soon as she might, she went after her uncle. He and Mr. Mewtas stood facing each other in the great tower window of the hall where the bow racks stood. Mr. Mewtas was a big well-looking man of about thirty, both fine and neat from his curling fair hair and short beard to his broad-toed velvet shoes, for he had had time to shift from his wet clothes into a suit of fine black cloth with carnation colored sleeves; there were jewels in his ears that gave a winking flash in the firelight when he moved his head.

Robert Aske, dribbling bog water from his boots, coat, and hosen, stood with his head bent over a letter. His hood was off, and he held it dangling beside his knee; Julian, watching him from the shadow of the screens, could see that his jaw was very set, and that the hand that held the hood shook, though ever so little. She thought, with a sort of pang, "He's frightened," and was both shocked and horribly daunted. Then she called herself a fool. Of course it was the chill of his drenched clothes. She moved forward, and he turned quickly and saw her.

She knew, by the way he turned and by his look, that he had needed someone. She was glad to be that one who had come. But she dropped her eyes as she curtseyed, lest Mr. Mewtas should divine from a glance that there was any confederacy between them.

"Niece," Aske said, "will you be pleased to send us some wine. And let someone set me dry stuff ready in my chamber."

"I will see to it, sir," she said, and went.

She wanted to bring the wine again herself, but did not because he had said, "Send us wine," and she would exactly obey. But as she waited a long time upon the stairs, hearing below the voices of her father and mother, as well as those of Mr. Mewtas and Uncle Robin, her teeth were chattering, partly for excitement, partly for dread that she had not rightly understood him.

When he came up, and she saw how he spied about and how his face lit when he saw her, she knew that she had not mistaken.

"I have set everything ready," she told him.

He laughed silently, and whispered as he came up after her, "I said I must put off my wet clothes. I stood close to the fire till the bog mud stank, and Mr. Mewtas could not speak for holding his nose."

But when they were together in his room and the door shut he did not laugh.

"Julian," said he, "will you help me?"

She scowled at him because he needed to ask, and he understood and gave her a smile. "Find me Will, or Chris Clark," he said, "and send him for me to your Uncle Monkton at Ellerton."

She laughed out at that. "I have already sent Chris. I sent him as soon as that perfumed popinjay bird below came in."

"Tut! niece," he murmured, "the King's messenger. But—"

"Listen," she cried impatiently, and reached up her hands to untie his doublet at the neck. She did it with a sharp tug, and began to undo the buttons, telling him as she did so that, "that fellow's servants watch the stables, I think, but if you should go out by the orchard and so to the ings, it's like they shall not see you. I told Chris to tell Uncle Monkton to wait by the thicket of thorns. There are four horses down on the ings still. Arrowsmith's the best, and then Pippin. I told Chris to saddle those two."

He caught her by the wrists. "But for what?"

"To ride. To get away." She stamped her foot at him.

"Where should I ride? Into the sea? To the Scots?"

She understood then that all her plan was foolishness, and hung her head sullenly. "You will think I am a great goose."

"No." He did not smile, and there was no gentleness in his look, but she knew that this was how he searched a man's face, to judge his worth and his truth. "I think," he said, "that you are bold, ready, and faithful."

At that she flushed her finest crimson. "But," she said, "will you ride to the King?"

"This very day. Mr. Mewtas will have it so. He says it is the King's command, and indeed so the letter says, to use all dispatch. He says it must be today because there was snow near Lincoln yesterday. With this wind there is like to be more tomorrow. That is true—" Yet he was frowning as he turned to cast his doublet down on a bench.

It was then Julian remembered that he had said: "Find me Chris Clark." So, "What will you have Chris do?" she asked.

"This," he told her. "The King writes that I shall make no man privy to his letter. But my Lord Darcy I must tell of it, and send him a copy. Can you have it copied and sent, so that none knows but you and I, Chris Clark, who shall copy it, and your Uncle Monkton, who shall fetch it to my lord?"

"I shall do it," she said, and took the letter, and left him.

When she came back, and tapped on the door, she found that he was dressed, ready to ride. The suddenness of it struck her then with a great clap of fear, and she caught him by both elbows.

"Uncle, why must you go today?"

"Today or tomorrow is all one."

"But—must you go?"

He looked at her very soberly for a minute, before he said: "I must go. Some man must tell His Grace the truth of these matters. No one has told him yet how wholly all this part of his realm, lords, gentlemen, commons, are set against his proceedings. And besides these there are also many of our way of thinking in the South. If no one will tell him, then I will tell him." He smiled at her. "So it is good that the King should send for me."

"If it is good," she muttered, "why do you write secretly to my Lord Darcy?"

"You're a lawyer, are you?" he teased her, but she would not smile. "Because, though I think it is good, yet, if it should prove the contrary my lord should know on what credence and safe conduct I went."

"Uncle!" she cried, "don't—"

He shook his head at her, and she was silent.

"Now," he said, smiling at her, "down we go to meet again this—what name did you call him by?—this perfumed popin-jay bird. And like two true plotters let us look strangely on each other. And I shall chide my niece, and my niece will be froward with her uncle, which, I do fear, she is most apt to be."

She would not answer his smile, but gave him over her shoul-der a fierce, glowering look, as though she dared him to make light of himself, or of her, or of the affair in which together they were concerned. Yet the truth was she was near to tears, which she would not for the world have let him see.

Will Monkton came to Templehurst a little before sunset. It was snowing, though not heavily, and in the house it was so dark that the candles were lit already. They were just going to table when Monkton came in, so my lord bade them set for another at his own table, and Monkton sat down opposite my lord and Sir George Darcy.

It was Sir George who said, "You bring news from Master Aske?"

"Time enough after supper," said my lord, and, "You've no wine in your cup, George." But Sir George was not to be put off. "If it is a privy matter and urgent will you not, sir, speak at once apart with Master Monkton?" and he looked from one to the other. He was no wiser for what he saw in my lord's face, but it was plain that the big, slow man opposite sat, as it were, on thorns.

"Have you," my lord asked, "a letter?"

Will Monkton answered, after a pause, that he brought the copy of a letter.

"And a message?" Sir George suggested, but my lord was holding out his hand, and Monkton put the copy of the King's letter into it in silence.

When my lord had read it he laid it down beside his plate, on the side farther from his son, and began to talk about indifferent matters. But while he discoursed to Master Monkton of the price of lime and of the weight of fat porkers killed and salted last month Sir George was looking across him to the copy of the King's letter, spread open on the board. Suddenly Lord Darcy took it up and laid it before him—"For else," said he, "I can see that your eyes will take a lasting cast, from glancing so long aside."

Sir George flushed very hot at that, but he read the letter and then said to his father—yet looking also at Master Monkton:

"Will Master Aske, think you, do well to go?"

"I think," said my lord, "that he will do well, having the King's word for his safe conduct."

After that Sir George was silent, and when supper was over one of his servants came in, saying that the horses were ready and the snow falling heavy.

"So," said my lord, "you must haste away, or you shall not make Gateforth before dark."

Sir George went, having kissed his father's hand, and given Will Monkton a sour good night.

Then my lord led Monkton to a window. It was cold here away from the fire, for the wind was clotting the flakes thickly against the glass, and chill air came filtering through the lead of the window frames. But it was private, and that was what they needed.

"When," my lord asked, "will he go?"

"By now he is already some hours gone."

"Gone?"

"My niece sent this word: 'Tell my lord—he would go.'"

"Tchk!" Darcy said, and then, "By the Rood! yes. That he would." He dabbled absently with his fingertips in some of the melted snow that dribbled through the casement, and shook the drops off.

"How many did he take with him?"

"Six, and a horse boy."

"Good men? Trusty?"

"All born at Aughton."

"And that means the same." Darcy gave a little laugh. Then— "Can you catch him up if you should ride now?"

"I could try. I ride heavy."

"You shall have a good horse. Come up with him if you can, and tell him he shall leave a man and a horse at divers places along the road—Which now?" He screwed up his eyes, peering through the muffled and darkening window, but seeing the long road that led to London, and the towns strung out along it. "At Lincoln," he said, "and at Stamford, Huntingdon, Royston, and at Ware. Then if this letter and safe conduct be a trap to take him, that servant who comes with him to London can warn his fellow at Ware, and so each the next, and in a day or but little more I shall know of it. And then—" my lord drove his staff down upon the stone floor of the window—"By God's Death, I'll fetch him out of the Tower if it should cost twenty thousand men's lives."

Monkton said: "Where is the horse?"

But very late that night he knocked again at the gate of Templehurst. When they brought him in they had to lift him down from the saddle, so stiff he was with cold. He had lost himself hours ago, and ridden, he supposed, in a circle. At last, because there was nothing else for it, he had laid the reins on the horse's neck, and let it find its own way home.

December 21

Lord Privy Seal was in the great closet, overlooking the tiltyard. Before him on the table lay lists of the King's debts, under three heads—"Merchants that be contented to forbear unto a longer day," "Small sums to be paid forthwith," and "Greater sums to be paid forthwith." Privy Seal was working down the second list, checking from another paper those names against which a clerk had written, "Sol": to show that the bill was paid.

"Henry Annottes, fish monger.

"Humphrey Barrows, ire monger.

"John Sturgeon, haberdasher.

"John Horn, tallow chandler."

There was a knock at the door, and a gentleman put his head inside the room.

"My lord," said he, "His Grace comes even now through the great gallery."

Cromwell looked up, nodded, and went on with his work. Yet his ears were pricking. When the King came in he was half-way to the door, and his cap in his hand.

The King let himself down into the chair that stood beyond the table, and near to the fire. It was a fine chair, very wide and ample, and its red Spanish leather was stamped with roses and lions, and fringed with gilt and crimson. He bit his lip and eased one leg to a better position, then shot a glance at Cromwell as if he warned him not to know that the King's ulcer pained him; Cromwell stood like any clerk, pen in one hand, cap in the other, and eyes cast down demurely; yet he missed nothing.

The King said, "You sent me word he was come."

"Last night, Your Grace, late."

"Well, what manner of man?"

"A man with one eye. A little man with a big voice." Cromwell, not forgetting that the King's voice was small and high-pitched for his great bulk, added, "Over big."

The King snapped, "As to his eye, we had been told that already. As to his bigness and voice we can see for ourselves. Of what manner is he in the inward man?"

If Privy Seal had been less quick he would have accepted the rebuke. But instead he turned it neatly. "Surely," said he, "Your Grace's wit will pierce more sharply into the inward man of him than could mine. But so far as I was able to perceive he is very confident."

"Of our clemency?"

"Of that, and, as I think, also of himself."

There was a silence in which Privy Seal turned away to lay the pen in his fingers beside the others on the table.

"He came," the King asked in his voice of dangerous gentleness, "he came then willingly and without delay?"

"Doubtless," said Cromwell, "in his heart he feared, remembering his late horrid treasons. But for all Master Mewtas could see, he came willingly and cheerfully. He talked much, Master Mewtas said, by the way."

"Talked?" The King leapt on the word. "Of what?"

"Of light matters, such as shooting with the long bow."

Master Mewtas had reported, not without malice, that Master Aske had spoken very freely of the hatred which the whole North Country bore to Lord Privy Seal, being so angry with him that they would, Master Aske said, in a manner eat him.

That had not prepared Cromwell to like Aske, nor had their interview last night bettered matters, since Cromwell had found him not at all respectful.

For my Lord Privy Seal had begun graciously, promising that Master Aske should find him good lord to him.

Aske thanked him gravely for that.

"And you, for your part," said Cromwell, "shall be plain with me, opening freely to me your whole mind and stomach."

"My lord," Aske said, "I am, I think, plain with all men. But my whole mind and stomach I shall open to the King alone."

"I am His Grace's servant."

"Yes," said Aske, and left a very definite silence.

So now Cromwell said, watching the King, yet not seeming to watch him, "Of light matters, such as shooting with the long bow." He saw the King's hand clench on the handle of the little dagger that hung by a gold lace about his shoulders, and added hastily, since for him policy came before private malice—"I think, with my Lord of Norfolk, that if Your Grace uses him with fair words he will tell much, both of himself and the other traitors."

The King uncrooked his fingers from about the handle of the dagger. "You shall see how I shall use him. Have him in."

When Aske came in he saw Privy Seal first and made a gesture with his hand to his cap. Then he saw the King. He pulled his cap off and went down on his knees.

"Well, Master Aske," the King leaned forward, staring into his face, "you have come. For what have you come?"

"To hear your most merciful pardon from Your Grace's own mouth, that I have already under your Great Seal. And to answer plainly and frankly as your Grace commands, whatever it shall please you to ask me."

The King heaved himself up from his chair. He went to the window, and came back, tramping heavily, forgetting altogether to disguise the lameness of his diseased leg. He stood over Aske; Aske raised his head and they looked each other between the eyes.

"I shall," said Aske, "if Your Grace gives me good leave, tell you the truth of the causes of our pilgrimage."

There was a silence. Then the King said to Privy Seal:

"Go. Leave us alone. See that we are not interrupted."

Cromwell went out very thoughtful. It might be—he hoped it was—that His Grace could not endure that any should see him so braved. It might be—he hoped it was not—that His Grace had taken a liking to Master Aske. For the King could like, at times, a bold man, and certainly this man was extreme bold.

December 22

Master Laurence Machyn and his wife sat late at breakfast. The servants had finished theirs and gone away on their several occasions; every now and then one or other of them would go past the screens to the street door with a bundle of mourning robes over his arm, or a sheaf of long candles, or a load of painted buckram escutcheons upon staves, for there was a great burial today at St. Laurence Pountney. But Laurence and his wife sat on; they had argued all breakfast time, and the argument was not yet concluded.

July said: "Well, sir, if you will not go, I cannot."

"Oh, sweet! It's not that I will not go. I cannot. I must be at this great burial."

July flung down upon the board that one of Laurence's big gilt spoons of the apostles with the figure of St. Peter on it, as if it had been no better than a spoon of tin.

"Why should they bury him today, when the King goes to Greenwich?"

"He has been dead four days."

"There's a quarter of mutton in the larder," she declared callously, "that's been dead longer than that. In this great frost—"

But he stopped her there with a fair show of sternness, which, however, he knew he should not be able to keep up for long. And true enough, when he saw July sit there, drooping glumly over the table, all light gone from her face, he had to think of a way of setting things right.

"I'll tell you, wife, what I shall do." He stood up, and, standing so, felt that he could speak as a husband should, who, if he chose to be indulgent, was firm withal.

"I'll send the boy to fetch Mistress Holland. She loves a show. You shall go together." July was picking with her fingernail at the blue stripe that was woven across the board cloth. She did not look up. "And Mat shall go with you, so you shall have a man to attend you in the crowd." Mat was Laurence's eldest journeyman; to send him away on a busy day meant much, and July knew it; but still she sulked.

"There, sweet," Laurence cast from him the last rag of simulated firmness, and pleaded openly. "There, sweet, be merry. Give me a kiss, and you shall have a gold noble to spend."

When he had taken his kiss, and paid his gold noble, he went away to see to all that he had promised July before he set to work on the business of the burial. He told himself that he had a dutiful wife—she was dutiful, he repeated to himself, in the main. Also she was hardly more than a child; whenever he chose to make a stand, then she must yield.

Yet the truth was not so, and he knew it. Already she took her way as freely as ever the first Mistress Machyn, and in return he got less comfort, for she would not be troubled to see after the maids. And lately, since he had given her a fine green nightgown lined with budge, she had shown herself a sad slug-a-bed, even trailing down to breakfast in it. He prepared a rebuke, yet when he saw her lay her cheek on the soft fur of the collar, and snuggle the green folds about her, his disapproval was quite swamped by pleasure in her pleasure, and pity for her pride in the gown, for, in her first delight, she had cried, "Oh! I never had none such before! My sister had no finer."

Laurence had spoken to Mat, who looked down and sidelong, disapproving. He stood for a moment at the door watching the boy go off on his errand to Mistress Holland. The briskness

of frost and sunshine had got into the lad's toes, and at the street
door he must take off in a great leap, so as to brush the lintel
with his hand; then he was away with a bound and a hoot, as
though he had escaped from a cage.

Laurence smiled and shut the door. In the darkness of the
passage he stood a moment, as his thoughts went back and hung
over July. He did not know how often in a day he would stand
like this, apparently vacant, but in reality searching, wondering,
learning.

Now he shook his head. He did not care if she was by no
means as meek as she had been. "One of her birth," he thought,
"must find it ill to be wife to such as I." With her growth—and
she had shot up tall since last autumn—she had put on a look as
of fugitive, proscribed nobility. Sometimes she was imperious,
though defiantly rather than with any confidence; sometimes,
when among company, there was a sort of dark sparkle about
her. "And if," thought Laurence "she be so set on this show, it's
but as it should be." It came to him with a pang of tenderness
that when she was first his wife she was so frightened a thing
as to have no heart for pleasure. He could not guess that she
would have had no heart for it today, only that she had heard
his friends talk last night of the Yorkshire rebels, saying that the
King had pardoned them every one. That was why she was so
set on holiday making.

The boy came back jigging on his toes and snapping his fingers behind Mistress Holland, who moved at a slow pace which
his feet could not well endure. Mistress Holland, having kissed
both July and Laurence, explained that she had been ready to

go out to watch the show with Mistress Pacey, but just before Laurence's lad came she had heard that Mistress Pacey could not go, she having fallen down the cellar steps, nine steps, and broken her leg. "I told her," said Mistress Holland, "I told her she would be sorry when she had the picture of the blessed St. Christopher in the parlor whitewashed over, and a motto—something about Fortune—painted over it. 'It may be the new fashion,' I said to her, 'but you'll be sorry therefor.'" Then she kissed July again, and pushed into her hands a little box of comfits.

So July, far from losing her dignity, was able to feel that she was doing Mistress Holland a kindness on going with her to watch the King riding to Greenwich, not as usual by water, but, because the Thames was quite frozen over, through London and over London Bridge.

They came through crowded streets, where the stones rang with frost, and the heaps of scattered garbage were hard almost as the stones, and laced over with patterns of white rime, to London Bridge, and following the crowd passed under the arches of the gatehouse there and a little way along the bridge till from a space between two of the houses they could look down upon the river, like a great dark green highway, with people walking about on it in the sunshine, and boys sliding, and some few people gliding at great speed upon bones tied under their feet; one of these, less skillful than the rest, was most popular with the crowd because of his frequent and comical tumbles.

But while Mistress Holland and Mat looked down July turned her back and looked up toward the sun, because its light was so blessed as it moved, in greater splendor than King Harry's across the sky which in these last days was empty of clouds from dawn to the red setting, and now of as clear a blue as any summer morning. She forgot everything in that pure light, and the delicate warmth on her cheeks, and, half-smiling, turned her eyes this way and that, enjoying everything without thought. There were many banners set out in their brackets over the gate today; they stirred a little, sleepily, unfolding their colors and their gold against the sun, then, drooping, hung close again. July looked below them, to the ledge just above the arch, and she startled Mistress Holland by catching her arm and letting out a shrill cackle of laughter.

"Oh!" she cried, "See him grin with never a tooth in his top jaw. And his hair—red hair—it moves in the wind."

Mistress Holland looked where July pointed, and pulled her hand down.

"Sh!" she said, low but very urgent. "That is one of the monks of the Charterhouse. They were holy men. Martyrs. You should not laugh."

July stopped laughing with a gulp. When she spoke, what with the way her voice shook and her teeth chattered, Mistress Holland could make little of it, and it seemed no explanation at all for July to say—if that was what she did say—'I laughed because they will not do so to the Yorkshiremen now.'"

Mistress Holland could see, however, that the girl was near now to tears. "Tut! Tut!" she said, comfortingly, tucked July's arm under hers and talked cheerfully of easy, everyday things. She also took some pains to shake off Mat so that she could ask July a few close questions; but July gave her none of the answers she hoped for, and certainly the girl was thin as a rake handle with no signs yet that she was breeding.

Soon the King and Queen went by, and small, pale Lady Mary, the King's elder daughter, who had once been Princess of Wales, close after them. The Queen smiled, and drew her hand out of her mantle of Russian furs to wave to the people as they shouted, and the King looked about too, with a gracious expression, and put up his hand to his cap now and then. But the Lady Mary went by them with a look like a sleepwalker.

After that Mistress Holland and July went down by Old Swan Stairs onto the ice, stepping on it very gingerly at first, then with more confidence. It was deep green, it showed feet thick, and had bubbles in it. July, staring down, thought it beautiful, and thought of the river flowing beneath the ice, all alone in its own silence, seen and yet unseen, for though the ice was clearish, like thick green glass, you could not see the water through it; or else you did not know which was water and which was the ice through which you saw the water. She thought that the river must feel now very safe, moving thus solitary below its frozen skin.

When they had had enough of walking about July and Mistress Holland began to look for Mat, but could not find him. "Well, we'll stand and wait," said Mistress Holland, and they stood back to back, the vintner's wife scanning the crowds on the ice, July looking up at the wharf above, till her eyes were dazzled by the bright sky beyond the people's heads.

Behind her she heard, among many scraps of meaningless talk, this, spoken in a man's voice:

" . . . A great brush and a pail of ink, and he inked every sign from Paul's to Old Bailey."

Whoever spoke had gone by now. Another voice answered him from farther away with a great laugh, and, "Ha! you lie!"

July whipped round.

Master Aske and a taller man had passed, and were swinging on up toward the Vintry at a good pace. July seized Mistress Holland by the hand. "There he is," she cried, and dragged her along. Mistress Holland, in her anxiety to recover Mat, was willing to show what nimbleness she could. Only when she found that July was plucking by the sleeve a strange gentleman did she pull her back, assuring her hastily that, "This is not Mat, Mistress Machyn."

Master Aske had stopped and turned. He looked first blank, then astonished, and then pleased.

"Mass!" he said. "Mistress July here!"

July stood dumb, only looking at him. If there were any thought in her mind it was that it would be enough for her could she look at him always and listen when he spoke. The perfection and quiescence of her sudden joy so warmed and lit her face as to make her, for those few moments, almost beautiful.

But Mistress Holland was insisting that she should know who was this gentleman.

July told her, "Master Aske."

"Not—not the captain of the Yorkshire men?"

July, without taking her eyes for a moment from his face, said yes, this was he. She did not remember, and would not have cared had she remembered, that she had lied to Mistress Holland, saying that she knew none of the Yorkshire gentlemen.

Mistress Holland herself did not precisely remember it yet, though it lurked in her mind, creating a slight confusion there. But of one thing she was sure, since little Mistress Machyn was acquainted with Master Aske, she herself should shake him by the hand, and having shaken him by the hand would bid him home to supper, and his friend too.

His friend it seemed was promised forth. Master Aske, after an instant's hesitation, remembered that the chimney at the "Cardinal's Hat" smoked, and said he'd come, and gladly.

At the vintner's house they supped and drank well, and afterward in the last colored light went to an upper parlor that looked upon the river. A servant poured more wine, and set down wafers, sugar comfits, and a dish of oranges. When he had shut the door and gone away Master Holland stood up.

"Sir," said he, "we and all England may well thank you, under God, for you and your fellows have saved religion," and he drank to Master Aske, standing.

Aske flushed and his eye shone. He was as ready to tell them about the pilgrimage as they were to hear. "And," said he at last, "now there is nothing to fear. The King is a very gracious Prince. He only needed to know the truth, which was kept from him."

Mistress Holland cried out that she'd said so all along. "It's that Cromwell," she said.

The vintner asked quickly, "Was Lord Privy Seal there while you spoke with the King?"

"At first, but the King drove him out."

"Is it possible?" said Master Holland. He looked shrewdly at Aske. "The King heard you patiently?"

"He heard me." Aske leaned forward looking from one to another, half smiling. "I'll tell you now what I've told no man. I rode here in great fear of my life. But the King's no dissembler. If he'd been smooth with me I'd have doubted him. But he was not so. I knelt there for half an hour, I think, while he rated me. But then, at the last, he said I should write down all that I had been telling him of the grievances of the North, and he would take counsel on them."

"Ho!" said the vintner, "you spoke of grievances to him?"

"When he let me speak." Aske gave a little laugh. "I thought he'd have knocked his dagger about my ears before I'd done. Yet in the end he gave me his hand to kiss."

He sat for a moment in silence, staring down at his wine, which, in the silver cup, showed no color, but only a surface that was dark, and darkly shining. He could see again the King's hand laid on his own, a plump, wide, white hand, with finely tapering fingers and many rings. He said, thinking aloud, "It's strange how when you have stood against any true man you love him all the better for it. There's Sir Robert Constable. We had each other always in displeasure in the old days. But now I know him, and he me. So too with my Lord Darcy. And so with the King's Grace; I never would have done him hurt, but now I'd die for him."

He looked up, and this time was aware of how July was watching him. He smiled at her. "He gave me a crimson satin jacket of his own," he said, "so you'll see me going very fine."

She dropped her eyes from his face to his breast for a second. "Is that it?" she asked, in a bemused sort of way, though the jacket he wore was of cloth, pretty well worn and not at all fine.

"Goose!" he said, and laughed. "Not this one. And that jacket will have to be mightily cut down or I wear it, so much bigger a man is the King than I. I told His Grace it'd be as in the fable of the ass and the lion's skin." He turned to the others and said, to explain his familiarity with July, "This maid I have known for many years since she was so high," and showed them with his hand.

But Mistress Holland cried out, "Maid? She's a married wife this three months."

"*Benedicite*!" said Master Aske, and looked again at July, more narrowly and more kindly. He thought to himself that he had never before seen her eyes so shining; he was glad to think that this must mean she'd got a good man, and was at last, as it were, warm, sheltered, and out of the wind.

1537

January 2

After the dullness of gray ice the pool in the old knot garden at Wilton gleamed dark with the reflection of the wall and the yew trees, bright with the pale sky. It was pleasant to see the water quiver as a breath of wind touched it, after so long immobility, just as it was pleasant to walk in the air, and feel it soft and clean on the cheek, after the biting chills or heat of great fires in

perfumed, shuttered rooms, which all had endured for the last
weeks. So Sir John Bulmer and Sir Francis Bigod paced together
in the garden, followed by Meg with a nurse carrying her latest
born, a boy now a month old.

Here, in Dame Anne's time it had not been thought amiss
to dry linen yarn or new bleached cloths along the flat, clipped
tops of box that edged the convoluted beds. But now that it
was Dame Meg instead of Dame Anne such things were not
done in the old knot garden: indeed already part of it had
been grubbed up to make Dame Meg one of those newer gardens, such as the King had, and some great nobles, where the
owner's coat armor was most cunningly picked out in colors,
with, for gold, yellow sand or crumbled and pounded Flanders
tile, chalk or well-burnt plaster for the herald's argent, sifted
coaldust for sable, bricks broken to dust for red, and so on.
This display of coat armor, where Bulmer impaled Stafford
(and Stafford with no sinister bend), had been Meg's first
flourish in her altered state, when from mistress she became
a lawful wedded wife. She had set the gardeners about it in
the first fine days of last spring, before even she began to root
through all those coffers and chests which contained Dame
Anne's stuff—old-fashioned, enormously ample gowns, hosen
of gigantic proportions, shoes easy, large, and slovenly trodden over. Of all these things Meg had made great mock to her
women, though not when Sir John was there, for he exacted
more respect for a dead wife than he had done for one alive
and going heavily about her duties at Wilton with an invin-
cible silent patience.

For a while Meg carried in her arms the stiff little bundle that was young John Bulmer of Pinchinthorpe, rocking him, making sweet silly noises to him, bidding him watch the birds as they flew, and bending her lovely face above him, lovelier than ever after the stress of childbirth. Partly she did it for sheer pleasure, because she was proud to be the mother of a true-born son, but also she was aware how Sir Francis Bigod marked her, as he and Sir John turned; his eyes lingered as if he saw her in a new guise, and with new kindness; that being so, and she what she was, she could not keep her claws from him, though she might hide them in the most demure gentleness of approach.

So, when John of Pinchinthorpe set up a high thin wall, Meg pushed the child into the nurse's arms. "In! In with him!" she said. "For I can see he's cold—oh, such cold cheeks!" She let her lips travel with a bee's light cruising kiss over the child's face, then caught Sir John's arm and leaned upon him, looking across him to Sir Francis with a faint smile.

For a little the three of them moved in silence. They came so to the small round pool, and stood, looking down. Then Sir John said:

"Frank will not believe the word that Rafe sent me from Marrick, sweetheart."

"No," said Bigod, "I will not think Master Aske a man to accuse his fellows to the King in London. Rather I fear that it's true what they are saying at Fountains—that when he came to London the King had him headed."

"Jesu Mercy!" cried Meg, but Sir John, giving over for a moment biting his nails, muttered that whether it were so, or t'other way about, yet Rafe's counsel was good—"that for no fair letters nor fair words we should not stir forth of the North Country."

Sir Francis looked from one to other of them with that lit, wild look of the Bigods.

"I tell you, Jack, that's not enough—to stay still nor stir not. For my part I am sworn to go forward again with the commons."

"No!" Sir John said, "No!" with his fingers at his mouth. "When my Lord of Norfolk comes—"

"When he comes I doubt he will rather bring us into captivity with them of Lincolnshire, than fulfill our petitions."

"But," Sir John persisted, "the commons'll not follow you, Frank. See how near they came to killing you at Pomfret for your traffic with Cromwell and your known learning in these English Scriptures."

"Yea," Sir Francis cried, "but now it is not so. They know me and acknowledge my truth," and he began to explain, not for the first time, how he had come to take arms with the commons, saying that it was manifestly against God's will for a secular man, a King, to be supreme head over the church; and he went on from there, subtly dividing what authority might belong to the pope, what to a bishop, and what to a king.

At the end of it all Sir John put up his hands to his head and tugged at his hair. "So it may be. So it may be. But to rise again! And if Aske hath betrayed us—or is taken—what can we do?"

"Shame!" cried Meg so suddenly, and with such a sharp and ringing note in her voice, that they who had taken no account of her at all in their argument were astonished into silence. And then she began, urging as Francis Bigod had urged, but with more vehemence, that to stay still was to lose all, that these ships which Rafe Bulmer wrote of from Swaledale were sent north by the King so that they might set on the North Country; that it was now, or else never, and that the commons were ready if only they should find leaders; and she caught a hand of each and looked into their eyes, eagerness quickening her beauty as wind draws up a flame, so that for a moment they could only stare at her.

Sir Francis cried, "God be my judge, all this is true," but Sir John tore his hand away and went off, crying that he'd hear no more—not one word.

Yet he did hear more, and that which came nearer the truth, when he lay beside Meg that night in the darkness. For when he tried to fondle her she struck his hands away and would have none of him.

"You," she cried, "you, of a great house, yet who will take no part, but to follow other men, littler men such as Robin Aske! And now he is high in the King's favor, and you—"

"Or he is dead—headed or hanged, as Frank says."

"He?" she cried. "Never! He's not one to let himself be tricked, but to climb upon other men's heads to a high place. Did you not see it in the old days? But I did. I knew it in him. As the devil he is ambitious."

"Well!" He was sullen. "What then can I do?"

"Do? Nothing. You'll do nothing. No, but if the commons need a leader it shall be little Robin Aske, or that madman Bigod, but never Sir John Bulmer."

They wrangled for a time, but at last he pleaded, half promised, then wholly promised that he would be forward to lead, if there were those who would follow. Only then would she yield. When he slept she lay awake awhile in the dark, remembering how this morning, when both Sir John and Frank Bigod left her, she had stood alone by the coldly shining, lightly shivering pool. She had leaned forward, to see her own face in the water; it showed there, wan and deathly, but she knew it well enough in her glass to know what beauty it was that that proud fellow, whom she had once loved, had despised. For that was the truth, which she had known all along; though she had made a pretense to herself that he loved her only too well; the truth was that he had despised her. And this was he, forsooth, who, if he were dead, all the courage of the North Country must die too.

But, truly, she could not think him dead. Then, if alive, he was at court, high in the King's favor, richly rewarded. "Yet," she told herself, "the last word's not spoken. If one, then another can prosper by that same means. And shall, if I can goad him to it."

January 5

There were several young gentlemen sitting at cards outside the door of the King's privy chamber at Greenwich. "He must," said one of them as another dealt from the pack, "he must have been with His Grace the best part of an hour."

"They say the King favors him greatly."

"Were I the King," cried one of them, "I'd have sent him home with never a tongue, the scurvy little traitor with his one eye."

"Did you hear how he spoke to the King's Grace?"

"What did he say?"

"It wasn't the words. I heard them not. It was how he spoke."

They fell to play again, but at the end of that game one of them, who had lost more than he could well afford, got up saying he had played enough, and began to ramble about the room, picking up a book and ruffling the leaves, twanging with his fingers the strings of a lute which lay on a bench. His aimless wanderings brought him near to the door of the King's chamber. He stood still a moment, then beckoned to the others. "Listen!" he said.

They cried fie on him! and told him he'd be losing his ears in the pillory.

"I cannot hear their words. It is, as you said, how he speaks."

The others did not leave their play, but he stayed a few moments listening. Inside the King's privy chamber a man's voice, confident, resonant, positive, went on and on. It was not the King's voice.

Master Aske came out at last. He looked hard at the young men with his one eye, but saw them not at all. He saw instead a work accomplished, and it was a work that he had never fully believed could be brought to a good end. It seemed to him now a small thing that this morning a man had come to the Cardinal's Hat—a man he did not know—bringing news of fresh trouble in the North. This fellow said he had it from a friend at Buntingford, who knew a man at Royston, whose cousin. . . . Aske could guess that if you went back over the slot you would trace it stage by stage, from mouth to mouth, all the way between London and Yorkshire.

The news was that the North was all of a floughter. Some were saying that the grand captain had been bought by the King; some that he was dead, or in the Tower. And the man who had a friend at Buntingford put into Aske's hand a soiled strip of parchment which must have been torn from an old book of church-wardens' accounts, for there were on the one side of it entries of money spent on candles for the rood-loft, wine for the altar, and beer for the ringers. But on the other was written in a staggering, scrawling hand—

"Commons keep well your harness. Trust you no gentlemen. Rise all at once. God shall be your governor and I shall be your captain."

It was signed at the bottom by the word "Poverty," and at each of the four corners the parchment was rent, because it had been snatched from the church door to which it had been nailed. So now Aske thought, "I must make haste home, to stay the people with the good news." But he thought that would be an easy thing to do.

A few minutes after he had left the King's bell jangled. That young gentleman who answered it came back and went away toward the gallery. The others questioned him in silence with lifted eyebrows, and he answered them in a whisper—"Privy Seal."

When Cromwell came to the privy chamber the King sat at the table bent over some papers. He gave no sign that he knew of Cromwell's presence, but, after Privy Seal had been on his knees a second or two, the King's hand made a motion for him to stand. So he stood, and let his eyes flicker lightly over the King, from his hair, once red-gold but grizzling and paling now; by the round roll of fat above the gold-stitched collar, the wide purple brocade shoulders, and so to the hands; as the King stooped over a bundle of papers his fingers drummed upon the table. It was certain that the King was angry; Cromwell would have given much to know against whom his anger was directed.

"This," said the King in his sharpest voice, "is the declaration of Aske. I have dismissed him to go North again." He looked up and suddenly cast the papers across the table. "Read it," he said, and sat back in the chair, his chin sunk on his chest.

Cromwell sat down, and began to read—"The manner of the taking of Robert Aske in Lincolnshire, and the use of the same Robert unto his passage to York." It took a long time, but the King now sat in silence, and quite still, except that the fingers of one hand twined and untwined about themselves the gold chain that hung round his neck, so that the jewel which swung from it tinkled on the emerald buttons of his doublet.

Cromwell read it through carefully, but as quickly as he might; only toward the end he read more slowly.

And the said Aske saith that in all parts of the realm men's hearts grudge, with the suppression of the abbeys and first fruits, by reason the same would be the destruction of the whole religion of England. And their especial grudge is against the Lord Cromwell, being reputed the destroyer of the Commonwealth, as well amongst the most part of the lords as all other worshipful men and commons, for as far as the said Aske can perceive there is none earthly man so evil beloved as the Lord Cromwell is with the commons, albeit the said

Aske saith that the Lord Cromwell never gave him occasion
to report of him, but he only doth declare the hearts of Your
Grace's people.

There was not much more after that, but when he had finished
Cromwell sat feigning still to read, while he weighed two different means of penetrating the King's intentions. Should he sigh
and say, "Alas! I am content to be misjudged in Your Grace's
service," or should he, speaking in a frank open manner, say,
"Here's a very honest man"?

He chose the latter, as being more provocative, but since
he did not dare to meet the King's eye he shaded his own with
his hand.

The King looked across at him, then down at the table. A
sluggish winter fly crept there. His Grace put his thumb down
slowly and firmly upon the creature; when he lifted it again
he looked for a long instant at what had been a fly, before he
scraped off the mess on the board's edge.

"Honest?" he said in a voice that told Cromwell nothing.
"Yea, I think he is honest."

The Duke of Norfolk, loitering alone in a small oriel that looked
from the southern side of the great gallery toward the river, con-
gratulated himself that it was Cromwell and not he who had
been sent for by the King, and had been with him for so long a
time. The duke, and almost everyone else in the palace, knew
that the King was in a rage; who had incensed His Grace mattered little, those that came near him would suffer.

There was a small desk in the oriel, and a stool. On the desk lay a Book of Hours bound in stamped leather. Norfolk set his knee on the bench, and began to turn the pages. It was a sumptuous work, not new, for it had belonged to the King's father before him, but none the less beautiful in the duke's eyes for that. He let the silky, strong parchment leaves slip crackling by under his fingers, catching glimpses of opulent gold, scarlet, lapis-blue: there were initial letters that held all of a scripture story, or only a grotesque animal: pictured pages where the golden haloes of saints beamed among English farms and fields: margins all a spray of flowers and leaves, and among the twined tendrils a monkey beating a drum, an archer aiming at a black and white magpie, half as big as himself, or a chaffinch painted to the life in his proper tinctures.

"What's the new printing," the duke said to himself, "to this?" and he thought scorn of all those worthy folk who must buy printed books because they could not pay the price of such craftsmanship. Yet there was uneasiness mingled in his scorn; Howards needed not to buy cheap; he might still commission as costly a book as this—yet it would not be so fair. In his mind he felt the breath of change, chilling as the east wind in blackthorn winter. Nothing new was quite the same, and God only knew how far mutation would reach.

Someone tapped him on the shoulder and he whipped round to find the King standing beside him. Cromwell was just beyond, pale, and placidly twinkling as ever. If the King had trounced him, none could guess it from his look; not even the tips of ears were burning, but already Norfolk felt the color climbing toward his own eyes.

"A fair work," he said hastily, waving toward the book the cap he had snatched off.

"Humph." The King put out his hand, and slapped the pages over angrily and hastily, searching for something.

Cromwell said he had seen in Italy a book printed for one of the Strozzi more perfect than a man could imagine, so exact yet flowing the letters of it, and the miniatures painted so graciously. "I remember," he said, "a grove of laurel painted there. A man might have walked into it to shade himself from the sun, and laid himself down under those trees, so masterly was the painter's hand."

"Humph!" said the King again, belittling the Strozzi's book. Then he said, "Ha! See here, Thomas Howard, you that are papist at heart and a friend of naughty monks."

They looked down then, and saw that his finger pointed to where there was a blank in one of the prayers, where some words had been scratched and scrubbed out, leaving the parchment's smooth surface blurred; neither of them needed to be told whose name had stood there before the King decreed that in Rome there was but a bishop, and he no greater in honor than any other.

"Before God!" cried Norfolk. "Your Grace is misinformed. I am no papist, nor no favorer of naughty religious persons. Nay! by Christ's Passion! but when I was in the North parts, and lay of necessity at one of the abbeys, several of my gentlemen warned me to take heed, for fear of poison, of what I drank there, so roundly I had spoken against them."

Cromwell put in eagerly, as if to help a friend, that such words had been reported to him. "My lord speaks the truth," said he.

The duke blinked at that, as if a glove had been flipped across his mouth. But the King said harshly that words were easy things. "And what lieth in a man's heart and stomach appeareth not so much by his words as by his deeds." When Norfolk began to protest that by words and deeds his true heart should appear, the King stopped him.

"Do you then," he asked, and let his small, keen eyes bore into the duke's, "do you in your conscience approve and heartily embrace the laws that we have made in all these causes of religion?"

Norfolk pressed his two hands together. "Your Majesty, I do know you to be a Prince of such virtue and knowledge, that whatsoever laws you have in times past made, or hereafter shall make, I shall to the extremity of my power stick unto them."

"Well," said the King, "if that were true, it were enough."

January 7

Master Purefoy, a master scrivener and a very distant cousin of Laurence Machyn, sat for a while upstairs in the parlor of the Machyn house, waiting for Laurence to come home. He sat all the time with his head between his fists, never lifting it. Sometimes he muttered to himself, between his teeth. "He might 'a lived. He might 'a lived." And once, at a thought of one of the boy's merry sayings, he wrung his hands together and groaned aloud. But for the most part he was too smitten to feel anything other than the great weight of loss for the son who had died yesterday; the one son, and the one child.

At the end of half an hour he could endure his thoughts no longer. He must be moving, though he knew that far or fast as he might go sorrow would come after, close as his shadow, not to be shaken off. So he went down into the hall below, and, finding none there, let himself out into the street, and turned in the direction of Paul's. He had not gone far when Laurence Machyn stopped him by putting a hand on his shoulder, for he had heard the news and could not let Master Purefoy go by, solitary in his grief. Yet now that he had held him up Laurence could think of nothing to say, but stood, with averted face, gripping the scrivener's shoulder.

His meaning was clear though, for kind intent can speak in a silence, and after a moment Master Purefoy turned, and went along beside him, telling of the little lad, and letting the tears run as they would. Laurence walked him up and down Knightrider Street for a long time, and heard, all in a jumble, of the boy's death, of his pretty ways, of how he had fallen sick, and what a solemn burial it should be. Laurence must see to that, "and stint nothing—stint nothing. For it was all for him, and now I care not to save, since now he—" "Ah, peace! peace!" said Laurence. "He is at peace."

When it was growing dusk they parted. Master Purefoy would not go back to the house with Laurence, and had not said, because in his grief he had quite forgotten, that ever he had gone in and waited, and come away again without a word.

So when the young shock-headed prentice lad Dickon, who opened the door to Laurence, told his master that he'd let in a gentleman and set him in the parlor upstairs, and yet he wasn't there now, and no one had seen him go, and no one knew what he had come for, Laurence could make nothing of it. "Who was the gentleman?" But Dickon, who had only been a week in the Machyn house, knew him not. Of what like then? Dickon had not noticed, but to get himself out of the scrape he muttered that the mistress would know, because she had been within in the bedchamber.

Just then July came out of the kitchen carrying a lighted candle. Laurence cuffed the boy, but not hard, and told him he must be more heedful. "By not asking his name," said he, "you might have lost a customer."

He caught July just as she came to the foot of the stairs, put his arm about her and kissed her.

She pushed him away crying, "Keep off! Your breath smells most ill favoredly."

"It is my teeth," he said meekly, and let her go.

"Then you should have 'em pulled out."

She began to go up, but he said, "Wife!" and she paused. "Who was this gentleman who came and who went again?"

"Gentleman? I know of no gentleman."

"Dickon let one in."

"Then ask Dickon."

"He knew him not."

"Well," said July, "and I saw him not," and she went on upstairs, leaving Laurence to come up after her.

Yet July had seen Master Purefoy very well, both coming and going, from the garret window, for she had spent all this afternoon in turning out an old chest up there. There were gowns in the chest, stuffy-smelling, stained, and some of them moth-eaten. There were swaddling bands for children, and little white embroidered caps, yellowish through being laid by. There was an old, a very old, headdress of tattered grass green silk and gilded wire; it was crumpled, but she straightened out the frame, pulled off her own white linen cap and veil, and put on the other. When she looked in an old steel mirror which she found wrapped in a bit of kidskin she could not but laugh at the strange fashion.

Time had passed pleasantly up there, for the sun came warmly through the window, and as she toyed with the stuff in the chest she could think her own thoughts. But she did not wish Laurence to know that she had idled away the afternoon, instead of seeing that the maids set the house to rights after the disorder of the Days of Christmas. And now she remembered that she had left the stuff all about the floor of the garret, having come down hastily because one of the maids had called her.

So she went straight on up the stairs, saying nothing more to Laurence, but with her ears, as it were, cast back like a dog's, to hear what he would do.

She heard him stop outside the parlor door, and then turn in. So she was alone again, except for the living candle flame that swayed in the draft like a dancer, like a spirit in cloth of gold. She stood on the stair to let the light steady, and stared at it till her eyes were dazzled; it was a pale saffron crocus, growing within a golden yellow crocus; it was a joyful thing to see. It was joyful because today Master Aske (he had said so) would be riding home, free and safe. As she moved on, groping with her hand, yet with her eyes still fixed on the candle flame, July began to sing.

Laurence heard her and stood still.

"Who?" he said to himself, and, "Jesu! I never heard her sing before," and he began to smile. Then something pierced painfully into his mind, like a needle into the quick under a fingernail, as he remembered how this afternoon Master Holland, the vintner, had spoken of "your good wife's friend, that same Master Aske that was captain of the Northern men." And Mistress Holland had said, "To think that your little July should have known him since she was a child," yet July had said of Aske that she knew him not; and now Laurence remembered with a sort of horror how she had lain shaking in bed beside him, the night he told her that Aske was captain of the Northern men. And this afternoon a man had come to the house and gone again, without leaving any word. Yet July had said that she saw him not. And now she began to sing, sudden and sweet as a wren in the hedge, for the first time since she came to this house.

Laurence went to the settle and plumped down on it. He began to gnaw his knuckles; then he wiped his forehead with his hand.

"It was because she has been frightened that she will lie," he told himself; but that which had comforted him often was nothing to the point now. After a moment he sprang up as if the settle was red-hot, because a thought which he would not entertain had shown him the two of them sitting there together. "It will prove to be some other. It will prove to be nothing," he assured himself. "I shall find out." But he knew that he could not dare to ask anyone who might be able to give him the true answer.

January 8

Malle opened the door of the bread oven beside the hearth and peered in. This time the loaves were well risen; she thanked God for that, and when they were all set out on the table, fresh, sweet-smelling, pale brown mounds, each with a bloom of flour upon it, she hung over them sniffing up the sweet savor and smiling.

While the loaves were still warm, but after she had redded up the houseplace and set bowls and spoons out for supper, she cut some thick spongy slices off one of the loaves and spread them thick with the herb-scented lard which the priory cook had given to Gib. Then she tied the bread into a corner of her apron and went out looking for Wat.

She found him where she expected, gathering sticks for kindling along the edge of the wood. It was growing dusk, with a small moon in an empty sky; there would be a hoarfrost before morning; already the grass felt crisp under foot.

She stooped to gather with him, and then straightened herself to wipe the back of her hand across her nose. "Wat, there's naught anymore to fear. For already, already God has done it. Whatsoever ill news cometh, that good news cometh after. Already, already it is done."

They saw Gib go by beneath them along the road; he did not look their way, but they kept very still till he was out of sight.

"Already! Already!" Malle said, as though that word was key to a marvel. She ruffled Wat's hair with her hand. "'What's done?' says you? Why, that you know well, having seen him. It's his work, it's God's great work that is done. Afore time was he thought it, and as he built the world he built his own hurt into the walls of it, for mortar to hold the walls to stand forever."

She said—"See here, what I have brought you for your supper," and untied the corner of her apron, so that Wat grabbed at the bread and began to eat. "So," said Malle, "you needn't be seen by your father this night."

"Wuf!" said Wat, and "Gur!" for that pleased him as much as the fine fresh bread, oozy with half-melted lard.

"So it is," said Malle, "that already, little as they may know it, he hath all men taken in his net. And when he will, he may hale in, to bring us all home. How else? Shall that strong One fail of his purpose? Or that Wise, who made all, be mistook?"

January 10

Archbishop Lee said, in a whisper, though the door was safe shut, and no one in the little warm room, with its painted and gilded wainscot, but himself and Gib Dawe, "You have the letter safe?"

"In my shoe's sole."

"They will give you a horse at the stables. I have put money in your purse. If you are questioned show the other letter, the one to the bishop of London."

Gib bowed his head and said nothing. There was no need for the archbishop to tell him all this again, since he was, he

conceived, no fool. He looked down at the archbishop's delicate hands, poised over his silver plate; one held a knife with a
silver-gilt handle, the other a little two-pronged thing, also of
silver-gilt, with which he now spitted the body of a wild duck,
in an action that seemed to Gib intolerably and fantastically
dainty.

"You understand? You will show the other letter to none,
till you come to my Lord Privy Seal. Then give it to him, and
such news as he will have of you of the new rebellious stirrings
here." Having thus delivered his final instructions the archbishop popped into his mouth a neat sliver of the wild duck.
"Go now, go now," he said, and was raising the cup of wine to
his lips as Gib laid his hand on the latch. The archbishop's blessing, an afterthought, and hasty, followed Gib into the passage,
and then he shut the door of this prince of the church, snug as a
hare in her form, and as timid—thought Gib—eating his meat
off silver (like a fine court lady) too dainty to touch it with his
fingers; duck for him, and beans and bacon for such as us . . . So,
as if jolted by each step of the stairs, the little spurts of malice
jetted up in his mind. "And a poor wretched nag it will be that
they'll give me," he thought, forgetting to be glad that he would
have a nag at all for his journey to London.

The horse was, indeed, nothing much to look at, but it proved
itself a serviceable beast, so that he went through Doncaster as
the sun drew near to setting. Beyond Doncaster, where the road
ran up a hill beside a wood, with a village a little way below upon
the right, he stopped, and for a moment looked back, and around
him. The quiet sunny afternoon was closing in peace; the village,

with the veiled orange glow of the sunset behind it, and the big stacks standing up almost as tall as the houses, seemed to fold itself in a smiling security, as much at ease as a man sitting down on his settle by the fire in the twilight, slipping off his shoes, warming his fingers and toes, thinking of his meat.

Gib, having cast one last glance back over his shoulder toward the North, where all was gray, and night coming up in a creeping mist, turned down the lane to the village. He too was at ease in his mind, wonderfully at ease.

Clearly, he thought to himself, as he jogged down toward the gathering of small houses and big stacks among the elm trees—clearly it was a man's duty to his Prince to carry news of treasonable words, discontented mutterings, threatenings of insurrection. Yet this, which had been his pretext when he came yesterday to the archbishop at Cawood, and found him, surely by the dispensation of providence, in need of a secret messenger, was not the chief cause of Gib's inner content.

That which had begun in pure, simple, almost physical relief, just to be clear of the dale, of Richmond, and of any country he knew, had grown deeper as he rode, had become, he was sure of it—most sure, God he thanked—a refreshment of the spirit such as he could not have dreamed of, nor hoped.

For he had confessed to God, not, as the papist idolators, to man, not in a church made with man's hands, but under no less a vault than the floor of heaven itself built before the world— his thoughts swinging in widening arcs, like a hawk mounting, lost touch with words. He only again remembered the melting as of frost, as of grief into tears, that came when he had cried

in his heart, "Lord, I have failed. Lord, I am not able to do it."
And then, out of a great self-loathing and despair, "Master, if
thou wilt, thou canst make me clean." At that moment came the
melting, and the tears, and a great welling-up of comfort and
humble confidence. He told himself now, "I am a sinner and
can do no good thing. But I am forgiven." And once in London
he would strive, not only against God's enemies, but against
himself, God's worthless servant.

He came to where, as it reached the village, the road narrowed
sharply, hemmed in between a steep bank with the churchyard
wall on top, and the stone flank of a barn on the other side;
beyond these it swung left-handed, so that the corner was blind
as well as narrow. And there Gib knew that had the Angel stood
in his way, and had the archbishop's nag turned aside crushing
his foot against the wall, as the ass crushed Balaam's foot, then
he would have beaten the nag till he had forced it on, or he
would have gone by on foot, or he would have gone about. But
not for God's own angel would he have turned and ridden back
again to Marrick. He knew this, but he shut the door upon the
knowledge, locked the door, and drowned the key.

No angel stood in his way. He rounded the corner, saw the
geese on the green and cows driven home, and heard the bell
begin to jow in the church. Everything was sweet, kindly, and
at peace.

January 15

When it was suppertime Dame Eleanor Maxwell came into the
prioress's chamber and settled herself at table, with noisy sighs

and breathings of which she herself heard nothing. The prioress did not yet move from her chair beside the fire. A servant was laying for supper, a pewter plate and a wooden plate, the prioress's great cup, and the little horn cup that was used by whichever of the ladies sat with her at table. She set on cheese and bread, a dish of lemons, and a jug of ale. Now she went off to fetch the salt herrings, and the eels, for today was Friday.

Dame Eleanor sighed yet more loudly and said, "Now that the priest's gone—and God knows where—the woman and that child will starve."

The prioress said nothing. It was useless to say anything to Dame Eleanor; only a shout in her ear could penetrate her deafness. But she nodded to show that she knew what the old lady was talking about.

"If," said Dame Eleanor, "Malle should come back here—the henwife's rheumatism is worse each year." A few minutes later she said, "Why should she not come back?" and she looked at the prioress and waited.

"Now," thought Christabel, "neither to nod nor shake my head will answer her that." Nor did she truly know how to answer. Now that Marrick Priory had the King's letter for its continuance, and, on top of that, now that this late rebellion had braved the King for the sake of the abbeys, she need not fear. Surely it would take more than a fool's babbling to endanger the house.

She nodded her head.

"Ah!" cried Dame Eleanor, and pressed her hands together. "Then she may come back and bring the child with her?"

The prioress nodded again, and so it was settled. After that they sat in silence, except that the prioress who had a lute upon her knee let her fingers toy with the strings, plucking no more than a tingling silver thrill from the minikin strings, and from the solemn bass a humming reverberation.

She bent her head; she would not look again at Dame Eleanor, because beyond her was the little secret recess which the master carpenter had made when he wainscoted the chamber. Not half an hour ago, with the door barred, the prioress had drawn from her breast the key, warm with the warmth of her flesh, and set it in the cunningly hidden lock. She had opened the door panel and looked in; even in that dark corner the firelight found the jewels in the little golden pyx inside the recess; the gold was in a buckskin bag lined with scarlet damask silk—rose nobles and angels—in value still a good sum, and always the same in the beauty of its sultry sullen gleam, as she poured it out upon her palm, and, covering it with the other, clenched both hands upon it.

Now, with Dame Eleanor in the room she would not look that way, but she thought of the pyx, and of the gold. Not for all their talking should the ladies have the pyx back again in the church. Let them guess, and guess again, whether or how the King's visitors had laid hands on it and taken it away. It should not go back into the church, to be seen and coveted by other new visitors that might be sent by the King; next time, there was no telling, these visitors might come to take away the holy vessels, such as were of value. And then the ladies would be sorry. But the little pyx was safe where it lay; and moreover while it was in the hidden recess it was as good as her own.

"No," said Christabel Cowper in her mind, as if Dame Eleanor had spoken an accusation, instead of only venting one of her wordless grunts. "It is not that I am avaricious. The pyx I keep for the sake of the house"—almost she was able to think "for the sake of God,"—but let that pass; she'd be honest and set her claim too low rather than too high. "And the gold," she thought, "it is not that I love the gold itself." She bent lower over the strings of her lute. Gold was a soft cushion to sit on. Gold was a rod to rule with. Gold bought things of good craftsmanship, things that were beautiful, things that made the heart rejoice. Without gold man in this world went very nakedly and wretchedly; with gold, strong and hearty, he might the better praise God. "Gold," she thought, "it's gold that bought this fair lute," and suddenly struck a full chord in which the voice of the strings mingled tingling sweetness and a somber compassionate solemnity. She listened while the notes pulsated, dwindled, and died.

Without raising her head she looked up at the old woman who sat mumbling with her lips like a rabbit.

"Surely," said the prioress, in a low but defiant tone, "surely gold is good."

Dame Eleanor sighed deeply.

January 16

It was a bright open day, cold, with a strong wind that went through the three beech trees on top of the moot-hill at Settrington like a tide of hurrying water, but with little noise because of their winter bareness. Now and again the wind sent up a cloud of dead leaves from the fallen drifts under the trees, lifting and spinning them against the blue sky; even when almost all had dropped again a few would loiter high in the sunshine, like butterflies.

Thirty or so husbandmen stood on the moot-hill looking down toward Settrington, and talking together, but neither loudly nor freely, for none knew why they were here, except that Settrington beacon had been fired last night, and that could only mean tidings of discomfort.

At last one said, "There's horsemen coming through the Coppins!" and all could see the winking flicker of sunshine on the steel caps of horsemen down there. So after that they waited in silence while Sir Francis Bigod and close on forty gentlemen and yeomen came up the hill.

Sir Francis was armed, except for a helmet. When he had wheeled his horse amongst the beech trees he pulled off his cap, waved it to them all, and began to tell them why the beacon had been fired.

It was indeed ill news. At the first he made them catch their breath by telling them that if they did not look well upon many causes, all they should shortly be destroyed.

"For," said he, "the gentlemen of the country have deceived the commons."

He let that sink in, and then, looking about and smiling, promised them that the bishopric and Cleveland were up under Sir John Bulmer, to ensure that the commons be not tricked, "trusting," said he, "that you will not leave them in the dust, seeing that they took your part before, and that it is in the defense of all your weals."

He waited then for a shout, but though there was a murmur, most looked on their neighbors silently and with glum faces. So he went on, leaning forward in the saddle, his voice rising higher and the wild Bigod look more apparent in his glance.

"For my Lord of Norfolk comes with twenty thousand men to take Hull and Scarborough, and other haven towns, which shall be our destruction unless we prevent him therein, and take them before; and so I and my fellow Hallom purpose to do."

They shouted then for the first time, for Hallom was one of themselves, and if he were in this—! They pressed closer, and Sir Francis, seeing it, took fire, and from this time on he had them hanging on him, so that they groaned when he said that they were deceived by the color of a pardon, which though it were called a pardon was none, but a proclamation; and one cried out to curse Privy Seal. Then they were silent again as death, while he read over to them the words of that same so-called pardon.

"But that," he told them, when he had done, "is no more but as I would say unto you, 'The King's Grace will give you a pardon,' and bade you go to the Chancery to fetch it. Also herein you are called rebels, by the which ye shall acknowledge yourselves to have done against the King, which is contrary to your oath."

They all began to cry out then, one saying, "The King hath sent us the faucet but keepeth the spigot. Which is to say we shall none of us taste of the ale." And another shouted that as for the pardon it makes no matter whether we have any or not, for we never offended the King nor his laws." "Nay," said another, "therefore we need no pardon."

"Well then," Sir Francis stopped there, and again they looked, all of them, to him. "Hear you further. A Parliament is appointed, as they say, but neither the place nor the time is appointed. And also here," and he tapped on the pardon with his fingers, "here is written that the King should have care both of your body and soul, which is plain false, for it is against the gospel of Christ, and that I will justify, even to my death."

He looked about at them with his eyes burning in his head, and then cast up his right hand clenched.

"And therefore," he cried, "if ye will take my part in this and defend it, I will not fail you so long as I live, to the uttermost of my power; and who will do so, assure me by your hands and hold them up."

Upon which up went all their hands, and they shouted so that a plowman tramping down the furrow a mile away heard the cry and stopped the horses to listen and wonder what might be afoot.

Then Sir Francis told them what must be done—he to go to Hull, which by now Hallom should have command of, others to make sure of Scarborough, and a letter to be sent to bring out Sir Thomas Percy on their side—and so he and his horsemen rode away down the hill. The others watched them go; the morning was cheerful, and their spirits warmed by enthusiasm and indignation at once.

"Blessed is the day," one told another, "that Sir Francis Bigod and Jack Hallom met together; for an if they had not set their heads together, this matter had not been bolted out."

Then, after a little talk and some argument, they broke up, to fetch their horses, and meet again at the White Cross, and so march against Scarborough.

January 19

Julian Aske came, abruptly as usual, into the winter parlor, having just put Dickon to bed. Her father and mother sat side by side, yet apart, on the settle; Tony and Chris were on the bench under the window, making an appearance of learning their Latin; a little apart her mother's waiting gentlewoman was busy cutting down one of Tony's old coats for Dickon.

When Julian opened the door they were all, except the gentlewoman, talking at once. But when she shut it after her they were silent. Then her mother cried, as if for the last of many times—

"Then you will do nothing! Nothing!"

"I can't," said her father, "turn away mine own brother from his house."

Julian went over to the fire. She set her foot on the raised brick hearth and rested one hand on the chimney. She did not think that just so her uncle would stand, nor how like him she was now, with her eyes bright and her mouth set hard.

"Then," her mother said, in the same sharp voice, "then must we flee away from it ourselves, all of us, as we did in the first insurrection."

Jack fidgeted with the pages of a book he had open on his knee. He said that this time it was different. No man could have done more than Robin to stay the people.

"Why!" Nell laughed. "So he does, with the one hand, and with the other he is trying to shield these traitors. You heard him say how he and Constable wrote that Frank Bigod's messengers should be set free, because, forsooth, 'It's none honest,' says he, 'to keep messengers.'"

"They're poor ignorant fellows—" Jack put in, but half-heartedly.

"Oh! He's taught you. But I'm not so tender of poor ignorant fellows. Let him be tender of his brother and of his father's house. *We* shall suffer for his tenderness."

Tony said, in his new man's voice, and with the air of importance he had grown into since Hob left home—"I think my mother is right. Why should he not go to my Uncle Will Monkton's. Or to one of these great men with whom he sorted in the insurrection. Let them have him. We do not hold with him in his treasons."

"Speak for your own self!" July said so suddenly and so fiercely that they all started and stared. "I do. I hold with him. But it's no treason, but lawful petition of grievances made by all the commonalty and gentry of the North."

"Hold your tongue!" her mother cried; and Tony, "Parrot! Parrot! Who taught you words to speak so pat?" "Quiet! Quiet!" Jack bade all of them.

When he had got silence he began to explain to July, with far more patience than any of the others liked, just why all that her uncle had done before the pardon was treason and needed pardon.

"He says," Julian muttered obstinately, "that he could not in his conscience have let such things happen, as the destruction of the abbeys, and preaching of heretics."

"Well then," said her father, still reasonable and patient, "what will be the end, if every man, because his conscience grudges at what the King does, shall count himself free to move war. Will it not be as in the days of the two Roses? Will it not be so? Come. Answer me."

Julian's face was burning, and she hung her head.

"I can't answer. But he could."

"Ho!" cried Tony, and he and Chris laughed loudly and insultingly at her.

Julian lifted her head, and looked at her mother. "But," she said, "if he goes from this house, I go too."

"God's Passion!" Nell sprang up. "Nay, but you shall go. I'll send you waiting woman to my sister, till you be married to a man that shall teach you reverence and quietness, and that soon."

When Julian had said that she would go from the house she had meant it, but as soon as it was said she thought, with a great jolt, "Where shall I go?" Something came into her mind, giving her answer. She lifted her chin, and scowled back at her mother over her shoulder as she went to the door. She had her finger on the latch, then turned.

"You shall send me where you will. But you shall not marry me. For I will be a nun."

In the darkness outside, when she had shut herself out from them, she was conscious at first only of the impressiveness of the moment she had created, at random as it were, almost it seemed now, out of nothing. But once more she realized the practical difficulty with which she was faced. What should she do now? It would be altogether tame if she returned to the parlor. It was too early to go to bed. The hall would be cluttered with servants getting ready for supper. She could not well lurk on the stairway till it was bedtime. Then she knew where she could go, and her heart lifted again to the height of her defiance, yet this time not angrily but in solemnity. She could go to church.

Outside was a night of full moon, heavily clouded: it was too dark to see, but she could hear a great noise of wind in the orchard trees and in the elms of the churchyard, where the branches strained and ground together, as the gale poured itself through them from the flat countryside. She reached the church porch and only then remembered she had not brought the key, which hung always at the end of the passage by the screens. But just as she realized this, her fingers, groping over the door, touched the cold iron of the key standing in the lock. "Huh!" she thought, as she pushed the door open, "the old man's forgotten again," for the priest from Ellerton, who came here to sing Vespers, was a careless, forgetful old thing.

She shut herself into the church, and into a different world. Here it was black dark, wholly quiet, except for a thin, wailing noise the wind made in the tower; and that seemed to come from a long way off. The air here, though it was still, and smelt of damp, stale rushes, of incense and candle reek, was colder than the living air outside.

She stood for a moment, because it was so dark, and suddenly so quiet, then moved forward. She could see nothing, but knew that the way was clear, if she avoided the bench which stood against the wall just beyond the door.

Then she tripped over something, cried, "Oh!" almost fell, and saved herself by clutching the man's arm who sat there with his feet sprawling out in front of him.

"Who? It's you, Julian!"

The voice was sufficiently like her uncle's voice for her to know him by it. It was so very unlike as to give her a new fright.

"Oh!" she cried again, "what is it? What are you doing here?" and her hands began to feel over him, but he put them away, and said:

"Doing? Nothing."

She had forgotten herself and the reason that brought her here. She sat down by him and laid her hands on his arm.

"Uncle Robin, what is wrong?"

He took a long time to answer and then spoke with a sort of harsh lightness.

"God's Passion! I think everything is wrong."

"Tell me. You must tell me, sir."

"Why? You know it," he cried, as if he could not endure her importunity. Then he muttered, "They took Hallom of the Wold in an attempt on Hull. They've taken Bigod now."

She felt his arm harden under her hands and knew that he clenched his fist.

"And that Bigod's taken, I thank God. For it was he that set Hallom on after I had stayed him and the rest from rising at Beverley. Let Bigod suffer!" Close to her ear in the darkness she heard his teeth grind together, and the sound appalled her by its force and fury. Yet when he spoke it was not anger that altered his voice.

"Hallom's this manner man, July. They say that when none would rise in Hull to take his part, he came safe out of the gate, and as far as the windmill, whence he might without pain have come clear away. But one cried out on him, 'Fie! Will ye go your ways and leave your men behind you?' So he turned back and came to the gate. And so they took him."

"And so," he said after there had been a long silence, "I sit here doing—nothing. I can do nothing. But that I can I will. I have written that they should not try Hallom yet, saying that the North's all dry tinder that a spark will set afire—and that's the truth. And I've sent your Uncle Monkton to bid them—Whom? Oh! Rafe Ellerker and the rest—to bid them a God's name let go on bail all those poor souls taken with Hallom and with Bigod, except only the leaders. So, by the duke comes, they may be forgotten and escape judgment. But I think," he ended bitterly, "I think Rafe Ellerker, like many another, remembers too near how he was with us to dare show mercy."

She hunted in her mind for comfort, but there seemed none to give him.

Then she thought of one who could help. "The King," she began uncertainly—

"I have written to the King," he took her up. "Constable said I wrote too plain, and that he may be displeased. Yet how can I write but the truth? And truth *is* plain."

"He has promised," Julian began. This time he had not spoken, but something rigid in his silence stopped her short.

He said, speaking in a hurry after a long time, "He has promised—I told them so at Beverley. I told them he was gracious lord to us all. So he is. There must be hangings after this late rising, for it's treason, though the people were misled. But he'll keep his promise that he made. I don't doubt it."

"No," she said.

"No. With his own mouth he—"

He started up, and went a few steps away from her.

"I say—'no,'" he said out of the darkness. "But now they may say that we have broken the appointment, so the King need not keep his promise to us."

She knew then what had brought him to lurk here in the church, and for a moment it struck her dumb.

Then she remembered, and was startled to think that she had forgotten why she herself had come there. So she told him.

He did not for a moment take it in. "A nun?" he repeated—"You, a nun? Why, niece?"

"Because I will undertake Christ's cause, and in that stand beside you as I may. And—and—he will prevail." She had begun grandly, but the grandeur tailed off as she thought, "It doesn't sound like the truth. Yet it is the truth."

He knew it for that, but he made no answer, except to say under his breath, "Jesu! Savior!" and then after a long pause—

"There was a poor wench at Marrick, a servant. They said she had seen him go over Grinton Bridge on a peddler's donkey. She would have it he was here, in the realm, now."

Julian could not understand why he told her this, unless it were because she had said, "Christ will prevail," and this was a sign to confirm that saying. Yet it seemed to her that he spoke not at all in triumph, but as if he was reluctant to recall what the woman had seen.

So they sat together, following their own thoughts. She saw herself declared, committed, sealed to the cause of Christ which he had chosen. Once more his mind looked, shrinking, down a road the end of which he dreaded to see. Tonight, as if distress had cleared his sight, he saw farther along it than ever before. Were Christ, he asked himself, were Christ in the realm now, and came to London, a poor man, speaking humbleness, poverty, truth, and the compassion of God, should he prevail, or should he be judged as a malefactor, and so, again, die?

February 3

Very early this morning, when the town of Pomfret was just beginning to stir, and the castle gate had not long been opened, Lord Darcy's litter, with a pretty good number of gentlemen and men-at-arms riding behind it, came to the gate of the Barbican. My lord's litter came through into the ward beyond the gate, but then the guard, who were George Darcy's men, stopped the rest before they could pass in. So Lord Darcy pulled open the leather curtains of the litter, and asked, "Why do you stop here?" and cried, "Get on! Get on!" to the boy riding the leading horse, and then, looking round, seemed for the first time to see the guard there at the gate, with their halberds set against his men outside, and a gentleman of Sir George's who now came out toward the litter.

"Oh!" said he. "It's you, Baynton, is it?"

Master Baynton pulled off his cap. But he said that Sir George had straightly commanded him to admit no one.

"Did he say you should keep out the Constable of the Honor and Castle of Pomfret?"

"No." Master Baynton looked down at his feet, and felt an inclination to shuffle them. "No." But he understood well enough what Sir George's intention had been. The order had been the same for the last three days, but till today the guard had been much stronger, for Sir George had expected the old lord to have been here before this.

"Well," said Darcy pleasantly, but with that in his eyes that Baynton found hard to meet, "It's I now, the constable, that command you let in my people," and leaning out of the litter he said not very loud, but curt and sharp, "Stand back, fellows!"

The men stood back, and Master Baynton had to skip out of the way pretty quick, for the old lord's gentlemen knew what they must do, and they and the men-at-arms came on smartly, packed close in line, knee to knee.

So they were all in the first ward, and my lord's litter going on to the second gate when Sir George came out of that, with his hair and beard not so trim as usual, clutching up his hosen, and with most of the points dangling from under his doublet, for he had just tumbled out of bed, hearing that his father was at the gate.

Lord Darcy beckoned to one of his own gentlemen, and with his help got down from the litter, and stood, taller yet than his son by half a head, all in crimson cloth lined with furs, and an old-fashioned bycoket hat with a brim of fur pulled on over his hood.

"Son George," said he, leaning on his stick, "who in your fantasy is keeper of this castle? Is it thou, or I?"

George Darcy did not like straight questions; he was a man that found crooked answers easiest. So he said—

"Sir, I have letters from the King."

"And I, His Grace's Commission." Lord Darcy began to go under the gate.

"What preparations have you for the duke's refreshment?" he asked over his shoulder, "For I hear he comes from Doncaster this day."

The Duke of Norfolk arrived about dinner time, so after he had dined he and my lord and Sir George went into the privy chamber, and there sat down by the fire with wine, wafers, and a dish of late apples. The duke was just now thawed after a cold ride; he drank, and sighed, and stretched out his feet to the warmth. But though he might have been glad to take his ease he did not forget his duty as the King's lieutenant, and began to ask shrewd questions as to the state of the North, and how many prisoners had been apprehended in the last troubles, who kept them, and had any yet been judged?

The other two, sitting one on each side of him, answered what he asked; sometimes one held the word, sometimes the other was too quick for him, tripped him up and came in first. Sir George leaned forward to it, very earnest, very eager to have the duke's favor, for that, he thought, might mean advancement in times to come. Lord Darcy seemed to play it as a game, with dancing sparks, almost of laughter, in his eyes, although he conceived that to have the duke's good word might, in times to come, mean the difference that lay between life and death.

After they had talked for some time the duke asked my lord to give him leave to speak alone with Sir George.

Darcy got up. "Gladly," he said, flipped George's shoulder as he passed him, as though they were the best of friends, and bade the duke refresh himself well after his journey.

But in the little room over the gate, with Thomas Grice his steward, he frowned over the account books which they spread out before them on the desk.

"I have offered," said he, "to keep Pomfret at my own charges, and that, if the duke consents, will tear the bottom out of my purse. Yet it is most necessary I should keep Pomfret in these days. It'd look ill to hand it over as if I knew myself guilty. And—" he laughed out loud now, "you should ha' seen Sir George's face!"

Sir George, not much later, left the duke alone to repose himself. He was not so merry as his father, though he had nothing to fear, and though the duke had expressed great confidence in him, and bade him be ready always with his men to come to Pomfret at an hour's warning.

February 5

The prioress called from the door of her chamber:

"Shut the gate. Shut the gate, Jankin! Shut the gate, you whoreson!"

Jankin did shut the gate just in time, and then the wild fellows outside began to pelt it with stones, to beat upon it with their quarterstaves and the butts of their pikes, and to shout, "Open, let us in!" At that the ladies, who had crowded out of the cloister, set up such a crying and shrieking as might have been raised in Troy when the Greeks tumbled out of the belly of the wooden horse.

The prioress came down into the great court. She had not screamed, and she turned to shake her fist at those who did, though she would not waste her breath by telling them to stop. She went up to Jankin, who was shoring up the gate with a piece of timber from the pile that was laid ready for sawing. The noise of stones and staves on the door filled the archway, and from the great court behind came the screams of the ladies.

"Who are they?" she shouted in Jankin's ear, and he shouted back that they must be men going to the new muster of the commons at Middleham. There had been bills set up on the church doors the last few days calling out the commons, just as in the first insurrection last October; but these were not like those who had risen then; being poorer, wilder, and more ignorant; some of them came from the savage parts at the head of the dale; some came even from as far as over Westmorland way.

"What do they want?"

But Jankin, no more than the prioress, could make anything of the confusion of voices outside.

"I must find out," the prioress said. "I'll go up to the guest-house chamber." And leaving Jankin to strengthen the door as best he might, she went to fetch the keys, which hung on the wall in his room; even in this emergency she remained sufficiently nice to nip her nose between two fingers as she went in, so potent were the mingled smells of cheese, garlic, Jankin, leather, and mice.

The guesthouse chamber above the gate was rarely entered during the winter, and the lock was stiff to turn, but she got the door open and went in. The room, when there were no strangers upon the road, was apt to be used for lumber, so now besides the settle and stools there were in it a couple of naked bedsteads, an old horse collar with the stuffing coming out of it, a pail of which the wooden strakes had sprung, and a spinning wheel that lacked a treadle. The room was also very dusty, and almost dark, because the tall arched windows at either end were shuttered, and the only light came through a little low window under the eaves on the side facing outward on the cartway.

The prioress picked up a sack, and swept a space clean from dust, and the dry, light bodies of last year's wasps and flies. Then she knelt down on the floor, and looked out upon the rabble below. There were perhaps thirty shaggy, dirty fellows; most of them were standing a little back at this moment; only one of them beat on the door with the haft of a rusty pike, and demanded, with plenty of foul words, that the nuns should open their doors, and give them to eat, "for," said he, "ye nuns, ye have too much, and we have nothing."

The prioress put her head out of the window.

"Stop your knocking on my door," she said, "I cannot hear myself speak."

He obeyed, gaping up at her; they all gaped.

She asked them what did they want.

They said again they wanted meat, of which, they knew, the nuns had store.

She told them, "Who said so, lied. For this long winter has eaten up all that was laid in."

They said let her give them money then, to buy victual withal.

She said, "I have no money," and at that one of them threw a stone. She pulled her head in. Another stone just missed her, and fell among the stuff on the floor.

She stood clear of the window. Let them shy their stones, she thought, and bawl themselves tired, for so they'll pass on the sooner. But she picked up one stone, and with a tight smile flung it back through the little window, a shrewd throw. Someone outside gave a sort of yelp, as much of surprise as pain, and she laughed.

But then she heard something that was no laughing matter. That was a new outcry, but this time the voices came from the great court and cried, "They're in by the stable! They're in by the stable!"

The prioress beat her hands together as she remembered what she had till now forgotten. When a piece of the stable roof had fallen in last year the nuns had not mended it, because of all the money that had gone to buy Lord Cromwell's favor, since it was at a corner and no beasts stood just there. She stamped her foot, and went toward the stair. But when she tried to open the door she could not. She shook it, and hammered on it with her fists, but no one came to let her out.

A good deal later Jankin came and opened for her, but he knew not, he said, and stoutly maintained, who had turned the key.

Nor did anyone else know, or would admit to knowing it. By no means could the prioress discover either who had done it, or their motive—whether of kindness to the Lady, to keep her out of harm's way, or of favor to the rabble who had broken in.

But the damage which these fellows had done was only too easy to ascertain. While the prioress paced up and down the guesthouse chamber, now stamping on the floor and shouting, now silently biting her nails, they had eaten up the ladies' dinner, and when they went away they carried with them a pannier full of white sweet cheeses, as well as two sides of bacon, four hams, the whole of one of the ladies' salted beeves, a firkin of sprats, a dozen hens, and the red cock.

February 6

Today all the gentlemen of Yorkshire were to come to York to take a fresh oath of allegiance to the King, seeing that their first had been so largely broken. Robert Aske left Aughton very early, so early that only plowmen and ditchers and such were on the roads. He would not wait for Jack, because he knew that while Jack would not have refused that they should ride together, yet he had some qualms about it. As for Mistress Nell, the thought that Jack should appear in York at the side of the chief rebel of all had fretted her almost into a fever.

Inside the gate of York the first man that Aske met was Will Bapthorpe, who came out of his lodging with a frowning brow and important air. He, Aske knew, had gone to the duke at Doncaster, and followed him since. He waved a hand to Aske, and then walked alongside, and whispered so that Aske had to stoop from the saddle to hear him.

"You got my letter?"

"Yes. And thanks to you for it."

"You understand? The duke, being the King's Grace's lieutenant, cannot—" He looked aslant at Aske and gestured with his hands in a way that he meant should be eloquent.

"Cannot what?"

"Sh! Cannot show himself gracious to any—to one—to you who—"

"To me, having the King's pardon?"

"Will you not speak low?"

"No," said Aske, "why should I? But it was kindly in you to write and assure me of the duke's favor."

Master Bapthorpe had, however, stiffened. He drew up the fur collar of his coat, dipping his chin deep into it, and stepped aside to let Aske and his people pass on.

The next to hail Aske was Rudston, who leaned out of an upper window just above his head, and cried, "Turn in! Turn in, neighbor Aske, and we'll drink together." He was dressed remarkably fine in plum-colored velvet, and a gilt chain swung out from his breast as he leaned from the window, and shone in the frosty sunlight.

Aske lifted his head and looked him between the eyes.

"Not so early," said he, "but later I'll think of some treason-ous words to speak, that you may report on them."

Except for these two no one whom he knew seemed to be pleased to speak with him. Either they avoided his eye, or, at most, gave him a hasty greeting, and turned away. It was so as he went to his lodging that morning, and through the day, and as he waited with the others to take the oath. It was not difficult for him to get the measure of it; only those sure of the duke's favor, such as Bapthorpe, or nosing about like Nick Rudston for information, the disclosure of which should dem-onstrate their own loyalty, would willingly consort with him; the others would avoid him as his fellows avoid a man that may carry the plague.

That afternoon, in an early dusk, as he knelt in the cathedral after Vespers, the singing having died away, and the footsteps of the singers rustled into silence on their way to the cloister, someone tapped him on the shoulder.

"Master Robert Aske?"

Aske stood up and said he was that same.

"I am one of the Duke of Norfolk's gentlemen. My lord would have a word with you."

Aske went with him. The duke's gentleman suggested that it would be well if he hid his face as much as he could in his cloak, and he did so.

The duke was at Sir George Lawson's house, and sat in that same room, and in that same chair where Aske himself had sat, only last October, and had heard music go through the streets as the people brought the monks back to their houses.

The duke did not rise, but, greeting Aske with a kind of high and distant courtesy which became his rank and reputation, waved him to a stool, and then, wrapping himself closer in his fur-lined, black velvet gown, said:

"Mr. Bapthorpe wrote to you that I would open to you in secret the reasons whereby I cannot show you very friendly countenance?"

Aske bowed his head, and replied that he had received the letter.

"But I did not show Master Bapthorpe those reasons, Master Aske."

Aske bowed again, thinking, "Mass! for a breath of fresh air and plain dealing." The room was very hot, as well as sweet with perfume. Sir George Lawson was eager to do all that he could in honor of the King's lieutenant, and my Lord of Norfolk was known to be of a very chilly humor.

"But with you," said the duke, "I will be plain. It was because I dared not."

Aske almost gaped at him. Here was plain dealing indeed.

"If, Master Aske, you knew the crafty drifts used here to bring me out of credit, you would say that I am not well handled."

For once Aske was at a loss for words. Craft and intrigue— that had been the very burden of his own thoughts, but the marvel was that the duke should share it with him. He could only stare into Norfolk's long face, with its sagging flesh, heavy hooked nose, and eyelids drooping over eyes that seemed weary to look out on the world.

"Tell me," the duke leaned toward him, watching him narrowly, "do men here in the North hold me for one who stands for the old ways, or as one of those who for fear or favor will consent to this New Learning which you call heresy?"

Aske chose his words with care. "When we came to Doncaster, all men, my lord, thought the first."

"And now?"

"Some still think it."

"And you?"

"I have thought both the one and the other."

"The one then, the other now?"

Aske said, with his eye on the duke's, "The first then, the second now."

The duke looked down at his hands, not as if abashed, but considering. At last he smiled. "I like you, Master Aske."

At the duke's tone, and at his friendly look, Aske felt as if his heart had tripped. What the duke had said was nothing, he knew, but how he said it—that was a different matter. For the first time since he had come back from the King, a month ago, he saw a gleam of daylight ahead.

"Sir," he said, and in so eager a voice that it was as though another man spoke, "my Lord Darcy told me that, before ever this pilgrimage was made, fifteen great lords swore together to suppress heresy and its maintainers. If you—"

"Fifteen great lords?" Norfolk had spoken sharply enough to interrupt, but now his tone was slow and reflective—"Who were they then?"

"He never told me their names."

Norfolk leaned back again in his chair. "Well, I can guess their names. Go on."

"My Lord Darcy told me this to put me in comfort not to fear the heretics," Aske explained. "The appointment of those lords took none effect. But if the great nobles are of our part, and if they will come forward in time, then our cause is not lost. But they must come forward in time. They must come forward now, or all will be to do again."

"Master Aske," said the duke, "will you raise war in the realm as it was in my father's and your grandfather's time?"

"That was different. That was House against House, and King against King. The cause now—I hold it to be of God."

"But you would move war against your Prince, for any cause?"

"My lord," said Aske steadily, "I have always thought, as did we all, that it were best to get the statutes reformed first by petition, but if we could not so obtain, then to get them reformed by sword and battle."

"Now," he thought, "he must dismiss me." But the silence lengthened. Aske looked beyond the duke's shoulder to where, pictured on the woven hangings of the room, a dog came out of a lake carrying a duck in its mouth; beside the lake a tree stood, on which a huge hawk perched; the tree bore six leaves as big as trenchers, and three acorns. It was the same hanging that had been here on the night when he sat writing the oath of the pilgrims; in the silence now, as then, the cathedral bells spilled out their notes on the air with the same cool, sweet deliberation.

Because his blind side was toward the duke he did not know how closely he was being studied, but at last the duke spoke.

"Master Aske," said he, "what I shall tell you, I should tell few other men. Will you promise me that you will keep my words to yourself?"

Aske promised, and as he did so thought, mistakenly— "None but an honest man would think an honest man's word enough."

"Have you," the duke said, "ever considered that patience and endurance may better serve than to resist? No. Don't answer me yet. You are a man of the law, they tell me; you will have read in the histories of old time, both of this realm and of others, how some things continue ever, some cease, and some, after mutations, return. And how, above all, there is no man, *no man*, Master Aske, but is mortal."

Now he waited, and Aske said, "You mean—the cardinal died, and—"

Norfolk held up his hand. "Enough. We understand each other." Then he sighed. "All this that has come upon the realm has come of a wench's black eyes, and I wish, though she were my niece, that she had never been born.

"But consider. For close on a thousand years there have been monks in England, and holy church has been one through Christendom. Is it likely that in one day one man, and that man not the King but a lowborn fellow, shall pull down the one, and cleave asunder the other, forever?"

Aske shook his head.

"No!" said the duke, looking pleased, but he had mistaken Aske's meaning.

"No," said Aske again. "Yet it could be so did none take a hand to stay it, neither in this day, nor in time to come."

"I cannot much fear it," the duke said loftily. "But even if we fear it, how we should best stay it is the question.

"Take my case," he leaned forward, incredibly gracious and familiar. "Say I let my likings show, what will happen? I know. I can tell you. At the best I shall be at Kenninghall, in the country, speaking my counsel to the ditches and the willows, but never to the King's ear. What can I do then? And that is at the best. At the worst it will be Tower Hill on some threadbare pretext.

"But if I serve loyally my Prince, I may the better also serve Holy Church, since if I serve not my Prince, other men, and worser, will be in my place."

They were silent again then. Aske, though unconvinced, did not, for respect's sake, wish to insist on that which he had already made clear as a line. The cathedral bells chimed again, and then there came another sound at which the duke turned his head toward the shuttered windows. The sound grew till the hoofs of the hard-ridden horse rang below them on the cobbles of the street and stopped with a clattering slide. There was some shouting, a door slammed, then another door, so that the house shook. Before even Master Appleyard had tapped, Norfolk cried, "Open there! Open!" Behind Appleyard came in a messenger, booted, and cloaked, with his cap in his hand, but his hood yet on his head.

"From the King's Grace," he said. Norfolk dropped on his knees and took the letter. "Go," he said to Aske, and already his long fingers were picking at the seal.

Aske moved toward the door after the other two who had already gone out. But he lingered, because he had remembered something which, when he came into the room, he would not have believed himself able to forget.

"My lord," he said, "there is one thing I must speak of, if I have leave."

"I've no leisure now," said the duke.

"Yet I must," Aske said, and at his voice and his stubborn look the duke stared, but could not stare Aske down.

"Well, be brief."

"I charged Master Bapthorpe," said Aske, "with a message about one Levening—I do not think he gave it."

"Levening that's a prisoner now? No. He did not."

Aske plunged into it then. Levening was innocent of treason. Bigod had forced him to come out in that last insurrection, and Hallom had threatened to burn his farms if he did not.

The duke turned his back, and moved away now to the fire. He gave Aske barely time to finish, then said:

"Why do you tell me this?"

"I promised him I would speak for him. He came to me because he feared he would be indicted."

"He was right to fear. I must do justice, Master Aske, and terrible justice."

"It would not be justice to hang Levening."

Norfolk looked at him over his shoulder.

"Master Aske, Bapthorpe knew, but it seems you know not, that it is dangerous to speak so."

"Not to speak so to you, my lord."

"Well, you have spoken." The duke turned away again, and Aske knew that he was dismissed.

When he came by the minster on his way back to his lodging the moon, not quite full, shone on the east end, making the glass of the windows shine white like ice. He looked up at the great bulk of stone upon which the nearer details showed softly and solemnly, while the shadows of every buttress towered up, densely black.

More than once he walked about the circuit of that huge creature of men's hands, revolving in his mind the duke's words and looks, and the tones of his voice, recalling to himself that once he had doubted my Lord Darcy, and how needlessly; and once he had doubted the King, yet he had been gracious. At last he stopped walking, and stood with his head bent, not looking up at the height of stone above him, but very conscious of it. "Shall I doubt God?" he asked himself.

February 13

The prioress found her little greyhound bitch gracefully sprawling upon her new coverlet. The coverlet was of light green verders, embroidered with white butterflies and true lovers' knots, and the little bitch had been rooting in a muddy corner of the great court: the prioress's rebuke was therefore severe, and her attention so absorbed by the damage to the coverlet that she took no notice of an outcry in the court below. She was indeed used to such outcries, few of which needed her interference any more than those others, not so dissimilar, which arose from rivalries among the priory poultry.

But now, as she stooped over the fawning apologetic animal, the door opened, and Dame Bess Dalton came in, her face crimson and her voice a squeak.

"They are come," she cried. "They are come to turn us out. And O! Chrissie, to take you away and hang you," and she threw her arms round the prioress, remembering only the old years when they were Bess and Chrissie, whispering and tittering together behind the ladies' backs.

The prioress, who was not thinking of those days at all, disengaged herself decisively. Her mind was wholly on the present, and in that present, no longer ago than yesterday, and no farther away than York, nine men, three of whom wore the monk's cowl, had been condemned to death for their part in the late troubles.

To do her justice, however, her thought was not wholly on this news of hangings which had been served up to the ladies this morning with their mixtum. "They cannot," she said, and the little greyhound cowered down again at the sound of her voice. "We have license to continue. They cannot turn us out. Who is come?" she asked sharply.

Dame Bess Dalton did not know who it was. But his men held the gate now, and had shut into the cloister all the ladies except herself and Dame Margery. And when she had mentioned the chambress Dame Bess wrung her hands together.

"Dame Margery laid herself down across the gate. She said the men should come in over her body only."

"And did they?"

Dame Bess mumbled that they did. "They stepped over. And then she sat up."

Even at this moment of crisis the prioress laughed aloud, then composed her face. She heard voices close outside.

"They are at the door. Open to them," she said.

The gentleman sent by the duke came in first, with a disdainful look; he was a big man, and in half-armor, so that the floor timbers groaned under him where a joist was weak. Sir Rafe Bulmer came in after him, but patently unwilling. The prioress, having found time to seat herself in her chair, rose with dignity and welcomed them.

Dame Bess, who had to tell the story many times before bedtime that night, did full justice to the prioress's conduct of the interview.

The duke's gentleman had spoken very high at first of traitors and of naughty papistical persons. "'Therefore,' quod he," so Dame Bess reported the kernel of the conversation—"'Therefore you must come with me, madame, and for the rest of you, I shall turn you out of doors and leave my men here to take charge,' and thereupon he looked at me, so that I quaked.

"But the Lady, she says, 'The first, and welcome. But the second you may not.'"

"'May not?' quod he. 'May not? May not turn forth a nest of traitors that have given shelter and comfort to the King's enemies in this last treasonous disorder?'

"'Sir,' then said the Lady, 'shelter nor comfort we never gave but they broke in on us and spoiled us. But turn out the ladies of this house you may not, who have the King's own license to continue. Lord Privy Seal also,' says she, 'being good lord to us.'"

"Mass!" cried Dame Anne Ladyman triumphantly. "That would give him to think on."

Dame Bess agreed, "Aye, for though he did fret and fume awhile yet he spoke no more of turning us out."

Dame Anne called down a blessing on Lord Privy Seal at that, and even those that in general had little liking for him looked at each other with a sort of covert pride in having such a protector.

"But poor Malle! They will not hurt her, will they? There was never harm in those things she saw. Why did the Lady have her go with them to the duke? And that poor lubber Wat too?"

For a moment no one answered Dame Margaret Lovechild. Then, "Tush!" cried Dame Anne, "she did not take Wat, but he ran after them. And who cares for a creature like Malle?"

That was further than some of them would have gone, and there was danger of a division arising among them. Yet when Dame Bess explained that the prioress had taken Malle to the duke "because the man said that we are evil reported on to him, for the sake of her visions," even the most tender-hearted were impressed.

"And there," said Dame Anne, "is our prioress given over to the malice of evil men, and some of us think of mad Malle!"

So they ceased to think of her, and returned to their questions about the prioress.

"Tell us again," said one, "what were her last words before she went away."

"We left her alone for a while," began Dame Bess, "as she commanded us."

"Did she pray when you left her?"

"We could not see. She bade us wait at the foot of the stairs."

"And then?" they prompted.

"She called us up again and said, 'Tell the ladies I have that shall stand me, and the house, and all of us in good stead.'"

They questioned among themselves what she had meant.

"Surely it was God's help she spoke of," Dame Margery Conyers said, and flushed to the edge of her coif, while her eyes filled with tears.

They all exclaimed that truly it must be so. But some of them would have felt more confidence had they known that the prioress spoke of the precious little pyx and the bag of gold that had lain hidden in the secret recess, and which she had taken out during those few minutes when she was left alone.

For a long time that evening the ladies sat around the dying fire in the warming house, discussing the case of the prioress, and their own case, while the candles guttered and flared unnoticed. At first they were inclined to be hopeful, but as the night deepened round them their spirits sank, and they began to fear not only for the Lady's life, but also the onset of every imaginable enemy, whether of rats in the ceiling, or rough men from the upper dale, or soldiers sent to fetch them after the prioress, or those ghosts and ghouls that wake when hearts beat weakest. Though at another time they would have reveled in this long, late, garrulous sitting, tonight they would have been only too glad to hear the prioress's voice, chiding them off to the beds they longed for but did not dare to seek for the perils that thronged on every side of their way upstairs.

February 16

The castle and town of Richmond were crammed with men and horses, and more coming in every hour, for the Duke of Norfolk had called on the gentlemen of Yorkshire to go with him to put down the poor commons in Cumberland, who had risen, and were besieging Carlisle.

This was a sore business for the duke, who feared to be blamed for it, as he feared to be blamed for anything that went wrong in the North, now he was the King's lieutenant in those parts. So his temper was frayed and his patience short as he sat by a sea-coal fire in a room that led off the great old Norman hall in the castle, conning lists of victuals and fodder for beasts, of pikes, of guns, of barrels of arrows, while a couple of clerks wrote busily, a group of gentlemen conversed quietly by one of the windows, and men came and went incessantly with messages and questions and the duke's orders. Far below the castle the Swale ran full over its ledges of rock, making in its falls a great noise, which came up to the duke's ears as a hush, like the sound of wind sifting through dry autumn leaves.

Now and again, when the door into the great hall was opened, the noise of men talking there quite drowned the sound of the river. At one time indeed, even with the door shut, the voices outside rose so angrily that the duke, frowning, sent one of the gentlemen to order the disputants to observe more propriety.

"Who," the duke snapped, "was brawling?"

"Master Aske," said he who had gone out.

Norfolk looked up sharply, then down. "Ah?" he said, "and of what did he dispute?"

"He maintained that these commons of Cumberland rise not against the King, but to defend their goods and wives against Clifford's horsemen, who, says he, are all strong thieves of the Westlands, and themselves fitter to stretch halters than the poor men of Kirby."

"It might have been thought," said Norfolk acidly, "that one so lately and so deeply dipped in treason would have held his tongue in such a matter as this."

"Yea! Yea!" said they all with great fervor, most of them having been among the Pilgrims of Grace last year, and not liking the memory of it.

But Norfolk stooping again over his papers felt the thought of Aske as unwelcome in his mind as a stone would have been in his shoe. He fairly hated the man, so sure of himself, so glorious even yet as to boast that he would know if there were any stirring in the North and would warn my lord of it.

And now he spoke openly the truth about this business at Carlisle and Kirby as he had spoken it privily to the duke himself. "Yet," the duke answered his own conscience or else it was his pride which pricked him—"Yet I myself wrote much the same to the King's Grace," and he plumed himself on that for a minute, and then regretted it when he remembered, with a jolt and a sudden qualm, the King's hard, bullying look one day when he had said how men whispered that for favor my Lord of Norfolk had forborne to fight the North Countrymen at

Doncaster. That made the duke glad to remember another letter he had written, this one to Sir Christopher Dacres, ordering him to set on the commons before Carlisle—"and spare not," he had written, "to slay plenty of these false rebels." He had the copy of that letter, and could, if there were need, produce it.

That evening when all preparations were completed, the duke, having a little leisure before bedtime, consented to see this prioress of Marrick for whom he had sent, and who, since her coming, had given the officers no rest, importuning them always that she should be brought to my lord.

When she was brought to him, between two pikemen, he frowned upon her blackly, and then, the more to awe her, said nothing, but looked down at the papers in his hand, or spoke to his clerk, or to one or other of those gentlemen who were with him. But his intention miscarried, for he gave her what she needed—an opportunity to study his face, just as old Andrew had used to study a new buyer of his wool. In her mind she summed him up quickly—he was proud, that of course, since he was first and greatest of the old noble blood; and he was subtle, she knew it by the underlook of his lowered eyes; but was he so sure of himself, or of his footing, as his dignity pretended? "We'll see," she thought.

"Hah!" he said at last, as if he had only now realized her presence—"Another of these naughty papist religious. And I hear that you were instant to be brought to me. I wonder, Madame, that you do not tremble, seeing that I bear the King's sword here for justice on all papists and traitors."

The prioress went down on her knees, but she kept her chin high. She said in her clear voice that she was no papist, and that she did not tremble since the King's loyal subjects had nothing to fear from His Grace's lieutenant.

"Nothing to fear?" he scoffed at her, and began to rail upon monks and nuns.

But the prioress watching him saw that hotly as he spoke, as if from the heart, yet he kept on looking now at the clerks, now at the gentlemen by the window, with a sort of calculation in his glance, that ill-suited the freedom of his words. So she said to herself, "All this for show!"

"I've a mind," cried the duke, "to send you and your wench to London, to answer before the King's Grace and his honorable Privy Council—you for your treasons, and she for these pretensed visions. For it may be," said he, with a very piercing look, "that as in time past sundry great persons were, with traitorous intent, confederate with that Nun of Kent against the King's person and health, so now once more. And what will ye answer to that?" But he looked triumphantly toward the gentlemen, and not at the prioress.

"Sir," said she, "that I will go right gladly, and at my own charges."

"What?" he said, and now stared at her, quite taken aback. So serene was her face that he could only think she spoke the truth, as indeed she did.

"Give me license, my lord," said she, "to go to London, where I may plead the cause of our poor house, taking with me our poor fool—"

"Fool?" Norfolk was sharp, for this was a new idea. He would look the fool if he sent a poor want-wit all the way to London with a charge founded upon idle tittle-tattle.

The prioress read him. "The wench," she said, "is a poor thing, but she has this strange manner visions. If there be evil persons who think to use her, of whom I know not, that matter should be bolted out."

She dropped her eyes humbly, but within herself she smiled. If—and she would have wagered Marrick's best crucifix that it was so—if the duke feared to be ill reported of to the King, and to Lord Privy Seal, now he would hesitate to keep this matter in his own hand.

He crossed one knee over the other, and drummed with his fingers on the arm of the settle on which he sat. She looked no higher than his foot, and saw that fidget and swing. Neatly and quietly she drove in her last nail. "I have," said she, "already sent a letter to my Lord Privy Seal in this matter, seeing that he is so good lord to us, and as it were our second founder, asking his license to come to him."

There was no more then to be said. Norfolk dismissed the prioress, informing her, with a rigid and impressive dignity, that he would take order in her case to send her to the King. Yet though his dignity might appear to be unimpaired he was conscious that this woman had gone beyond him. Yet he took comfort. He would waste no money over her, since she would go at her own charges. And if she went hardly at all as a prisoner, his own part in it would be, if necessary, the easier to disavow.

He got up at last, yawned, and called for his gentlemen to bring wine and candles. "Tomorrow," said he, "we must set out betimes. There's bad roads between us and Cumberland."

February 24

After the trial of the seventy-four rebels of the commons in the hall of Carlisle Castle, the Duke of Norfolk walked awhile on the walls with Sir Rafe Ellerker and Master Robert Bowes. The trial, though briskly conducted, had been, necessarily, because of the number of the accused, a longish business, and the hall uncomfortably hot, for these last days had been more like early May than February.

Now therefore it was pleasant to walk in the fresh air, and the duke spoke cheerfully, though with a proper sobriety, of the work they had together been engaged in, Sir Rafe having been marshal in the late trial, and Master Bowes attorney for the King.

"Truly," said the duke, "had I proceeded by jury, rather than by martial law with the King's banner displayed, I think not the fifth man of them would have been condemned."

He looked at Bowes, and Bowes nodded. Knowing him for a silent man the duke found that enough, and went on:

"For you heard how the poor caitiffs said, 'I came out for fear of my life, or for fear of burning of my houses, and destroying of my wife and children.' And here, in these parts, a small excuse would have been well believed by a jury, where much pity and affection of neighbors doth reign." The duke looked at each of them again, thinking, "They shall know that I do not fear to speak my mind," and thinking, "There's no disloyalty in that."

They stood for a moment at the turn, feeling the light breeze that touched their faces pleasantly. From within the castle came sounds of voices and a busy stir, but outside, though knots of men stood about the streets, the town lay strangely quiet; they could hear someone chop wood, and a woman chide a crying child, but otherwise it might have seemed that those who went about walked in their sleep.

The three turned and began to go back again.

"So I hope that His Grace will be content with our doings," said the duke, "for though the number be nothing so great as their deserts did require to have suffered, seeing that of six thousand I reserved only seventy-four for punishment, yet I think the like number hath not been heard of put to execution at one time."

And again he looked from one to another, and rubbed his hands together.

"Come," said he, "you must be glad to have so well discharged your duty to your Prince."

They said then, Sir Rafe leading, that they were glad.

"And that you shall surely know you have done what shall please His Grace," Norfolk said, "I shall read you a letter." He took it out from his pouch, and spread it out upon the coping of the wall, and ran his finger along the lines to find his place.

"'Our pleasure,'" he read, "'is that before ye shall close up our Banner again, you shall in any wise cause such dreadful execution to be done upon a good number of the inhabitants of every town, village, and hamlet, that have offended in this rebellion, as well by hanging of them up in trees, as by quartering of them, and setting up their heads and quarters in every town great and small, and in all such other places as they may be a perfect spectacle.'"

He folded up the paper again, and then looked into their faces.

"So," said he, "you see that both you and I have well served the King. Lawyers may say, '*Fiat Justitia, ruat coelum.*' But it is better that these, whom blind Justice might have spared, should suffer, when by the example of such a dreadful severity, many more may be prevented from light doings."

They said, the two Yorkshire gentlemen, that it was better, and that the King was a most gracious, godly, and wise Prince.

February 26

The Duke of Norfolk and the muster of gentlemen who had followed him from Richmond to Barnard Castle, and Barnard Castle to Carlisle, came down from the high, bleak moors to the gentle valley of the South Tyne. The sun was low, warm upon their backs, and flashing upon the pikes and halberd blades, when they came within sight of the town of Hexham, sheltered among its orchards. The great bulk of the priory showed above the walls, piling itself up to the high-ridged roof and tower of the church itself. From the priory tomorrow the canons would be put out, and the King's receiver put in to assess the value of their stuff, and of the stuff in that church, one of the most ancient in the realm, and for the North perhaps the holiest. So

Aske, who rode ahead with those of the duke's gentlemen who were to prepare for his coming, would look everywhere in the golden green sunset valley, except at the priory.

After supper, because he did not care to listen to the talk of a parcel of young men who were boasting of the lesson that the saucy commons had received at the duke's hands, he went out, and wandered aimlessly about the town. It was growing dusk when he came to the place where the brook ran out under the wall of the canons' garden; the evening air was still and pure, with a deep blue dusk; a thrush sang in one of the taller trees; the stars were coming out and there was a tang of frost as well as the scent of wood smoke from the evening fires. He leaned on the rail of the little foot bridge, listening to the voice of the water with its sweet chucklings and whisperings.

A bell began to ring, uncertainly at first, then steady and insistent. Someone in the priory had not forgotten that it was time for Compline, even if it were the last time that Compline should be sung. Aske listened for a minute, then began in a great hurry to go round the wall toward the church.

He reached the cloister as the bell jangled into silence. Three of the canons were going into the church by the door in the northeast corner. He made haste to come up with them, and when he reached the door found that one of them was waiting, who now laid his arm across the open door, barring the way.

Aske stood still. He had come here in haste, because of great need, and for a moment he could find no words. He looked at the canon, a man of about his own age, but long, lean, and already gray. The canon, bending forward in the gathering dusk, saw a man with one eye. "Who are you?" he said sharply.

Some obscure eddy of discarded habit put the answer into Aske's mouth.

"The great captain," he said, and then—"A man desperate."

"Come in, my son," the canon answered him.

In the silent and darkening church Aske knelt down beside a pillar, leaning his shoulder and forehead against the stone. Far away in the choir the three canons began their Vespers; their voices attenuated and deadened by the emptiness around, but answering steadily and promptly, one to another, in the familiar responses. The darkness grew deeper, so that the one candle that they had lit began to cast strong shadows, while the windows turned blank and black with the night outside. Once, when one of the canons passed between the candle flame and the wall of the choir, his shadow leapt up, monstrous, to the very clerestory.

When Compline was over Aske heard their footsteps die away and the door into the cloister clap to. It had seemed to him that one of the canons lingered, as if expecting him to get up from his knees and come away, but he had not moved, being ashamed of the tears that ran down his face.

At last he got up, stiff and dazed, and groped to the door. He had his hand stretched out to unlatch it when it swung inward, and he saw, in the swimming light of a number of torches, a small company, and upon the very threshold of the doorway, one man alone. Aske stood still, his eye dazzled and his mind amazed, till he recognized in the gentleman who stood almost foot to foot with him the Duke of Norfolk.

"My lord!" he said, "My lord, you must hear me!"

Norfolk had for a second stood staring, almost as startled as the man who had blundered at him out of the dark church.

Then he saw who it was; he saw the disorder of Aske's face, and along with disgust and quickened dislike came the thought—"In this state that he is in he might speak more freely than he means."

So, leaving the others to begin the business of the inventory of the stuff in the church, he turned back, and into the warming house. One of the servants stuck a torch into a bracket and tried to stir up the fire, but the ashes were dead, so he went away, shutting the door upon the duke and Robert Aske.

The duke sat down. "Well, what must I hear of you?" After a minute, restraining his impatience, he said in a mild tone, "Come, Mr. Aske."

He did not, however, learn much, or not much to the purpose. At first Mr. Aske clamored, in a manner almost distraught, that the duke should have mercy upon the poor ignorant commons, closing the King's banner, and pardoning such as had not suffered. When he began to grow calmer, the duke put certain questions to him, about Lord Darcy, Sir Robert Constable, and others. But then he would speak only in their favor, stoutly maintaining that there never had been any acquaintance between my Lord Darcy and himself before he came to Pomfret, and that nor the old lord, nor Constable, nor he had intended treason, but lawfully to petition the King.

Yet—as the duke remarked afterward to Mr. Appleyard—such tenderness toward those taken in treason argued little loyalty to the King's Grace, and that great faithfulness and kindness that was manifest between Lord Darcy and this man Aske—he being but a gentleman of no great House—might in itself be held as worthy of suspicion.

The duke stopped there, and regarded Mr. Appleyard closely, though covertly, wondering, "Will he report to the King my faithful carefulness in His Grace's service?"

March 4

July said, standing beside Mistress Holland at the vintner's door: "Hear me while I say it again. Is this right?

> Take new cheese and grind it fair
> In mortar with eggs without disware.
> Put powder thereto of sugar I say,
> Color it with saffron full well thou may.
> Put it in coffins that be fair,
> And bare it forth, I thee pray!

"Thou hast it, sweet," cried Mistress Holland, patting July's shoulder. "That is how I make my flawnes."

"But," said July, stepping down into the street, where already Laurence's prentice boy was waiting to see her home, "it's the pie crust for the coffins that I cannot make as you make it, so crumbly and light."

"Lord!" Mistress Holland waved her hand over July's head to a neighbor going by. "Lord! there are who can make pie crust, and who cannot. But chiefly ye must keep it ever dry. Your wet crust is your hard sad crust."

"Well, I must e'en try," said July, and sighed.

"There!" Mistress Holland leaned down from the step and kissed her, then whispered in the shelter of July's big white kerchief, "Never fear for thy pie crust, sweet, to please thy husband. Tell him what thou hast told me. That's how best to please him."

So July went off, with the boy close behind her. She said to herself—"Friday dinner, herrings and flawnes, and ling in that green sauce." She sighed again. She was not averse to pleasing Laurence, since he was always so kind, but she would have preferred to have pleased him by making light crisp crumbly flawnes than in that way which had caused Mistress Holland such delight to hear of. She did not want a child, yet it seemed that she carried one now. She felt as she had felt when Mistress Holland had told her—a little scared, and much more perturbed, but most of all as if she had suddenly become a different person, or two persons—July, whom she had always known, and, as well, this stranger that housed a stranger. Yet, though perturbing, the situation was not, she decided, without its advantages, since she felt herself vastly more important than she had ever been. Looked upon in that light the event should, she thought, be celebrated. She stopped therefore and bought some caraway comfits which she and the boy enjoyed on the way home; July treated him fair; each drew out one at a time and ate till all were gone.

March 6

The prioress of Marrick, making use of the privilege of a guest and the pretext of an aching tooth to abstain from Terce, went up instead to the prioress's chamber in the priory of St. Helen's,

Bishopgate Street, in London. Not for the first time since she came here a fortnight ago, she was struck, as she stood looking round the spacious room, vaulted and painted above, wainscoted and painted below, with the opulence of its design, and the poverty of its garnishings. On the tall carved livery cupboard there was nothing of silver, but wooden bowls and horn cups only; there were no cushions to give ease upon the settle by the hearth; the prioress's bed stood bare, with naked tester and sparver; when the prioress of Marrick sat down on it, instead of sinking into the softness of feathers, she heard the harsh rustle of straw.

"God's Passion!" she cried softly to herself, throwing up her clenched hands, and bringing them down upon her knees. It was a relief to be alone, and able to express the impatience that bore hard on her. This waiting of hers upon the pleasure of Lord Privy Seal was made no easier for her by the punctuality and assiduity with which these ladies of St. Helen's kept their Hours, and she began to move restlessly about the room, remembering how near Privy Seal's house was, almost next door, in Broad Street, yet she had not succeeded in finding a means of coming to his presence. And then she began to reckon what money had been spent already, and what yet remained to spend in the buckskin bag, and to try to fathom the bailiff's report of his efforts to obtain Lord Privy Seal's ear. "Is he cheating me?" she thought, or perhaps it was rather, "How much doth he cheat me?"

In her impatient wanderings she came again to the foot of the prioress's bed. A big hutch stood there, an old-fashioned but very handsome piece of furniture, carved with foliated circles, and arches traceried like church windows.

To divert her thoughts from trouble the prioress of Marrick jerked it open, and looked inside; it was full to the top. She laid back the lid upon the bed, and began to go through the stuff there, turning it up carefully at one corner so as to make no disturbance.

There were silk embroidered coverlets, and curtains of fine needlework for the bed; under these she came upon cushions, tasseled, fringed, and worked with roses, butterflies, birds; there were carpets for the cupboard and table, and at the bottom, wrapped separately in soft leather, such silver cups that at the sight Christabel Cowper's eyes widened, and color came up to her cheekbones as she remembered how she had led the conversation round about till she could boast about her own great cup Edward; but Edward was a poor thing compared with the least of these. There were also, among the silver things, two pairs of very gay shoes, one of red leather, the other of green.

"Mass!" said the prioress to herself, and, "Why?" Then she laughed aloud. It must be that these things were laid by because it was Lent; such might well be the fashion among these dutiful daughters of St. Benedict. She made all neat again, and shut the lid, lingering only for a second as she considered whether to take out and use one of the cushions. But though the prioress of St. Helen's was a vague, elderly dame, and timid (Christabel thought) as a sheep, and though Christabel might be on occasion peremptory, contradictory, or scornful with her, yet there was that in her (perhaps it came to her by birth and blood) which made the prioress of Marrick unwilling to take such a liberty as this. So, shutting the hutch with a little slam, she went again restlessly about the room.

There were three arched windows along one side of the room; that side looked out upon the church, which, tall, new, and stately, took all the sun, except for a short time at noon. On the other side and at the end farthest from the hearth, was another window, but it was shuttered, and she had never seen it open. This morning, because the prioress of St. Helen's and the ladies were so devout, and because, since it was Lent, she must, forsooth, sit without cushions, and because she was sure the bailiff was cheating her, and because she was by no means sure that her long journey here would not end in failure—because of all these vexations, she laid hands on the shutters, unbarred and swung them inward.

With them came, like a wave pouring into the room, all the noise, stir, and color of a busy street, that was also full of sunshine. "By St. Eustace!" the prioress murmured, and leaned out, smiling, partly in derision at those who so regarded Lent, and partly from pure pleasure in the lively light and the moving crowd.

A little way along Bishopgate Street a gentleman and his servants were coming out of the yard of a big hostelry, where was the sign of the Bull hung out over the archway. They came past just below the prioress, so that she caught the winking flash of the jewel in the gentleman's ear, and got an excellent view of the strong curling black hairs of his clipped beard, and of the gold chain over his shoulder; so fine he was, in scarlet velvet and white hosen, that she must suppose he was on his way to court; as he went out of sight her heart went with him there.

Then her ear was caught by a run of notes played upon a lute, and her eyes were drawn to a window which stood open almost opposite the window in which she stood. A plump, very comely young woman sat there, with half-shut eyes and a half smile, placid as a cat which sits purring in the sunshine. From beyond her shoulder leaned a young man's face that looked hungrily on her, while a boy in the room behind them sang:

> Alone I live, alone,
> And sore I sigh for one.
> No wonder though I mourning make
> For grievous sighs that mine heart doth take,
> And all is for my lady's sake.
> Alone I live, alone,
> And sore I sigh. . . .*

The prioress of Marrick could see how during the song the young man's hand stole out and was laid upon the young woman's honey-colored satin lap; she saw too how the young woman took it up by the wrist, between two of her fingers, as though it were a thing she were loth to touch, and so removed it from her knee. The prioress smiled, yet sighed; she liked the young woman's action, which seemed to show a decision of character such as she must approve; yet she was grieved for the young man, whose face wore such a look of loving and longing. She was sorry when, as the song ended, the two of them went away from the window.

---

*Music and lyrics for this song can be found on page 558.

But still there was plenty to watch; a funeral passed, with candles and torches pale in the sunshine, and many painted escutcheons, priests in plenty, and a long tail of mourners following like a black shadow. Then, in the midst of the street, for a moment empty, a young girl in gray woolen gown and white coif met a tall prentice lad. The girl put her hand on the lad's shoulder, and lifted her face, fresh as a flower, to be kissed. The boy, more shy than she, stooped, a little awkwardly, and kissed her.

The prioress laughed at that, so pretty a thing it was, and so aptly redressing the balance tipped by the proud young woman in honey-colored satin, against love and the springtime. She heard the door of the room behind her open, and turned, still smiling.

"When gorse is out of bloom," she said to the prioress of St. Helen's, hesitating behind her, "kissing's out of season. Here have I been watching the prettiest shows as if I were at a masking."

The prioress of St. Helen's came closer; she was nearsighted, with a plain, old, wrinkled face and indeterminate expression. She glanced out of the window, went away, came again, and said:

"Madame—that window—we keep it shut nowadays." When the prioress of Marrick made no reply other than to raise her eyebrows, the Lady of St. Helen's stepped back, but again returned and with a very high color and flustered air, reached past the guest, and pushed the shutters to.

"Jesu!" said the prioress of Marrick, "this is indeed to keep Lent."

"Lent?"

"Why, yes. Is not all this—" Christabel Cowper waved her hand to the bare poles of the bed. "Is it not for Lent?"

The older woman, flushed and confused, dropped her eyes, and muttered that, no, it was not for Lent, and then with a rush of words—"but it is for our sins, that we lived in religion so worldly for a long time, till God's chastisement (I mean the fear we now live in) remembered us of our Rule. So now," she said, her hands picking at her gown, "so now, hoping that God may be merciful, and turn from us his anger, and save us—we—we—"

"I should ha' thought," the prioress of Marrick broke in, "that a plump purse given to my Lord Privy Seal had been of more service in saving your house."

"Forsooth!" said the other, with great simplicity, "that we have given already, or rather we have given him an annuity."

Christabel Cowper laughed. "Then why not sit on your cushions and look out on the sunshine and the street?" said she, but the other did not answer, except by shaking her head with a troubled air, so that there was silence till the prioress of St. Helen's asked haltingly whether the Marrick bailiff had sped any better this day.

"No better—yet it cost him four angels—so he says."

"Alas!" The prioress of St. Helen's sighed and hung her head; then after some fidgeting and clearing of her throat brought out a question.

"And the poor woman you brought from the North, that the sheriff's officers took away to prison in the Fleet— Is she . . .

Have you . . . Do you hear of her? And the poor little knave that would not be parted from her?"

The prioress of Marrick turned. Was she to be questioned by this shrinking creature, and concerning Malle, the crazed fool that had helped to bring Marrick to this pass? She stared hardily into the other's eyes, but this time she could not look them down.

"I hear nothing. The matter lieth not now in my hand."

She was at the door before the prioress of St. Helen's mumbled, "Yet they are of your people. You are . . . you . . ."

"I," said Christabel Cowper, "am a loyal subject of the King's Grace," and on that she opened the door and went out.

March 21

The old lame tailor had come to the castle at Pomfret to try on Lord Darcy's new gown; black velvet it was, trimmed and lined with black sarcenet. He stood now, reaching up and breathing hard through his nose as he untied the laces at the neck of my lord's doublet. Darcy, his head turned aside, could see where the gown lay across the coverlet of the great bed, on which an embroidery of swans and cocks, cunningly disposed, made a trelliswise pattern of white, black, and tawny.

The tailor got the laces undone, and the buttons, and Darcy turned, slipping the doublet from his arms, just as one of his gentlemen came in with a look startled and discomposed.

"What now, George?" Darcy hailed him. George Nevill had been in my lord's household since his boyhood.

"A letter, sir."

Darcy took it. When he saw the mark of the King's signet he understood Nevill's look, and moved a few steps away while he opened and read it.

Nevill watched him, though covertly, and when he could discover on my lord's face no alteration of expression he let out a small sigh. Darcy heard it, turned, caught his eye, and with a lift of the shoulders and a shake of the head gave him a close, hard smile. Meanwhile the tailor, unconscious of all but his craft, stooped over the gown as it lay on the bed, contentedly touching the stuff of the sleeve with the back of his knotted deft fingers.

Darcy dropped the letter down on a stool and came back to where the old man waited; he caught with his fingers the cuffs of his shirt, and so holding them, stretched his arms behind him, while the tailor slipped on the gown. "Ah!" the old man breathed, as it went on, and when he had fastened it at the breast with pins, he stepped back a few paces, and stood, his head slanted, regarding my lord. Nevill's eyes were on my lord too, but he was not thinking of the set of the gown.

"Forsooth!" said the tailor, "it fits well. A good gown! A fair gown. But the sleeve there—" He ran forward and began to pull and ease the stuff on one shoulder.

"It is a fair gown," said Darcy, looking down at the tailor's bent head with its thin graying hair. "But you must have it ready for me soon, lest I go up to the King's Grace at Easter time."

Nevill said, "Sir—" and stopped at Darcy's glance. But the tailor lamented aloud.

"Alas! my lord. If the gown be for a court gown— Alas, had I known, it should have never been sarcenet but satin at least, or damask. Your Lordship was never wont to wear sarcenet for your gowns at court. Alas! it will shame me. Suffer me to—"

Darcy interrupted him. "It will serve. It will serve. And"—he spoke now over the little man's head to George Nevill at the door—"it may be the King's Grace will be gracious lord to me, giving me, in consideration of my infirmities, license to remain in the North parts."

The tailor, his mouth full of pins, made a little, indefinite humming noise, and then mumbled that in no time he could put satin in place of the sarcenet. "Some say," he added, "that a man may journey more easily by sea than by land."

"Surely," said Darcy, "I should journey more easily by sea," and he laughed, but as if angrily. Then he touched the tailor lightly on the shoulder. "I can see that you would have me go to court."

"Why, yes," said the old man simply.

When the tailor had finished and gone away with the gown over his arm, still bemoaning the unsuitability of a lining of sarcenet for one of my lord's station, George Nevill said:

"Sir, have I leave to ask?"

"What do you want to know?"

"Will you go to court by sea?"

"By sea," said Darcy, "I shall not go. For neither will the King give me leave so to come to him, nor if I could get myself a ship should I go to his court, but rather to that of the Emperor in Flanders."

"Then . . ."

"I shall wait," said Darcy, "till I am sent for and fetched. And it may be, George, that I shall yet die in my bed." And he laughed and gave George Nevill a buffet on the shoulder.

But when Nevill had gone away he sat long looking through his letter books, weighing in his mind which, out of all those copied there, might be twisted into meaning treason. He read with a very grim face, and afterward brooded a long time before he took up the pen and wrote—

"For I peremptor feel my broken heart, and great diseases without remedy, to the death of my body, which God not offended I most desire after his pleasure and my soul's health; and he be my judge never lost the King truer servant and subject without any cause but lack of furniture and by false reports of pickthanks. God save the King; though I be without recover."

What they would make of that? He did not know. But it could do no harm and was as near the truth as he could, or dared to, go.

The old serving woman who had taken the prioress's money let her into the parlor of Thomas Cromwell's house and slipped away again, furtive as a mouse, behind the carved and gilt screen that stood across the doorway. The prioress heard the lightest click of the latch, and knew that she was alone, and that now, if her luck held, she would need none other to speak for her, but herself would speak to my Lord Privy Seal.

There was an oriel window at the far end of the room where she would not be seen at once by anyone coming in; so she went

and sat down there upon a little gilt stool; sunshine came colored through the tall window, and brighter and cleaner through
a casement which stood open upon a little inner garden.

From the stool the prioress set herself systematically to
observe the furnishings of the noble chamber; she did it partly
to calm her breathing, but partly also for genuine curiosity.

There was a tapestry carpet on the floor in the oriel. A greater
carpet lay on the floor of the parlor, a very costly thing and such as
the prioress had never seen before, but at once she began to picture
her chamber at Marrick with another like it, though of course far
smaller. Round the walls there were hangings of red and green say,
and on the two carved settles which stood one on either side of the
hearth there were cushions of green velvet embroidered each with
a rose, the single wild rose which was the King's.

As she sat there waiting, and listening, she could hear not
only the noises of the street, dulled by distance, but also the
closer, smaller noises of the house; someone in a room above was
playing a recorder, and in the kitchen a servant chopped herbs.
She heard a bustle begin outside; dogs barked, there were voices,
and the sound of footsteps. Then the door opened and from
behind the screen came a rather portly gentleman in a well-worn
coat of russet faced with black lamb. He had a broad, fleshy face,
small eyes, and a mouth that pouted out full in the middle, but
which narrowed to a thin line at each corner, and there turned
up, like the mouth of a cat. He was pulling off a hawking glove
and now he threw it down on the table; the bell that had been
jangling as he tugged at the glove rattled once on the board and
then was silent.

"You've lost your wager," said this gentleman to one among those others who followed him. "There's no tercel this side the sea can match my Archangel." Then he saw the prioress.

"Who is this?" he said, very sharp and quick, to the gentleman behind him; and to the prioress, "How did you come here?"

She was the first to answer, but not before she had made a reverence of the deepest and humblest that she knew. She said:

"By paying."

"Ho! And paying whom?"

"My lord, if I told you that, I might not find him—or her—so able or so willing to help me to your presence another time."

"No," said Cromwell. "You might not." He looked at her hard, but before he had made up his mind to call the servants and tell them to take her away, she spoke again.

"But it's alone that I should see you."

Her effrontery amused him, and besides he thought she looked too sensible a woman to have come empty-handed.

"Did you pay for that too?" he asked.

She said no; only my lord himself had that to sell.

"To sell!" Cromwell laughed, and said to the others, "Leave us."

As they went out he came to the window and took the Flanders chair of painted leather that stood there. The prioress sat down again upon the stool.

"Do you not know," said he, "that a religious should not be forth of the cloister? And if she must so, she is bound by her Rule to have two of the nuns with her."

The prioress said she knew it well. "Yet when there is sore need—" she said; and then, "As for the ladies, they would have been afraid to leave our house."

He laughed again. Though her words were of the simplest this woman's tone gave them salt.

"And where is your house?"

"At Marrick on Swale in the County of Yorkshire."

"Marrick," he repeated, and was silent for a minute sucking with his tongue at a hollow tooth. "St. Ambrose— no—St. Andrew of Marrick had license to continue—last autumn—September." He seemed to reflect again, and then told her the amount they had sent to him as a gift, and reminded her that half their year's rents had also been promised. "And there are other matters," he said, stabbing into her face with his sharp eyes. "Other matters which make me to well remember the name of your house. Is it to speak of these that you have paid?" and he smiled, but acidly.

She held out the buckskin bag that she had carried clasped in both hands.

"My lord, there is the rents."

He took the bag, weighing it in his hand before he untied the thongs, and let the gold run out into his palm. "Correct," he said, when he had counted it. "But for those other matters—"

She did not pretend to be ignorant of what he meant, but affirmed, briefly yet categorically, that those men of the Western dales who had raised insurrection had broken into the priory by force, and by force taken from the nuns' table and the nuns' store;

she told him precisely what they had taken, even to the red cock and the firkin of sprats, seeing that she could not regard these things as unimportant, and he, listening attentively, seemed to agree with her in that.

"But," he said, when she had finished, "there is, besides all, this woman, your servant, who—"

"Whom I myself, my lord," she urged, "brought hither, that if there were in her sayings any treason it should be bolted out."

"True." He nodded. "Well, it shall be bolted out." He sat silent, his hands on his knees, his small sharp eyes looking out into the garden. Except for something taut in his stillness he might have been meditating; but she knew that he listened and waited. She knew also that here was her cue.

"My lord," she said, "I have no fear that you shall find treason, for the woman's but a poor fool."

"I shall know that, when she hath been examined on these matters. If she is innocent she shall be set free."

"As to that," said the prioress, "I care not, whether or no. But," she got up from her stool now, and did him a reverence; when he turned to look at her, he saw that she held out to him a small thing wrapped in leather.

"What is this?" He took it from her hand and unwrapped it. It was the little pyx, which, as he held it, caught the sun with the pure luster of gold and the sharper refraction of light from the faceted jewels.

"What we ask," said the prioress, standing meek and empty-handed before him, "is that the King's Grace and you should know our loyalty. And that we may have and retain your gracious favor, to whom we look as to our second founder, to preserve our house in these unquiet, scrambling times."

He was examining the pyx, turning it round in his fat, strong hands. As she watched it she felt a sharp pang of loss, for the precious, pretty thing.

"Madame, why are you so resolved that even at a great price your house shall continue? Is it because you are one of those false papist religious who tender more the rags of their outworn corrupt superstitions, than the new light of the true gospel? Come, why is it?"

If he thought, by the sharpness of his look and tone, to abash the prioress, he had misread her. She paused for a moment before she answered, but it was for calculation, and not confusion, that she needed time.

"Sir," she said, "I shall tell you. As you would be loth to see this realm invaded by the King of France, or to see the Turk, or any other, triumph here, being yourself not only a member of the Commonwealth, but also, under the King's Grace, the chief ruler of it—so I."

Cromwell did not laugh aloud, but she saw his big body shake as he chuckled. "So you," he said, "being under God, the chief ruler of Marrick—"

He stood up. "Well, madame, if I find that your wench is, as you say, nothing but a poor crazed thing, your house shall take no hurt." He laid the little golden pyx to his cheek, as though it were a thing he loved, and he nodded to dismiss her.

March 22

Aske sat in the Cross and Martlets Inn at York. He had a book on his knee because if he seemed to read it was easier to keep out of the talk. There were close on a dozen other gentlemen sitting about the room, everyone being indoors this wild evening, and the talk was lively, for now that the duke's progress of justice was completed, except for the trials and hangings to be done at York, most of these gentlemen expected to have license to return home; they spoke therefore of their stewards, their farms, and household affairs.

But a few of them, close to where Aske sat, left such matters for a moment to talk instead of the trial of Master Levening of Acklam, which would be tomorrow.

"He will be hanged," said the most elderly of the three. "No jury dare acquit." He added quickly, "And that is well." But yet he hung his head down and spoke with a harassed look.

"Ellerker will see that he is cast," said another. "The King has granted Ellerker a parcel of Levening's lands."

"Fie!" the elderly man rebuked him. "The King will grant no man's land before he be attainted."

"It's common knowledge Ellerker is promised it."

"Well," said the elderly man, "whether that be so or no, they'll cast him in an hour."

"No," said an elegant young man with a most assured manner, and a lisp in his speech. "I think otherwise. For they say that Sir Robert Constable has said he would not for a hundred pounds have Levening hung."

"Sir Robert Constable!" someone scoffed. "And how long shall his will weigh with a jury? Know you not that he is sent for, and my Lord Darcy also sent for by the King?"

They began to argue then whether that were true. Some said yes, others no, others that Sir Robert but not my Lord Darcy had been summoned to the King.

"And if it be so," lisped the young man again, "what then?"

"Then let them go, and they shall find that they lie in the Tower," someone answered promptly, "along with Tom Percy and his brother."

"Sh!" said another; and Aske knew, though his eye was on his book, that they looked at him. They began then to talk of other things.

After a few minutes Aske got up and went out. He had thought he needed quiet in which to make up his mind, but when he came on young Ned Acroyd in the way to the kitchens, he found that it was already made.

"Take this book," said he, "and fetch my coat and your own. I'm going out."

While he waited for the boy, Aske stood in the covered way that led from the street to the inn yard. The lantern that hung just over his head sent shadows sliding over the roof timbers as it swung in the gusty wind that fluttered the heavy cobwebs there, and tapped the hanging rope of a bell against the plaster wall. The rain spattered in, and down the gutter outside ran a thin wreathed line of dark water caught here and there by the gleam of the lantern. Now, as he waited, Aske felt his heart knock because of that to which he had, by a simple word to Ned, committed himself.

Ned came back with his coat and a lantern.

"Whither, master?" he asked.

"To the duke."

"Then I hope," said Ned, and laughed, "that it's to take leave. They say it's all finished now and that we shall go home. But I would you should take me with you to London, master, when you go back to Gray's Inn."

Aske told him sharply that he talked too much, so after that Ned held his tongue, and Aske was sorry.

The duke had supped, said Master Appleyard, his gentleman usher, and he would receive Master Aske. Aske went up the stair, and into the room where he had sat with the duke in February, and where he had sat alone last October. The only difference seemed to be that tonight there was a posy of daffodils set upon the table.

Aske had had it in mind to move his business at once, but the duke gave him no time, calling to him in the most friendly way to come in. "Come in, Master Aske, I want your counsel." When he had made Aske sit, and Master Appleyard had been told to send up wine and wafers, the duke began to talk about the late pacification of the wild lands of Tynedale and Redesdale, and from that slid off to mention Levening and tomorrow's trial, and then began to question Aske straitly— "What think you of this—or this—or that?" Aske gave him the answers, in a mechanical sort of way, since all this was to go over old ground. Not only had they spoken together of these things, but Aske had written down particulars of certain matters at the duke's request.

And then the duke said: "It would be well if the King had many servants as honest as you, Master Aske."

"Now!" thought Aske, and again felt his heart knock in his chest. But instead of saying what he had come here to say—"Would His Grace listen?" he asked.

The duke leaned forward. "I do think he would, did he know one he could entirely trust. For me—I put my life in your hands, Master Aske—for such as me, who am of the great nobles, he has a jealousy. (Why should I fear to say what all have known, both of himself and of the King his father before him?) So he will never trust us. And for the base-born servants he has—well, I'll speak no ill of them. Every man must have his beginning, as my Lord Darcy saith. But it is to you, and gentlemen like you, that the King would listen, if there were one of you that dared to speak the truth."

He stopped there and waited. He wondered if he had said enough. Master Aske's eye was bent on the ground, his mouth was hard. The duke thought, "Does he doubt me? Is he taking the measure of his danger? Or does he believe that it is as I say?"

Aske lifted his head. He had hardly heard the duke's last words. He had indeed been taking the measure—not of the danger, for that he thought he knew—but of his own strength.

He said—"My lord, do you say that I can serve the King by telling the truth to His Grace, and serve too in clearing unjust suspicions from my Lord Darcy, and Sir Robert Constable and others?"

"I do. I do."

"And that I should, to that end, repair to His Grace?"

"You cannot speak so freely, Master Aske, by letter. It is when you speak to the King as you have spoken to me, face to face, and openly, that His Grace will be convinced of your truth and loyalty."

"Will you—" said Aske, omitting any title of courtesy, because the words that he was about to speak had to be driven out by force—"Will you give me license to go up to London to the King's Grace?"

"I will, most surely." The duke clapped him on the shoulder. "And I will write letters in your favor to the King and to my Lord Privy Seal."

Aske thanked him, and when the duke stood up he knew that he might go away.

As soon as the duke was alone he called for Master Appleyard.

"It is done, Hal!" he said, most cheerfully. "I have by policy brought him to desire of me license to ride to London. I shall write him letters, and other letters that will show His Grace and my Lord Privy Seal in what sort to take my commendations of him."

He went away to the table, and lifting the jar of daffodils sniffed at the fresh sweetness of spring in them.

"I shall," he said, "counsel His Grace to use him with fair words, as if he had great trust in him, so that the fellow may cough out all that he knows about those other two traitors, Darcy and Constable." He put down the flowers, and looked at

Appleyard, with something like a smile on his face. "So well he loves them he must always be speaking of them, justifying them in their treasons. It will go hard if the King's Grace and my Lord Privy Seal cannot pick out something from it all that will be to the purpose."

March 23

The archbishop's officer and his men started off in the chill of a mist-choked dawn to bring the Marrick Priory serving woman from the house of the archbishop, where she had been examined, to the Benedictine Priory of St. Helen's in Bishopgate Street, where her mistress the prioress lay, and where the woman should be set free.

If, however, on such a raw, nipping morning, a man should meet a friend and turn in to drink with him, it is but nature. And if a man's servant turn in too, it is but nature again, for what's sauce for the goose is sauce for the gander. And if, while they sit drinking, and talking neither of profanity nor wantonness, but of sober and godly matters, the woman and her brat, who had been told to sit still on the bench outside, wander away and are lost, what can a man and his servant do to find them, in all the streets and lanes of London? The archbishop's officer and his servant spent an hour searching, then gave it up. It was twenty to one that any would inquire what had happened to the wench, who could besides ask her own way, having a tongue in her head, though the lad was dumb.

Later that morning, but still early, Thomas Cromwell, Lord Privy Seal, came to visit Thomas Cranmer, archbishop of Canterbury, in the Palace of Lambeth.

The remains of the archbishop's breakfast still lay upon the table with a book open beside the plate; so the two of them stood together in an oriel. Beyond the little leaded quarrels of the window lay the river; the blown glass dipped all the outside world into a dim, watery green, and across its concentric flaws the passing wherries seemed to wriggle and bend like so many caterpillars. The sun was beginning to shine through the mist, though palely, and the tide was at the full.

Cromwell took from his pouch a little silver and enamel box, and offered it to the archbishop; there were dried French plums in it. The archbishop would not take one; this was a foreign habit which Privy Seal had picked up abroad; every autumn his agent bought these dried and sugared French plums for him at Antwerp and sent them to London. While Cromwell bent his head over the box, daintily choosing his fruit, and while he popped it into his mouth, the archbishop continued to hold forth upon the necessity there was for a new Great Bible in English. Cromwell, consuming the plum with pouted lips and critical deliberation, listened, bowing his head from time to time without interrupting the archbishop's eloquence.

"But," said the archbishop, "it must be fairly printed, large and plain and not so costly neither that all may not buy."

Cromwell saw that his advice was now required. The archbishop would concern himself with the spiritual benefits of a new Bible, and judge between the merits of the translations—

old versions of Wycliffe, new versions of Master Tyndale and Master Coverdale—but when it came to matters of business, then it was time for Privy Seal.

"Then," said he, "I have the very man for you, one Grafton. And if it shall be well printed, it must be printed abroad. Paris it shall be, for there they have the best printers, and the fairest paper." And he, in turn, favored the archbishop with a discourse on that subject.

But, when he had finished, and had opened his little silver box again, and again taken out a plum, he held it between his fingers, looking keenly and yet a little smiling into the archbishop's face.

"Mass!" said he, "and I had forgotten what brought me here."

Thomas Cranmer shook his head, so that his soft cheeks quivered a little; he too smiled, as if to indicate that he was not so simple as to suppose that there was anything that Privy Seal ever forgot.

"Tell me," said Cromwell, "whether ye have commoned with that woman from Swaledale that I wrote you of?"

"I have."

"Well, is there treason in her sayings?" He was watching the archbishop, but not now smiling at all.

"There was none."

"None, you mean, that you could discern."

"None at all," said the archbishop, who could occasionally be obstinate.

"Not when a woman declares she has seen a king in Swaledale, coming to take his kingdom?"

"None."

"Then," Cromwell scoffed, "her visions are from God."

"Nor that neither," said the archbishop placidly, "but from a distempered wit. Yet that there is nothing unhonest in the poor creature I am assured by certain words she spoke."

Cromwell did not ask what the words were, but, reaching past the archbishop, opened the window, so letting into the close still room fresh air and many sounds—the voices of men, walling and laughter of the gulls, the creak of a well wheel, and through all, the soft, insistent lapping of the tide.

"Those words," said the archbishop, when his slight pause exacted no question, "were these. 'Of the increase of his government and peace shall be no end.'"

Cromwell, looking out of the window, observed—"Well, that had a loyal sound."

The archbishop smiled with indulgent superiority. "She spoke not of the King's Grace. But those very words are written in the English scriptures, and therefore I say there is no treason in her. For, surely if any man hath taught the poor creature to speak these things, that man is no papist, but one who knows the New Learning and the very gospel of Christ."

"That is sure proof of loyalty?"

"Sure proof," the archbishop said, with the same bland smile.

"Then Sir Francis Bigod is either no traitor or ignorant of the English scriptures."

"Oh!" said the archbishop, and his smile died.

"I shall," said Cromwell, "myself examine the woman."

He put his hand to his cap and moved toward the door.

"I have set her free," the archbishop told him in a voice that he tried to make confident.

"You—*you* have set her free?"

"Or rather," the archbishop maintained his dignity with an effort, "or rather by now she is free. For I gave orders to take her this morning to her mistress, the prioress of Marrick. Who lies," he added, "at the Priory of St. Helen's in Bishopgate Street."

"I know that," Cromwell snapped at him, and went out quickly.

From daybreak to close on noon except when he went down to church to sing Mass, Gib taught the boys that came to the chantry for their schooling. Except for what small reward he received from Lord Privy Seal for his writings, this chantry and school were all Gib's living. He owed them to Friar Lawrence's good offices, and knew that he should be grateful. But to teach the children was a hair shirt upon his shoulders.

Today was no worse for Gib than other days. The red-haired boy he birched three times, and the squinting boy twice. Someone slung ink at someone else, but the offender was not to be discovered, even though Gib threatened to flog all; he began to carry out his threat, but while he dealt with the second victim one behind his back threw his English Testament across the room. He plunged to rescue it, and as he stooped heard a scuffling and giggling behind him. When he stood up he saw that they had all fled—he who had been under the birch went last of all, with his bare behind showing pink between his shirt and the hosen which he huddled up about him as well as he could.

So there was Gib, left standing alone in the little dusty room, hearing their scurrying footsteps, laughter, and derisive hooting die away down the stairs. With raging disgust in his heart he looked round at the empty benches and all the mess and litter of their childish heedlessness. There were some marbles under one bench end; he picked them up and threw them through the window. Sticking out of the pages of Stanbridge's *Accidentia* there was a colored paper; when he looked closer he saw that it was one of those painted wood-cut pictures of saints which devout persons buy at pilgrimage places, and afterward give away to their friends. This was a picture of the rood; angels, with skirts curled up like the tails of mermaids, hovered to receive into a chalice the blood which poured from the wounded side of the Christ. Gib tore the paper into four pieces and stamped on it. Before he shut the book his eye caught sight of the picture on the title page; eight well-groomed docile scholars, disposed in two orderly attentive lines, waited upon the instruction of their master; the effect of serenity and seemliness was a little weakened by a big slobber of dried brown blood which had probably been spilt from someone's nose after combat, but even so it was cruelly far from the truth, and Gib slapped the book down upon the bench. However, when he had for a while gnawed his knuckles, the extremity of his irritation passed, and he decided that he might as well make the most of his freedom. He unlocked a cupboard, took out a packet of writings, pulled on his hood and began to go downstairs; if he went out at this hour he would miss dinner here, but he would be able to hang about the kitchen door of Lord Privy Seal's house, and in this way he might more than make up for what he lost at home.

When he came down to the lower room he found that the old Kat had been drinking already and was very quarrelsome. She lurched toward him as he went through, and he thought that if she could have lifted from the hook the pot where white puddings were boiling she would have soused him with it. As it was she followed him to the door and stood screeching after him down the street.

But when a couple of hours later, he came away from Lord Privy Seal's house in Throgmorton Street, he had money in his pouch and even a word of commendation from that chaplain of my lord who had scanned through his writing against the papist superstition of pilgrimages. He had also herring, bread, and beer in his belly. So he went more cheerfully; it pleased him that the porter wagged his head as he passed and gave him good-day. "Here," he thought, "I have a place. Here they know me for what I am." It warmed him against the cold east wind that had kept the day huddled in a November-seeming murk. He thought, "Perhaps when my lord reads more of what I write he will have me into his household." He saw himself a chaplain there, well fed, warm, with a little room to study in, having in it a curtained bed, a desk, a shelf of books, as that chaplain had before whom he had stood today. Then, even as he went through the street, he raised his fist and struck himself on the breast, horrified at himself because, for those writings of his which should have been only to advance God's kingdom, he hoped to receive worldly reward.

And, in the meantime, he must go back to the chantry and to old Kat, by now most likely sodden and snoring.

He came to Cornhill and stood hesitating while a dray piled with a brewer's hogsheads went by. He decided not to go home yet, so he crossed the street and went on down Birchin Lane, meaning to fetch a compass and return by Lombard Street.

He had already turned under the low archway leading to St. Edmund's Church, when he found that a crowd filled the way. There was a scaffolding up against the church, and workmen standing on it, not working, but looking down. The crowd too was looking the same way, at a place below the scaffolding.

Gib did not care what they stared at, and walked more slowly so that he should not have to shoulder his way through them. As he drew near people began to move away.

"Marry!" said a fat woman as she came past Gib, "I marvel the poor wench was not killed."

"That fellow that let so heavy a stone fall into the street should taste of a rope's end," said the man.

"Poor soul!" said another. "It were a charity to bring her to her home, wherever it may be. I myself am in haste, or . . ." and he passed on.

So now Gib had come to that part of the street where the crowd had been, which now had melted away, and there was Malle, the poor foolish wench from Marrick, sitting with her head cast back against the wall of St. Edmund's porch, and

Wat, his son, fondling and fumbling at her, and making strange noises in his throat.

Gib thought—"If I had gone the shorter way—" He thought also—"She does not know me," and Wat never looked his way.

Gib went three steps or four, with a skulking glance back over his shoulder. His heart gave a great jump. Malle turned her face toward him. He wrenched his head round, and went on, stepping softly, listening for her voice. At the corner of the street he did not look back.

March 24

There was a northeast wind blowing down the length of Broad Street as Gib went toward Lord Privy Seal's house. He tucked his hands into his sleeves to keep them warm, but, whether he would or no, instead of putting his head down into the wind he must keep it up to peer about, looking for—he would not let himself know what. Instead he muttered under his breath, "Whew! Winter's come again. Early spring is never sure," and he tried to think of fire and supper waiting for him when he went back. Old Kat might natter at him, but she would go out sooner or later to the ale house, and then he could read by the firelight, or if he chose could go out to one that he knew, and talk with him of the coming reformation of all things—a heartening subject, for not only did New Jerusalem gleam before them, very pleasant and lovely, but also there was the enemy to be thought of, and his downfall, the enemy who was not only Satan, but also such bishops as Winchester, such nobles as Exeter, as well as the great part of monks and nuns, all such in fact as with malicious perversity would not look up to see the heavenly city descending upon them.

He came opposite the gate of a woodyard, and heard a dog begin to bark wildly there. "Some naughty thief," he thought. "There's none honesty in these days." He paused to watch the fellow bolted out, saving to himself that he should, if occasion served, speak a word to him of rebuke and of salvation.

But instead of some rough fellow a woman and a lad came out of the yard and trailed away along the street in front of him. They had not seen Gib. He could easily, by turning back, or simply by waiting a while, avoid their notice.

But when he knew them, after a bump of his heart, and a great perturbation of mind, peace came to him. Like a full bucket dropping back into the well with a dizzy whirring of the winch, and a heavy plop and splash—like that, all in a second, he knew that here was mercy, here was forgiveness, here was his chance of salvation offered to him once more by the unimaginable patience of God.

He overtook the two of them.

"*Pax vobiscum*," he said, standing in their way.

Wat stepped behind Malle; she faced him, but there was no look of recognition in her face.

He said: "You know me."

She only mumbled something about darkness.

"What? Are you blind?"

She shook her head, but said again that it was dark.

"Where do you live?" he asked her.

She said: "We do not know where to go."

"Well," said he, "I shall take you where I live—till I can provide better. Come on." When she did not move he said again,
"Come on," and at the sound of his own voice his heart sank
and trembled. To attain salvation he must love these two, as the
Samaritan loved the traveler. Yet already he heard in his tone
sharp exasperation at her stupidity.

March 26

Aske waited till the grayness of the new day was in the room.
Then he got up and wakened Ned Acroyd. Ned lit a candle
and, stifling huge yawns, began to dress his master. Being so
sleepy he was, for once, silent, and Aske was glad of it; like
a physical pain this day's departure from Aughton bounded
and consumed all his thoughts; he did not so much remember as feel in himself all the other days of summer, winter,
spring upon which he had stood in this same room. Those
days, and the little room, and all Aughton, were, it seemed,
lodged somewhere in his body, and they were being plucked
away from him with a long, sore wrench. He thought, "If only
I were taking Will with me instead of this lad!" And on the
thought Will Wall came in.

Aske looked at Will over the top of Ned's bright brown head
as the boy stooped to button his doublet. Will's face was gray;
he was as thin as a garden rake. Aske thought, "By the Rood!
however I needed him, he could not come with me."

"Master," said Will, "send away the lad."

Ned turned round, grinned, stared, then looked up at Aske.
He nodded, so Ned went away. Will shut the door upon him,

and with his back to his master said, in a wisp of a voice, "You are going to London?"

"Yes."

Will turned, throwing up his hands to clutch his hair with a gesture and look so wild that it startled Aske, who stretched his arm out to catch him if he should fall.

Will took his wrist with both hands.

"Master," he said. "I will not drink. I swear it as I hope for mercy. I will not touch drink but only water, if you will forgive me, and I may come with you."

"It is not that," Aske told him hastily. "You should have come. But you are not fit to ride such a long gate."

Will let go his wrist. He stood there with his head hanging, and said, not wildly now, but so low that Aske could hardly hear, and indistinctly as if he was powerless even to move his lips—"I shall die if I may not go."

"Will!" Aske said, and then, not knowing what he did, went over to the window and flung open the shutters. Outside in a drenched gray dawn a blackbird called nearby, sudden and urgent as a trumpet, but announcing only peace.

"Master, I have always been with you. There never has been a time—never—always—" Will muttered.

"Oh, Will!" Aske began, then stopped short. "If you can ride," he said, "you shall come."

He expected and feared some passionate demonstration of feeling. But Will only stood silent for a moment and then spoke quietly. "You've heard me promise," said he. "If I fail you this time also, may my Maker, when next I receive him, be my damnation." He opened the door. "I'll see have they a breakfast ready," he said, and went out.

Julian was in the parlor and sat with her uncle while he breakfasted, but they said very little once he had told her that he would leave a servant at Buntingford. "To bring home news how—to bring home news," he said. When he had finished they went out through the hall and to the court. Julian looked sharply at her uncle when she saw Will Wall in the saddle instead of Ned Acroyd. But after that glance she made no comment.

Aske mounted, and she stood at his knee with her hand laid on the horse's neck. He had not kissed her, and now they avoided each other's eye as if they were two plotters guilty and unmasked.

He said: "Keep my little coffer for me, niece. You know where it lies."

She nodded. He had charged her with it last night.

"It may be," he said, "that the King's Grace will be persuaded to hear me. Then it will be well that I have made this journey."

She nodded to that too.

"God be with you, niece," he said, touching her head lightly with his hand. She felt the horse move from under her fingers. She looked at him then, meeting his eye.

"God—" she said, and shut her lips tight, and nodded hard.

He did not look back at all. Will Wall and the other men wheeled their horses and followed him. So he was gone, with all that there was to say left unsaid. She went back into the hall and stood there irresolute what to do now, because there was nothing to be done. She heard little Dickon upstairs calling out, as joyfully ready for the new day as the birds outside.

Gib sat down to supper alone. Old Kat had gone off to the tavern; Wat had snatched what he could get and gone away to eat it in some corner, like an animal; Malle would not stir from where she sat by the hearth. She did not plague him with her chatter now; but he was finding her silence worse.

When he had brought her in the other day old Kat had made a great scene, screaming at him to take away his drab and his bastard, whose presence she seemed to think an insult to her virtuous respectability.

But now, though she still railed on him, when she could find him alone, for bringing these two, it was on a different ground. For this morning she had announced that the wench was bewitched, and the lad a warlock. "Surely," she said, "Satan has them both in his power. For when I speak to her, saying she should fetch or carry for me (and heavy my work is with you all), what will she say but one word over and over. 'There's darkness,' says she, 'darkness, deep, deep darkness.'"

So now, though he despised himself for it, Gib hitched his chair round a little so that he could, out of the corner of his eye, see her if she moved. Yet all he could see was that now and again she would raise her hand, and holding it spread out before her eyes, would strike it up and down a few times; but whether to hide something from herself, or to clear away some obscurity, he could not tell.

Every time she did it, however, the skin of his back seemed to prickle. He even envied Wat's escape, who now seemed to shrink from Malle as much as he had before used to cling to her.

March 27

The baggage was packed, the trussing coffer locked, and one of the two saddlebags corded, and the prioress of Marrick stood in the midst of the guest chamber at St. Helen's Priory, looking about at the litter of things upon the floor yet to be put in—a girdle, a comb, a little painted box, some shifts, and a pair of shoes. During the last weeks this room had grown familiar, from the painted Passion emblems on its carved ceiling to the worn red brick of the hearth, and the hanging of green verders, paled to the color of pea soup near the windows where the light caught them. Now, because of the disarray of her packing, and the empty perches where her gown and cloak had hung, it was once more strange. The sun came out with a sudden harsh gleam, filling it with brightness which faded as suddenly as it had shone.

"Tchk!" said the prioress impatiently. The man who had been sent to fetch more cord, and the woman who had taken the prioress's riding coat away to brush it—both should have been back by now. She opened the door and listened. Besides the sound of the ladies of St. Helen's chanting Prime, she could hear voices below. "How they must ever be talking!" she said to herself, and came in again to walk restlessly up and down the room, and at last stand looking down at the trussing coffer, impatience giving way in her to pride and pleasure as she thought of things bought yesterday which were packed inside it.

For the house there was a little silver plate, and skeins of silk enough to last Dame Ladyman through several years of embroidery, besides a reel of wonderful gold thread. There was also a length of sanguine brocade, very rich, very lustrous. But for the prioress herself there was a small goblet of glass from Venice, almost as clear as water; with bubbles such as rise through water caught and prisoned in it; yet it had been made by the hands of men, and by fire. It had cost nearly all that was left of the money she had so painfully wrung from Marrick lands to save the priory from suppression. Well, she deserved the pretty thing, for the priory was saved, and by her doing.

The serving man came back again; at least he seemed to have made haste at the last, for he was out of breath.

"Come now," she said briskly, "cord it up and then load the beasts and we'll—"

"Madame," he interrupted her, "he says we shall not go till we deliver her up again."

"'He' says? Who is he? And deliver whom?"

"He says he is a servant of Lord Privy Seal and that we must give up mad Malle."

"*He* is mad!" cried the prioress courageously, but yet her heart sank. When she came down to the court she found a tall young gentleman with a loud voice, a heavy gold chain, and much assurance; his manner was rough and hectoring but he was certainly not mad.

During their conversation, since the young man would not speak low, quite a number of people collected, at a discreet distance but well within hearing. The prioress could see, beyond the wide shoulders of Lord Privy Seal's gentleman, a little mob of nuns jammed in the doorway of the cloister; they wrung their hands together, and she could hear their voices shrill and shaking, protesting that they were the King's most loyal subjects any day of the week, and that they harbored no such woman, and that she was none of theirs, but the prioress of Marrick's servant. The prioress led the young gentleman farther apart, and spoke with him for a long time. He nodded at last; aloud he said, "See to it that you find her," but he winked one eye at the prioress.

When he had gone away she returned to the chamber which she had thought so soon to leave, but in which she must now endure yet more waiting. Another time she might have taken comfort to herself from the manner in which she had conducted this last negotiation—from her own sagacity, firmness, and address—but the blow had been so sharp that she could feel only the bitterness of impotent resentment.

This resentment was not directed against Cromwell, nor against his gentleman, though it was to Cromwell that she had sent, as a humble gift, the little cup of Venice glass, and it was to reward the young gentleman for his good offices in bringing the cup to his master, and word to her again, that the length of sanguine brocade would have to be once more converted to silver pieces.

Christabel Cowper's resentment was aimed rather against Malle, and against the prioress of St. Helen's, and against something—or perhaps it was someone—behind Malle and the old prioress, in alliance with, or in support of them. Her thought here became obscure, and she did not try to resolve the obscurity, but she knew that the something or someone was set to gainsay her, as she was set to have her own way, maugre any gainsaying.

Laurence Machyn opened the door of the solar where July sat on the settle beside the fire. As he came in he could see that she did not turn her head, but remained stooping forward, holding out her hands to the flames. She was very idle these days, doleful and tetchy by turns; the child to come seemed nothing to her but an enemy that drained her life.

Laurence knew all that, was sharply wounded by it, and loved her all the more. He came softly behind her now, leaned over the back of the settle, and laid one hand over her eyes. Then, before she could start away, he brought the other hand forward, so that what his fingers held was just under her nose.

"Guess what it is," he said, and dabbed it, soft, faintly fragrant, and cool upon her lips.

"Flowers," she said, not striking his hand away. He was so glad at that that he laughed.

"But what flowers?"

She sniffed at the little posy, and cried, "Oh! Sir, primroses!"

He let her go then, feeling himself well paid by the joy in her voice, and almost overpaid when, sitting beside her, he saw her bend over the tight little bunch with its frill of green leaves as she held them cupped in her hands. She looked up at him and they smiled at each other. It was for a minute as though they were very close to each other, and very young together with the young flowers of the year between them.

March 29

Very early on this morning Lord Privy Seal's gentleman came once more knocking at the gate of St. Helen's Priory. They told

him he might not enter. He said enter he must, and speak with
the prioress of Marrick. He had a letter for the prioress from
his master, telling her that he took in good part her gift, and
would be gracious lord to the priory (so long as the ladies should
show themselves to deserve it), and would in no wise recall their
backslidings, but only their humble supplication and good will
to himward. But the young gentleman said nothing of the letter,
insisting that he must speak with the prioress.

So down came Dame Christabel while the bells were ringing for Prime; she had a velvet purse gripped in her hand in
which was the price of the sanguine brocade. She received the
letter from the young man, and gave him thanks, and the little
purse in recompense of his good offices with his master. What
she had bought of him was worth the price, and yet she felt a
pang when he took the purse from her fingers, and tossed it in
the air, before he shoved it in his pouch, kissed her hand and
went away.

It was just about that same moment that Malle, coming in suddenly, caught Wat lapping cream from the top of the milk. He
thought her hand on his shoulder was Gib's, and he jumped
aside as nimbly as a flea. He had his arms up to guard his ears,
and when he saw Malle he let them drop, but he edged away
from her as far as he might, until the wall stopped him.

Malle said: "Darkness, and God moving nigh-hand in the
darkness. The cloud eats up the sky, black cloud, so that the ash
trees are white against it as clean bone, and the elms show green.
Down there's the priory. Look, you can see the nuns' court and

the orchard, and the church in the midst. And there's Hodge in his red hood carting dung.

"O Jerusalem!" she cried. "If thou hadst known those things that belong unto thy peace. But now are they hid from thine eyes."

She heard Wat's teeth chatter, and stretched out a hand to comfort him. He endured her touch, but only as an animal that stands because it is too terrified to run.

She said: "He has bowed the heavens down, and their darkness is under his feet, and dark water in the clouds of the air. And now with the wind he winnows snow from the cloud.

"Look, Wat!" she cried, and pointed toward the naked mud and wattle of the wall, but neither of them saw it. "Look! There he comes down the daleside with the young bracken uncurling like rams' horns, spreading like wings about his feet. The head of him and his hairs are as white as white wool, and as snow."

As Wat tried to dive away under her hand she grasped him tighter.

"He's Love," she said, "and that is greedy as a lion, and may not stint till it has ate us to the bare bones.

"For how can he," she said, "give us the whole height of heaven till we come begging to him with empty pokes? How can he bear us up in his hand while we grovel safe on ground? How can he lap us close and dear in his love when we are girded with housen and cattle, and cloaked about with gold?

"Today—" she said, "now—we must find the Lady and tell her."

An hour or so later the prioress of Marrick came into the cloister to take leave of the prioress of St. Helen's, just as fourteen old dames, dot-and-carry-one on crutches, twisted with rheumatism, or bent under the mere load of years, went into the ladies' frater to eat their breakfast, for it was Maundy Thursday. She heard their clacking yet feeble voices, saw their deformities, and, smelling them also, pinched her nose between her fingers and pulled a disgusted face.

The prioress of St. Helen's, summoned from the frater, came out, still wearing the apron patched with damp in which she had knelt to wash the knobbled, twisted feet of an old creature from Portsokenward. She was flustered to see Dame Christabel, because, having been moved by pity and excitement, she had let herself cry, and she guessed that the prioress of Marrick would not miss the redness of her eyes.

"Will you go, Madame?" she fussed. "Will you not stay with us over the Feast? Why must you ride today?"

"Because my business is done," Christabel Cowper said, and no more. She was not going to explain by telling about the visit of Lord Privy Seal's gentleman.

"But hearken!" she said to the prioress of St. Helen's. "Here comes to me again, this very morning, that same serving wench that I brought here, and for whose sake Lord Privy Seal had me in anger. Well, I have had my man send her packing. And if she comes again to your gate do you the same. I tell you friendly.

Else she will bring you into trouble with her talk of visions. Even now she would have had me listen to some madness of visions, but I would not hear her."

She snorted through her nose, and gave a derisive laugh. "I gave my man silver to give her, though he's a sad knave and may have put it into his pouch. I cannot help that. Let her fend. I'll have no more to do with her. And now, Madame," she said, in a different smooth tone, proper to one great person speaking ceremoniously with another, "and now, Madame, I am come to take my leave, and to give you thanks for—"

"If she comes again," the prioress of St. Helen's broke in, speaking breathlessly, "I shall succor her. And I shall hear her visions if she will tell them."

"Ho!" said the prioress of Marrick, without any affectation of respect, "will you so? Well so you may, if you care not whether your house stand or fall."

"It is better," said the prioress of St. Helen's, pressing her soft wrinkled hands together, "better it should fall, if thereby shall come peace between us and God. For I think it is for our sins, Madame, that he has chastened us. And if he take from us all we have, it is to make us, who have cleaved to worldly wealth, cleave only to him, so that he may bless us."

The prioress of Marrick stared to hear this gentle creature turn upon her. She was even a little impressed; not very much, but enough to make her argue the point.

"But though he bless," she said, "what then?"

"What then?"

"If we—if you shall have lost all, and are turned out and the house fall . . . ? Then it will be too late."

"Too late for what?"

The prioress of Marrick, thinking in terms of a bargain between buyer and seller, found herself unwilling to use the first words that came to her tongue. "Too late for payment." She would not say that; she even rejected the word "reward." "For his help. For comfort," she said at last, for once preferring propriety to sincerity.

But the old prioress answered sincerely, though with a most undignified shaken voice, and a great sniff after she had spoken:

"Let him alone for that. He will see to our help, and he will know how to comfort."

They stood facing each other a moment longer. From the open door of the frater came the cackle of the old folks' voices, even, now and again, the smacking sound they made as they ate. Someone belched; someone choked on a draft of beer and began to cough.

The prioress of Marrick let her lip curl. She had Moses and the Prophets; half an hour ago she had had mad Malle babbling of the insatiable tender love of God. Now she had the old prioress of St. Helen's. She had not listened to any of these, nor would she have listened though one rose from the dead.

She moved away, not very tall, but in her fur-lined riding cloak bulky and very stately.

"Tush!" she said, and no other word of farewell.

✻ *The Chronicle of Christabel Cowper, prioress of Marrick, ends here.*

March 31

Lord Darcy had dined at the house of the mayor of Pomfret. He came back to the castle in the afternoon, going slowly on foot, leaning on a silver-knobbed staff, with one of his gentlemen on either side and two servants behind. The boys and girls were coming back from the fields with primroses. Lord Darcy stopped a string of the smallest of them, and asked for a posy. A little girl, all blue eyes, smudged rosy cheeks, and open silly-sweet mouth, gave him her handful, and then backed away, still staring. He kissed the flowers to her, told the servant go give her a penny, and went on, holding the posy under his nose.

When he came into the first ward he found a number of horses standing; evidently they had just come in, for the marks of the saddles and girths were still dark upon them. A stranger came toward him, a broad-faced, freckled, sandy man, who pulled off his cap and held out a letter.

Lord Darcy went on till they were close; then he too uncovered.

"Welcome," he said, "to you in the King's livery, and wearing the King's badge."

Because he smiled, and spoke so lightly, the other conceived that he must talk big.

"I've sufficient force with me—" he began.

"To take me? Why so you shall—when you will." And my lord went on at his usual slow pace. His two gentlemen and the servants thrust by also, stiff as dogs that square up for a fight.

The King's man looked after them, hesitated, then followed, but at a little distance.

April 2

Aske had waited at court all day since Mass, standing first on one foot, then on the other, in a kind of blank suspension of feeling. He had handed over to a gentleman of the bedchamber the letters which the Duke of Norfolk had given him; and now he could only wait. He did not know whether he would wait in vain, to be turned out this evening when the presence chamber was cleared, or whether some officer of the guard would come with a warrant and pikemen, and so he would sleep tonight in prison; or whether the King would send for him, and he would have that opportunity to speak, for which he had come to London. He longed, against his will, that it should be the first; he expected the second; he dared not hope for the last.

When a yeoman usher came to his elbow, and said that the King had sent for him, his heart gave so great a jump that it sent the blood drumming into his ears. If the King would see him on this Easter Sunday evening, when the court was crowded with all the great nobles and ambassadors, then perhaps the King would hear him speak, if not today, then some other day. At least, he said to himself, following the usher through many passages and up and down stairs, it must mean that all's not lost.

They came to a door in the farther part of the palace; here were the offices in which the chancellor of the augmentations and his clerks pursued their business, but Aske did not know that. The usher stopped with his head bent to listen, and knocked. Then he pushed open the door and motioned Aske to enter.

There were five or six persons standing together in the dusty sunshine of the room; their backs were toward him and all

looked down at something at their feet. The room was unfur-
nished except for a big table and a couple of stools, but piles
of leather and folded canvas lay about, and against one wall a
number of wicker hampers were stacked.

The men standing there turned about, and Aske saw that
the King was in their midst, and went down on his knee. He
saw also that Cromwell was on one side of the King and Lord
Chancellor Rich, chancellor of the augmentations, on the other;
and what hope he had conceived, died at that sight.

"Well, Mr. Aske?" said the King.

Aske got up from his knees and came nearer; they were
watching him, all of them; he knelt down again and asked for
leave to kiss the King's hand. The King held it out, white and
scented; he kissed it, but the King had already turned away,
leaving him kneeling in the midst of them.

It was then that he saw what they had been looking at when
he came in. An open hamper stood there half full of hay. Gold
gleamed among the hay, and jewels, like small colored eyes. On
the floor in front of the hamper lay tumbled together gold chal-
ices and silver, jeweled and enameled reliquaries, the crook of an
ancient and beautiful crozier, a small image of silver. Aske looked
at these, and knew that the others still had their eyes on him.

"Well, Master Aske," said the King again, "you have said
that the Act of Suppression of the Abbeys was the greatest cause
of the detestable treasons of your North Country men, and that
the hearts of the commons most grudged at it. Now tell me
again—in your conscience do you think it was so?"

"Surely," said Aske, "it was so."

"And as for you yourself?"

They had to wait for the answer. Then Aske said, "I and all others grudged at it."

"And do you now grudge at it?"

During the still longer pause, the King stretched out his foot, broad-toed as a duck's webbed foot in its yellow velvet shoe. He rested it lightly on the curve of an overturned chalice, rolling the vessel backward and forward under the sole of his foot.

"Your Grace," said Aske at last, "has the whole of the North Country altogether at Your mercy."

"I'll have no mercy on traitors, Master Aske," said the King. He gave the chalice a push with his foot so that it rang against the rim of a big alms dish. He waved his hand in Aske's face saying, "Go! You may go!"

So Aske went out of the room. As he found his way back through the palace he kept his head up, but he was thinking, "Here goes a man that came to London to speak plain, and was afraid to speak." He was aware that he would not have been permitted to speak. Besides that, the outrage of seeing the King tumble the consecrated cup with his foot had strangled every word upon his tongue; but still, he knew that he had been afraid to speak.

When the door had shut behind him Cromwell murmured as if to himself—

"I marvel how such a traitor, seeing his treason utterly defeated, dare speak so stoutly."

"A murrain," cried Rich, "upon so cankered a heart!"

"He is a man much unbroken and rude," said Cromwell.

"As yet unbroken," said the King, moving away from them. They followed him out of the room.

Aske came away from Westminster by water and told the boatman to put him down at Blackfriars' Stairs. This way he could go as easily to Gray's Inn as to the Cardinal's Hat. At Gray's Inn he would find, he knew, men not very ready to be seen in his company; at the Cardinal's Hat, he could guess, he would find Will Wall, drunk as a lord.

He had not made up his mind which way he would choose to take when he came to Ludgate, and so hung on his heel a moment under the gate arch. From the west the setting sun poured into the street a flood of gold; when he looked that way his eye, half blinded, could see only dark shapes of people moving, fringed about with silver. He turned to go back up Bowyer Row toward St. Paul's and heard someone behind him cry, "Sir, Master Aske! O sir!" and there was little July Savage tugging his arm with one hand, and hauling after her by the other a young, rambling puppy at the end of a scarlet ribbon leash.

He took in first her shining look of joy, then the glance that she threw over her shoulder toward a slight young man with straw-colored hair, in his Easter Sunday best of tawny doublet and white hosen. If this were July's husband he looked a poor rag of a man, but by his expression a gentle and kindly one.

"Sir," cried July, speaking first to one then to another, and sometimes, it seemed, to both of them. "You must come home with us. He must come home. Sir, I pray you! Sir, ask him! Oh, it must be so!"

Aske laughed. "This little maid and I," said he to Laurence Machyn—"I must still so think of her—we have been friends many a year now."

"Oh, many a year!" cried July.

Laurence said if Master Aske were not pressed—because it was not far to go—he—his wife—they would take it kindly—

"It's but round the corner," said July, "and surely you may not refuse."

As they walked together Laurence was planning that when they reached home he would make an excuse and go out again, and leave them there. Yet when it came to the point he found himself unable to do it. They sat round the fire in the solar upstairs talking little, for it seemed that when July had announced that she and Laurence had been walking in the fields beyond Temple Bar, she thought of nothing else but to sit watching Master Aske, with such a light on her face as would have been proper had he been, thought Laurence, an angel from heaven.

Laurence had sent for wine, and a plate of nuts. He plied Aske with these, and made perfunctory remarks, eyeing his guest furtively most of the time (since he could not endure to look at July), and hating Aske on every count upon which one man may hate another. Aske was a gentleman, and therefore he sat with his chin on his breast in disdainful silence; he was July's leman, fretting that her husband should be gone and leave him to stretch out his hand, to draw her to him, to—Laurence swallowed hard there, and wriggled on the settle so that July flung him a quick, impatient, chiding glance. Master Aske cracked the nuts in his fine white teeth, and Laurence hated him for that. The man was even hateful for his dark hair, though it gave Laurence some comfort to see in it quite a scattering of gray.

During one of the many long silences they all heard some- one knock, and knock again on the street door below. Laurence turned, listening. "That boy's run forth again," he said, half to himself. He missed, therefore, how though Aske neither turned nor stirred, the hand that lay on his knee became clenched till the knuckles showed white. But July saw it, and saw how he sat there, stiff as wood, then slowly turned his head toward the open door of the inner room, where a corner of the Machyn's blue and yellow curtained bed showed, and beyond it a window.

Laurence got up and found that July was on her feet.

"No," said he sharply, "I'll answer. It may be some drunken fellow."

He had hardly gone out when July's hand was on the latch.

"Out through the window there," she whispered. "I'll keep them as long as I may."

"No—no," said Aske, but she had gone, and he was left to realize how close fear had followed at his heels, that he should have been even for an instant so unreasonable as to think that the King might have sent to take him here. Yet he sat very still, and must listen with all his ears, and gave a great start when July came in again, shutting the door softly behind her.

"It's only the matter of a corpse to be buried," she said, and then, "What do you fear? What has happened?"

He said shortly, "Nothing." But because at that she looked so miserably chidden he would not leave it there. "Nothing," he said again, "indeed. Yet I think they will take me, in spite of the pardon."

She shut her eyes, leaning back with her arms spread and the palms of her hands pressed against the door. It was apparent as she so stood, though he only later remembered it, that she was with child.

She opened her eyes, and turned her head, listening.

"He's coming back," she said. "Quick. Promise me. If—if they do, find means to send me word."

He said hastily, "If I'm taken, I'll send Will Wall."

Then Laurence came in.

April 6

Aske had not meant to come again to the Machyns' house, since he felt himself to be like a man who has detected in his body the unmistakable signs of the plague. But this evening, having vainly waited all day outside the presence chamber, as he had waited every day since Easter Sunday, he did, though with compunction, and shame at his own weakness, come to the house in Knightrider Street, and knock. The master was not in, but the mistress, they told him, was in the garden, and they took him through the house, and out under the arched passage into the little pleached garden beyond. The honeysuckle was showing gray-green leaves though the vine and the big old mulberry tree were still stark bare, and there were tufts of primroses flowering in the grass.

But July was not here, so the boy left him to go and find her, and Aske sat down on the built-up grass bank below the honeysuckle. Above, the setting sun caught and glorified the chimneys of a neighbor's house, dyeing them with fiery sanguine, but the small hidden garden was full of shadow, and of peace. As he waited there in the quiet for a little while he almost forgot the blackness of the present.

July, sitting with her face toward the screens at the end of the servants' table in the hall, had seen him go by to the garden. So had the little gray-haired man, wearing Lord Privy Seal's livery, who sat opposite her, but neither had made any comment. Master John Heath, a cousin of Master Henry Machyn, and so, though distantly, a cousin of Laurence's, was a man of an orderly habit of mind. The sight of Aske in the house had been a surprise to him, and certainly must be looked into, but he would first pursue that inquiry for the sake of which he had come, and only afterward attend to the other.

"So," said he, "you have had no communication with your sister since you came hither to London?"

"I have told you—none."

"No letters? No messages? Come, sweet cousin, it's not that you are thought to favor her treasons, but if she wrote to you, there might drop a word, to you innocent, but to us disclosing or confirming her guilt."

"I have had no letter, nor message. I never thought to have."

Cousin Heath rooted thoughtfully in his ear, watching her. "Yet," said he, with a cunning look, "you do not ask, 'What treason?'"

"Because," said July, "I do not care. I do not care what she has done. I do not care what she suffers for it."

If she had spoken wildly he might have thought that she lied because she was frightened. But here, he could not but know, was the calm and deadly truth.

He leaned toward her, and began to explain how, hearing that his cousin Laurence's wife was sister to this traitor, he had begged that he himself might question her, rather than another, sure as he was that there was nothing but innocence and loyalty in Mistress July—"as I now hear and can vouch for," he said.

July, thinking of Aske in the garden, looked at him with a blank face.

"But," said Laurence's kinsman, "besides that your sister and her paramour have raised insurrection lately, sending hither and thither to call men out, it was she, we know surely, who set on Bigod to rise, whose detestable conspiracy has given the King's Grace fresh cause to have those of the North Country in his dread displeasure."

"She did that?" July cried, not calmly now. "If she did that—"

"Tut! Tut!" he said, and tried to pat her hands as they tore at each other on her lap, but she took them out of his reach. He began to find her agitation suspicious.

"'If she did that,'" he said, "and so she did, she will die for it. Do you know how?"

July shook her head. She was thinking—"It is her doing. It is her doing that he is endangered."

"She will be burned alive."

"She will deserve to be so," said July, and again he could not but recognize the very accent of truth.

"Well," he said, "I can see that indeed you favor not your sister's doings, so we will let that alone.

"Yet there is another matter."

He hitched his chair nearer to hers, and said, speaking low, "This man Aske, that I saw come in— Will he speak openly to you if you should put questions to him?"

When he had sat in the garden perhaps a quarter of an hour Aske began to suspect that July had been told by her husband to have no more dealings with him. As that was but too probable, the only thing to do was to leave, making some excuse if he saw anyone on his way out.

So he came back to the house, and opened the door leading to the screens passage. The door opposite him was open on the street; July stood there, and with her a small gray-haired man, who leaned close and whispered in her ear. Robert Aske saw Cromwell's livery color; before he knew what he would do, he had shut the door softly, and gone back a few steps into the garden. He remembered now that July's sister was a whore, and July herself a liar. He thought, "She is to betray me to them."

July found him standing there. She was so glad to see him, for all her fear, that she thought nothing of the sternness of his look, except that for a few minutes she might be able to soften it.

"Come," she said, "come beyond," and went past him toward the farther garden. For a moment he thought to turn and go away without a word, yet he followed her.

But when she sat down on the grass bank, patting it to show that he should sit beside her, he would not, and standing in front of her he said, "That man you spoke with—he is one of Cromwell's."

She nodded. "He is a cousin of my husband."

He looked down at her, and now her eyes shrank from his, and she turned her face away.

"And," he said, "when I have talked to you, you shall report my words to him."

She did not look up, or speak, or even shake her head.

Nor could he find any more to say. If it was true there was nothing to be said. But then—how he did not know—but he knew that it was not true, and that he could trust her, if no other. He said suddenly:

"I did not think you would betray me," and, "Nor I do not think it. Surely I know you will not."

She broke down at that, caught his hand and clutched it in both of hers, bowing herself over it, so that he felt her tears fall on his fingers. She told him, so far as he was able to distinguish her words, that indeed she could not—"Oh! do you not know that I could not?"

He sat down by her on the bank, leaving his hand in hers, and hoping that she would become calm; but she did not seem able to stop crying, now that she had begun. At last it distressed him too much to be borne longer.

"Sweeting," he said, "let's be merry a little. Will you for my sake?"

She gave a great gulp, and sat still, and apparently without breathing, for a long instant. Then she released his hand, and in silence wiped her eyes, not making any attempt to turn away, but doing it simply, carefully, openly.

The sun had gone down, and a half moon looked into the garden from a sky that was still bright but whose color was chilling away. With a sudden flurry of wings, a blackbird alighted in the mulberry tree, bowed, swung up his tail, and began his song.

"How sweet he sings," said July, not in the low voice of one who is near to tears, but in a high, clear tone, that brought startlingly to Aske's mind the wild beauty of her sister. "But whether he thinks on the moon or upon worms," said July, "none knoweth." And she laughed.

When Laurence came into the garden, the moon, instead of a thin white flake with the blue showing through, was a well of purest cold light. As he came through the passage he heard voices; at the farther end he stood looking at them.

Aske, stooping down, was playing idly with a pebble, dandling and jumping it in his cupped palm. July sat gazing at him with a little smile and a look of inly bleeding tenderness. This was not that look which a woman bends upon her lover; to Laurence it was something worse than that. It was the look, at last on July's face, of a woman, not of a child; of a woman gazing on her child.

Laurence knew too well in himself the kind of love of which that look came, to mistake it in another. But to see her pour it over the bent head of this man was worse, he thought, than to find them breast to breast.

April 7

Aske heard them driving the nails into his coffin. He braced himself, straining to heave off the lid. He tried to shout, and wakened himself by a groan. It was a dream. He was awake now, but the knocking went on, and someone below shouted, "In the King's name!"

He was out of bed, with his hand on Will's shoulder, shaking him. But Will only rolled over in bed with a snore, and Aske remembered that a few hours ago he had come back to the Cardinal's Hat dead drunk. So there was no help in him.

There was no help anywhere, nor anything to do but dress and be ready. He could hear them opening the doors below. His knees were shaking, and in the dark he could find only shirt, drawers, and shoes. By the time he had these on a light shone on the ceiling and slid to the floor, as they came clattering upstairs.

They burst in, half a dozen of them, armed archers of the guard, and he could hear more outside. They said they had come to apprehend him for new treasons lately discovered, and laid hold of his wrists. Will wakened just at that moment, yawned, stared, and lurched out of bed.

"Will! Stop!" Aske cried, but Will went at the men, clawing and screaming like a maniac, to be knocked down as clean as a skittlepin. Those two who held Aske drove him to the door. He could do nothing, but as they dragged him downstairs he shouted, "Don't hurt the fellow. He's drunk. He means no harm."

Out in the inn yard, where the sharp night air met him, he remembered that he was not half dressed, and tried to hang back, asking that one would fetch his clothes, or give him time to get them on. They said they were not his body servants, nor his nurse neither, to put on his hosen, and tie his points, and wipe his breach for him.

As they thrust him into the street he experienced for the first time, with rage and fear, the impotence of a prisoner.

April 8

The litter halted, and Lord Darcy in its black interior heard someone beat with the butt end of a pike upon a gate. As the bars rumbled into their sockets, and the gates clattered back upon the walls, the litter moved on, swinging the leather curtains for a second aside, so that a little trickle of the swaying torchlight dodged in, and was blotted again. The litter stopped once more, and just then, from high up above, came the strokes of a great bell, telling the hour. It was ten of the clock, and the great bell of the King's Tower of London had struck it out.

Darcy pulled the curtain aside, and got his foot over the edge of the litter. He was not going to show these fellows any unwillingness to arrive. But for a moment, dazzled by the crowded torches, he could only blink, unable to make out any of the surrounding faces clearly. Then he saw Mr. Lieutenant, Sir Arthur Kingston, lean and tawny brown as a Berkshire hog.

"Good Master Lieutenant," said he, "you give me a kindly welcome."

"Sorry I am, my lord," replied Kingston stiffly, "to give you any welcome to this place."

"Nor should you," said Darcy, "if honest men were up, and rogues down. Well, show me the way."

They showed him the way to the Beauchamp Tower, and there he found, sitting about the remains of a very meager fire— but in the Tower that small handful of fuel cost as much as a bushel of sea-coal anywhere else—Sir Thomas and Sir Ingram Percy, strangely pale after their weeks of captivity; and Sir Robert Constable. They had heard of his coming from the guard, and so had saved some of their supper, and made him welcome to it, prizing him not only as a comrade but also, for this night at least, as a novelty, and an event.

So when he had eaten they sat a long while talking, till the two Percys, having wearied themselves out with railing against Cromwell, began to yawn, and lay down under their cloaks. Soon they slept, Thomas with sudden starts, and now and again a sharp cry, and a hand flung out; Ingram with the blank look of death upon his upturned face.

The older men lay down too, but did not sleep. Instead they murmured together of the apparent dangers of their case, or of such slight hopes as they might discern.

Darcy himself had none of these hopes, saying roundly, "Cromwell is set to pull down all nobles. So I shall go, and those two, yet you may scape."

Sir Robert argued a bit against him; yet was brought to confess that indeed, as a distant kinsman of the Queen, he might, at the worst, find one with power to procure his pardon.

"Yet—" he cried, "Yet—'pardon!' For us who have done no treason since that pardon we were freely given!" Darcy heard him grind his teeth in the darkness, and then mutter, "I do not wonder to hear those two curse and swear."

"Well," said Darcy, speaking slowly after a silence, "I shall not hope but for one thing. Shall I tell you what?"

"What then?"

"That God in his mercy will take my death as if I had died fighting for his cross."

"Say you so?" muttered Constable, startled and solemnized.

"And maybe, in his good time, he will rise up to defend his honor, and holy church, and to tumble down," said Darcy, "these heretics and Privy Seals," and he laughed, sharply and angrily.

April 9

Laurence Machyn heard his wife sigh. It was a very small breath, and she was unconscious of it, but to him it was as dreadful as the sound of the passing bell. And again she sat very still, yet with her eyes roving, as though she listened and waited. Laurence groaned within himself, thinking, "She sighs for him."

He laid down his knife beside the ham-bone he was picking and said abruptly:

"They took him to the Tower on Saturday. One told me of it this morning."

He had not meant that there should be the least note of triumph in his voice, and he was ashamed to detect it. Yet it did not matter, since July missed it. The news itself was all she cared for.

She turned her face toward him, and he saw horror quicken it; then, before his eyes it seemed to die, so white and empty did it grow. She said nothing, and her eyes looked past him. After a minute she laid her hands on the table and stood up.

"I have finished," she said, and went out. He heard her climb the stairs, and thought he would hear her footsteps in the room above, which was theirs. But no—she went on to the attics. He knew that she went there so that he should not come in upon her, and he felt as if something had laid a hand upon his heart, squeezing it cruelly.

Upstairs Julian stood in the little closet under the roof, leaning a hand against one of the beams, and looking down, without seeing it, at the old cow-hide trussing coffer. Her thought was not, as yet, precisely of Robert Aske, but rather—"It has come." All her life she had been expecting the worst, and now the worst had come.

April 16

Quite a score of mounted archers, riding close, surrounded the litter in which Lord Darcy was brought from the Tower for examination by the lords of the council in Lord Chancellor Audeley's house. They rode into the courtyard, and then the sergeant of them, dismounting, unlaced the leather curtains, and said to my lord, "Sir, you are to follow me."

The fine new staircase which the lord chancellor had lately had built was of an easy and broad tread, but when a gentleman usher opened a door at the top, and beckoned my lord in, he paused, leaning heavily on his staff. Then he lifted his head and went into the room.

It was a sunny place, and the windows were open upon the tops of the apple trees which showed, among their fresh leaves, round bright pink buds. A small company of gentlemen stood talking together in the pleasant air and sunshine. There was Fitzwilliam, broad and black; Paulet with his smooth look, Edward Seymour the Queen's brother, now Lord Beauchamp, looking, as always, like one who knows himself to be better than his company. Suffolk, who liked to ape the King when he was not by, stood with his fine legs straddled wide, swinging from his fingers a jewel that hung about his neck. At the board's head, apart from all these, sat Cromwell, with a heap of papers before him, licking his thumb and flicking them over as calmly as if they were bills of lading, instead of articles framed against the King's enemies; as if he were once more a merchant among the merchants of Amsterdam, instead of Lord Privy Seal, presiding over the King's Most Honorable Council.

Darcy stopped inside the door, his eyes snapping bright, and seeming, for all that in these days his great height was bowed, to look down on the whole company. Some of them avoided his glance, some gave him look for look, as they came back from the windows, and settled themselves in the chairs set about the table. Mr. Pollard, the King's remembrancer, who sat in place of any common clerk at a further small table, dipped his pen in the ink, and held it poised.

"Well," said Darcy, speaking to them all but looking only at Cromwell, "I am here now at your pleasure. Ye may do your pleasure with me. Yet I have read of men that have been in such favor with their Princes as ye be now, that have come at last to the same end that ye would now bring me to. And so may ye come to the same."

"Keep that door!" cried Cromwell, and the gentleman usher, who was one of Norfolk's gentlemen, namely Perce Cresswell, hastily slammed the door and set his shoulders against it, as though that would prevent Lord Darcy's voice, strong still, and still with a sound of youth in it, penetrating the oak of the paneling.

"Outside!" said Cromwell, "Fool!" So Perce went out.

There was an interrogatory of over a hundred questions, and time wore on as Cromwell put them to Darcy, Darcy answered, and Mr. Pollard wrote his answers down. Now and again one of the other lords would break in, for Darcy spared none, hitting here and there in his replies, and that was easy for one with such a long memory as his, which could range back, through things done and said in court or camp for twenty, thirty, forty years.

"You," said he, mocking at them all, "you that think you can pull down the walls and leave the thatch standing! His ribalds and his scribblers," and he pointed his staff right at Cromwell's face, "they go about to teach the commons to grudge and murmur and scoff at holy church. Take ye heed that they come not to grudge at us noble men, and when they have pulled down the church pull down also the whole nobles of the realm, and so rule all, tag-rag."

Cromwell let him finish, and then he smiled, a small thin smile.

"You say the nobility shall be pulled down. God's Bread! but it is you yourself and your fellows who pull it down by treasons against your Prince. Mr. Pollard," he said, turning to the little table at the wall, "put to him that question as to . . ." He ran his finger down the paper. "The one hundred and twentieth," he said.

Mr. Pollard read it out.

"If all things had succeeded according to your intention, what would ye have done, first touching the King's person, and then touching every man of his council?"

"Enough!" said Cromwell. "Let him answer so far first."

"Shall I answer?"

"You shall."

Darcy straightened his back. His face was flushed and his eyes a bright frosty blue, so that for all the chills of the Tower, and his age and weakness, for a moment he looked the quick and dangerous fighter he had been.

"For the King," he said, "not a hair of his head should have been touched. For the ancient and noble blood upon the council, our intent was to preserve it. But the villain blood that is there, that should have been taken and judged."

"Meaning—" Cromwell asked. Now he was not smiling.

"Thee, Master Cromwell." Darcy's look as much as the curt words stripped an upstart of his Privy Seal, and of all his importance.

"For it is thou," he went on, "that art the chief causer of all this rebellion and mischief, and art likewise causer of the apprehension of us that be noble men, and dost daily earnestly travail to bring us to our end, and to strike off our heads. And

I trust, before thou die, though thou wouldst procure all the noblemen's heads within the realm to be stricken off, yet shall one head remain that shall strike off thy head."

Cromwell got out of his chair, and began to beat with his fist on the table. "Strike him on the mouth," he cried, but there was no one there would do it for him.

April 20

Lord Privy Seal was among the crowd which waited upon the King as he came out from chapel. The King waved his hand to put away from him all the others, and went with Cromwell to a window looking upon the gardens.

"Well?"

"From my Lord Darcy," says Cromwell, "nothing but saucy words and high cracks."

"And from Aske?"

"Nothing of moment. Though plenty to hang the man himself," he added.

"You sent to him?"

"I went to him myself. First I told him that his own brother had given information of his treasonous proceedings."

"And he said?"

"Nothing to the purpose. Yet I think it touched him nearly. For he said, 'God help me!' and then, 'Which brother?' I said, 'Your second brother, Christopher Aske.'"

"And then?"

"No more on that head. But I said that he should have pardon for speaking the truth; that if when he comes to trial he should chance to be condemned I should be his intercessor; that no harm was meant to them all, but only to preserve the honor of Your Grace, which would be much touched if rebels should not be judged by law; but that once judged all those shall have mercy that have not offended since the pardon, 'as,' said I, 'His Grace knoweth that you have not. So you may speak freely.'"

"What did he say to that?"

"That for his own part he would always be ready to declare such things as come to his remembrance. But that if he bought his life by condemning other, he would be a thing to be abhorred of all good men, and his life worth naught."

Cromwell dared only to give a slinking glance at the King's face, but it was enough to show him how it had grown red and bloated as Henry stood silent, throttling down his rage. Just then the horns blew for supper, and Cromwell caught a glimpse, beyond the King's shoulder, of the pages and gentlemen of the chamber, waiting with towel, ewer, and basin for the King to wash his hands.

"Tcha!" said the King at last. "He'll speak before long. You shall see. He hath an ill conscience before God for his treasons. He'll not endure."

Cromwell thought of the man he had seen this morning, whose teeth chattered with the cold, but whose look was resolved far beyond defiance. He shook his head. "He answers still very stoutly. And they say at the Tower that though he has had the colic and has moreover a sore cough, yet he will most often be merry when they bring his porridge."

"Merry!" cried the King. "Who sends him help then?"

Cromwell said no one could have sent him anything. "At the foot of his last writing he asks the lords of the council for the love of God that he may send for money and clothes, 'for I am not able to live,' says he, 'seeing none of my friends will do nothing for me.'"

"And yet," said the King, "he will not speak! Vile villain!" he said, and there was a kind of incredulity in his anger. "Has he no care for his soul?" he asked.

Cromwell did not undertake to answer that. He said, reflectively, that the fellow might be put down into a straiter place, and a worse. "Or there is the rack."

"No. Not yet." The King brooded. A pleasant strain of music reached them from the presence chamber, and a pleasant smell also, of roasted and spiced meat.

"No," said the King again. "Try this." He spread out his hands, and looked down at them, half drew off a sapphire ring, slipped it back into place, and held out to Cromwell a circle of twisted gold, with white enamel and green interlacing tiny pearls.

"If he does not trust you, me he will trust. Say to him that there is his Prince's token to ensure him of pardon, if he will speak the truth."

"Sir," said Cromwell after some hesitation, looking down at the ring upon his palm, "should you pardon this man—"

"He must by some means be induced to tell the names of those others," the King answered in a gentle voice. "But as for pardon—" He turned away, and beckoned for the ewer and basin.

May 12

As July was buying mackerel at the door a man came by who hesitated, turned, and then stood as if uncertain of his way. He was a stranger and yet to July there was that about him which reminded her of someone. She caught his eye and looked hastily down at the fish in the huckster's basket, barred with black ripple marks of the sea, and gleaming with the sea's blue green. She bought half a dozen, had the man lay them on the stone paving of the screens' passage, and was about to shut the door. But as the huckster moved away, that other, who had loitered near, came to her. He had the appearance of a harmless worthy man, and yet there was something in the way he glanced about that made her fear him, though he himself had a look of fright.

"You want my husband?" she said.

"Are you Mistress Machyn?"

She nodded and thought to shut the door. Yet that likeness of his, that she could not account for, made her pause.

"My brother," he said, "made me swear on the cross I should come to you. He could have no ease till I swore it. I'd have come sooner, but" (he dropped his voice very low) "they had me in Newgate, to question me."

"Come in," said July.

"No. Better not." He glanced about again. "The sooner I'm away, the better for you. But I promised Will—"

"Who is Will?"

"My brother. Will Wall. But Will's dead. He was Mr. Aske's servant."

July could say nothing because of the loudness of that name in her ears, or else it was the blood drumming there.

"Will died a week after they took Master Aske. He came to me at Ware before daylight, for they'd taken his master about midnight. I knew then that Will was a dead man. The moment I saw him I knew it. He raved all that week, clawing and striking at his breast, saying it was he that had brought his master into treason, crying out, 'He was hid, and I brought them to him,' and crying out, 'Oh my master, my master, they will draw him, and hang him, and quarter him!'"

"Stop," cried July, but she had not voice enough to make him hear her.

"He made me swear I should tell you Mr. Aske was taken, for so, he said, he had promised to do. And just before he died he said I should tell you also that his master was taken by night in naught but his shirt and shoes. I'd 'a' come before, but they took me—" He stopped then because the young woman had shut the door in his face.

Laurence came in a while after and shouted for July. She heard him well enough from the kitchen, but did not answer. Then she heard him go upstairs. After a moment he called again, "July! July!" and came to the kitchen door, so she had to go out to him.

"Wife," he said, "I can nowhere find my blue hosen."

July put her hand to her mouth, looking not at him, but out toward the garden. The sun shone through the open door; a bee came in, lingered, and then went off again. There was summer in his humming, and in the silence he left behind him, and in the smell of chopped mint that came from the kitchen. But her mind was frozen; only her heart ached as she felt it beat heavily. The hiss of a pot boiling over, a shriek and a peal of laughter from the maids, made her start, but still she felt that she was not properly awake.

"Why do you want them?" she asked.

"I've torn these on a nail. That fool Nick's no craftsman. I shall turn him off."

"I mended your gray," said July, with a huge effort.

"It is not warm enough yet for them."

"I—I am busy. Can you not find something? You have plenty."

Her voice nearly broke on that. She turned and went away into the kitchen. "Plenty of hosen." So he had, and coats, and doublets, everything. He was warmed, fed, and cared for. She would have been glad, that moment, to do him an injury for being so.

She had forgotten Laurence, because her thoughts clung so tormentedly to the other, when she heard her husband call again, "July, come here."

As she climbed the stairs he went back into their chamber. She found him standing in the midst; the floor was strewn with clothes, tossed here and there, gowns, shifts and shirts, doublets and petticoats.

He said, "My black doublet is gone too, and that red camlet coat, and two of my best shirts."

When she said nothing, and did not even look at him, he asked, "Where are they?" and came nearer to her, to say again, and louder, "Where are they?"

"Master Aske—" she began.

Laurence stepped back. His foot caught in one of her gowns so that he almost fell. Now he could not look at her, any more than she could look at him.

She said in the smallest voice, but it was steady, "He has been there this two months, through all these late frosts and cold, in but his shirt and his shoes."

Stealing a glance at her he saw her whole face shake, and again grow still. She looked straight before her through the window, but she pointed to where the curtains of the bed moved gently in the sweet air. "They are there," she said, "under the bed. I should have sent them to him."

"How?"

She said, "I do not know."

The look of her and her voice so cut him to the heart that he could not endure it. He went past her, downstairs, and out into the street.

Outside the Tower that evening a man hung about till it was almost time for the drawbridge to be lifted and the gates shut. Then, seeing a sour-looking grizzled fellow going in, he seemed to take courage, stepped forward and stopped him.

"Gossip," said he, "there's a gentleman in there called Aske."

"There is," the old fellow agreed.

"Can I . . . How can I get this to him?" With one hand he held out a bundle, and with the other fumbled in his purse.

"Are you a friend of his?"

Laurence dropped the angel that he had between his fingers.

"My wife—" he began, and then stood dumb, his eyes downcast, the very picture of a shamed but acquiescent cuckold.

The old man chuckled softly. "By Cock!" he said, "so it is with these gentlemen, and this one with his filed tongue would be harder for a wench to resist than another. And he mettle. I know something of mettle. I've seen prisoners enough in my day, but this one—" He seemed to recollect himself, and growled, "Saving that he's a pestilent traitor."

Laurence shoved the bundle at him, and said with more violence than so gentle a man could have been thought capable of, "Here. Will you take it or no?"

The old man took it. "Aye. He shall have it tomorrow. A murrain on him for a traitor." He picked up Laurence's angel out of the dust, and stumped away across the bridge.

In bed that night, with the candle blown out, Laurence kept silence a long time. Then he cried out in a harsh, rough voice:

"I took that bundle. The jailer says he shall have it tomorrow."

After that they lay far apart in the wide bed, awake and silent. She could not speak, and he would not.

May 13

The sunshine, which when Aske first came to this place had only touched the stones of the wall and brought its fleeting warmth as low as to his knees, now, unless clouds cheated him, lay for a longer time each day upon the floor, so that he could even warm his feet in it for a little while. He was standing in the precious sunshine, turning himself slowly about when he heard the key rattle in the lock, and old Ned Stringer came in, shut the door, and tossed a bundle on the floor between them.

"There's what you've been asking for," said Ned, with his sourest face.

"What is it?" Aske stared at him, then at the bundle.

"Looks to me like a coat for your back."

Aske stooped. He fumbled at the knot before he could get it open. Then he looked blankly at Ned. "But these are not mine."

Ned cackled at him. "Do them on. Who cares if they're yours? No, they're not yours neither, but they're from your leman, master, brought by her own husband. (Out on you for a rank seducer!) Though he seemed a poor fellow, yon husband, with his foul teeth, and lank hair; and women's hearts are frail."

Aske, looking down at the open bundle and hearing Ned's words, saw again Laurence Machyn coming across the little twilight garden in this same black doublet with the crimson sleeves; a poor, awkward creature Aske had thought him then.

But now he said: "Hold your tongue, you fool. She's no leman of mine, and may God reward him for his good charity, for he's a truer friend to me than any other."

"Tell me that!" said Ned, and went away sniggering.

May 14

Just before dusk Mr. Kingston, lieutenant of the Tower, came to inform Lord Darcy that his trial would be tomorrow, at Westminster. Darcy sat over the fire, alone, for today the two Percys and Constable had been moved to other quarters, and Kingston, seeing him as if for the first time, said to himself, "He is old. He is ill." He tried to remember how old the old man must be, but could not.

And then Darcy looked up at him with such a quick frosty gleam in his blue eyes that Kingston could not think of him as old at all.

"So Master Cromwell has his false witnesses ready at his tail," said my lord, and laughed.

"Do you doubt," said Mr. Lieutenant, "that you shall have justice?"

"I doubt it sorely," said Darcy in a friendly, open tone.

Kingston shook his head.

"Sir," said he, "I shall show you that you mistake if you think the judgment is foregone, or that my Lord Privy Seal is your enemy."

"Oh! I mistake?"

"Truly you do. As we drank wine but now in my lodging, Beauchamp, Audeley, and some others being present, my Lord Privy Seal spoke of your trial. Quod he, 'My lord's peers may condemn him, for the King's honor's sake, but by God's Passion, I myself will travail to obtain his pardon, the which I am well persuaded the King will not refuse to grant.'"

Darcy had his hands spread out upon his knees and seemed to study them.

"Cromwell said that?" he asked softly.

"He did. He did. I heard him speak so with my own ears."

"I remember," said Darcy, "that the old Cardinal" (he meant Wolsey) "said one day to me that he knew no deeper head than this Cromwell's. And I'd say, 'Nor no blacker heart.'"

"Fie!" cried Master Lieutenant, "How can you so rail on one that would befriend you?" And he began to pace about the chamber till he came to a stand near Darcy, looking down upon him with a reproving frown.

"Well," said Darcy, tilting his head to look up at Kingston, and speaking with a mocking lightness, "I never thought that in these days my peers would do for me what I and others did for my Lord Dacre, maugre the King's and Cromwell's teeth—namely, to acquit me of treason. But now, these words of Cromwell's being known, there is none that may wish me well but will, for the King's honor's sake, cheerfully cast me as guilty, supposing that my life will be spared."

"And then my Lord Privy Seal will get your pardon."

"Master Lieutenant, are you so simple?" He put out a hand, and waved it to move the lieutenant from his side. "I'll ask you," said he, "as Diogenes the Greek asked King Alexander, to get out of my sunlight, or rather my firelight, for either is very dear to us prisoners."

Master Kingston did not stop after that. Darcy sat on, wrapping himself closer as the fire died down, turning over in his mind all the charges that they might bring against him tomorrow, and his answers; recalling as much as he could of the letters which they might have seized, besides words of his which they might have by report of persons indiscreet or malicious.

"Well," he thought, "it's not from the answers I have given to their interrogations that I shall be charged," and he laughed to himself as he recalled those taunts of his which the clerks had written down word for word, until Privy Seal had cried,

"Enough. Enough. Write no more of that." For when they questioned him of his doings he had replied by accusations, and these not against his companions in rebellion, but against those very men who sat at the council table, and others, not present but in favor, such as my Lord of Norfolk, and his son Surrey.

So he rehearsed his case in his mind, wary as a fox, fierce as an old wild boar. "And we shall see," he said to himself, "when we come to Westminster Hall, whether they will muzzle me so that I cannot speak."

Yet, because he was, for all his spirit, an old man and frail, more and more his thoughts began to slide from what must be tomorrow to what had been, and especially to what had been long ago; so that in his mind he was in the little chapel at Templehurst, which he remembered as far back as he remembered anything. There was the smell of incense, and the fume of snuffed candles hanging in the air; there was the great painted crucifix above. And at the same time he saw all the candles that stood upon his father's hearse in the chapel blow one way, so that the light slid and rippled over the pall of black and gold tissue. And now, because he himself was little Tom once more, his father stood before his eyes, immensely tall. The servants were dressing him in a gown of rayed cloth that had many gold buttons fastening it all the way down the front from the high collar to the fur-trimmed hem. And little Tom had a pair of wooden knights, carved and painted, and each man jointed on his saddle, that rode at each other as you pulled the strings underneath. They met with a crack, and he woke at a great jerk of his head nodding forward on his breast.

It was time to sleep, since his wits must be keen tomorrow. He got up, and beat on the door to let them know that his servant should come to him.

May 17

July went out shopping very early, with Dickon to carry her basket. She bought a young sucking pig in Newgate Street, and told Dickon to carry it home, saying that she would go on to Goldsmiths' Row because she desired a new silver cup. But when she had watched him out of sight she set off to walk to Westminster.

She found that she should have reached the great hall there an hour earlier if she wished to see anything, or even to hear much of this trial of the Northern rebels. All she could do was to press into the crowd that filled the farther end, and there stand wedged, hearing less of the trial itself than of the conversation that went on round about her. For, since all thereabouts must needs miss most of what was going on, they took no pains to listen, but talked, comfortably and pleasantly, among themselves. "And he with the one eye was the traitor Aske?" said a woman. "God put out his other!" "By Cock!" said a big man, "but they'll have their deserts. You shall see that they'll be cast, as Lord Darcy was two days ago, and so they'll hang one and all." "Nay," said another, "but lords die by the axe." And then they disputed of that, and of the hanging and drawing of lesser traitors. But when July took her hands down from under her veil, unstopping her ears for a minute, they were saying how slow in hatching their goslings were this year. "Ah! That's this long drought," said a man, and then a thin woman cried, "Chip their shells for them, neighbor, chip their shells."

So July kept her thumbs out of her ears, and strained to hear what was spoken beyond the crowd, where Master Aske was being tried for his life. But someone over there would cough and cough, so that though she listened for his voice she could never be sure that she heard it.

By dint of squeezing and pushing, which brought her black looks from those she pressed against, she managed after a while to draw nearer. But now it was the man with the cough who was answering questions, and what with the huskiness of his voice and his fits of coughing she could make nothing of what he said, and grew almost as impatient with him as the judge was, who would often break in, crying, "Well, I cannot hear you," and to the King's sergeant-at-law, "Go on to the next point, since he cannot or will not answer."

And Aske, almost voiceless and fighting for his life, felt a rage, and a cramping fear at this malignant injustice which was grappling him down. They were charging him with those things for which the King had granted pardon, and with those things which he had done to keep the country stayed when Bigod rose, only there they twisted his honest deeds and words to treason. For treason they made it that he had not disclosed how Levening had desired his intercession with the Duke of Norfolk; yet to the duke himself he had disclosed it, when he interceded with him for Levening. And, had he not disclosed it, of what had he then been guilty, seeing that the jury at York had acquitted Levening of treason?

But now it was treason even to have trusted that the King should keep the promises which he made. The blank wrong, he thought, would have kept him dumb, even if his voice had not failed him; and his brain also seemed both blind and bound. Yet, because he was a lawyer, he fought them inch by inch, beating them off from one charge after another; and all to no purpose, for like a sea tide they always came back over the same ground, and if any charge might not in itself amount to treason, "Well," said they at last, "each one plainly showeth your cankered traitorous heart, and together amount to very great treason."

"Jesu!" cried Aske then, finding a little his voice, "now know I what I never learned before, that ten white pullets make one white swan."

"It shall not profit you," said the judge, "to jest at the King's justice."

At last July realized that the judge's voice, which had spoken so long in a dry, unbroken drone, like a bluebottle shut in a room, had ceased. There was a stir, and the sound of footsteps; far off a door whined, and then shut. A pause followed during which her neighbors in the crowd shuffled their feet and shifted restlessly, telling each other that dinner would be cold if the jurymen were long. This period was broken by the sound of raised voices from the direction of the court. "What's that? What do they say?" Everyone lent an ear, and then the words came, passed back from mouth to mouth—"They plead guilty."

"Who? Who? All?" So it was questioned, impatiently, for this was a tame ending for a trial. But July only shut her eyes, and shut her lips and waited, almost not breathing, till someone said, "Nay, not all. Only the Percys, Sir John Bulmer, and Hammerton . . ." "And Bulmer's whore," the word came next. That was the first time July knew that Meg was there among the prisoners. It meant nothing to her.

For a second time a hush spread in a fluttering, whispering way over all the crowd, till they heard the footsteps of the twelve men returning. In the awful quiet the voice of the judge came now quite clearly as he read out the names of the prisoners: Robert Constable, Francis Bigod, George Lumley, John Bulmer, Margaret Cheyne, Robert Aske. To each name the jurors replied with the word "Guilty."

At the end the prisoners were asked had they aught they would say. "Constable?"

"Nothing."

"Bigod?"

"Nothing, except— Nothing."

"Hammerton? Lumley?" Each answered, "No."

"Aske?"

There was a little pause, for Aske was coughing. Then he said, "Nothing." And at last July knew that she had heard his voice.

The prisoners were brought back through crowded streets where people stared and nudged, whispering together, except where some prentice lads booed at the men, and whistled to make Meg look their way. Just inside Ludgate they were halted for a few moments because a horse was down, and the wagon, loaded with bulging sarplers of wool, blocked the way. The mounted archers' horses came jostling back on the prisoners, and then they all stood, in the open, bland heat of the day, for the sun was now high above the housetops.

In the slight confusion Sir Robert Constable came abreast of Aske. They had not met since they had been together at Templehurst, months ago, but Constable saw that Aske regarded him with as little interest as if they had parted yesterday.

"Heart up, Cousin Aske," said Sir Robert, when Aske turned away a dull, indifferent eye; and then—"Look!"

Aske looked down where the other pointed, and saw, spilt upon the street close beside them, a handful of bluebells and red campion; some young creatures coming back from the fields this morning must have let them fall, for they were still quite fresh.

Sir Robert stooped quickly and picked them up. He smelt them, and laughed, as if at his own foolishness, and yet for pleasure too.

"So sweet they smell," he said, "and bring to mind sweet things. Take some."

But Aske shook his head as if he were angry, pushing Constable's hand aside, and then the archers moved on, and they were separated.

That evening when Ned Stringer unlocked the door to tell Aske it was time for him to take his turn at the privy, he found the prisoner lying face downward on the straw, his forehead on his crossed arms.

"Come, master," he said, and turned away, to stand swinging his keys, awkwardly silent.

"Come, master," he said again, "I never thought I'd see you set down. What then? Do not we all die? And if the pains be sharp, yet they're over before long." He looked round now, and saw that Aske was standing on his feet; he held out one hand toward Ned.

"Here," said he, "take that if you will."

Ned came nearer, and stared at the ring that lay on Aske's palm. It was a very pretty thing, of gold, pearls, and enamel, green and white.

"What's that?" he asked. "I never saw that on your finger."

"I plaited threads from my shirt and hung it round my neck."

"What is it then?"

"It's a token from the King."

"What for? And you'd give it to me! What is it a token for?"

"To promise me pardon for speaking the truth."

Ned cried, "By Cock! You're mad then. You'd give it to me? Why man! there's nothing to fear if you have the King's token."

Aske gave him a look which the old man could not make out; however, he kept the ring and went away down the stairs.

When he came back Ned stared hard at his hands, but there was no ring on any finger.

"What have you done with it?" he cried.

"Cast it down the privy."

"God's Death! You did not!"

"It meant," said Aske, "nothing."

"The King's token—nothing?"

"I am persuaded—nothing. And besides that," said Aske, as he sat down and let his head drop on his clenched fists, "it's justice I want, not mercy. And there's no justice, nor no mercy either. None, I think, under the floor of heaven."

May 18

It was not yet light indoors when the great gross old doctor of divinity from the Our Lady Friars in Fleet Street wallowed up the narrow turning stair of the Beauchamp Tower, blowing heavily. The warder stopped, and opened a door. The friar went in past him. Lord Darcy was in the room; he got up, as gaunt as the other was fat, so that they might have passed in a Morality for Gluttony and Abstinence.

"I came betimes—" said the friar, still gasping.

"I thank you for that." Lord Darcy spoke with a very stately courtesy. Then he smiled, and laid his hand a moment on the friar's shoulder; they had known each other for many years, and it was as plain that the friar was moved as that he was unwilling to let it be seen that he was moved. So my lord went on talking, partly to give him time, partly for sheer delight in talking; for to any captive a listener is as a drink of water to a thirsty man.

"Yesterday," said he, "they told me I should die today. Well, 'twas a strange thing, Father. At first I could think of two things only, swinging betwixt them like a clock's pendulum. The one was—'I die—*I* die o' Saturday,' and t'other—'It cannot be I.'"

The priest nodded. He might have spoken, but my lord was not now to be stopped.

"Soon," he said, "why, very soon, in an hour—by the Rood! It was no more—the thing was no longer strange. And then I knew that though I had little time, yet I had to spare for what must be done. For it is indeed a thing remarkable, how few cares trouble a man who is come close to the day of his death."

"There is," said the friar, "one needful care only, and it is that for which I am here."

The old man, with his heavy pouching cheeks and great belly, was one of those whose souls, strenuous and austere, are masked in fat; abstinence bloated him, penance puffed him out. Only if you looked closely at the red, fleshy face, you could see in its grossness, courage, gentleness, and a humble spirit. So now, for all his noisy breathing and purpled face, he had put on dignity as if he had put on a vestment.

Darcy went slowly down on his knees to make his last confession.

That was hardly done when there came a knock at the door.

"*Nunc dimittis, Domine, servum tuum in pace,*" murmured my lord, whose face, purged of passion by the solemnities and mercies of his late concernments, was still as a carved face on a tomb.

The lieutenant of the Tower came in. Darcy moved toward the door, but Kingston waved him back. He said there was word from the King's Grace that my lord should not die today.

"If not today—when?" Darcy asked, sooner than either of the others had thought he would find his voice.

Mr. Kingston did not know.

"Well," said Darcy, and was able to smile, "I may yet die in my bed. And yet I care not, whether it be so or no."

But the two could see that he was still shaken by the stress of not knowing when he should die, though that was the very state in which he had passed all his life until yesterday.

So the fat old friar, disregarding Kingston's gesture toward the door, plumped himself down upon one stool, and my lord sat upon the other, and when Kingston had gone they were silent for a long time, looking, each of them, at the ashes upon that hearth where Darcy had not expected to see another fire kindled.

Wat had seen the window in the roof change from the coping of a well into which you looked upward and saw only deep darkness and slowly wheeling stars, to a square of faint gray, and, at last, of pallid light. He got up and crawled along the loft softly so as not to waken Malle. But she was awake, and, though he scowled and shook his head at her, she followed him down the ladder, and when he got into the street she was beside him. So they went together toward the river, Wat walking on the balls of his feet and crabwise, ready to spring away did she try to catch him.

The sky above the houses was invisible, and a cold mist lay close over all; sometimes it moved at a puff of light wind, but for the most part it clung, still and white, to the chimneys and rooftops, growing thicker and more chilling as they came closer to the Thames.

At the top of the Tower Wharf Steps they met some fishermen going up homeward, bare-legged, bare-footed, with their hoods pushed back on their shoulders, carrying the wet, sharply-reeking nets over their shoulders, and dripping creels of fish.

At the foot of the steps, since the tide had already run far out, there was sand, firm, smooth, and clean as though this was the first of days, and the world just come new from God's making. Moored beyond the lowest dropping of the tide lay the fishermen's boat, and the track of their feet led up from the water's edge, with here and there a swept patch of sand where a trailing lappet of the nets had dragged behind them. Round about the boat, on the sleek, gray, sleepily swinging water, the gulls sailed, or dozed upon the boat's gunwale.

Malle sat down on a rock beside a little pool. The water in the pool was clear almost as the air; the sand at the bottom was sharply ribbed in the semblance of ripples, one ripple following another, and each smooth, regular, perfect—motion translated into form by the cunning, fingerless hands of the tide, which had worked this craftsmanship during the night.

Wat went on toward the water's edge, following the shallow winding channel which the escaping water had made as it slipped from the brimming pool back to the river. The channel was empty of water now but still marked with the waving lines of its flowing, and edged with tiny cliffs, sharply cut as if built of rock, but all of the cessile sand, and all less than an inch in height.

Down by the water's edge that same bright brown sand was dark with wetness, yet the wetness was bright too, as if it were a shining skin laid over the sand. Wat's footsteps squeezed it dry and pale for an instant, then, as he passed, the water seeped up again so that there was no trace to show where he had trod. Here and there smooth stones broke the gleaming film, clear cold blue, red with a streak of buff, yellow flawed with green; all watery colors brought to life by water. A little farther out the shallowest sliding edge of the receding tide slipped in and out with a hiss, and along this Wat moved slowly, all his life in the soles of his feet to feel the stir of the prawns under the sand, and then to snatch them out and drop them into his canvas pouch for breakfast-time.

Long before he had as many prawns as he wished he heard Malle calling, "Wat! Wat! Come!"

He went to her, lagging, and when he was near would not come within reach of her hands.

She said: "There is darkness, and God moving nigh-hand in the darkness."

Wat made a growling noise in his throat and swung away on one foot. But he could not go. So he stayed to listen, a shoulder bunched between him and her.

Malle said: "All the black night, with not one candle left, not one star, they've dragged him with them, and now they have him to judgment before the dawn comes. The fire's lit and burning, and there's a window the blind morning looks through, and another, and that way's the moon; so day and dark may see the light that made them taken in the hands of men."

She turned away and looked up to where above the empty strand and the wharf the great bulk of the Tower loomed, huge and sullen in the mist. High up the King's banner hung dead upon its staff.

"Man," said Malle, "would take swords, bows, and bills to save him. And the angels wait to break heaven and let burning justice and the naked spirit flake down in flame to heat to scorched souls those men that bear God to die, that so they may know their Maker.

"But he will not. Look, Wat, look! There he is, and holdeth in his hands that glass vessel, clear, precious, brimmed full with clean righteousness. So he hath carried it without spilling, through life and now through death. That shining water's his pure righteousness to wash clean all the world's sins.

"Ah!" she cried, "stay them! Stay them! lest with their swords they shatter the glass and so the water is spilled, for we need it every drop."

She looked at Wat, and he cowered away.

"Sword cannot save righteousness—only spill it for the thirsty ground to drink. And that he knoweth."

She said: "There was the old lord who came to Marrick saying he was a merchant man. Come and tell him this thing."

But though the two of them managed to come within the Tower by following a young girl who brought in eggs to the house of Master Partridge of the Mint, they did not come to my Lord Darcy. For near the Beauchamp Tower one of Master Kingston's men met and questioned them, and set his pikestaff about their shoulders, and drove them, with blows, and much shouting, out of the place again.

At the distant noise of that commotion Lord Darcy jerked his head round to listen and drew in his breath sharply. When there was silence again he turned back, but now he smiled bitterly.

"They should have had my head this morning. By now I had passed, and I was ready to die."

He brought his fist down on his knee.

"Now," he said, "I am not ready. Now I must hope to live, and yet look to die. Yea, and if I die, I die for the faith of Christ, for which we of that pilgrimage took arms; yet, if I die, I die because we Northern men were betrayed by the rest," and he began to rail upon the Marquis of Exeter, "a sheep," he called him; and Lord Montague, "that will stumble at any molehill, and the other Poles but leaves in the wind."

"So now," he said, "is the King and this Cromwell set higher than ever.

"My son—"

Darcy did not let the friar say further. "My Father!" he mocked, and shot out his finger at the other's face, "if you, you the spiritual men, had but called upon all the realm, gentlemen, nobles, and commons to rise, they had risen, for holy church, and Christ, and for righteousness' sake."

"My son," said the friar, "whether you die tomorrow, or whether you live, put aside from you those thoughts. For I tell you surely, that's not God's way."

"Not—" cried Darcy; and then, while the friar held his eyes, he grumbled angrily, "Is it not then? Well, an' if it be not? Tell me how, then? What other way? How? How? Is it not foolishness to think—"

He did not finish, for the old friar stood up.

"*Stultitia Dei*," he said. "It is foolishness. It is God's foolishness that is wiser than men."

Darcy did not move nor speak for a long time. At last he raised his head, and the friar saw something that was almost a smile on his face.

"Well," said my lord lightly, but as men speak lightly before a last, hopeless fight, "I am not of so holy a mind as to be able to take God's way. But," he said, and met the friar's eyes, "I'll not grudge to die. It may be he will accept that for service."

Then he stretched out his hand, and said good-bye.

✤ *The Chronicle of Thomas, Lord Darcy, ends here.*

May 14

When Gib came to Lord Privy Seal's house in Throgmorton Street, and asked for my lord's chaplain, he was told that there were orders that he should be brought up to my lord himself. "Ha!" thought Gib, as he went after the servant through a big hall, and along a passage, "so my lord has taken note of my writings. He would not have sent for me, but to commend me."

The servant let him into a small, pleasant, sunny room with a big painted mappemonde on the wall, all scarlet and blue, with ships here and there upon the seas, and cities, walled and bristling with towers and spires. At the table sat Lord Privy Seal, and his two hands lay upon a page of writing that Gib knew very well, for it was his own.

"This," said Cromwell, not even waiting till the servant had shut the door, "this will not serve," and he rapped the backs of his fingers on the page.

Gib was so surprised that he fairly gaped.

"No one," said my lord, "would laugh at this that you call, 'An Interlude of the Seven Deadly Sins.'"

"They are not meant to laugh," cried Gib, angry now.

"If they laugh not, they listen not," said Cromwell, and threw the papers across the table toward Gib. "Mend it," said he, "or I'll not buy."

That was all. He waved his hand, and the big diamond on his forefinger blazed as the sun caught it. Then Gib was outside the door, and raging.

May 28

Until the bent, sour-looking little man's hand furtively twitched her sleeve, July had not realized that this morning, wherever she went, he had been near. Now, as she turned and looked at him, she knew it, and fright seized her; but before she could call out to Mat, who went in front, the man muttered, "Word from him you love." That for July meant one only; she never doubted whom, nor hesitated what she should do.

"Mat," she said, "Mat," and when he turned, "I forgot, at the Cow in Boots, to buy cardamons. Go back quickly and buy two ounces." When Mat had gone—"Now," said she to the old man, "Quick!"

But he would not be quick, objecting that the Cheap was too crowded for such privy business as his, so they turned into Milk Street, and there, under a gray white cloud of a flowering cherry tree that branched above them over a wall, he pulled out of his doublet some writings.

"A letter?" cried July, "I can't read writings." But her hand stretched out to take it, for at least his hands had touched the paper.

"Aye," said Ned Stringer, putting her fingers by. "For the King, and for Privy Seal," and he told her, sharply and angrily, as if he hated the whole business, that yon fellow, the traitor Aske, in the Tower, had written to them begging mercy.

"Mercy?" July whispered it. She had never thought of mercy.

"Aye. But he's stiff-necked. I told him, 'Down on your knees to 'em. Confess your fault. Beg! Pray! Howl if you will. What matter so you scape the pains you dread when they cut you down.'" And in July's sight the man made an awful pantomime of the executioner's business; and then stared at her, and grinned in her face.

"For he doth dread them. He says, 'If I might but be full dead before I be dismembered—' Oh! I promise you he dreads them well enough, however he may feign. I can see him turning the thought over and over like hay in a wet June. Well—well. So I brought him paper, and 'Write,' I says, 'and none of your pride,' says I. But what will he write? No goodly humbleness, but only 'for the reverence of God and for charity.'"

"Give them to me," said July, through her teeth, and tried to snatch the letters. But again he fended her off.

"Na! Na! Wait till I tell you. There's that one, on the big sheet to the King's Grace, for that was the fairest piece I could come by. And this other is to Privy Seal, and that little bit too goes with it, for at the last he remembered, said he, one in Yorkshire, a poor man whom he had, so he said, defrauded of his land, though unwitting, and now would right him." He held the papers out now to July and she laid her hand on them, but he did not yet let go.

"Will ye swear that ye will take them to the King and Privy Seal?"

"I will take them," said July.

"Well," said the old man, his eyes boring into her face, "I believe you will," and he cackled suddenly as if lovers and their love were a sour jest.

"Did he—" asked July, looking down at the papers which their two hands held. "Did he—at once think of me to carry them? Of me—before all other?"

Ned looked at her. He read, in her averted face and hesitating speech, misgiving and withdrawal. He could not know how July did not dare to look up, desiring so greatly the answer "Yes," knowing that the answer must be "No."

And it was "No." For old Ned began to excuse Aske. 'Twasn't him thought on you. 'Twas I. He says, 'None will dare take it.' So then I says, 'There's your leman,' says I. 'Try her.' But he was angry with me for that, only at the last he said, 'Tell her then that she shall run into no danger for me. For that,' says he, 'would be worse to me than death, seeing I have been cause of bringing so many into danger. Yet,' he says, 'if she may without danger, tell her I'll pray God bless her for it forever.'"

He waited a moment, and then made as if to take back the papers. But July snatched them then from him.

"Will ye do it then?" he said, but got no answer from her, as she turned away and left him standing there.

May 31

July met Master John Heath, Laurence's cousin's cousin, the one who was in Lord Privy Seal's household, as he had appointed at the West end of St. Paul's. It was raining, a soft, misting rain after a great fall during the night, and she was glad of it because she could muffle herself up in her cloak in such a way that none would know her.

From Paul's they went down together to take a boat at the Cranes for Westminster. July was too breathless to talk, seeing that the child was growing a heavy burden, and Master Heath, not liking the business, hurried on always a little ahead of her. Once he pulled up where a pool had swilled out of the blocked kennel and halfway across the road.

"You tell the truth when you say you formerly were affianced to this man?"

"Surely I was," said July, hastening to tell her tale once more, "but then my sister's husband would not pay my dower, and therefore—"

"And," Master Heath continued, without letting her finish, "and it's true also that you came then together, being betrothed."

"It is true."

Well," said Master Heath, "I've promised you, and so I shall bring you to the Queen. Woman's frail, and if you thought of this fellow Aske as your husband, and if he so used you before you were married to my cousin—"

"He had me in the North Country before I came here to my marriage—just before," said July.

"Well," he looked her up and down with suspicion, "I've never seen a wench carry what must be nigh a nine months' child with as little show as you."

"All women," said July, "are not the same." Then she laughed, as if the matter were a light one and as if she were not desperate with fear lest he should, even now, refuse to help her. "And surely it is I that should know whose is the child."

He laughed too, and leered at her with a familiar, insulting look. But then again he hesitated.

"It's the truth you say? I'll not help you if you've wronged my cousin's bed."

"It's the truth, as God shall judge me. I'll swear it on my Maker at the next church, if you will."

But he said No, he'd believe her, only it went sore against his mind that it should be a rank traitor that had her maidenhead, and he hurried her on again.

By the time they reached Westminster the rain had taken off and the sun shone, so that all the puddles flashed, and the roads steamed; when they came into the palace gardens the rosebushes were dressed with diamonds, and the briar rose leaves smelt of sun-warmed apples. As they drew nearer to the palace there were no rosebushes but tall posts striped white and green, set in puncheons painted with the same colors; the posts had painted and gilded beasts and escutcheons of arms on top. There were too, instead of grass, curious beds of pounded colors set among clipped borders; the gardeners were busy here smoothing away the pock marks which the rain had left in the King's coat of arms, and the Queen's.

The sun was bringing other people out too, besides the gardeners. As July and Master Heath went by the long range of buildings two young men came through a little low doorway; they stooped because they were so tall; and because they were so broad in their puffed sleeves the silks whistled against the stone of the doorway as they came through. They went past laughing, and with only a sliding glance that took in July's pale pinched face and brown stuff gown. July did not look at them at all, but she saw them well enough to hate them for being free and in no danger of the hangman's knife.

She and Master Heath turned into a little paved court, where a dog was busy with a bone; then by an open stairway into a gallery which was bare of tapestries and swept of its strawing herbs. Servants were just then casting down fresh strawings out of big bundles of sacking, and raking them into smooth swathes. As the sweet herbs and rushes tumbled out all the gallery smelt as if the summer fields were come within its four walls.

After that gallery they went on through passages, upstairs, downstairs, through rooms great and small, some empty, some furnished; in some there were ladies, young and old, and children, as well as men reverend and men saucily or grandly young. It was more like going through a whole street of houses than through one house.

At last Master Heath stopped in a gallery where there was a small oriel jutting out, and told July to wait there till he could find out at what hour the Queen would pass by on her way to the chamber of presence. July went to the oriel and sat down. She felt the child kick strongly in her body; clutching her hands tight across him, and shutting her eyes, she went over once more the lies that she would tell, not liking them at all since they dishonored Master Aske, but trying them on her tongue so as to be sure that they were plausible and likely to move another woman, also great with child.

She heard a door open and started up; she had not thought that Master Heath would so soon have returned. But it was not Master Heath. A dozen or so ladies were coming into the room preceded by two elderly persons in black velvet with gold chains, one of whom carried in his hand a white wand. Among the ladies was one young, very fair in complexion, with a pleasant prim face; she wore as many jewels, sewn upon her gown, and loading her neck and fingers, as a May Day Queen wears flowers. Behind her, with one hand on her shoulder, puffed and huge in purple and cloth of gold, came the King, rolling in his walk, and limping a little,

July went out from the shelter of the window, and sank down on her knees, less for reverence than for fear lest she should fall.

"Your Grace . . ." she cried, and dragged Aske's petition from where it lay between her breasts. "Madame, have mercy on an unhappy man, and thereby upon a most wretched woman."

The King took the letter; he read it. July saw the small mouth tighten and sneer. She averted her eyes from his face, and, looking nowhere but at the Queen, began to pour out that same tale she had told to Cousin Heath—all lies, yet the Queen listened, as July harped desperately upon that one string: "the child—the child—his child."

But the King broke in.

"You ask mercy, Mistress, for a traitor, because you carry his bastard," and at that the Queen flushed and turned her head away.

July laid hold of the skirt of her gown and felt the jewels and the gold stitching harsh and crisp under her fingers. The Queen tried to free herself, but July clenched her hands tighter.

She could say no more. To beg mercy for love's sake was impossible, for that would trench upon the truth, huge, inmost, which might not be come at in speech. But she thought—"I'll not let her go. I can't let her go," since to let the Queen go would deliver him to torment.

She heard the King cry, "Off! Pull her off!" But then Queen Jane's eyes met hers again. She said no word, but none was needed.

July loosed her hold, and the Queen laid her hand upon the King's sleeve.

"Sir," she said, "Sir, if I asked mercy for my sake? I do ask it."

"He shall not live."

"Oh!" July cried, repeating the words that Ned Stringer had used, and which had never been silent since in her mind. "Oh! if he could but be full dead before he be dismembered!"

The King's glance, oblique and contemptuous, came back to her face.

"Will that content you? And—him?" He watched her while she nodded. "You think it will? Well then, he shall have that. Tell him that surely he shall hang till he be full dead."

He went away. July had only time to snatch the Queen's hand and kiss it before she too went after the King.

June 15

July, who, was alone in the kitchen, the women both being out, heard Laurence come into the house, and go upstairs. After a while, since she must go up sooner or later, she took the dish of honey cakes which she had been baking, and going slowly through the Hall began to climb the stairs. She had her head bent, so that it gave her a start when she saw his feet upon the stair above her; she raised her eyes and found him standing looking down at her.

"Strumpet!" he said, speaking quite softly, and struck at her face with his fist.

It was a wild, swinging blow, and she dodged it easily, but in doing so she lost her footing, tried to grab the rail, and began to fall. As she fell she heard him cry, "July!" and again, "Strumpet!"

She picked herself up at the bottom of the stairs, and, dazed and shaken, began to collect the cakes, but then the pains began. He came down to where she leaned against the wall, peering at her and whispering to know what was the matter. Yet really he knew at once what it must be, though July could only shake her head in answer.

So he got her upstairs as best he could and then rushed out to find a woman to help her.

June 30

July sat in Laurence's father's chair, which the journeyman had brought out into the sun for her. Every now and then one of the women would put her head through the open kitchen window and ask if she needed anything. Oftener than that Laurence would come from the workshop, and look at her, and go back again. July answered the maids, because they asked her a question. As Laurence said nothing, but only looked, she did not need to answer him, nor did she turn her head when he came out, though she knew quite well that he was there. She sat staring before her at the bellflowers, sweet Williams, and tall white lilies, and at the washing hung out on the line, men's breeches, women's smocks and sheets and kitchen clouts. Not one of these things, from the lilies to the oldest torn clout, was more lovely to her eyes than any other, or of more significance.

She heard from the house the sound of the women talking, clattering their pails, or churning the clothes in the big tub with the wooden dolly peg. From farther away came the noises of the street—grinding of wheels, boy's whistling, sing-song cries of hucksters of lavender, fish, milk, and just now of fine raspberries. She heard, without remarking, one of the women open the street door and begin to haggle over a price. Then the elder of the two came into the garden, and set on her knees an earthen pot full of raspberries.

"There, mistress!" she said. "There's the first of the season." She was a woman with a kind, plain, lined face. "And for the one child that miscarried," she said, "there'll be plenty more in time to come," and before she went away she gave July's shoulder a little pat with her hand, which was pale purple, soft, wet and wrinkled from the washtub.

July looked down at the smoldering soft crimson of the raspberries. She did not want them. Nor did she want another child.

Nor did she want the one that passed from dark to dark. The one thing she wanted was to know if Master Aske were alive or dead, and here there was no one to tell her, since she could not ask Laurence, and the maids would not know.

Laurence came out of the workshop again, and this time he did not go back, but instead threw down upon the ground a big pair of cloth shears which he had in his hands, and came toward her. There was a little low stool beside her chair, upon which she had set the raspberries. He took them up and sat down on it, looking up at her as she looked down at him. Then each turned away.

He began to take the raspberries one by one and put them into his mouth, as if he were very hungry. But in a moment he spun round on the stool and laid the pot down on the ground, and so turned away from her he said—

"Wife, do you forgive me?"

"Oh! Yes." July was indifferent.

"When I thought you would die I did not care whether—I did not care for anything but that you should live, and should forgive me. You do forgive?"

"Yes," she said again, as evenly.

He was fidgeting with his foot so that he tossed the pot over and the raspberries tumbled out on the ground. He at once began to pick them up as if the matter were one of the greatest moment and urgency. "Yet," he said as he stooped, "if you could tell me truly—if I knew whether—if the child was his— You told the King so."

"Yes. It is. It was. Yes, I told the King," she said, not even wondering how he had come to hear so much, but thinking how she might learn if Master Aske were dead, and safe from pain.

He sat quite still for a moment, then he said, "It makes no difference now. You are all that I love, and that is all I know."

When she heard him say that she was pricked by a thin small shaft of remorse. Yet though she was sorry, she hardened her heart, for she thought, "If I say it was a lie, and the King should hear of it, he might be angry and take a vengeance on him." But then, with a quick pang of hope and dread, another thought came— "If I first made him swear to tell no one, I might find out from him whether he still lives."

So she asked him, would he swear? "And I'll tell you the truth," she said.

He swore, his eyes on hers, and she told him, and he turned from her once more, "So I killed my son," he said, and after what seemed to her a great while, "But we shall have more. Shall we not?"

"Yes," she said. "Yes," speaking hastily because she could contain herself no longer. She was aware neither that her hands were gripped together on her lap till they shook, nor that he watched them.

"Sir," she whispered, not trusting her voice if she spoke louder, "is he dead?"

He said nothing, and now she dared not look at him. At last he got up. "I will go and find out," he said, and left her.

He went, not knowing clearly why he went at once so far, nor what he should do when he got there, straight through London to the Tower. He had some idea of asking a porter at the gate, or one of the guard, but it turned out to be easier still than that. When he came by the foot of the green space to the north of the Tower, he found several men working on a temporary scaffold which had been set up there, and which they were now pulling down. Two others were forking together, and pitching into a cart, straw that was sodden in places with dark brownish red, and one of these was the old fellow to whom Laurence had given the bundle of clothes, and who, it was clear, at once remembered him, and was ready to talk.

There was plenty to talk about, for today Lord Darcy had been beheaded on that scaffold, and the old man was full of it. He knew also the latest news of the two last surviving prisoners of the North Country insurrection, Constable and Aske, so that Laurence had not to put a single question.

When he got back July was sitting in the garden where he had left her.

He said, "They took him from the Tower two days ago. It is to be done at York."

"How long will it take them to get to York?"

But Laurence could not tell her.

She said, "I thank you," and after a minute he left her and went back to the workshop.

July 15

July stood by the kitchen table absently fingering the leaves of the rue that lay tumbled on it. There was a bowl of clean water to wash the rue, and an iron pot in which to boil it when washed. Rue boiled long, and strained, was good for the kidneys; Laurence believed much in it, and had asked for it last Christmas when the snow fell, and had lamented the lack of it through the long cold spring. So now she was preparing it against next winter.

Yet if you looked through the kitchen door you might think that there would never be winter again, so gallant was the little space with flowers. The last of the sweet Williams had been overtaken by pinks, carnations, and the first of the snapdragons; above, in the bright sky, the swifts fled like arrows, and turning, flashed like dark wet gold against the sun. Over all lay the triumphant, open heat of perfect summer weather.

But July was thinking neither of the rue on the table nor of the summer shows outside. She was listening to the bell of St. Andrew in the Wardrobe tolling for a burial. This was not one of Laurence's burials, but July knew all about it, because his cousin Henry Machyn was furnishing it, and Laurence had gone out to help him, and had lent him hangings for the church, and two dozen staff torches; Cousin Henry had on this same day another funeral, almost as great, at St. Martin's, Charing Cross, so he had needed to borrow from Laurence.

When July had listened to the bell for quite a time she suddenly began to bestir herself, bundling the rue into its washing water, and from that, with scant care, into the pot. Calling to one of the women to have an eye on it, she went upstairs for her cloak and hood, and then to the workshop. It was empty except for young Dickon, who had been left behind with plenty to do in cleaning of brushes and grinding of paints. But when July came in he pocketed a pair of dice, and jumped up. "Get the basket," said July, "and come with me."

But she was not going shopping—at least, not yet, and she told Dickon, "I shall go first to church."

"Aye," said the boy, politely though without enthusiasm; but when he understood that she would go to St. Andrew's to see them bring in the corpse of Sir William Laxton, knight and grocer and alderman of London, it was a very different matter.

And even as they came to the church door they could see the procession moving toward them up the street. "Ooh!" cried Dickon, jumping up and down to see better, and then climbing up on the plinth of the church porch, and clinging to the stone like a tomtit to a tree. "Ooh! here they come! See the escutcheons nid-nodding. And the candles, so many!" July looked back from the steps. The crowded escutcheons of arms upon their poles were bright as a garden of flowers, and beyond them the great candles moved close as a thicket, but the flames of these, borne backward as the procession moved, made but a pale show against the sunshine. She gave one glance and then went on into the church.

Here, when the door swung to behind her, there was sudden darkness and quiet, with a sour and solemn smell of old incense, damp, and stale rushes. Two priests moved about in the sanctuary; they looked round as they heard her lift the latch, but she slipped away behind a pillar and knelt down out of sight.

Only when all the train of choirmen and boys, bearers and mourners, had brought the dead grocer into church and set him down below the painted rood, did July shuffle out cautiously from where she lurked. Now, in the dimness of the church, the colors of the escutcheons showed only gloomily, but the candle flames, winking and fluttering, were warm gold and very bright. In the midst, where the light was brightest from the clustered candles set on the hearse, she could just see the crimson and cloth of gold pall which covered the coffin.

Requiem aeternam dona eis, Domine; et lux perpetua luceat eis.

The voices rose and fell in the chant, answering each other in words which she did not understand, yet knew, as she knew, mistily, the intent of them.

In diebus illis: Audivi vocem de caelo: dicentem mihi, Scribe. Beate mortui: qui in Domine moriuntur. Amodo jam dicit Spiritus: ut requiescant a laboribus suis . . .

Requiem aeternam dona eis Domine: et lux perpetua luceat eis . . .

"Give him rest eternal . . . Give him light . . . A voice from heaven saying, 'Blessed are the dead, for they rest . . . Rest, and light.'"

So the words went by in July's mind, yet less akin to words than to musical sounds, disembodied, piercing home beyond the reach of words.

For her it was not the body of that prosperous knight and grocer which lay under the crimson, golden-gleaming pall. It was Robert Aske's body, and it was his spirit that waited now its dismissal among all lovely and loving shows, lights, singing, and the presence of friends and lovers. For surely now he must be dead; and if he was dead, then at peace. And perhaps, thought July, death is the best thing, and I need not have feared, because there is always death, and it will not have hurt him long. And surely he must be dead.

She got up from her knees, and was surprised to find Dickon at her elbow, for she had forgotten him.

"Where do we go now, mistress?" he asked, skipping along beside her, but whispering because of the solemnity of the church.

"To buy some cucumbers," said July.

On that same day, and at about the same time that July was in church, Robert Aske made his confession, received absolution, and took upon his tongue the consecrated wafer. Dr. Curwen, the priest, gave him also, as to a man dying, the sacrament of extreme unction. Now he knelt for a moment longer in the little chapel of the keep at York. When he stood up he must go to the top of the tower to his hanging.

He found himself upon his feet.

"Sir," he said, "I am ready. And I pray God bless the King's Grace for letting me pass without those pains which—"

He stopped, not because Dr. Curwen had said anything, or even moved. Yet he stopped, and waited for the priest to speak.

Dr. Curwen cleared his throat. He looked at the altar, he looked at the floor. He said: "Aske, it is the King's will, that since you think it a religion to keep hidden between God and you the names of those traitorous persons whom you know of in the South parts—it is his will that you shall hang in chains until you die."

Aske felt his cheek grow cold and his heart begin to jump, before, it seemed, his brain understood what it was that Curwen had said. Then he understood it fully.

"God!" he whispered, and cried again, "God!" so loud that his voice cracked on the word.

Jack Aske, and the other Yorkshire gentlemen bidden to York by the Duke of Norfolk, and now waiting on top of the keep, heard the cry. More than one of them started, looked aside at his neighbor, and then as quickly away. Jack shut his eyes, and hoped not to fall. In the silence that followed they heard the soft purr of the wind against the battlement, and except for that nothing but the sounds (and they were very slight sounds) of the crowd below. Yet it was a great crowd, York being full for market day, and all the market now deserted for this business of the hanging of the great captain of the pilgrims.

There was a stir at the open door of the stair which came out on the roundway. The duke's foot soldiers came up, and among them, but alone, the prisoner. Jack shrank back, but even so if he had reached out a hand he could have touched Robin as he passed by with a blank face, and his blank eye socket ("Thank God!" thought Jack) on this side.

Then up came the Duke of Norfolk, whom Jack and all those other gentlemen must salute, as he saluted them with a grave but courteous air. And all the time, as Robin's brother uncovered, and as he received the duke's greeting, he was in an agony lest Robin should see him there.

He need not have feared. Robert Aske had no wits just now to see anyone. He stood, dumb and still, while they fixed the irons about him, brought him to the ladder, and helped and hauled him up it. He heard Dr. Curwen's voice saying the prayers that he knew, and by some compulsion in him, when the doctor's voice stopped, he made the necessary responses. But all his mind and will were bent upon one thing only, and that was so to rule his body that when he was cast off it should neither struggle nor scream.

He could not altogether rule it. When he swung out, and the irons bit him, he did struggle, because he must. One of his shoes came off, and it seemed to him a frightful thing that he should have to go short of a shoe, until he remembered that he would not ever again tread upon anything but the empty air.

He was alone now. Close beside him the roundway was empty, but when he glanced down into the sickening depth below his feet, he could see that the green space was full of white faces turned up to him.

With a groaning of iron upon iron, he was turning slowly round. The minster came into sight just as the bells sounded, tossing out their bubbles of sweet sound upon the air. Still he turned; now he saw Fishergate Bar, half ruinous since it had been blocked up for so long, now the wide country beyond, patched golden with harvest, and far away the low hills beyond Aughton.

The hours wore on, and pain grew. Toward evening he began to suffer from thirst.

July 18

July was in Mistress Holland's parlor upstairs when the vintner brought in another man of his mystery, but a stranger, and not of the London guild. He was a fine old man, with a handsome, kind, quiet face; his name was Master Oldroyd. He and Master Holland sat down in the window seat, and when they all had wine and wafers and cherries ready to hand, the two men talked of men's affairs in low voices, and it seemed sadly, and Mistress Holland continued her interrupted account of the qualities of a new serving woman. In a few minutes she got up and went out to fetch a new coif to show July, and July sat, not listening nor looking toward the men till she caught a word that Master Oldroyd spoke:

"York?" she said then. Mr. Oldroyd turned to her.

"Do you know York, mistress?" said he, leaning forward toward her, because he liked young things.

She nodded, though indeed she knew nothing of York but that she had passed through it, once to go north with Meg, once to come to London to her wedding—that, and a fact that filled the earth—that Master Aske had been hanged there.

Master Holland heaved up his hand, let it fall on his thigh with a great clap, and sighed deeply.

"Alas!" said he. "Tell her what you've told me. It will be sad news for her, for Mistress July knows him, and brought him once here to us, and there he sat."

He pointed, and July followed his finger to the place where Master Aske had sat on a settle beside the hearth which was full now of green boughs for summer. Then her eyes came back to Master Oldroyd's face.

"God have mercy on him," said he, "and send him death soon. I tell you it struck me through the heart the other morning when I came by under the keep, and saw him move—as, poor soul, he will move yet for many a day."

"Move yet?" said July.

"It was but the day after his hanging, for they hanged him last market day, and men that are hanged in chains live longer, much longer, God help him, than that."

July looked down at her hands as they lay on her lap, but she did not see them or anything else in this room. She only heard the King say, "Surely he shall hang till he be full dead."

Master Oldroyd sighed. "God help him," he said again. "But did you indeed know him, mistress?"

"Since I was a young child," July said out of a dead body.

She did not leave at once. Mistress Holland came back with the coif, and turned it about to show it off, and July said it was pretty. Master Oldroyd got up, and took his leave, and he and Master Holland went away. Mistress Holland peered at July, patted her hands and said that indeed she looked but poorly yet.

It was then that July said that she must go, and followed Mistress Holland downstairs. It seemed to her to be ages of years after the time that Master Oldroyd had come into the room.

She said good-bye to Mistress Holland, was kissed, was given—and said thanks for—a basket of cherries. There was no hurry. Master Oldroyd had said that he would live a long time yet.

But once she had parted from the vintner's wife haste devoured her and she fled through the streets, seeing nothing, hearing nothing; needing, before she dared to think, one thing—to be alone.

That morning Malle and Wat had to carry a big pannier of clean, washed linen to the hostess of the Dolphin. They came back along Bishopgate, Malle going in front and Wat keeping warily off, a few paces after. But just before the gate Malle turned.

"Wat!" she said. "Wat!" and though it was broad day her hands went out as though she felt about for him in a dark place.

He slipped away, so as to put a man with a barrowload of fresh lettuce between them. Then he made as if to run, yet turned and came again to her, though shrinkingly.

She said: "Darkness, and God moving nigh-hand in the darkness."

Wat seized a handful of her gown and dragged her with him till they were out of the busy street and upon one of the little paths that led, vagrant as sheep tracks, among the thorn bushes in the narrow space between the houses here and the Town Ditch. There was no one about except two old men fishing, a few children, and some tethered goats. Wat pushed Malle down on a little bank where butter-and-eggs and pale vetch grew; he went a little way from her and crouched down, keeping his eyes on her face, as still as a rabbit before a stoat.

Malle said: "Darkness is made over all the earth, deep as the sea, hissing bitter and black with pain, salted sharp with all men's sins. And he drowns there, hanging from the nails they have stricken through his hands."

Wat moaned and grumbled in his throat, and below them beside the water one of the old men swept up his float and cast it back again with a little plop.

Malle said, "So is he gone down under those waves." She lifted her head and her eyes widened. "Look!" she said. "The dale's full of light. He has set on fire the sea. Not even the deep waters can quench him, but he comes again, flaming and shining with the bitter sea itself to be his new coat. Hurt and harm are his coat, and a glory that the young stars didn't know. Light has licked up the dark water. Love has drunk sorrow, rejoicing, and the great Angel of Pain is redeemed."

She stood up.

"Come, little knave," she said, "there's one at the manor that needs must be told."

But when they found July, hurrying through the streets, and Malle went along with her, telling her what she had seen, and pulling now and again at July's arm to make sure she heard, July only struck her off.

Indeed July marked her no more than one passing through the woods in summer marks the tower of gnats that swims above his head as he goes.

When she came into the house, having slammed the door upon Malle, there was no one in the hall, so she stood a moment, looking down into the hearth, filled with green boughs for summer, but blackened by fire. She was alone at last; yet now she found that to be alone gave Master Oldroyd's words more room to swell, and swell.

One of the serving maids came in and asked her a question. What the words meant July could not tell. She said, "I do not know. You must see to it," and the answer seemed to fit, because the woman went away. But that had shown July that she could not endure to be found again, and spoken to, especially to be found by Laurence, with his piercing, anxious love.

Then she remembered, as if it had been a thing told her many years ago, that he would be out all this morning, and the men too, preparing a great burial, so that the workshops would be empty. She went out into the yard. The young dog, which was lying in the sun, leapt up, wagging and fawning. He followed her to the door, but she shoved him from it with her foot and shut him out, and stood a moment, staring, but blindly, about the workshop, with its litter of brushes, spilt, powdered colors, and clean cold smell of the lime tempering over all. Yet because she had not gone far enough till she had gone as far as she could, she went on, and climbed the ladder to the loft above, where today there was nothing but dust, dust and cobwebs, some odd bits of rope lying about, and one long length hanging from the truss of the roof timbers.

The rope hung dangling before her eyes. It hung.

Laurence found the dog scratching and yelping at the work-shop door. It was an eager ratter, so he said to it, "Good dog. Rats!" and let it in. But it rushed to the foot of the ladder, floundered up a few rungs, and when it slipped back, lifted its head and howled.

So he went up and found July. He shouted till one of the men came, and they were able to get her down. Then, in the thick dust, they worked on her. When they had almost given up hope; she breathed.

The first thing July knew was the sparver of the bed above her as she lay on her back. She heard, and seemed for a long time to have heard, a little regular clicking noise. She turned her head with a sudden huge pain, and saw that Laurence sat on a stool beside the bed; he slipped his beads briskly through his fingers but his eyes were on her face.

It was as he got up and leaned over her that she remembered, and she whispered before he could speak—

"He hangs alive in chains. He is not dead."

Laurence sat down again. Now she did not even hear the click of his beads, and again she lay, simply staring upward.

"Wife," said Laurence suddenly, "we must pray God for him."

She cried, so that it tore her throat—"No. He made pain, he chose it for himself." That was all she could say, and Laurence must guess the rest. God who had made pain, so that all the universe was corrupt with it, God would do nothing to help one who, hanging in chains, moved yet.

Laurence stood up, and again bent over her. But this time he took her hands in his and held them closely.

"You do not understand," he said. "There's nothing to fear in pain. Love makes it all different. I love you. If I might suffer for you I would be *glad*."

Her eyes came to him, startled, staring wide, and her face changed as she slipped back from him into unconsciousness. Seeing that change he thought she was slipping right away from him into death, and he rushed to the door and shouted for the women.

❋ *The Chronicle of Julian Savage ends here.*

July 20

Gib had just birched one of the bigger boys, thereby obtaining a silence, sudden, uneasy, and charged with rebellion. But at least it was a silence, for which he was thankful, especially when Master Hawkes opened the door and walked in. He was pleased also to see Master Hawkes, who was a Mercer, a man of substance and a great favorer of the gospel. "He knows me," thought Gib, "for what I am. He sees that I am a man of parts. He is my fellow Christian, like-minded with me and with all who care for God's honor." That was the second thought which he substituted for the first, yet not so quickly but that he was aware, and ashamed of the other.

"Now," said he to the boys, "con your books," and he brought Master Hawkes away to his own chair, and sitting him down there led him into conversation of this commission that had been set up to determine beliefs. Now and again he had to scowl over his shoulder as the tide of noise began again to flow. At first it was only a rustling. Soon one of the youngsters yelped like a puppy as someone jabbed his seat with a knife point; someone else dropped a book and there was a scuffling of feet and sound of hard breathing and stifled laughter, as they covertly fought over it. That was the worst of children; you could never be free of the care of them as long as they were with you. Shallow-witted, idle, and frivolous themselves, so that a man must be always straining to dwarf himself to their littleness, they would never allow him to be at peace to speak with another man. So Gib could have only half his mind upon these articles of the bishops, which were to bring all England to a conformity in belief, and of which Master Hawkes was discoursing; it fretted him the more that this was so, because Master Hawkes had private knowledge of what went on behind closed doors, he having a cousin in the household of Hugh Latimer, bishop of Worcester.

"Tunstall and Stokesley," said the Mercer, "gave and took many shrewd raps that day, so I hear."

"Yet they shall not have the better, proud papist prelates that they are," cried Gib, with a tight smile, "That I'll warrant."

The other rubbed his plump, firm jowl with one finger.

"As I see it," said he, "the issue pleases and displeases both them and us. For they have had their own way over their seven sacraments—"

"Fie!" said Gib. "Shall we never be free of this prating of sacraments?"

"Yet faith is set clear above any sacrament."

"That's well done!"

"And as clear our men have made it that faith alone justifieth."

"So," said Gib, "that is very well." Yet he did not meet the other's eye, nor did he seem in his appearance at all jubilant, but kept looking down at the floor. For though theologically he was convinced of the truth of that doctrine, he was not able to feel it true in himself. All the faith which he had, and it seemed to him to burn clear as a great fire, was not enough to enable him to do that simplest first work of all—merely to love his neighbor and receive those little ones, scrabbling and tittering behind him, as if each one were Christ. Without that, should faith save him?

The Mercer chuckled.

"None will wholly rejoice," said he, "excepting the bishop of Worcester."

"Why he?" Gib asked quickly.

"By the Mass! Because he is not learned in these subtleties and thinks it's all one, so as pilgrimages and relics and images are brought down, with purgatory, and so as justice be done between high and low; for that last has always been in especial his constant sharp concern."

"I know it has. I have heard it."

Twelve o'clock struck with dilatory halting concurrence from all the steeples near, and from farther off came the faint floating sound of other bells.

"Go! Go!" Gib flung over his shoulder at the lads, and they rushed out. The pounding of their feet on the boards ceased; from the yard outside rose the sharp babble of their voices. He turned to Master Hawkes and asked would he bring him to the bishop of Worcester.

"Well," said the Mercer slowly, and with a cautious look, "if I could do so, what would you have of him?"

"That he should set me to work. He's a man after mine own heart," cried Gib. "If I could preach or write—" He thought, but did not say—"If I should mightily set forth God's word, that might suffice."

"You write for my Lord Privy Seal."

"He," said Gib, "has done much for the gospel. Yet he is a worldly man. He minds power and policy, aye, and lucre, more than he minds God's matters."

He looked at Master Hawkes, righteous indignation now contending with the resentment of a rejected author in his face. "Will you bring me to the bishop?" he urged.

The Mercer, unwilling to meddle further than he need in Gib's affairs, consented, but stiffly. He brought Gib to the bishop's house and then handed him over to a small, square priest who had the figure and complexion of a plowman, rather than of a clerk, and whose perfunctory, brief questions made Gib chafe.

Yet within half an hour he found himself sitting at a table opposite Hugh Latimer, lord bishop of Worcester, no stately person like Archbishop Lee, but a lean, stooping man, in an old gown and rubbed fur tippet, and with great horse teeth pushing out his lips in the midst of his graying beard.

Before him lay the remains of his dinner—the backbone of a herring on a notched wooden plate, salad, bread, and a horn cup of ale. He made Gib eat and drink too, sending away the square-shouldered chaplain for another fish, another penny loaf and more ale.

So it was easy for Gib to speak to this man, though he were a bishop, and Latimer sat and listened, only chumbling with his lips in a way he had, as if he could never arrange them over his teeth quite to his liking.

When Gib had finished both his dinner and his explanation—which was a great deal of the lads at the chantry school, and a little of Lord Privy Seal, and nothing at all of Malle and dumb Wat—Latimer leaned back in his chair.

"As clear as it is to me," said he, "that you are a man who can preach, so clear it is that you are not one made to teach. And as for these massing matters in your chantry, neither you nor I see aught but blind superstition in them. So, if you, having as I can hear heart and will for it too, consent to come with me to my diocese, I will set you to preach God's word to those who have not heard it this many a day."

Gib stared at him across the table.

"I—I—I can write," he stammered, and seemed altogether taken aback, and not at all as if this was that very thing he had hoped. "That is no less to advance God's cause than if I preach."

"But I," said the bishop, "cannot maintain you here for that end. If you will write, you must go to Lord Privy Seal for your reward."

"I could remain at the chantry. It is enough without more reward."

"And the chantry, you tell me, is torment to you."

Gib blundered up, pitching back the stool he sat on.

"It is. It is. If I could come—" He covered his eyes and Latimer saw his throat work.

"Well, Master Dawe," he said coldly, "I can do no more for you than this. I had not done so much, perhaps, but that you sent up word that you were a man poor, and in danger of the judgment."

"Oh!" cried Gib, "shall I have time to think?"

"Humph!" said the bishop, with some not unnatural impatience. Then he said, "Well, you shall have time. Come again within this week and ask me if you will."

Gib went down the bishop's stairs knowing that far from escaping the judgment, he had brought himself to it. For once more he must choose whether to bide or to run.

Thunder came after dark and with it rain, a rushing sluice of unseen waters that mashed down great swathes of the tall, head-heavy wheat. Rain beating on his head and neck brought Aske back for a little while out of nightmare into conscious horror. He saw in the scribble of lightning which split black night the sheer drop of the wall beside him; the green far away below.

And as his eye told him of the sickening depth below his body, and as his mind foreknew the lagging endlessness of torment before him, so, as if the lightning had brought an inner illumination also, he knew the greater gulf of despair above which his spirit hung, helpless and aghast.

God did not now, nor would in any furthest future, prevail. Once he had come, and died. If he came again, again he would die, and again, and so forever, by his own will rendered powerless against the free and evil wills of men.

Then Aske met the full assault of darkness without reprieve of hoped-for light, for God ultimately vanquished was no God at all. But yet, though God was not God, as the head of the dumb worm turns, so his spirit turned, blindly, gropingly, hopelessly loyal, toward that good, that holy, that merciful, which though not God, though vanquished, was still the last dear love of a vanquished and tortured man.

July 22

By this time that which dangled from the top of the keep at York, moving only as the wind swung it, knew neither day nor night, nor that it had been Robert Aske, nor even that it had been a man.

Even now, however, it was not quite insentient. Drowning yet never drowned, far below the levels of daylight consciousness, it suffered. There was darkness and noise, noise intolerably vast or unendurably near, drilling inward as a screw bites and turns, and the screw was pain. Sometimes noise, pain, darkness, and that blind thing that dangled were separate; sometimes they ran together and became one.

That evening Wat came skulking into the chantry chapel to be out of the way while his father and old Kat quarreled upstairs. Kat had returned from the tavern very drunk and in good fighting trim, so it was likely they would both be at it for some time.

When he had shut the door behind him he was sorry and turned to steal out again; but a stick fallen from one of the jackdaws' nests in the roof snapped under his foot, and Malle, who stood near the altar with her hands over her face, turned, saw him, and called "Wat!"

He went edging toward her, stepping lightly, as if at a word he would run. Yet she did not touch him when he came, but plumped down on the altar steps, and looked up at him standing a little way off.

She said, "Darkness, and God moving nigh-hand in the darkness." Her hands wrenched one against the other, then dropped lax on her knees, and she smiled. In the long silence that followed they could hear the sound of Gib's voice and old Kat's voice, and the bump of something heavy that might have been a bench overturned in the room above.

Then Malle said: "The darkness is done. The sun's risen, just one morning like any other sunshine morning, with folks about their business and wives baking bread, and the mill wheel turning. It's all light in the churchyard, young new light, the color of green apples when they're golding over."

Wat crept a little nearer, but he was shaking.

"God 'a mercy!" Malle cried, "God 'a mercy! Here he comes between the graves, out of the grave.

"When he was born a man," she said, "he put on the leaden shroud that's man's dying body. And on the cross it bore him down, sore heavy, dragging against the great nails, muffling God, blinding him to the blindness of a man. But there, darkened within that shroud of mortal lead, beyond the furthest edge of hope, God had courage to trust yet in hopeless, helpless things, in gentle mercy, holiness, love crucified.

"And that courage, Wat, it was too rare and keen and quick a thing for sullen lead to prison, but instead it broke through, thinning lead, fining it to purest shining glass, to be a lamp for God to burn in.

"So men may have courage," she said, and caught Wat by the skirt of his coat as she stood up. "Then they will see how bright God shines.

"Come," she said, dragging Wat toward the door, "and tell him that's been taken far from here to die."

But Robert Aske had gone too far, nor did he need now that Malle should tell him.

For now (yet with no greater fissure between then and now than as a man's eyes are aware, where no star was, of the first star of night), now he was aware of One—vanquished God, Savior who could as little save others as himself.

But now, beside him and beyond was nothing, and he was silence and light.

❖ *The Chronicle of Robert Aske, Squire, ends here.*

November 2

Wat came in late for dinner. He stumbled into the room, leaving the door wide. When Gib cried, "Shut the door!" he turned and lurched toward it, but fell before he reached it. Up jumped Kat, to stare at him as he lay on the floor.

"The sickness," she said.

There it was, in a word, for they all knew that the Great Sweat was still about in London since the unseasonable warm autumn.

As the disease had struck Wat suddenly, so it worked quickly upon him. By evening Gib could endure the sights and sounds of the lad's malady no longer. He got up, tucked his book under his arm, and said there was an errand he must do, and not to bar the door, for he might be back late.

"Aye, by God's Teeth," said Kat, busy stirring something over the fire. "Go forth if ye're afraid of the Sweat."

Gib was not afraid, and for a moment he hung on his heel, willing to show her that her taunt was unjust. But he cast a look upon Wat, and then he hurried out. He had not thought where he would go, and now did not choose his way with any very clear intention, yet when once he started he went in a great hurry, as if he were late for an appointment. And he was indeed very late. Bishop Latimer had said—"Come to me again next week," but that was months ago. No use to go now. "He'll not see me," thought Gib; and then—"Nor I'll not ask that he shall—only look upon the house when I go by." Yet there lurked in his mind a thought that it was the finger of providence which had brought the bishop here to London to preach dead Queen Jane's funeral sermon, just at this very time.

When he came to the house, and saw the broad, brown-faced plowman of a chaplain even now going in, he was sure that providence was pointing him in too. And by that sheer conviction he got in, and up to the same small plain room where the bishop sat reading by the light of a candle, and blowing his nose loudly and frequently, for he had a great cold.

"Well," said Hugh Latimer, when Gib stood before him, glowering at the floor, "what do you want with me this time?"

"Sir," Gib lifted his eyes, and Latimer, though in the throe of a great sneeze, did not miss the meaning of his look; he had known enough men that despaired of salvation to recognize one such when he saw him.

"Sir," said Gib, "is it better that he that knoweth himself to be a castaway should preach or be silent?"

"It is best," Latimer answered, after he had trumpeted into his handkerchief, "that he should by the grace of God be a man redeemed, and no castaway. But though he hath no assurance of salvation, yet he must preach. For," said he, warming to his subject, "our bishops and abbots adulterate the word of God, mingling it with the dreams of men, like taverners who pour good and bad together into one pot. Purgatory, which they preach, is, forsooth, a fiery furnace, for it has burned away many a poor man's pence. Go you to Canterbury, or even no farther than Westminster hereby, and you shall find images covered with gold, and dressed in silks, and lighted with wax candles, yea, even at noon, while Christ's living images are anhungered and thirst. Surely if we who know the light of the true gospel shall hold our peace, the very stones will cry out against us that let their preaching go unanswered."

Gib, shuffling his feet, listened, but sullenly. All this was true. The bishop's counsel was also in effect what he wanted to hear. Yet he could not but consider the bishop's eloquence ill-timed. Shall one preacher preach to another?

However, at the end of it he said, humbly enough, "Then, sir, if you will, as you offered me before, set me to preach, I will be your bedeman with God for it."

"Good," said the bishop, and worked his lips a while in silence, snuffling heavily, and at last asked when Gib would be ready.

"I am ready."

"Come then tomorrow. There is a church in Worcester—" and the bishop began to tell Gib about it; the benefice was no great matter, but there were souls to save, and bitter enmity to meet of papist priests, informers, adversaries of the true light.

November 4

All through the dark morning hours Gib lay waking and wrestling, but whether he wrestled with the devil or with the Angel of the Lord he did not know; nor did he know, when the light came, whether he had won or lost.

The scholars found him by turns absent and savage; yet for once he regretted their going, for he must now return to the room below, where Malle and old Kat watched over the sick lad. There, when they had eaten, he plumped down in a corner, and with fingers stuffed into his ears, and face averted, he tried to read; at least he kept the book open on his knee.

Toward evening, seeing that Wat lay quiet, Kat mumbled that she'd go forth a while, but not for long. She had not been to the tavern either yesterday or today, so she went now with eagerness, yet with a backward look. "Not for long," she said again before she shut the door.

When Malle had blown up the fire, and set bread and bacon and a jug of penny ale on the table for supper she drowsed with her head against the wall. So she did not see Gib wrap the New Testament and *The Prick of Conscience* inside two clean shirts and his best gown with a budge fur tippet, and take his staff in one hand and half the bacon clapped between two pieces of bread in the other, and go softly to the door. He, like old Kat, looked back before he shut it behind him, but he did not speak.

The short afternoon was almost gone when Malle woke. She did not look about her, not even to see whether Wat slept, but sat for a long time quite still, her hands in her lap, staring straight in front of her, with her mouth a little open, and her eyes very wide.

At last she got up and came to Wat. He lay quite still, just as he lay before she fell asleep, his face turned to the wall, and one hand under his cheek. She bent down over him, so that she could whisper in his ear.

She said: "No darkness, no darkness, for God hath come so high in the darkness that it tore all to tatters, and now is quite done away."

When he did not stir she stretched out her hand and, touching his neck, found him as cold as any little frog. So she cried over him for a while, but then, without wiping away her tears, she began to talk to him, though, simple as she was, she knew that he could not hear.

"Wat," she said, "listen how the wind blows, as if it were a great water rushing. All the trees in the wood toss their branches, and the leaves hiss and sigh. And though the doors are shut, in church it speaks too, groaning in the tower, for he groans with us. But the candle flames burn bright, lovely fire that we pluck from the empty air, so close he comes to us, for us to lay hold on in our need. So is the triumph of that High One great and

peaceable, homely and glorious, and now and forever he sitteth
down to his feast, waiting till we sit down with him, and all the
children have come home. But it is he himself who bringeth us,
each one upon his shoulder. We have but to stay still until he
lift and carry us."

She leaned her head closer, as if she waited for an answer.
Then she said:

"Stay till I come. I must tell your father."

But she could not tell Gib, because he had run away, for the last
time, and would not come back again, and that very hour rode
out of London beside one of the bishop of Worcester's servants,
going toward the West.

It was a cheerless evening, and the sun set forlornly in a haze
of chill yet tarnished light. Gib hung his head down as he went,
and would neither speak nor look up, so beaten to the ground
was he by shame, while his soul chawed upon something compared with the bitterness of which the salt smart of penitence
would have been sweet as honey.

For now he knew that though God might save every other
man, Gib Dawe he could not save. Once he had seen his sin as
a thing that clung close as his shadow clung to his heels; now
he knew that it was the very stuff of his soul. Never could he,
a leaking bucket not to be mended, retain God's saving grace,
however freely outpoured. Never could he, that heavy lump
of sin, do any other than sink, and sink again, however often
Christ, walking on the waves, should stretch his hand to lift and
bring him safe.

He did not know that though the bucket be leaky it matters not at all when it is deep in the deep sea, and the water both without it and within. He did not know, because he was too proud to know, that a man must endure to sink, and sink again, but always crying upon God, never for shame ceasing to cry, until the day when he shall find himself lifted by the bland swell of that power, inward, secret, as little to be known as to be doubted, the power of omnipotent grace in tranquil, irresistible operation.

As they passed Paul's great church it stood up to the south, between them and the drab ending of the day. But the light that smudged the sunset sky so mournfully, glowed warm rose through the clear grisaille of the clerestory, and blazed fire-red in the west window, as though a feast were prepared within, with lights in plenty and flame leaping from the hearth, for the celebration of some high holy day; as if a great King held carousal there, with all his joyful people around him, with all his children brought safe home.

But because Gib fled, and because he was ashamed that he fled, he did not look up, and he did not see.

✶ *The Chronicle of Sir Gilbert Dawe, Priest, ends here.*

The End and the Beginning

Though Gib did not come back to the chantry, no one else came to turn the two women out, so they stayed where they were. A week before Christmas a priest knocked at the door. He was a little old man who had a face like a mouse, wistful and eager, with very bright yet soft eyes; a tall lad behind him, in the livery of some gentleman, carried a bundle in which the sharp corners of books showed among the softer contours.

Malle came to the door, her arms white with flour, for she was baking, and the old priest told her that his name was Thomas Barker. He seemed to think it natural that he should come in, and the boy came in too and put down the big bundle on the floor. When the priest had given him a groat he went away, but the old man sat down by the hearth where the dough was plumping up and smelling most sweetly.

Malle had retreated into the farthest corner, where Gib's birch rod stood, and was watching him from there. He did not seem dangerous. He looked round the room once, and smiled at her. Then he drew some plain beads from the folds of his gown, and sat with his eyes shut, letting them slide ticking through his fingers. Malle stole from her corner at last, and lifted the cloth from the dough which was ready for baking. He did not glance at her, but when she came near again with the loaves he made the holy sign over them, and said something softly which she knew was a blessing on the bread, before she slid them into the bake oven.

In a little while old Kat came back from the tavern, swaying and quarrelsome. She did not leave him to sit there without questioning, and soon found out that he was the new chantry priest. When she heard that, she turned from truculent to maudlin, and flopped down on a stool whimpering that, aye, she had always known it, so might she and the poor fool now go packing.

"If you go," said he, "who'll look after the helpless silly old man?"

For quite a time after that Malle expected that another old man, who was helpless and silly, would come to the chantry, but he never came. Only the old priest was there. He slipped as easily into their life as oil into a rusty lock.

Once a big black-bearded gentleman visited him, who seemed, in his high white leather riding boots, and wide-skirted green fustian coat, to fill the room, so that Malle was frightened, especially as he had two dogs with him. But the old priest talked to him with very familiar cheerfulness, calling him Jack, and even Jackanapes, while the large gentleman called him nothing but "Sir," and "my Father."

At supper that night the old man told them that this had been Sir John Uvedale, "whom," said he, "I taught whatsoever latinity could be driven into his thick skull. No scholar—oh, no, no, no—yet a good lad. Surely a very good lad." He went on, in that way he had, nodding and murmuring to himself. At last he looked across at Malle and Kat with bright, gentle eyes:

"I cannot think it right, my daughters, that they pull down the abbeys, and he is among them that do it. But if it is sin in him, then I pray God to set against it his goodness to me." He seemed to forget his supper then, because he shut his eyes, and they saw his lips move.

In the spring old Kat died. She fell suddenly to the floor one evening, and lay there twitching and groaning. They got her to bed, but she could neither speak nor move, and her face was puckered horribly as if she snarled at them. In a week she was dead, but Malle stayed on with the old priest, cooking and doing for him in her muddled way. She was not frightened of him now, for he was never angry, and would sit and read, or tell his beads, with his feet under the bench and the skirts of his gown drawn close, while the worst of household disorders weltered around him. Malle talked to him while she worked, chattering as she had used to do with Wat, garrulous as a sparrow, but never about Gib or Wat, or anything that was in the past. Sometimes, though not often, he would check her, saying gently, "Peace, good wench. There are times for silence." Then she would clap her hand over her mouth, and tiptoe about her work, breathing heavily, and overturning or dropping more things than ever in her efforts to be quiet.

One day, nearly two years after he had come to the chantry, she came back from buying pigs' trotters and hocks for making brawn, to find him reading a letter, which, he told her, the carrier had brought him out of Yorkshire. It was from Sir John Uvedale, and he sent, the old priest said, to fetch him back to the North Country—"where I was born," said he. "For I was born a long way from here, at a place called Topcliffe on Swale."

Malle looked out of the window. In the street the rain was falling straight as rods. But she saw a fair early morning when she and Wat had driven Black Thomas, the ladies' mule, across the river, and he had rubbed the sack of rye off the saddle against a tree.

"The Swale," said she, "was very cold that day and the little knave slipped when the stones rolled under his feet and nearly got a dousing."

"What!" said the old man, "are you also of Topcliffe? No—for I should know if you came from any village in ten miles and more around."

She shook her head, and murmured, as if it were a word she had long forgotten, and must try again on her tongue to know how it sounded "Marrick . . . Marrick."

"God 'a mercy!" said he, "that's stranger still. For Sir John will have me to be parson of Marrick, and if you will come you shall keep my house for me there."

She looked at him in her slow way, and then cried very eagerly—

"Will *he* be there? Shall I find *him* there?"

He could not get from her the name of him whom she hoped to find at Marrick, but because she grew so wild, at last he took her hand and held it between his own.

"Child," he said, "whomsoever we find there, God's Christ we shall find, if we seek for him."

"Ah!" she said, with a long sigh. "When shall we go?"

They reached Marrick on the very day that the ladies went away, and Sir John Uvedale's people at once became very busy setting things to rights against his coming in the evening. The old priest left them to it and went down to the riverside, to walk up and down by the Swale in the sweet faint sunshine of November, telling his beads in quietness.

But Malle hunted about both outside and inside the priory—up to the little gate at the foot of the nuns' steps, into the kitchen, the prioress's chamber, the guest chamber; into the cloister, where she picked up some of the bravely painted pages of the books which Uvedale's man had torn and scattered there. Then, because two of them shouted at her, she bolted out of the cloister and went across the great court to the dove house and stable. But back she came after a little while to the church, still seeking and peering.

At last she came to the frater, where, on the table, lay the litter of the ladies' last meal. Among the crumbled bread and empty egg shells there lay upon one dish what was left of a piece of broiled fish, and upon another half a honeycomb.

She knew then that he had been there, and that they had given him to eat of these things so short a time before that the comb still oozed into the dish transparent gold from its severed cells.

She hurried away down the steep meadow to the banks of the Swale. The old priest stopped his pacing and smiled at her.

"He *is* here," she said.

He nodded to her, glad that she had found the one she had hoped to find, and then continued to walk up and down.

Malle went and sat down where the grassy bank broke in a low sandy cliff, and set her feet upon the scoured, white, water-rounded stones left dry by the river, which though it was now November was still shrunken by a long autumn drought. One of these stones she laid carefully upon the painted pages which she had gathered up in the cloister, so that they should not be blown away. Then she began to fold them, one by one, into the shape of tiny boats.

The old priest drew near to see what she would be at. When he saw, it was in his mind to rebuke her for such a misuse of holy writings. But he did not, for, he thought, she is as innocent as ignorant. And then he thought, "Even so ignorantly, and almost as childishly, do we launch forth our prayers upon the silence and the dark. And to him they come, and after to us return; but what went out from us as these little boats of paper, he sends again to us, an argosy, deep-laden." So he only smiled at her when she looked up, and went back to his pacing and to his meditation, which had been of God's love and his great work in the redemption of the world.

For he had been thinking how God's plan had, by sin, been horribly wrested from its high and sweet perfection. It was, he thought, as if number itself had rebelled, forsaking congruity and order, so that not only must the children's sums go awry, but the whole fabric of reason split from crown to base, men's minds founder, and the sun and stars cease to keep due course. "No less a thing," he thought, "no lighter, have we men done with our sins. No less a thing, to make right again of that most monstrous wrong, has God done. To right it God came, and was a man. God did not only send, he came."

He thought—"I must tell her. Even she must learn and know this thing."

Yet when he came close to her again he could find no words to tell her, so sure he was that no words could make her understand so high a matter.

She had taken all the papers from under the stone, and now those which were not yet folded into boats lay in a bright litter at his feet; he looked down and read upon one the words:

> It is true, that sin is cause of all this pain; but all shall be well, and all manner of thing shall be well.

On another was written:

> See I am God: See I am in all things: See I do all things: See I never left my hands of my works, ne never shall without end: See I lead all things to the end that I ordain it to, from without beginning, by the same might, wisdom, and love, that I made it with. How should anything be amiss?

And on another:

What? wouldest thou wit thy Lord's meaning in this thing?
Wit it well: love was his meaning. Who sheweth it thee? Love.
Wherefore sheweth he it thee? For love. Hold thee therein,
thou shalt wit more in the same. But thou shalt never wit
therein other without end.

All those pages had initial letters of blue, or dusky blood-red,
painted upon the paper, but there were two which were of parchment, smaller but much more glorious, with borders of twined
flowers of all colors and golden letters, plumped up above gesso,
and burnished by long rubbing with a bear's tooth.

On one of these was written:

Deum de Deo: lumen de lumine: Deum verum de Deo vero.

And on the other:

Homo factus est.

When Malle had made all the little ships ready to sail, she set
them on the water, where it lapped, trembling and bright, close
to her feet. They bobbed and curtseyed there, loitering a minute
till the strength of the river caught them. Then they went dipping and dancing away toward the sea.

Historical Note

A great many historical persons appear in this book, of whom Henry VIII, Katherine of Aragon, Anne Boleyn, Cardinal Wolsey, Thomas Cromwell, Princess Mary, Sir Thomas More, and Archbishop Cranmer are the best known. Not all, but many of the episodes in which they appear are founded upon documentary evidence. To take a few examples: much of Foxe's report to the cardinal in 1528 is drawn from the letters of the English agents in Rome; what Queen Katherine said to Montfalconnet, to the nobles and clergy in 1531, and to Mountjoy was reported to the Emperor by his ambassador; Anne Boleyn's arrival at the Tower in 1536 and her conversation with Kingston were described by Kingston to the King.

The description of Marrick nunnery is founded upon the late sixteenth century plan, reproduced on pp. 556–557, as well as upon local knowledge. The names of the prioress and her nuns are drawn from the (slightly longer) list of those pensioned at the Dissolution. Owing to delays in publication caused by the war Archbishop Lee's last visitation of the nunnery was not available for reference, but though there is little evidence for the character of the prioress, that little is interesting, and, I think, suggestive of her personality.

Much of Lord Darcy's life is known from documents; these have been used in this reconstruction, and his rather puzzling character inferred from them. On the other hand Julian Savage and Gilbert Dawe are imagined and without any historical foundation. Of Robert Aske's life before 1536 practically nothing is known except his connection with the Percys and his entrance into Gray's Inn; his association with Margaret Cheyne is entirely fictitious. Margaret herself is, however, historical, though it is doubtful if she was in fact a daughter of Buckingham. The events of her life, again with the exception of her relations with Robert Aske, are taken from contemporary documents. From these I had already supposed her character when I found my supposition confirmed by the fact that up to the early years of the nineteenth century she was still remembered in Yorkshire under the name of Madge Wildfire.

For the Pilgrimage of Grace, in which the historical theme of the book culminates, there is a mass of evidence, so that almost all the scenes connected with the rising are founded upon documents. To take some instances: Robert Aske's report to the King gives an account of his own movements during the first few days of his connection with the Lincolnshire rising. Lancaster Herald described his mission to Pontefract in a long document, much of which has been used verbatim; the Duke of Norfolk's dealings with the leaders of the pilgrimage are revealed in his own letters and in such confessions as that of Cresswell. Aske's replies to examination in the Tower throw much light both on his character and on the motives of the pilgrims, and I have made use of these, as well as of many other depositions, though unfortunately, again owing to the war, I could not, except in a very few instances, go behind the printed version to the original manuscript.

To indicate to what degree and where this book reproduces authentic history would need, however, far greater space than can be spared in a note. This is a novel, and much in it is, necessarily, imaginary. But I have been scrupulous to preserve undistorted any fact known to me, with two minor exceptions.* In broad outline the account which I have given of historical events is as correct as I have been able to make it, and there are besides, indistinguishable to the reader among the imaginary scenes and persons, many such intimate yet authentic facts as the devotion of Aske's servant to his master, the dislike of Anne Boleyn for monkeys, or the quarrel of Mr. Patchett's servant with the ostler at Cambridge. The music of the song on p. 418 may be found on page 558, reproduced from the *Antiquaries' Journal*, vol. XV, 1935, p. 21.

---

*The name of Robert Aske's servant was Robert Wall, but the name was changed to avoid confusion. The disposition of the buildings of St. Helen's, Bishopsgate, was not that which is here described. In one important particular I have differed from other writers upon the Pilgrimage of Grace. My authority for the King's vengeance upon Robert Aske is Wriothesley's detailed account of the execution of the leaders of the pilgrimage, in which he mentions the punishment which each received, and distinguishes between the hanging of Sir Robert Constable and that of Robert Aske (Wriothesley I, 65).

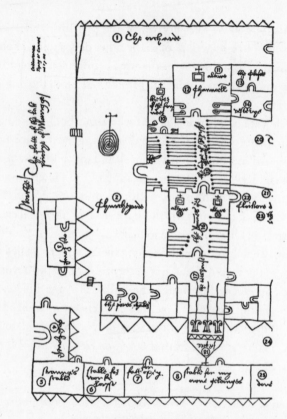

MARRICK PRIORY.

From a plan drawn up probably about fifty years after the Dissolution.

(Reproduced from Collectanea Topographica et Genealogica, 1838.)

1. The orcharde.
2. Churchyarde.
3. oxe house.
4. gate house.
5. straungers stable.
6. table for worke horsse.
7. for fatt oxen.
8. stable for my owne geldinges.
9. the priores chamber.
10. the quier of the founder.
11. altare.
12. Chancell.
13. the Closett.
14. vestereye.
15. the bodye of the paryshe churche.
16. the Nonnes quier.
17. the bell house.
18. stepell.

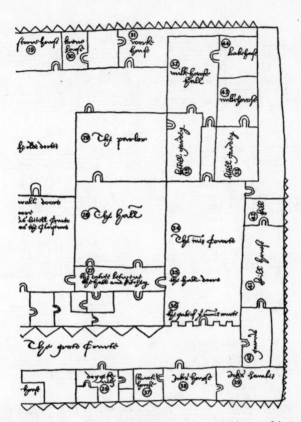

19. stoore house.
20. The olde dorter.
21. wall doore.
22. Cloistore doore.
23. This littell Courte was the Cloisture.
24. The grate Courte.
25. dove house.
26. dogge kenels.
27. the entree betwene the hall and the kitchen.
28. The hall.
29. The parlor.
30. brewe house.
31. worke house.
32. milk house hall.
33. littell gardne.
34. The inner Courte.
35. the hall doore.
36. the gate of the inner courte.
37. slawter house.
38. Joks house.
39. Joks chamber.
40. garners.
41. Still house.
42. Still.
43. milk house.
44. bake house.

Questions for Reflection and Discussion

Use the following questions as guides to deeper individual understanding of the novel or for group discussion.

1. What is the mystery that surrounds the death of Katherine of Aragon? (5–8; January 7, 1536)

2. What were the King's visitors looking for when they came to Marrick? What was their impression of Marrick Priory? What was their interest in Malle? (10–22; January 18, 19, 1536)

3. What consequences loom for Anne Boleyn due to the miscarriage of her second child? (22–26; January 29, 1536)

4. After the King's visitors leave, what seems to be the future of Marrick and all monasteries and priories? (33–37; March 6, 1536)

5. Describe Malle's and Wat's vision. Which image of what they saw is most personally meaningful for you? (38–42; March 28, 1536)

6. What is the impact of Malle's vision on the nuns in the priory? (49–55; April 8, 1536)

7. How does Lord Darcy learn of the changing winds in Anne Boleyn's life? What is his opinion of Cromwell? (55–60; April 12, 1536)

8. How does Anne Boleyn react when she hears that, "'The poorest subject the King hath,' he told her, 'hath justice'"? Why would she react in such a way? (63–66; May 2, 1536)

9. What is Lord Darcy looking for in seeking out Malle to hear of her visions? What does he hope God will do to help those who want to fight tyranny? (68–73; May 18, 1536)

10. What kind of response is Robert Aske looking for in his conversations with Malle? (95–103; August 29, 1536)

11. What does Cromwell's letter to Robert Aske's family reveal about Cromwell's willingness to use power to further his own ends? (114–17; September 8, 1536)

12. What is the quarrel between Robert Aske and his family concerning the issues that are now created by the King's tax and social policies? What is chilling to Aske's family about Will's suggestion? (130–38; September 14, 1536)

13. How does the man from Lincolnshire describe the tax policies that are becoming more oppressive? What role do they begin to see Robert Aske playing in presenting their grievances? (138–42; September 17, 1536)

14. In what way does Robert Aske seem to be irresistibly drawn into the rebellion? What choices does he have? What kind of future does he imagine for himself? (153–57; September 30, 1536)

15. What values was Robert Aske trying to preserve by writing the Oath of the Honorable Men? Who did he see as the agents of evil? How did he see the King? What was his fatal error? (210–15; October 16, 1536)

16. In what way does Lord Darcy show his sympathy for the rebellion? What was the reaction of the archbishop? (234–44; October 19, 1536)

17. What is King Henry's reaction to the Pilgrimage of Grace? How did the King strategize to respond? (278–84; November 2, 1536)

18. What decision does Darcy make that will determine his future? Robert Aske knew a line had been passed. What did it mean in terms of his conflict with the King? (284–94; November 10, 1536)

19. What was Cromwell's reaction to Lord Darcy's decision to honor his word to Robert Aske? (295–99; November 14, 1536)

20. How strongly does the King think the consciences of his subjects should be bound? What does this say to those who rebel against his government to seek justice? (299–306; November 18, 1536)

21. Why does Robert Aske accept the King's offer of pardon? What does this mean for the Pilgrimage of Grace? What kind of reception does he get from the King? Why does this make Cromwell nervous? (324–36; December 18, 21, 1536)

22. In his declaration to the King, what does Robert Aske identify as the issues he thought were important? What does the King and Cromwell think of his declaration? What do they plan to do eventually with Aske and anyone else who defied the King? (351–58; January 5, 1537)

23. How did Christabel plan to deal with the ongoing threat to close Marrick? What does it say about her values? (367–70; January 15, 1537)

24. What are the indications that life has changed for Marrick Priory? (385–88; February 5, 1537)

25. How does the questioning of Aske by the Duke of Norfolk show that things are getting dangerous for Robert Aske? What kind of doubts does this begin to raise for Aske? (388–97; February 6, 1537)

26. What is the King's response to the latest signs of rebellion? What kind of justice does he order his soldiers to carry out? (407–9; February 24, 1537)

27. How does the Duke of Norfolk use Aske's distress over the treatment of the commons to implicate others in the rebellion against the King? (409–13; February 26, 1537)

28. How successful does Christabel Cowper think she is in saving Marrick Priory by bribing Thomas Cromwell? In what way is Christabel unable to accept the prophetic words concerning the future of Marrick Priory? (421–29, 452–57; March 21, 29, 1537)

29. How did Aske ask for mercy for the people in the North of England? What was the King's response? What were the consequences for Aske? (459–65, 471–72; April 2, 7, 1537)

30. What were the results of July's attempts to ask mercy for Aske? Is she willing to jeopardize her personal chance at happiness for Aske's sake? What action does it lead her to take? How does her husband bring her a message of healing? (507–13, 517–24, 524–30; May 31, June 15, July 18, 1537)

31. What message is the author communicating with the juxtaposition of Malle's visions and the slow, torturous death of Robert Aske? (536–38; July 22, 1537)

32. What final decision does Gib Dawe make for his life? What is his final sense of who he is as a person related to God? How does the author comment on Gib's opinion of himself in the context of the mercy of God? (541–44; November 4, 1537)

33. What messages of hope do we find in the final pages of *The Man on a Donkey*? (545–52; "The End and the Beginning")

About the Author

Hilda Frances Margaret Prescott was born in Latchford, Cheshire, on February 22, 1896, the daughter of an Anglican clergyman. A brilliant student, she studied modern history at Oxford University and medieval history at Manchester University, receiving master's degrees from both institutions.

Prescott taught in private schools for a time but in 1923 gave up full-time teaching for writing, though she maintained a connection with Oxford University as a tutor in history. Her first novel, *The Unhurrying Chase,* was published in 1925, followed by *The Lost Fight* in 1928 and *Son of Dust* in 1932. Each of these historical novels is set in medieval France and centers on a moral and sexual conflict in the midst of a harsh feudal world. All three novels were praised for their historical depth and their style, "a constant careful beauty which from the first page marks her work as both unusual and distinctive," as the *New Statesman* put it.

Prescott's most acclaimed work was *The Man on a Donkey,* a powerful historical novel of early Reformation England published in two volumes in 1952. Set mainly in Yorkshire, the novel is a multifaceted historical panorama of the Roman Catholic reaction against the new religious policies of Henry VIII. *Commonweal* lauded the book as "a profoundly moving chronicle, a beautifully executed piece of literature, and a massively impressive work of power, sensitivity and drama." Prescott also received acclaim for *Spanish Tudor: The Life of Bloody Mary,* a biography of Mary Tudor that won her the James Tait Black Memorial Prize.

While many of her historical novels are engrossing epics of romance and adventure, H. F. M. Prescott lived a quiet life for many years in Charlbury, Oxfordshire. A committed member of the Church of England, she had a great fondness for travel and the English countryside. She died in 1972.

Readers,

We'd like to hear from you! What other classic Catholic novels would you like to see in the Loyola Classics series? Please e-mail your suggestions and comments to **loyolaclassics@loyolapress.com** or mail them to:

Loyola Classics
Loyola Press
3441 N. Ashland Avenue
Chicago, IL 60657

LOYOLA & CLASSICS

Catholics	Brian Moore	978-0-8294-2333-4	$12.95
Cosmas or the Love of God	Pierre de Calan	978-0-8294-2395-2	$12.95
Dear James	Jon Hassler	978-0-8294-2430-0	$12.95
The Devil's Advocate	Morris L. West	978-0-8294-2156-9	$12.95
Do Black Patent Leather Shoes Really Reflect Up?	John R. Powers	978-0-8294-2143-9	$12.95
The Edge of Sadness	Edwin O'Connor	978-0-8294-2123-1	$13.95
Five for Sorrow, Ten for Joy	Rumer Godden	978-0-8294-2473-7	$13.95
Helena	Evelyn Waugh	978-0-8294-2122-4	$12.95
In This House of Brede	Rumer Godden	978-0-8294-2128-6	$13.95
The Keys of the Kingdom	A. J. Cronin	978-0-8294-2334-1	$13.95
The Last Catholic in America	John R. Powers	978-0-8294-2130-9	$12.95
The Man on a Donkey, Part 1	H. F. M. Prescott	978-0-8294-2639-7	$13.95
The Man on a Donkey, Part 2	H. F. M. Prescott	978-0-8294-2731-8	$13.95
Mr. Blue	Myles Connolly	978-0-8294-2131-6	$11.95
North of Hope	Jon Hassler	978-0-8294-2357-0	$13.95
Saint Francis	Nikos Kazantzakis	978-0-8294-2129-3	$13.95
The Silver Chalice	Thomas Costain	978-0-8294-2350-1	$13.95
Son of Dust	H. F. M. Prescott	978-0-8294-2352-5	$13.95
Things As They Are	Paul Horgan	978-0-8294-2332-7	$12.95
The Unoriginal Sinner and the Ice-Cream God	John R. Powers	978-0-8294-2429-4	$12.95
Vipers' Tangle	François Mauriac	978-0-8294-2211-5	$12.95

Available at your local bookstore, or visit **www.loyolabooks.org**
or call **800.621.1008** to order.

Join In. Speak Up. Help Out!

Would you like to help yourself and the greater Catholic community by simply talking about Catholic life and faith? Would you like to help Loyola Press improve our publications? Would you be willing to share your thoughts and opinions with us in return for rewards and prizes? If so, please consider becoming one of our *special Loyola Press Advisors*.

Loyola Press Advisors is a unique online community of people willing to share with us their perspectives about Catholic life, spirituality, and faith. From time to time, registered advisors are invited to participate in brief online surveys and discussion groups. As a show of our gratitude for their service, we recognize advisors' time and efforts with *gift certificates, cash, and other prizes*. Membership is free and easy. We invite you, and readers like yourself, to join us by registering at **www.SpiritedTalk.org**.

Your personal information gathered by SpiritedTalk.org is stored in a protected, *confidential* database. Your information will never be sold to or shared with a third party! And SpiritedTalk.org is for research purposes only; at no time will we use the Web site or your membership to try to sell you anything.

Once you have registered at SpiritedTalk.org, every now and then you will be invited to participate in surveys—most take less than ten minutes to complete. Survey topics include your thoughts and ideas regarding the products and services you use in relation to Catholic life and spiritual growth. You may also have the opportunity to evaluate new Loyola Press products and services before they are released for sale. For each survey you complete, you will earn gift certificates, points, or prizes! Membership is voluntary; you may opt out at any time.

Please consider this opportunity to help Loyola Press improve our products and better serve you and the greater Catholic community. We invite you to visit our Web site at **www.SpiritedTalk.org**, take a look, and register today!